TABLE OF

INTRODUCTION

❖ FEATURING ❖

WORLD-FAMOUS
SLUGGER

MICKEY
MANTLE

COMPOSER, LYRICIST
& JAZZ HALL OF FAMER

EUBIE BLAKE

OH, AND
**MURRAY
H.
EDWARDS**

CELEBRATED
AUTHOR AND
HUMORIST

MARK
TWAIN

JIMMY DURANTE
EXTRORDINAIRE

FILM ACTOR

PLUS CREEPY GUY WITH A NERU JACKET
AND... MAN WHO SWALLOWS TRASH CANS

Chicken Ranch Charm School

Handwritten inscription:

February 2012)

Katie –

Hope you enjoy this book as much as I enjoyed writing it –

Murray H. Edwards (signature)

Chicken Ranch Charm School

MURRAY H. EDWARDS

The Old Weather Bureau Publishing Company
Abliene, Texas

Library of Congress Control Number: 2012910501

ISBN 978-0-615-65089-0

Special Thanks to:

Cover and section openers by John-Morris Edwards of Austin, Texas, a wonderfully gifted artist and musical talent. His artwork is much better than the stories they illustrate.

Book Design by Tom Martens of Fort Worth, Texas, who has the patience and endurance of Job, but is much more creative.

Edits, suggestions, criticisms, and ideas by professionals and friends to whom I will always be grateful for their persistent encouragement and advice.

The Old Weather Bureau Publishing Company
The Old Weather Bureau Building
1482 North First Street
Abilene, Texas 79601

For my brothers, Weldon Lynn and David.

———————————————————

INTRODUCTION

Mickey Mantle, legendary New York Yankees slugger and party boy, is often credited with the gallows-humor observation, "If I'd have known I was going to live this long, I'd have taken better care of myself." The older I get, the more I appreciate the crusty wisdom of that statement. Well, it turns out The Mick recycled the phrase from jazz musician Eubie Blake, who recycled it from vaudevillian Jimmy Durante, who recycled it from humorist Mark Twain, who probably recycled it from some other poor soul whose name is forever lost to history.

Consciously or subconsciously, writers are always borrowing observations, themes, and plot lines from other writers. Some are even honest enough to admit

R.I.P.

1835-1910

Mark Twain

it. The truth is, the themes of man-versus-nature, man-versus-man, and man-loves-woman-but-loses-woman-only-to-win-her-back-in-the-end are as old and universal as the Book of Genesis. And most likely, the writer of Genesis borrowed the bulk of his material from oral storytellers, who sat around late-night campfires roasting the equivalent of prehistoric s'mores while recounting tales of chatting serpents, burning bushes, and parting seas.

In the collection of short fiction that follows, I'll admit to recycling some of these ancient themes, myself; hopefully, they're written in a way that brings a fresh, modern perspective to the genre. For example, in the man-versus-nature story, "Pirouette," a West Texas rancher faces a life-and-death struggle against a formidable, but very unusual, adversary. In "Press Six for Love," an out-of-work photo clerk exacts a measure of revenge against his homophobic, cold-hearted boss, a slightly off-kilter retooling of the man-versus-man theme. And then there's "Dirty Martinis," a man-loves-woman-etc. tale set in the exotic world of high-stakes private poker.

Jimmy
Durante

1893-1980

REST IN PEACE

The characters in my stories have also been recycled, but in this case, not from other authors (at least not intentionally). Instead, they're based on my interactions with people I've met over the years, sometimes chance encounters. The Walgreen's sales clerk in "No More or Less a Man" is modeled after a beautiful lady, whose name I don't remember, with whom I had a brief, but poignant, conversation in downtown Fort Worth several years ago. The narrator of "Tweeze" was inspired by a woman I crossed paths with in Brooklyn, under considerably less pleasant circumstances, when she angrily accused me of dawdling on the subway stairs, making her miss a connection. Unlike the story, no one pushed me in front of the next train, thereby saving me the indignity of being sliced in half. (Note to readers: never, under any circumstances, dawdle on New York subway stairs.)

Unfortunately, I had to exclude a couple of my favorite characters from the stories that follow, because they didn't fit well into any of the plots. For instance, I once met a guy who looked as if he swallowed a trashcan, whole, and then somehow fitted a white T-shirt over his oversized belly. Obviously proud, he occasionally patted it as if he were a nine-month-pregnant woman ready to deliver. While watching television, he would balance his beer bottle on top of his mega-tummy, using it as a giant coaster to prevent unsightly rings on the coffee table. Besides him, there was the greasy-haired young hustler, wearing a 1960's peace medallion over a Nehru jacket, who sold pre-paid legal services door-to-door. When I bluntly asked what he was selling, he cryptically replied, "Well, giving a simple answer to a complicated question like that would be like trying to give you a haircut over the phone." Hard to top that for weirdness.

Back to recycling. The point is, authors are sponge-like in their ability to absorb people, places, and themes. These days, with as many writers and bloggers as there are laptops, it's likely that anyone reading this book has already been compiled into a fictional character of some sort. Maybe into one of my stories.

One final thought: the next time you hear, "If I'd have known I was going to live this long, I'd have taken better care of myself," give the credit to Murray H. Edwards, instead of Mickey Mantle or Mark Twain. All of us borrowed the pithy phrase from someone else, and since the other guys are already dead, I'd be the only one who might actually benefit. Then, when I've gone to that Great Writing Desk in the Sky, you can claim the honor. ✪

asked the

Mik
woul
possible in Au   w, and
ne of the benefit   any d
living in an area v   her h
said, "everyone   every
everybody."   scular
barrel-c   a man w
grown up on o... of the Cz
arms outside of town and still h
calloused hands to prove it, Buck officed down t'
Aubrey. He and Claude were long-time friends, playing fo
graduati   contrast to her husb
the same age as Cal
all and talked on S
ter church, the la
ave St. Anne's pa
ot. The sheriff was ...
Aubrey called. From the background no...
could tell he was having dinner with his family. In
turmoil, Aubrey tried to keep her voice calm, just as she'
one during closing arguments on a child-molestation case earli
year. Buck said he'd dispatch a deputy and would als
to the ranch himself. The deputy arrived first, and less tha
te later. Buck drov   to the carport pulling into the slot Cla
y occupied.   w was waiting for th
men, havi   to her ranch-h
s and a gr   nylon coat, the o
sed wher   e took Callie and
ling on S days. Aubrey
large of the search.
aring for trial, st
nfolded and'
ead a large ra
nap on the hood
of th   iff's pick
ngine s
ing. Th
awmer
ed the
flash
r shou
hile s
sed a
o ma
he fe
oute

Pirouette

ONE

Pirouette

Claude's four-wheel drive Chevrolet bounced and lurched down the steep, deeply carved ruts toward the bull pasture, his next-to-last feeding stop of the day. Even though hostile clouds threatened bitter winds and snow flurries by sundown, the winter storm was of little concern to the fourth-generation cattleman. Keeping

➤

time to a melody looping over and over in his mind, Claude pleasantly tapped his fingers against the steering wheel. He was thinking about ballet.

After hearing a tinny, cassette-tape version of "Dance of the Snowflakes" playing in Callie's room every evening for the past three months, Claude knew the melody by heart, but very little about *The Nutcracker*. According to his wife Aubrey, the plot involved magic spells, dancing mice, and a sugar plum fairy. As unappealing at it sounded, Claude wouldn't trade this evening's performance for a corral full of high-priced cutting horses. Five-year-old Callie was one of the dancing snowflakes, and as far as he was concerned, the entire ballet revolved around a two-minute scene with her climactic *pirouette*.

For most of his adult life, the "old-school cowman," as he referred to himself, cultivated his reputation as a hard-shell bachelor. Then, just before his 52nd birthday, he met Aubrey Williamson, the newly elected county attorney. Unlike other women he'd dated, she had real *substance*. Whether discussing state politics or debating the merits of dry-rubbed barbeque, Aubrey more than held her ground. Claude put aside his never-in-a-million-years swagger and launched a determined and ultimately successful courtship for this once-in-a-lifetime woman. Two years later, Callie came along, and even though strangers often mistook her as his granddaughter, he didn't mind. The once hard-as-concrete rancher transformed into 220 pounds of supple Play-Doh, periodically molding into a guest at a teddy bear's tea party, a judge for a bubble-blowing contest, and now a ballet critic, who would offer rave reviews of the snowflake scene in *The Nutcracker*.

By the time Claude's truck passed through the gate, two of the three Herefords in the bull pasture, "Hidalgo" and "Lover Boy," assembled by the feed trough, already anticipating the daily ritual. The bulls' dinner table consisted of a twelve-foot-long, three-foot-wide slab of reinforced concrete standing eighteen inches off the ground, cradled and supported by thick-metal legs on each end. A pair of mourning doves landed on the trough, hoping to scavenge crumbles of feed. The lifelong rancher loved wildlife - birds in particular - and kept a reference guide on his dashboard in case he spotted some he hadn't seen before.

The third bull, several years older and nicknamed "Brick" because of his dark-red coloring, sequestered himself from the others in the post-oak brush. Crippled in his left shoulder, Brick especially kept his distance from Hidalgo, who was responsible for inflicting his old injury. The smallest bull, Lover Boy, avoided confrontation of any kind and was the most docile of the three. Although each animal weighed well over a ton, it was a hundred pounds less than at the beginning of the breeding season, the result of following a harem of approximately 30 cows all summer.

His mind still focused on Callie's debut later that evening, Claude unhinged the tailgate and loudly banged a 50-pound sack of range cubes against the pick-up bed. Hearing the familiar call to dinner, Brick emerged from the brush, a hundred yards away, and plodded methodically toward the trough and the other bulls. As was his custom, Claude delayed pouring the feed until all the cattle were gathered, preventing dominant males such as Hidalgo from intimidating the others and stealing their allotments. While waiting for Brick, Claude tried to coax Lover Boy into nibbling a cube from his outstretched hand. Perfecting the trick would amuse Callie and help calm his city-raised wife's fear of the colossal creatures.

When Brick sauntered within twenty yards of the other Herefords, Hidalgo made eye contact with his older rival and launched a long, deep-throated bawl, as if he were saying, *Stay away, this is my territory.* The crippled bull bugled in response, as if he had again mustered the courage to confront the schoolyard bully. Hidalgo, his head low to the ground and swinging side-to-side like a slow-motion pendulum, lumbered toward the approaching challenger.

Recognizing this hostile behavior, Claude quickly emptied his feed into the trough, hoping to create a distraction. True to his reputation, Lover Boy drifted over to his place at the dinner table, safe from the imminent conflict.

Hidalgo, his adrenaline rendering him oblivious to any distraction, accelerated to a trot and charged Brick, who braced for the impact. The bulls collided head-on, as if two eighteen-wheelers crashed together. Stirring up clouds of dust with their hooves, the angry males rammed each other repeatedly, grunting and snorting, each seeking the other's unconditional surrender, but neither gaining an advantage. Brick, his nose bloodied almost immediately, didn't yield to the bigger and more muscular Hidalgo, who now had stringy, scarlet mucous dripping from his own mouth. It was as if the eighteen-wheelers were unsatisfied with their initial collision and wanted to destroy each other in some sort of winner-take-all demolition derby.

Claude rarely interceded in fights between bulls, knowing they usually ended quickly, but hoping to protect Brick from further injury, he hurried to the pick-up truck and grabbed his rope.

Approaching the Herefords, but staying safely out of their combat zone, the old-school cowman made himself look more imposing by jumping and swinging his arms, like a football player taking calisthenics, and yelling as loudly as he could. Claude's diversionary ruckus failed to distract Brick and Hidalgo, so the rancher took a deep breath and moved within a yardstick's reach of the fighting giants. He smacked each bull across the horns with the lariat, the human equivalent of a sharp slap to the face. At first, the maneuver succeeded as the bulls paused their hostilities and glared at each other, their flared nostrils gasping for air. But within a few seconds, Hidalgo, seemingly unsatisfied with the truce, challenged Brick with a loud bellow and broke the fragile cease-fire. Interceding again, Claude repeatedly struck both cattle with the rope, until Brick, almost as if he sensed a referee was ending the fight, took two steps backward. Instead of pursuing the older bull, Hidalgo briefly hesitated, and when he did, Claude stepped in front of the larger male and hit him across the nose, the animal's most sensitive area. Flinching from the pain, Hidalgo retreated to the feed trough, now apparently satisfied with a draw rather than an outright knockout.

The conflict over, Claude turned toward his dusty Chevrolet, relieved that neither animal had been seriously injured. He could finish his feeding routine in plenty of time to get home, shower, and dress for *The Nutcracker*.

An instant after allowing his body to relax, Claude felt a crushing blow to his back and heard a crack, as though a wooden bat had hit a home run, which he instinctively knew was the sound of his own ribs breaking.

Before he could react, Claude tumbled facedown to the ground, dirt filling his mouth and cactus pin-cushioning his left hand. Brick loomed above him and head-butted the unprotected rancher's back and hips with the blow-after-blow impact of a 2,000-pound sledgehammer. It was as if the normally levelheaded bull had confused a human with Hidalgo and sensed an opportunity to settle a long-standing score. With the feed trough ten yards away and his pick-up another five yards beyond that, Claude instinctively curled into the fetal position. The unfamiliar movement seemed to bewilder the Hereford, who responded by slamming his thick head into his victim's body. This time, the cowman felt a sharp, electric jolt as one of Brick's horns bayoneted his shirt and sliced a gash across his abdomen.

While the crippled behemoth towered above him, Claude remained motionless, his eyes closed, trying not to panic. He felt as if someone had doused his stomach with gasoline and lit a match. As the bull's breath rippled across the rancher's now-sopping-wet shirt, Claude held his own breath as long as he was able. The slightest movement of his chest could provoke the crazed animal into ramming him again.

Then, just as the cowman had been sucker-punched minutes earlier, Brick was blindsided by Hidalgo, who returned to finish their fight. The two Herefords blasted each other, creating their own testosterone-fueled tango of dust, blood, and mucous. With the bulls distracted, Claude, unable to walk, crawled inch-by-painful-inch, to the feed trough. Using only his right hand, the other being smothered in prickly-pear thorns, he pulled himself alongside the metal legs and eased under the protective eighteen-inch crawlspace of the concrete trough. There he collapsed, temporarily safe from the fighting cattle, but afraid he would bleed to death.

9

Standing in front of her bathroom mirror, Aubrey applied eyeliner and anxiously checked her watch. In a few minutes, she and Callie would be leaving for the performance, and it wasn't like her husband to be late, particularly for an event involving their daughter. During the first year of marriage, Aubrey learned Claude was a bit over-the-top about punctuality, but now, in one of the ironies of their marriage, she had become equally obsessive. It evidently wasn't a genetic trait, however, because Callie had no sense of urgency, whatsoever.

Eight years earlier, Aubrey, then a 38-year-old assistant district attorney, lived in Austin. After a series of unsatisfying relationships, she'd concluded marriage and children wouldn't be a part of her life's story. Her criminal law practice had been far more satisfying, despite having to joust regularly with career criminals and sleazy defense attorneys. Eventually, Austin's weirdness grew tiresome; and Aubrey decided to leave town, wanting to find the "real" Texas. Answering an ad in a legal journal, she landed an associate's position with a small, West Texas law firm handling divorces and child custody cases. The delicately built woman gave notice, packed her things, and moved to Willow County, all within 45 days.

The job paid the bills, but Aubrey missed the rough and tumble of criminal law. A year later, when the Jurassic-aged county attorney retired, she launched a long-shot campaign against another "good-ol'-boy" for the position. Two weeks before the election, her opponent, arrested for driving drunk, withdrew from the race. Even so, only 54% of Willow County voters saw fit to put the "carpetbagger," as her adversary mocked her, into office. Four years later, she would be reelected with 78% of the vote.

Her former law associates in Austin said she was crazy to trade the comforts of city life for "nowhere," but Aubrey never regretted leaving behind never-ending traffic delays and revolving door dating. Once in Willow County, she fell in love with its big skies and larger-than-life characters, one of whom was Claude Morris.

She first met her husband-to-be, two weeks after being sworn-in as county attorney. Wearing a shirt barely fit for a homeless shelter and boots that smelled of cow manure, Claude marched into the courthouse to file charges against a persistent trespasser. Still red-faced from the encounter only an hour earlier, the handsome rancher said he'd caught the troublemaker and his birddog poaching for the third time in six months. The rancher matter-of-factly recounted how he'd aimed his loaded 30-06 at the offender and observed that it wasn't in his nature to kill an innocent dog, but he had absolutely no problem shooting a poacher.

Not certain if Claude was serious, Aubrey laughed anyway, realizing she'd traded Austin's hippies and goofballs for Willow County's rednecks and gun-toting bubbas. The moment she laughed, Claude looked at her differently. It was as if he had seen a rare goldfinch for the very first time, and he chuckled as well, probably realizing how silly and caricatured he must have sounded. He asked Aubrey to dinner that same day, but before giving an answer, she checked with a couple of courthouse people about her prospective date. Claude Morris was intelligent, the game warden said, in addition to being polite and generous to a fault. The women in the county clerk's office were considerably less charitable, noting the rancher was short-tempered, impatient, and more interested in birds than people. Plus, they sniped, he had "a short attention span with women."

The latter statement, Aubrey noted years later, was the one thing about

Claude they had all wrong.

She hurried to the kitchen to check on Callie who was perched on a kitchen stool wearing leotards, a pink tutu, and a silver headpiece resembling the latticework of a snowflake. Her daughter, looking like a miniature ballerina except for the cowboy boots on her feet, held her ballet slippers in one hand and a glass of milk in the other. She would change into the footwear, Callie informed her mother, when they arrived at the auditorium. The little girl loved her chocolate-colored boots with the green-stitched top, her first pair, and seldom took them off because they were just like Pappa's. Aubrey remembered two weeks ago when Claude and Callie danced "The Cotton-Eyed Joe" in the kitchen - the daughter clasping her father's hands and standing atop his giant boots as the two of them spun and kicked at the "whoop-whoop" of the country melody. When the song ended, Callie, as if performing an encore, turned a flawless *pirouette*.

Aubrey smiled at her daughter's firmly-in-control attitude. Claude sometimes joked that living with Callie was like having an assistant wife around the house, the way she took control of situations and tried to boss him. Truth was, he loved her assertive, independent nature.

Glancing at her watch one last time and now irritated at her husband's apparent tardiness, Aubrey decided not to wait any longer. Quickly scratching out a note, she wrote that Claude would have to come to the ballet by himself. She would save him a seat.

Drifting in and out of consciousness, Claude wasn't certain how long he'd been trapped under the concrete trough, his watch having been lost during Brick's assault. The ink-blue clouds draped like a massive shower curtain against the sky, and with the sun about to set, the temperature would drop quickly.

Every hammered muscle in the rancher's body ached, and his cracked ribs pinched his lungs each time he breathed. His hazy mind struggled to focus on what he could do to survive.

Whenever Claude tried to move, blood oozed from the slice across his abdomen. Using his good hand to rip off the buttons, he pulled his soggy shirt down from his shoulders and pressed it tightly against the gash, creating a makeshift compress. He was sure his left leg was broken and maybe his pelvis. With a stomach wound and bone fractures, it wouldn't be possible to drive the pick-up or open any gates. A more reasonable goal was to pull himself into the truck's cab before the winter storm hit. That way, he could at least start the engine and stay warm. Claude would use his cell phone, now resting uselessly in the passenger seat of his truck, to call for help.

Taking a deep but painful breath, Claude resolved to attempt the five-yard journey from the feed trough to his truck. He inched his head from under the concrete protection and concentrated on reaching the Chevrolet. There it was, a safe haven; but between the trough and the pick-up, something cast a long, end-of-day shadow. Moving his head a few inches more, Claude came face-to-face with Brick, whose eyes were wide with rage.

Saving an aisle seat for her husband, Aubrey made small talk with another snowflake mother and tried not to think about her husband's absence. At seven o'clock, during the ballet's overture, she excused herself to the foyer and called Claude's cell phone one last time. Directed to his voice mail, she left a second message, now sounding more concerned than irritated. She switched her phone to "vibrate" and returned to her seat.

The community's presentation of *The Nutcracker* lacked the quality of Ballet Austin's, as Aubrey expected, but it wasn't bad for "nowhere." Callie performed flawlessly, of course. At one point, she sneaked a quick wave to the audience, quietly asserting her independence, even though she'd been warned against doing anything like that.

When her husband hadn't called, nor arrived by the end of the snowflake scene, Aubrey knew something was wrong. Deciding not to wait until the end of the performance, she slipped to the back of the auditorium and found Anne Matthew, Callie's dance teacher. Anne agreed to take care of Callie after the ballet.

Aubrey hurried out of the auditorium and was greeted by a blast of frigid air and light snow flurries. Running to her car, she felt nauseous, imagining alternate visions of her headlights flashing upon Claude's wrecked four-wheel drive or walking in the house and finding him lying on the floor. Although her husband appeared to be excellent health, he was twenty-pounds heavier than when they first married. Aubrey warned him - Claude joked it was nagging - a man his age wasn't bulletproof from a heart attack or stroke.

Fearing the worst as she blasted along the highway, Aubrey felt relieved she didn't see Claude's vehicle overturned on the road. The empty space in the carport indicated her husband wasn't home; even so, she searched every room in the house, flipping on all the lights and calling his name. Seeing a bone-dry bathroom shower, she dialed 9-1-1 and tried to remain calm.

Aubrey asked the dispatcher to connect her directly to Alamo Mikeska, Willow County Sheriff. That wouldn't have been possible in Austin, she knew, and was one of the benefits, among several disadvantages, of living in an area where, as her husband had said, "everyone knows everything about everybody." A stout, barrel-chested Czech who'd grown up on a farm outside of town and still had the calloused hands to prove it, Alamo officed down the hall from Aubrey. Nicknamed "Alamo" in high school because of his do-or-die attitude on the football field, he and Claude played together on two undefeated teams. In contrast to her husband, Alamo married at nineteen and had a grandson three-years older than Callie. The two men hunted quail on the ranch every fall and talked on Sundays after church, the last to leave St. Felicity's parking lot.

The sheriff was home watching television when the dispatcher transferred Aubrey's call. In spite of her turmoil, Aubrey struggled to keep her voice calm, just as she'd done during closing arguments on a child-molestation case earlier in the year. Alamo said he'd dispatch a deputy and would hurry to the ranch himself.

The deputy arrived first. Less than a minute later, the sheriff pulled into the carport, taking the slot Claude's pick-up normally occupied. Aubrey was waiting for the lawmen, having changed into her ranch-hand jeans and a green, puffy-nylon coat, the one she used when Claude and "his girls" went feeding on Saturdays.

Aubrey immediately took charge of the mission. As if preparing for trial, she unfolded a large ranch map on the hood of the sheriff's pick-up, its engine still running. The two lawmen shined their flashlights over her shoulder while she used a ballpoint to mark the feeding route. Aubrey asked the deputy to loop around to the far side of the ranch and begin his search at Claude's first stop. She and Alamo would ride together and work in reverse order, from the last feeding station to the first. They would rendezvous in the middle of the ranch, assuming no one came across her husband's truck in the meantime.

It took less than five minutes for Alamo and Aubrey to reach the heifer pasture, which would have been Claude's last stop of the afternoon. Several bawling yearlings gathered by the fence, their snow-dusted heads turned downwind from the biting gale, still waiting to be fed. It was clear the rancher hadn't made it that far, so the pair headed for his next-to-last stop.

Aubrey acted as the gate opener as the sheriff drove his truck. She knew Alamo was an old-school gentleman and would have preferred opening the gates himself, but tonight, there was no time for West Texas protocol.

When the two arrived at the bull pasture, the sheriff switched on his truck's high-intensity spotlight, mounted on the top of his rig. It took a second for their eyes to adjust, but Alamo and Aubrey simultaneously recognized the outline of Claude's pick-up 40 yards ahead, beyond the gate and next to the trough.

Aubrey scrambled out of the sheriff's truck and opened the gate, shouting her husband's name as she fumbled with the ice-encrusted latch, and not bothering to close it once Alamo drove through. Sprinting back to the truck and climbing into her seat, Aubrey felt her face flush, dreading what might lie ahead.

Alamo quickly angled his vehicle alongside Claude's truck, focusing the spotlight toward its cab. There was no movement inside, and before Aubrey could say anything, the sheriff grabbed his flashlight and bolted for the Chevrolet.

She saw his flashlight light up the interior of her husband's truck, but no one was inside. Stepping back, the sheriff waved his light around the surrounding area, and Aubrey spotted a large, dark-red bull on the other side of the Chevrolet. It was Brick, his head high and posture erect.

Something about the Hereford's tense-looking stance, like an awkward dancer posing an arabesque, frightened Aubrey. She redirected Alamo's spotlight toward the animal. The light illuminated the entire area, including some sort of lumpy, oblong object underneath the concrete trough. She saw the sheriff move toward the form, but the bull lowered his head and projected a low, menacing bawl, as if he were saying, *If you know what's good for you, stay away.*

Evidently afraid to proceed any farther, Alamo stopped and pointed his flashlight toward the lumpy shape. Recognizing the outline of cowboy boots, Aubrey realized the oblong object was her husband.

The sheriff called for his friend in as calm a voice as he could muster, but heard no response. Alamo repeated Claude's name, increasing his volume and urgency each time, until at last, he shouted. Still, there was no answer.

Nearly panicked, Alamo retreated to his pick-up, unlocked the twelve-gauge shotgun he kept secured behind the front seat, and loaded two shells. They quietly considered their options. Although Aubrey had little experience with cattle, she sensed the bull was deranged and had hurt or perhaps killed her husband. The sheriff was concerned that if he fired at the animal, part of shot pattern would strike Claude as well. They decided Alamo would try to scare Brick away from his prey.

While Aubrey watched, the sheriff edged out of the truck. He took two steps toward the Hereford and shot into the air. Brick flinched at the noise, and when he did, the sheriff fired the second barrel. The wild-eyed animal took several steps backward, but as soon as the echo of the gunshot faded, he returned and hovered over the concrete trough, unfazed and resolute.

Alamo reloaded the shotgun. From the look on his face, Aubrey knew he had decided to kill Brick and take the chance of also shooting Claude.

Before he could pull the trigger, she opened the passenger door and dashed to the front of the sheriff's truck, confronting the Hereford, only ten yards away. Grasping the truck's ice-cold bumper with her left arm so she could swing herself onto the hood when the bull charged, Aubrey swallowed, her throat full of fear. She waved her right arm and shouted, as she'd seen Claude do.

Grasping the truck's ice-cold bumper with her left arm so she could swing herself onto the hood when the bull charged, Aubrey swallowed, her throat full of fear.

Alamo barked at Aubrey to get back into the cab. Like Callie asserting her independence earlier in the evening, she had already made up her mind. Her body trembling, Aubrey pulled off her puffy green coat and waved it over her head, like a flag snapping in the wind. Brick seemed mesmerized by the movement of the coat, and although he snorted and pawed the dirt, the hulking giant refused to abandon his prey.

Conceding the Hereford wasn't taking the bait, Aubrey released her hand from the truck's bumper and moved even closer to the belligerent animal, still swinging the coat and now fully exposing herself to the danger. This time, Brick eased away from the concrete trough and raised his powerful, regal head, loudly bellowing into the night. She sneaked a glance at Alamo, as he quietly inched toward his crumpled friend.

Now shivering uncontrollably, partly from the freezing wind and partly from terror, Aubrey continued her taunting, until the massive creature, no longer able to resist the challenge, lowered his head and slowly lumbered toward her. She held perfectly still until Brick was within a body length of smashing into her, then hurled her coat toward the bull's head, landing it right over his horns and eyes. The now-visionless animal stopped in his tracks and angrily shook his head, trying to rid himself of the nylon blindfold. Aubrey flashed to the front bumper and, using it as a kind of stepladder, clambered onto the hood of the sheriff's truck. A shock of metallic cold greeting her body, she stretched facedown all the way to the windshield, her feet dangling off the front of the vehicle.

While Aubrey clung to the hood of the truck, Alamo pulled his friend from under the concrete trough. She prayed silently as Alamo put his arms under her husband's exposed shoulders and dragged him around and behind the Chevrolet to the sheriff's pick-up. Between Brick's angry bawls piercing the night air, Aubrey heard Alamo open the driver's door. Grunting from a mighty surge of adrenaline, he pushed Claude into the front seat, shoving his body all the way to the passenger's side of the truck.

Slinging his head back and forth, Brick, his mouth lathered with roiling saliva, finally cast off the puffy blindfold. More agitated than ever, the ferocious-eyed bull spotted his tormentor, lying exposed on the hood of the sheriff's truck. Just as the Hereford charged with his final do-or-die assault, the sheriff started the pick-up and yelled at Aubrey to grab on to the windshield wipers. Alamo switched his headlights to high beam and aimed the intense spotlight toward the vengeful beast, temporarily blinding and disorienting him. Brick veered off course, but not before blasting the side of the sheriff's truck with his muscular head.

Aubrey clutched her icy lifeline and stiffened her arms. The sheriff shifted into gear, gunned the truck, and raced for the safety of the pasture gate.

To Claude's morphined mind, the dreamlike music reminded him of something he'd heard before, maybe a classical melody at a church service. But unlike the rich, full tones of St. Felicity's pipe organ, the familiar sound was thin and tinny. Vaguely aware he was no longer hiding under the feed trough, the rancher worried he was hearing the music at his own funeral service.

Claude slowly tilted his throbbing head toward a metal stand holding an IV bag and then to the linoleum floor, which seemed to be the source of the exotic sound. Through clouded eyes, he recognized a pair of small, chocolate-colored cowboy boots. The boots seemed to move with the rhythms of the strange melody, and for a moment, the rancher wondered if he was hallucinating or had gone to heaven. He mustered all his strength to raise his head a few inches off the pillow. A slightly built figure, dressed in pink and wearing a silver headpiece, energetically turned a *pirouette* at the foot of his bed. And then Claude realized, in fact, he was in heaven. ✪

Avanyu

"On the back row of the decommissioned Greyhound, a state highway worker, his face leathered from hours in a carcinogenic sun, snuggles with his dozing girlfriend. Inch-by-inch, careful not to awaken her, he slides his sore left arm from under her shoulders. A fresh tattoo slithers from his wrist to shoulder and honors the feathered skysnake, Avanyu, a holy symbol of the Navajo."

TWO

Avanyu

The air inside the bus reeks of rancid beer and stale perfume. Midway down the aisle, fresh urine soaks one of the empty seats and drips onto the floor. Passengers who are still awake, lulled by the diesel engine's Prozac-like noise, ignore the stench and surrender to the cadenced snoring of a big-bellied drunk on row seven.

➤➤

On the back row of the decommissioned Greyhound, a highway construction worker, his face leathered from hours in a carcinogenic sun, snuggles with his dozing girlfriend. Inch-by-inch, careful not to awaken her, he slides his sore left arm from under her shoulders. A fresh tattoo slithers from his wrist to shoulder and honors the feathered skysnake, Avanyu, a holy symbol of the Navajo.

Impulsively, the man decides to cruise the bus and video the other passengers, recording their impressions of an eighteen-hour "Gamblers' Holiday" to the Lucky Pelican Casino. He stands in the aisle and holds the Sony at arm's length, pointing it toward himself - a tenth-grade dropout, with a raven-colored ponytail and almond-shaped eyes, now a flagman on a road crew. Still high from smoking weed in the bus lavatory, he rambles through an introduction to his "documentary." He'll post the video on YouTube, he brags to the camera, but will not ask for anyone's permission.

A couple of rows in front of him, three tellers from a downtown bank nurse quart-sized cups of margaritas and chatter to the camcorder about their "no-husbands-allowed weekend." The pretty brunette, her eye shadow and mascara smudged into Rorschach blots, giggles as she describes how, on a dare, she kissed and offered to sleep with one of the blackjack dealers. On Monday morning, she'll return to her job cashing checks, wearing a tailored suit and sensible pumps, unaware of her X-rated confession's download to the internet.

Sitting in front of them, an unemployed Gulf War veteran wears a wool shirt more appropriate for December in Vermont than July in Texas. He raves about the Shreveport casino's all-you-can-eat buffet. "Better than the Frontier's or Sahara's in Vegas," he boasts to the camera, oblivious of other passengers' reluctance to sit next to someone whose shirt percolates body odor, and whose breath smells of fish and whiskey. Reaching into in his shirt pocket, he caresses the $28 he won at the video poker slots. "Plus, I won me some walkin'-around money."

Across from him, a second-year law student stares at the seat in front of her. Her passed-out boyfriend slumps against the bus' window, his crusty lips quivering as he snores. Irritated because he hasn't spoken to her for the past three hours, she's annoyed at the prospect of being interviewed. "I don't think so," she mumbles to the man with the camcorder, hoping he will move on.

He smiles and says he'd consider it "a real special favor." Without waiting for a response, he presses the Sony's record button.

She exhales loudly, her reluctance giving way to resignation. "Well, from my boyfriend's point of view, it was a good trip. He got drunk and got laid."

Looking through the viewfinder, the highway worker asks, "What about from your point of view?"

She bites her lip slightly, thinking of a response. "A little disappointing, I guess." Then, realizing her answer would be considered soft by law-school standards, the woman shakes her head and glares at the camera. "No, damn it, it was big-time disappointing."

"Yeah?"

"Yeah."

"How come?"

She flicks her head toward her puffy-faced boyfriend. "I'm just tired of living with a drunk and a slob, that's all."

"You guys live together?"

She hesitates. "Well . . . for the time being."

"The time being?"

"I'm thinking of moving out."

The highway worker presses the camcorder's pause button. "You know, you're a fine-lookin' woman." He lightly touches her shoulder. "Women like you don't have to live like that." Further emboldened by his lavatory toke, he leans to within an inch of her ear and whispers, "Need some help movin' out?"

She flicks her head toward her puffy-faced boyfriend. "I'm just tired of living with a drunk and a slob, that's all."

Something about his brashness attracts her, something almost primal. While the bus's engine hums a comforting white noise, she scribbles her phone number on a piece of paper.

He stuffs it in his pocket, having already decided to betray his sleeping girlfriend. All he needs is an alibi.

Later in the day, at an intersection on Weatherford Street, a rangy-looking runner presses two fingers to his neck and studies the second hand of a diamond-encrusted Rolex, counting his pulse. An attorney whose afternoon soap-opera commercials promise "compensation for your on-the-job injury," he wears a Rice University sweatshirt and custom athletic shoes. The sweat-drenched man impatiently jogs in place as he waits for the traffic signal to change.

A lime-green Pontiac, accessorized by a mismatched yellow door, pulls alongside the curb. It squats on treadbare tires purchased from a wrecking yard on the outskirts of town. The thin-faced driver wears an out-of-fashion, floral-print dress she scavenged at the fire department's annual garage sale. Slumped in the passenger seat, her 80-year-old mother stares vacantly ahead, no longer able to remember the sister she's about to visit. The old woman's crackled skin is jaundiced from years of smoking generic cigarettes and washing with harsh, bargain-counter soap.

The driver rolls down the passenger-side window and asks the runner, "Excuse me, sir, could I ask you a question?"

He stops jogging, knowing he has about twenty seconds before his pulse drops below the target range. "Yeah, sure." The woman's car, pockmarked with golf-ball-sized indentions, reminds him of the ones he's seen at the shelter where he sometimes volunteers.

"I can't remember where they moved the bus station," she says, her voice rasping as if her vocal chords were made of sandpaper. "Do you know where it is?"

Although he knows Fort Worth well, the man struggles to recall the station's exact location. He's ventured inside the bus station only once before, last fall when he bought a round-trip ticket for his cleaning lady to visit her dying mother in Hermosillo. "Let's see, I think you continue down this street for about four lights and turn right on Calhoun. Go another eight to ten blocks, and you should see it on your left," he says.

"Thank you," the woman says. "By the way, do you know the time?"

Instinctively, he glances at his Rolex. "Twelve-fifteen," he answers, forgetting that all his clocks are set ten-minutes fast. Self-conscious because his watch has twenty times the value of her automobile, the attorney, not wanting to embarrass the woman, discreetly pulls down his sweatshirt sleeve and covers the Rolex.

She notices the subtle movement of his hand, but interprets the gesture differently - as a frightened man hiding his property from a potential thief. The woman cannot imagine a person having any reason to fear her. Although only a government check away from destitution, she is not a criminal, nor will she become one. She's proud of her Navajo heritage and family - one son works a steady job in highway construction; the other is a sheriff's deputy. Though her husband is now disabled, he once performed with his own blues quartet.

The progressive-minded jogger recognizes the pain and heartbreak in the woman's eyes. Although worlds apart in their interpretation of his action, for a moment, both are deeply ashamed.

An hour later, in the same part of downtown Fort Worth, a half-dozen women wait outside an intimidating brick fortress. All but two look as if they're sleepwalking through a familiar nightmare. One, a fidgety, Hispanic teenager wearing too much make-up, has a panicked look on her face, as if she's somehow responsible for her man being in jail. The other, an anorexic-looking white woman, laughs crazily, still high from a morning of smoking crack.

The women patiently assemble in front of a locked steel door, as a sheriff's deputy fumbles with the key. Once inside, they'll pass through metal detectors to the visiting area and fulfill their once-a-week obligation and ordeal. They are the girlfriends or wives of men who, more likely than not, have beaten them because dinner wasn't ready on time, the beer wasn't cold enough, or . . . just because. When the women enter the soulless visitor's room, still stinking of harsh disinfectant, they try to please their insignificant others by looking sufficiently sad. Some are grateful their visits are limited to once a week and only 30 minutes.

Outside, on the other side of the street, a grandmother and her five-year-old grandson wait for the traffic light to change. The little boy holds his baby brother, not more than six-months old, and doesn't understand why his father must stay at this place or why his mother decided to go away.

The woman reaches to take the infant from the little boy. He awkwardly shoves the baby into his grandmother's arms, not intentionally, but because he is five-years-old and his brother is heavy. Angered at his clumsiness, she punches the little boy in the chest. The child, knocked back a step, looks terrified. Although he wants to cry, he doesn't, because he's learned that crying will only be rewarded by another punch.

They cross the street. The grandmother feels guilty about hitting the little boy, but is unable to control her actions for some reason.

When they reach the sidewalk, the sheriff's deputy, who watched the mini-drama from afar, opens the door for the woman and asks if he could speak to the little boy.

"I don't care," the grandmother says, "go ahead."

The officer, a full-blooded Navajo, who understands the difficulty of holding a family together when the breadwinner is in prison, kneels on one knee, face-to-face with the child. "Hey, you're a pretty big boy to be carrying your brother all by yourself."

"Here, I have a little something for you."
He reaches into his pocket and hands the
child a silver sheriff's badge.

The boy stares at the floor.

"You know what? When I was about your age, I came to a place like this every week to visit someone."

The child refuses to look at the sheriff's deputy. "Here, I have a little something for you." He reaches into his pocket and hands the child a silver sheriff's badge. It's a toy, one of many the officer has purchased over the years.

Hesitantly, the boy accepts the shiny badge and explores its ridges and grooves with his slender fingers. He looks up at the officer, cautiously studying the man with the kind eyes.

In the months ahead, he'll enjoy his visits with the sheriff's deputy, even more than the visits with his father. In the years ahead, the child will listen intently to the deputy's words of encouragement, and one day, he'll hand out toy sheriff's badges of his own.

———————

At dusk, as he does every evening, the silver-haired street musician unties a saxophone strapped to the side of his wheelchair. His eyes crusted with cataracts, the man plays for dimes and quarters under a light pole on Weatherford Street. Before doing hard time for selling cocaine, his blues quartet headlined in crowded jazz clubs in Memphis and Chicago.

After an hour, the street musician needs a rest and carefully places his tarnished-brass instrument on the sidewalk, beside his wheelchair. He smiles. As seen through the man's diseased eyes, the saxophone appears to move and coil, reminding him of a beautiful feathered skysnake.

He plays all night, collecting $36 in tips. Just before sunrise, the Lucky Pelican Casino bus passes through the Weatherford Street intersection, as it does every morning at the same time, its diesel engine humming a comforting white noise to the gamblers on board. Without looking at his eight-dollar Timex, the street musician mutters to himself, "Right on time." He slides the mouthpiece off his saxophone and labors to strap it to the side of his wheelchair.

Afterwards, a lime-green Pontiac, with a mismatched yellow door, pulls to the curb and takes him home for a traditional breakfast of flat bread and blue corn mush. ✪

Life&Leisure

A Traitor in our Midst?

Ask Mr. Mighty Brain

Editor's Note: Mr. Mighty Brain recently completed the final draft of a Pulitzer Prize acceptance speech. His advice column, which regularly appears in The San Antonio Reporter-Gazette, is virtually a shoo-in for this long-overdue honor. Forever humble, Mr. Mighty Brain plans to stay grounded and completely in touch with all the common people who remain his loyal readers.

Dear Mr. Mighty Brain,
I'm a lifetime member of the Daughters of the War of 1812. Unlike our more glamorous counterparts, the Daughters of the American Revolution and the Daughters of the Confederacy, our society toils in relative obscurity, promoting patriotism and educating the public about that noble, often-neglected conflict.

As the chapter parliamentarian for the [p]ast 41 years, I've faithfully attended [o]ur local chapter's formal teas, battle [re]enactments, and summer picnics at [th]e lake. During that time, I've only [mi]ssed one meeting, and that was [be]cause I was in the hospital, flat on [my] back with a bulging L4-L5 disc, after [hav]ing marched three miles with our [soci]ety in the Independence Day [para]de.

[Rece]ntly, however, I discovered an [obscu]re family letter that calls into [ques]tion my great-great-great-great [grand]father Cornelius' role in the war. [The d]ocument reveals he was a spy for

sophisticated," which, of course, he is. Your letter is another link in an amazing chain of good fortune for Mr. Mighty Brain. On Thursday, he received correspond-ence announcing he almost certainly holds the winning entry in the Publishers Clearinghouse Sweepstakes! Two days earlier, he was invited to an "all-expenses paid" trip to a Florida luxury resort, merely for participating in a "no obligation tour" of the resort's timeshare condos.
Additionally, one of his neighbors invited Mr. Mighty Brain to an Amway "get acquainted" meeting, where he expects to fulfill his dream of becoming financially

Dear Mr. Mighty Brain,
My sister, Lois, recently became obsessed with Catholic saints. She prays to them constantly and treats them as if they were her personal staff. It all started three months ago when Lois decided to drive to Tulsa for a new pair of orthotics. Why she couldn't have purchased them locally, I don't know. Anyway, she was worried to death about her old Pontiac breaking down on the way, so a Catholic friend suggested she buy a St. Christopher's medal for protection. My sister looked all over town and finally found a silver one at a pawnshop. The old rattletrap (the car, not my sister) made it all the way to Tulsa and back, and Lois believed it was all because of that medal.

THREE

Ask Mister Mighty Brain -
A Traitor in our Midst?

Editor's Note: Mr. Mighty Brain recently completed the final draft of a Pulitzer Prize acceptance speech. His advice column, which regularly appears in The San Antonio Reporter-Gazette, is virtually a shoo-in for this long-overdue honor. Forever humble, Mr. Mighty Brain plans to stay grounded and completely in touch with all the common people who remain his loyal readers.

Dear Mr. Mighty Brain,

My sister, Lois, recently became obsessed with Catholic saints. She prays to them constantly and treats them as if they were her personal staff.

It all started three months ago when Lois decided to drive to Tulsa for a new pair of orthotics. Why she couldn't have purchased them locally, I don't know. Anyway, she was worried to death about her old Pontiac breaking down on the way, so a Catholic friend suggested she buy a St. Christopher's medal for protection. My sister looked all over town and finally found a silver one at a pawnshop. The old rattletrap (the car, not my sister) made it all the way to Tulsa and back, and Lois believed it was all because of that medal.

Afterwards, Lois surfed the internet, downloaded all the Catholic saints and their specialties, and laminated a handwritten directory for her purse. Now, whenever she sees road kill on the highway, she immediately asks St. Francis of Assisi, the patron saint of animals, to bless the smushed possum's or armadillo's soul. Why she believes animals have souls, I don't know, but it's better not to argue with her now that she's tight with the saints. My sister loves to hike but wouldn't dream of doing so without first checking with St. Patrick, who's evidently in charge of snakes, and asking him to pen up all his crawling buddies. Lois claims her last root canal was a breeze after she talked with St. Apollonia, the dental saint, and her internet now runs faster after St. Isidore cleaned out some spyware from her computer.

The odd thing is, up until recently, Lois hasn't been particularly religious. Why she's become so interested in saints, I don't know, because our family isn't Catholic, Irish, or Mexican. In fact, the last time I remember my sister going inside a church of any kind was four years ago when the local Presbyterians closed their doors. At their "Going Out of Business Auction," she outbid a Methodist and a Lutheran for a pair of silver-plated candlesticks. Thankfully, no Episcopalians showed up, or she would have left empty-handed.

Mr. Mighty Brain, do you think Lois might be on to something? Even though I'm suspicious of all this mumbo-jumbo about saints, I wouldn't want to miss a good thing.

Signed,
Baffled Baptist

Dear Baffled Baptist (Isn't that redundant?),

Since Mr. Mighty Brain is not Catholic, he cannot claim to have perfect knowledge of all things spiritual. Nor is he infallible, an admission which may come as a surprise to some of his long-time readers. He is, however, able to imagine how heavenly matters of this nature are managed and resolved.

He envisions a Celestial Senate of the Saints - a marbled, columned chamber, similar to the U.S. Senate in Washington, where weighty matters are debated such as declaring war, confirming Supreme Court justices, and funding research on swine-odor management in Iowa.

In the heavenly chamber, saints are assigned desks, which are arranged in rows of concentric circles. Just as in Washington, an aisle separates the conservatives from the liberals. For example, Daniel, the patron saint of prisoners and an ACLU, card-carrying liberal, sits across the aisle from the ultra-conservative Adrian, the prison guards' law-and-order, tough-on-crime saint. Luke, the favorite of cosmetic surgeons, is opposite his nemesis, Raymond, patron saint of malpractice attorneys.

Mr. Mighty Brain further imagines a Speaker of the Saints, selected in an incense-filled back room, who presides over the august body with an iron fist. The Speaker dishes out choice committee assignments based upon support of his latest pork-barrel boondoggle, or whether another saint blackmailed him with indiscrete photos taken at last year's St. Valentine's party. (Perhaps the love saint himself has dirt on the Speaker, which is why he merits a holiday all to himself.)

Whenever an Earthly prayer comes to the floor of the Celestial Senate, the Speaker assigns it to the relevant saint for evaluation and action. In the case of conflicting constituent requests, such as whether a baby-seal safari would be successful, the patron saints of hunters and animals meet in committee and resolve the issue.

Each year, the Celestial Saints caucus behind closed doors and vote themselves and their staffers an unconscionable pay increase. They agree not to be bound by any of the onerous rules they've established for other spiritual beings. On filing their heavenly tax returns, they conveniently "forget" receiving rental income from their second homes in Eden and fail to report lobbyist-paid junkets to Shangri-la.

That said, Mr. Mighty Brain really has no idea whether your sister's requests to the saints are worthwhile, but sees no harm in the practice. However, he does wonder why a St. Christopher's medal would show up in a pawnshop.

Dear Mr. Mighty Brain,

I'm a lifetime member of the Daughters of the War of 1812. Unlike our more glamorous counterparts, the Daughters of the American Revolution and the Daughters of the Confederacy, our society toils in relative obscurity, promoting patriotism and educating the public about that noble, often-neglected conflict.

As the chapter parliamentarian for the past 41 years, I've faithfully attended our local chapter's formal teas, battle reenactments, and summer picnics at the lake. During that time, I've only missed one meeting, and that was because I was in the hospital, flat on my back with a bulging L4-L5 disc, after having marched three miles with our society in the Independence Day parade.

Recently, however, I discovered an obscure family letter that calls into question my great-great-great-great grandfather Cornelius' role in the war. The document reveals he was a spy for the British, not the patriot all of us believed.

Mr. Mighty Brain, this information was absolutely crushing, and if it became known to the other ladies, I'd be labeled as a fraud and a traitor, just like Cornelius. Rather than be unceremoniously stripped of my lifetime membership, I've considered resigning from the society "due to health reasons." That itself is a bit of a lie, but not as big as the lie I've been living for the past 41 years. What do you think I should do? Please do not reveal my name, nor my real city.

Signed,
Mata Benedict Rosenberg

Dear Descendent of a Man Who Chose a Country that Came in Second Place in the Two Wars We Fought Against Each Other and Thus Began a Gradual but Inexorable Decline into International Irrelevance in Spite of Their Current Belief to the Contrary,

Burn the letter.

Dear Mr. Mighty Brain,

Your name was given to me as someone who is completely trustworthy and financially sophisticated. The person who gave me your name asked that I not reveal his identity, so as a person of high integrity myself, I will respect his wishes.

My late father was a high-ranking executive with a Nigerian oil company. At his death, the family discovered he had secretly deposited approximately 27 million dollars (U.S.) into his personal security account in Ghana. The existence of the account remains unknown to the Nigerian oil company.

Unfortunately, our family has little experience in handling large sums of money. Also, the laws in Nigeria prevent us from wire-transferring funds from Ghana into Nigeria. However, the rules do permit wires from Ghana into the United States.

Because of that loophole, we are asking if you will assist our family by allowing

us to transfer this money into your personal bank account. You would take a 15% fee for your assistance plus, of course, any expenses you may incur in the process. You would then transfer the net proceeds to our family's bank account in Nigeria.

Naturally, I must solicit complete confidentiality in this transaction, by virtue of the sensitive nature of the matter. Please acknowledge receipt of this letter at your earliest convenience with your signature on your personal letterhead.

With Kindest Regards,
Simba Mufasa

Dear Simba,

Mr. Mighty Brain is flattered someone would consider him "trustworthy and financially sophisticated," which, of course, he is.

Your letter is another link in an amazing chain of good fortune for Mr. Mighty Brain. On Thursday, he received correspondence announcing he almost certainly holds the winning entry in the Publishers Clearinghouse Sweepstakes! Two days earlier, he was invited to an "all-expenses paid" trip to a Florida luxury resort, merely for participating in a "no obligation tour" of the resort's timeshare condos. Additionally, one of his neighbors invited Mr. Mighty Brain to an Amway "get acquainted" meeting, where he expects to fulfill his dream of becoming financially independent. And now, this opportunity!

As to your proposal, Mr. Mighty Brain plans to discuss the matter with his cousin, Ponzi Madoff, and will be in touch. ✪

"Sullivan guided me through the entryway to his living room, gesturing for me to have a seat on one of two damask-covered settees, placed parallel with each other. Separated by an ornate, glass-topped coffee table, we sat like mannequins, posing stiffly on crimson and gold-fringed settees, as uncomfortable as the atmosphere in the room."

FOUR

Dirty Martinis

Teague was late, as usual. Stingray and I waited in the Petrossian Lounge, just off the lobby and catty-cornered from the high-dollar blackjack tables. After three, maybe four rounds of dirty martinis, we gossiped like seventh-graders in PE class.

➤➤

Stingray was dating a Dallas trial lawyer who was so bad in bed, she said, he brought new definition to the term "legal brief."

"Oh, come on, he can't be that bad," I countered, offering a defense for someone I'd never met.

She leaned toward me, straining to be heard over the jazz pianist, fifteen-feet away. "Plus, the man's hairier than one of those Middle-Eastern suicide gorillas."

"You can't say stuff like that."

"Well, it's true," Stingray countered, stretching out the last word into a syllable and a half. "I figure the reason they're suicide bombers is because they can't get laid on earth. Don't they get, like, 70 or 80 virgins in paradise if they blow themselves up?"

We paused our conversation long enough to watch a liquored-up executive-type, on the downhill side of 50, meander into the bar with a leggy, sandy-blonde friend and veer over to the only available table, next to ours.

"Well, at least you can snuggle up with someone on occasion," I said, nodding toward the inebriated man. I tapped my faux-alligator purse, checking that it remained sandwiched between the chair and the layer of cellulite growing like kudzu on my thigh. In Vegas, pickpockets worked the Bellagio just like the Flamingo or any other casino on the strip. They just wore nicer clothes.

"You're not the one using a Dirt Devil to vacuum his side of the bed," Stingray complained, repositioning the olive in her glass. "He has fur on his back long enough to braid into pigtails, for God's sake." She downed the last of her martini. "Where the hell is Teague?"

With a hard-earned salon tan, fabulous hair, and a low-cut, aqua-blue blouse with sequins spelling out her professional name, Stingray seemed prepped for one of those glamour-photo shoots they do at the mall; except in her case, it was her everyday appearance. Granted, my face never shattered any mirrors, but Stingray's always caught the second glance, and although we were both 42, she looked a full-decade younger. Like a halo from a medieval painting of the Madonna, her sex appeal radiated about her, which Teague subtly used in arranging our traveling poker games.

At the next table, the inebriated executive ordered twin shots of chilled vodka, his Clark Kent glasses resting cockeyed on his nose. When he threw back his head and gulped the vodka, his blonde friend discretely glanced at her watch, no doubt regretting her decision to socialize with this very un-Super, Superman.

Stingray, twice divorced and no longer looking for permanence, mentioned trading her "lawyer ape" for her three-day-a-week personal trainer, Joaquin. "He's dumb as broccoli and probably makes a dollar over minimum wage . . ." She paused and moved within inches of my ear, practically shouting to be heard over the pianist's improvisational riff, "But I understand his barbells are Olympic-sized."

Even though Stingray and I had known each other forever, her trashiness still amazed me.

At the table next to us, a somewhat-woozy Clark Kent leaned over to kiss his friend. Not the least bit interested, she inched away and balanced herself at the very edge of her chair, which leaned at a precarious angle. Before she could push him away, Clark Kent made another lunge. The woman's chair tipped over and the two of them tumbled onto the floor, sprawling into some sort of coital-like wrestling pose. She screamed, causing the music to stop, as well as most of the conversation in the bar, leaving only the rhythmic sound of slot machines pinging in a distant part of the casino.

The cocktail waitress hurried over to the couple's table, helping them to their feet and collecting the liquor tab before security escorted them out of the bar. They were quickly joined by a heavily muscled Filipino man, in his early 30's, wearing wrap-around Oakley sunglasses that clung to his cleanly shaven, cue-ball-like head. Our partner, Teague, 30-minutes late, had appeared out of nowhere to assist the fallen couple.

Like a ballroom dancer furious at her clumsy partner, the embarrassed blonde straightened her dress, glared at Clark Kent, and stormed out of the Pretrossian. Looking as if he'd caused the pair to be eliminated from the ballroom competition, the executive threw his arm around Teague's shoulder as if they were old friends and commiserated with our partner for a couple of minutes. Then, somewhat unsteadily, a chastened Clark Kent wandered back into the casino.

The pianist, obviously a man with a sense of
humor, launched a swingy version of "Let's Fall in Love,"
as Teague glided over to our table.

The pianist, obviously a man with a sense of humor, launched a swingy version of "Let's Fall in Love," as Teague glided over to our table. "Hey, Stingray, Queen, sorry I'm late." He plopped down on the empty seat. "Heard a commotion and thought it might be you guys causing trouble."

"Wow, that was some kind of floor show," I said, shaking my head.

"You're late again, Cue Ball," said Stingray, clicking open a clamshell compact and checking her make-up. "Trolling in the men's room?"

"There you go, again," our partner said, dramatically crossing his arms in front of his thick chest, as if he were offended. "When you gonna shake that redneck attitude?" Teague didn't flaunt his sexuality, and even though he looked as if he'd be far more comfortable fighting in a martial-arts-death match than cruising a gay bar in a boa, he didn't deny being homosexual, either. He grinned and winked at Stingray. "For your information, Miss 'I'm-straight-and-the-whole-world-should-be-also,' I've been checkin' out the suite for tomorrow afternoon's session."

"Everyone coming?" I asked. At last count, Teague received five commitments for our private Texas Hold'em game. With a carefully cultivated reputation for running totally legitimate and first-class games, our partner rarely suffered a vacancy at the table.

"Yep. In fact, one of 'em was just here," he said.

"Who?" Stingray asked, using a small brush to powder a shiny place on her forehead.

"That drunk at the next table."

"You're kidding."

"Nope. Name's Sullivan. By the way, he asked me to apologize for his behavior. Said it was 'uncharacteristic.'"

"Yeah, I bet," I said. "About as uncharacteristic as spots on a Dalmatian. How'd he know who we were?"

"I told him you were my partners, in case he freaked tomorrow afternoon after he met you two," Teague said. "I've seen guys flake-out, pick up their money, and take the first flight home, if they're really uncomfortable or humiliated about somethin'. Guess it's a man thing."

Stingray asked, "So, a guy could be humiliated because two other women, who he's yet to meet, saw him commode-hugging drunk?" She reapplied her salmon-colored lipstick and polished her teeth with her index finger. "Men are so weird, sometimes." Using the tube of Clinique to signal the cocktail waitress, she ordered another round of drinks.

My earliest childhood memory is sitting on my father's lap, drinking milk from a sippy cup, and watching him deal cards. He taught me the difference between straights and flushes before Mom taught me my ABC's. A professional gambler, he provided well for his family; but we were always on the move - Memphis, Vegas, Denver, even Detroit, briefly, before finally settling in Fort Worth. Back in those days, poker kings had a bit of a sleazy reputation, so Mom told our neighbors he traveled the country selling plumbing supplies. Today, with the sport's glamour and made-for-television glitz, top poker pros have their own fan clubs and websites. If he were alive, I'm sure Dad would have his own line of logoed windbreakers and customized coffee mugs, probably something to do with his favorite saying, "Never bet the whole farm. Bet it an acre at a time." It

was his cardinal principle of always making careful, measured bets, never risking everything you had on one hand. It's a rule I've never broken.

I won my first big money during my junior year at TCU, skipping a Tri-Delt social one weekend for a private poker game at the Adolphus in downtown Dallas. That spring, I realized an Art History degree provided a standard of living just a half-link higher on the food chain than a student's, so I quit school to concentrate on cards. Because he assumed I'd be curating the Louvre some day, my father wasn't thrilled when he heard the news. But he understood the math.

A year later, I met the love of my life, another poker junkie. Also a college dropout, Curtis counted cards and calculated odds like a Toshiba laptop, but it was the kind, generous way he treated everyone he met that won me over. It didn't matter if people were Forbes 400 or stuck on food stamps, they were no different to him. Marrying a fellow gambler was a big risk, given the killer divorce rate in our profession; but ignoring the odds, we took a chance. It was a solid marriage, even with our gypsy lifestyle. Our little girl, Susan, lived a garden-variety childhood, playing in a backyard tree house, peddling Girl Scout cookies, and suffering through piano lessons. The family business probably stops with her; she's now sixteen and far more interested in college than cards.

Four years ago, Curtis developed stomach problems and rapidly lost weight, becoming jaundiced and tiring easily. Assuming it was all the travel and erratic hotel food, he delayed going to the doctor for a couple of months. When a specialist finally examined him, the verdict was stage IV pancreatic cancer, with a prognosis of four months, max. Playing a long shot, Curtis volunteered for an experimental treatment at M.D. Anderson, which offered the equivalent odds of drawing an inside straight. Unfortunately, he drew soft and lasted only 37 days. The Saturday before he died, Curtis mumbled something to his doctor about being taken off morphine long enough to clear his mind. He wanted me to invite a friend over to his hospital room for one last poker game. I phoned Stingray.

Curtis couldn't walk, so my best friend and I stood around his bed and played Texas Hold'em for a couple of hours, doing our best to leave our tears outside the room.

When the game ended and Curtis and I were alone, he asked me to crawl up on the bed and lie next to him. Sharing his pillow and holding hands, we talked about my life after he was gone. He wanted me to "find someone," even remarry. "Lindsay, you're too young and pretty not to have a special person," he said, adamantly. "Promise me you'll consider it."

I knew he meant every word. In his own very-male way, Curtis was attempting to look out for my wellbeing, even in death. At that moment, watching the man I loved teetering on the edge of life, it was inconceivable I'd ever love again. When I tried to speak, for the first time in my life my voice completely locked down, my throat aching as if someone had crushed my windpipe, as well as my heart.

Curtis' pain soon returned. Knowing the end was near, he asked for morphine and smiled one last good-bye. Two days later, he died peacefully.

For a while, Susan had difficulty accepting the finality of her father's death, constantly wearing his old shirts around the house and insisting we not clean out his closet. After six months, she dealt with her loss by obsessing about school, determined to become a research scientist and discover a cure for pancreatic cancer. In chemistry lab one day, when an experiment failed to work correctly, Susan angrily flung her rack of test tubes against the wall, shattering the glass. Fortunately, her teacher understood the source of Susan's rage and helped her clean up the mess.

As hard as Curtis's death was on my daughter, it was even tougher on me. I stayed home for two years, living off the insurance money, isolated and content to play endless hours of solitaire. Unable to escape the paralyzing grief and afraid of losing Susan or my mother, it was as if I was sitting at a poker table and passing on every hand, fearful of life itself.

Mom, recognizing my emotional paralysis and knowing my savings would eventually play out, offered to take care of Susan on weekends while I returned to the circuit. It was as if I'd been seeking permission to move ahead with my life, and my mother offered it. The first person I called was Stingray.

Teague met Stingray - then using her real name - at the prelims for Ultimate Texas Hold'em, a TV reality show, and although neither of them made the finals, the two hit it off and kept in touch. A couple of months later, Teague decided to retire from competitive poker, realizing he perspired like a sumo wrestler in a steam room every time he drew a good hand. His marketing instincts told him Stingray's good looks offered more lucrative opportunities for private poker sessions with wealthy businessmen than regular casino tournaments, so he offered to become her agent and unofficial bodyguard. For Stingray, who grumbled that playing the poker circuit was like swimming without a life preserver in a sea of testosterone, it was an attractive proposition. They shook hands on the deal and arranged private gigs all over the country.

After a year, the report card on Stingray's winnings was barely a C minus - the grade courtesy of a generous curve. "We make a Hamburger Helper living," she complained, "certainly not filet mignon." In truth, both were only a few months away from working cash registers at Home Depot or Hobby Lobby. Hearing about my "un-retirement," and knowing I was a more consistent winner (although it was never specifically mentioned), Stingray and Teague floated the idea of my joining their partnership.

For me, the notion of traveling with a "team," of sorts, was appealing, especially with Curtis gone. Hanging out with Stingray, always fun and edgy, would be Valium for my mental and emotional health, but I wasn't sure about Teague - a Filipino body-builder, ten-years younger than us girls. It was a huge gamble, all right; but after thinking it over, I agreed to an equal, three-way split, no matter who won. What developed was a symbiotic relationship - Teague's salesmanship and physical protection, Stingray's good looks and high-wattage personality, and my knack for reading an opponent and playing the right cards.

Three months later, we weren't always having filet mignon, but no one was eating Hamburger Helper or clerking at Home Depot.

The drill remained consistent for each party, with our male partner booking a VIP suite and providing food and beverage set-up. Since hotels and casinos frown on private gaming events held on their premises, Teague told management he was a software guru, providing specialized training for executives, and wasn't to be disturbed. He joked to Stingray and me it was the only time in his life when looking vaguely Oriental was a huge advantage. The evening before a session, the partners met for dirty martinis, one of several of our superstitious rituals. Teague ran late, of course - if he arrived on time, it was considered bad mojo - and part of the routine was to accuse him of trolling the men's room. Professional gamblers have more quirks and good-luck charms than NBA all-stars have tattoos.

The party would begin promptly at two the following afternoon and finished whenever one person won all the money or the remaining players agreed to a truce. Games occasionally lasted fourteen, fifteen hours, but normally ended by midnight. Teague extracted a non-refundable advance fee, or "rake," of $5,000 from each participant for organizing and producing the affair, which meant our travel and hotel expenses, plus a little extra, were always covered. Every player ponied up a stake of $25,000, which eliminated lightweights and wannabes. Thanks to Teague's salesmanship, the sessions routinely maxed-out.

The next afternoon, our suite provided a box-seat view of the Bellagio's outdoor dancing fountains, Sin City's favorite tourist attraction.

As the event's host, Teague, who became "Cue Ball" for our parties, greeted our guests at the door. He introduced them to "Stingray" and "The Queen of Diamonds," cocky-sounding nicknames he created so clients would believe they were playing with poker legends like Amarillo Slim or Texas Dolly. Even though I considered my professional name completely hokey, the clients were intrigued and somewhat intimidated by it, exactly Teague's intention.

As part of his preparations the evening before, our partner installed a customized, green-felt poker mat on the dining table, instantly transforming the area into a serious-looking, private casino. Joining Stingray and me around the table were Sullivan, our Clark Kent friend; "Elvis," a seriously handsome cotton farmer from Mississippi; "Knife," a trauma-room surgeon, who loved poker, he said, because it gave him "a better adrenaline rush" than an emergency room; Malcolm, an airline pilot, who, like Sullivan, actually used his real name; and a 40-something-year-old Philadelphia Italian, "Rambo," who never told us his profession.

Before beginning the session, Teague reviewed our house rules: three bidding rounds per hand; no cursing or off-color jokes; no leaving the table except for potty breaks every 30 minutes; and no smoking or using tobacco of any kind. Since he wasn't a part of the actual game, Teague acted as the banker - just as in Monopoly, except with real money - emptying and counting our guests' satchels of $100 bills and converting the cash into our own customized poker chips. He also served as part-time bartender, waiter, and once or twice, as referee.

An hour later, the atmosphere, as usual, was similar to a lunchtime basketball game at the YMCA - middle-aged guys, all macho-ed up, determined to prove they still had game. Stingray, always bubbly and flirty, only added to the hormonal fog, with Elvis and Knife jockeying for her attention.

Texas Hold'em has its own unique slang, and Elvis made sure everyone knew he savvied the lingo. Speaking in a thick delta drawl, he repeatedly referred to his face cards as "paint;" three or four cards not of the same suit were a "rainbow." Although I kept quiet, I knew the difference between paint and rainbows before I learned who Ken and Barbie were.

A genuinely polite man, Malcolm wasn't much of a poker player. Several times during the afternoon, he seemed distracted by Stingray's bosom and misplayed his cards. The first to go bankrupt, the friendly pilot graciously exited, thanking Teague for the chance to play. Earlier, when he left the table for a bathroom break, I noticed heavy fraying on his shirtsleeves and wondered whether he really had any business mingling with this high-rolling crowd. It wasn't my place to be a social worker or a psychologist; still, I felt sorry for the guy.

Knife, when he wasn't nervously sipping from his can of Diet Coke or adjusting his Nebraska Cornhusker ball cap, repeatedly tapped his fingers on the table, an annoyance to the other players. An hour into the game, Teague asked him to stop the finger-tapping, but Knife didn't take kindly to being reprimanded, no matter how gently, and responded with a don't-you-know-I'm-a-doctor glare. After two-and-a-half hours of hemorrhaging poker chips, the Cornhusker surrendered and departed with a flippant "See ya, I'm outta here," grabbing a fresh soda as he left.

Rambo had the look of someone you didn't want to anger. For the first hour, he didn't speak, finally grunting two sentences, one to complain the beer wasn't cold enough, and another to say he hated vinegar-and-salt pretzels. After three hours, Rambo caved-in and caught a red-eye back to Philly. He seemed like the kind of guy who, once he arrived back in the City of Brotherly Love, might decide luke-warm beer and crappy pretzels weren't worth 25 grand and send a couple of goons back to Vegas for a full refund. That's when Cue Ball earned every penny of his cut.

Sullivan was harder to figure. An excellent card player, he wagered aggressively, yet rarely over-played a hand, folding when the odds weren't in his favor. He seemed more like a gentleman who drank *Pinot Noir* and ran 5K's on weekends, not a drunk who'd tumble onto the Petrossian Lounge floor. Sullivan owned a Houston BMW dealership, and it turned out, he and our male partner had a long history. Teague, newly graduated from U of H, went to work for Sullivan, who taught him the fine art of selling over-priced, German cars. In return, Teague schooled his boss in the nuances of playing Texas Hold'em. They remained friends long after Teague left the dealership, turned poker pro, and nicknamed himself "Cue Ball." Self-assured and confident, you'd never suspect this was Sullivan's first swim in the Testosteronic Ocean of private gambling.

At seven o'clock, Stingray hoisted her white flag and wandered back to the suite's mini-kitchen to help Teague prepare chicken-and-cheese nachos, another of our quirky, but exacting, rituals. With our game on the hush-hush, room service was a no-no.

With Stingray now on the sidelines, three of us were left to duke it out: Sullivan and me, with near-equal arsenals of chips; and Elvis, down to a few remaining bullets.

At seven-thirty, everyone took a break. With Stingray in the kitchen lusting after the hunky cotton farmer, Sullivan and I refueled with peppered-up nachos. On the way back to the gaming table, he asked where I lived.

"Fort Worth."

"Yeah?" Sullivan perked up. "What part of town?"

"Mistletoe Heights. Just off Forest Park."

"Great area. I was just up in your neck of the woods a week ago giving waltz and two-step lessons."

"As in dancing?"

He smiled. "My daughter lives in Fort worth. She met this good-looking cowboy who invited her to Billy Bob's. She hadn't country-western danced in a while and didn't want to look bad. Hope she doesn't turn into a full-fledged diva." After a long pause, he chose his next words deliberately. "You know, I'd like to apologize about last night."

"I'm not sure if the lady was your wife or girlfriend, but she's probably the one who needs an apology."

"I'm not married, actually," Sullivan said, "not that being single made my actions any less distasteful." He glanced down toward the carpet. "She was a woman I met in another bar, after I'd been, shall we say, over-served a bit. It wasn't my normal —"

"Don't sweat it," I interrupted, sensing his discomfort.

"After I'd bought her a drink at the Petrossian, she decided to leave." He looked up and laughed, nervously. "I figured I'd at least get a good-night kiss out of my investment." He shrugged his shoulders. "Talk about doubling down on my stupidity."

"Well, it's really none of my business."

"I just want to apologize to you, that's all," he said. "Oh, and to Stingray, of course."

I shrugged my shoulders. "Everybody makes mistakes."

Sullivan seemed relieved. Then, impishly, he asked, "By the way, if you're the Queen of Diamonds, did your mother name your brother Jack or King?"

Sullivan seemed relieved. Then, impishly, he asked, "By the way, if you're the Queen of Diamonds, did your mother name your brother Jack or King?"

I smiled. "Oh, you know how Teague is. Always looking for a marketing angle."

"So, do you have a real name, or must I keep referring to you as 'Your Highness?'"

Smiling, I extended my hand. "I'm Lindsay. Lindsay Walton, although 'Your Highness' does have a certain ring to it."

Sullivan, his eyes twinkling, shook my hand firmly. "Nice to meet you, Your Highness Lindsay."

When we returned to our seats, Teague asked everyone's permission to increase the ante from $1,000 to $3,000 per hand, since there were now fewer players. My turn to shuffle, I riffled the cards and thought about Sullivan teasing me about being "royalty." It felt good, even coming from a semi-scoundrel like him.

Gathering his cards from the table, Elvis mocked the airline pilot, Malcolm. "What a 'donk,'" he said, using poker slang for someone who's a weak player. "Probably the first time he ever played in this kind of game." There was a slight smirk on his face, but it wasn't the sexy lip-curl of his Tupelo namesake - more of a melodrama villain's sneer. "Thankfully, it didn't take long to put him out of his misery."

"He wasn't such a donk," I lied, remembering how sorry I felt for Malcolm.

Across the table, Sullivan glared at the cotton farmer. "I don't think he was, either."

"Crap," Elvis said, ignoring our comments. He sorted his cards and leaned forward. "I've been 'drawin' dead' for the past hour."

The timing of his complaint seemed a bit suspicious. I noticed whenever our Mississippi buddy drew a good hand, he leaned forward in his chair, ever so slightly. His bold, first-round wagering confirmed my theory he was "reverse bluffing," and both Sullivan and I threw in the towel before the second round of betting.

Two hands later, Elvis leaned slightly back in his chair, while arranging his cards. Even though his body language suggested he'd drawn poorly, he bid the first round as if he had a royal flush. Whether Sullivan also noticed this chair-leaning quirk wasn't clear, but both of us wagered the limit on the second and third rounds, calling Elvis' bluff and forcing him to "bet the farm" and throw all his chips in the pot. If Dad were playing, he would have smiled, slyly.

At show-and-tell time, I presented a pair of nines.

Next, Elvis reluctantly produced a pair of fives, confirming the skinny bluff.

When it was Sullivan's turn, he cracked a half-smile. Laying three kings on the table, he said, softly, "Donk, donk, who's there?"

Elvis looked at Sullivan and shook his head. "Man, you just picked this cotton farmer clean." Then he glanced at me. "Actually, both of you did."

The Mississippi guy was the kind of person we dealt with all the time - an overconfident jackass who'd played plenty of Saturday-night poker with his buddies or watched the pros on TV, certifying him as a know-it-all piece of fruit, ripe for picking. Thanking everyone and promising to return to one of our parties, he drifted to the mini-kitchen and flirted with Stingray.

Teague delivered a fresh batch of nachos to the table. "Anyone need a refill?"

"Not for me," I said.

"I'm about up to my neck in nachos, Cue Ball." Sullivan smiled. "Look, her Highness and I have about the same amount of chips. It'd take us a week to wipe the other out." He glanced at his watch. "It's nearly nine. How 'bout we call a truce, and you, me, and Lindsay head down to *Le Cirque* for a real dinner? My treat."

It didn't seem to take long for Teague's mental calculator to compute we earned over $75,000 for the day, making the decision as easy as shuffling a broken-in deck. "Sounds good to me," he said.

I glanced at Stingray, who was laughing and touching Elvis lightly on the arm, and likely making plans for the rest of the evening. Given Sullivan's track record the prior evening, I was cautious about accepting his offer.

As if he were reading my mind, Sullivan looked at me and smiled. "Don't worry, we won't go anywhere near the Petrossian. I promise." Then, turning to Teague, he added, "Plus, Cue Ball can be your personal bodyguard."

I earned good money sizing up people and trusting my instincts. "OK, count me in. I'm ready for a filet mignon."

A month later, I accepted Stingray's long-standing invitation to join her health club. Ten minutes into our first treadmill session, my legs felt as if they were filled with sand rather than muscle.

"So, how's it going with the personal trainer?" I asked, trying not to sound as if I were gasping for breath. "'Joaquin,' isn't it?"

"Apparently, he isn't attracted to older women," Stingray said, looking straight ahead as she jogged.

"Oh? How old is he?"

"He's 30, but I told him I was 31." She switched her treadmill's setting up a level and angled her head toward at me. "And I was, once upon a time."

"Maybe he'd be more attracted to Teague, if you know what I mean."

"I don't think so." Stingray's face was glowing, unlike mine, which was sweating. "Actually, they met a couple of weeks ago, and Teague's gaydar didn't register any blips."

"You heard from Elvis any more?"

"He's called a couple of times, once to invite me to a boll-weevil symposium in Memphis." She wrinkled her nose. "Be still, my aching heart."

"Give him credit," I said, now unable to mask my gulps for air.

"Yeah," she said, somewhat clinically. "He should be in Hollywood making movies instead of God-Knows-Where, Mississippi, pulling weeds or whatever cotton farmers do." Stingray's face morphed from glowing to glistening, still relatively attractive compared to mine, which I imagined to be all sweat-hoggish. "Speaking of new friends, what's the deal with Sullivan?"

"We've been emailing every day, talking on the phone every night. Very weird."

"What's weird about it?"

"It's been a long time since anyone paid much attention to me."

"Lindsay, you're an attractive woman. Lots of men pay attention to you. You just don't pay any back."

"Sullivan's different. As much as I didn't care for him at first, he turned out to be such an eclectic man, definitely not a typical Houston bubba. More of a cashmere-sweater kind of guy." I lowered the speed of my treadmill, unable to match Stingray's pace. "Plus, he likes me. He wants to know what radio channels I listen to, what I think about politics. He really likes me."

"You act surprised."

"I guess I am, to a degree. That evening in Vegas, we seemed to connect on so many levels. After Teague went to his room, Sullivan and I talked until, maybe, three or four in the morning." Pausing for a hit of oxygen, I continued, "Every night since then, while Susan's doing her homework, we're on the phone for an hour, at least. Sometimes, a couple of hours. It's just so, well, comfortable."

Stingray raised her eyebrows. "Comfortable?"

"Yeah, I feel as if we can talk about anything, really. Curtis's illness and death, what we like and don't like about ourselves, my depression, a single mom raising a sixteen-year-old. I went to counseling for a solid year and never opened up like I do with him."

"Wow."

"Yeah, it's amazing, Stingray. Plus, he actually isn't afraid to express his emotions and talk about what he's feeling."

"This is a male you're talking about, right?"

"Come on, there are men who talk about things besides football and sex."

"There may be," she said, dryly, "but I've never met one. So, are you guys dating?"

"We've discussed it, but I don't know if I'm ready, at this point. And, to be honest, I haven't taken care of myself as I should have, which is why I'm on this stupid treadmill."

Stingray chuckled. "Is Sullivan OK with just being your buddy?"

"Well, he knows I'm unsure of my feelings about seeing someone. He says he's patient and willing to take things slow."

"Trust me, every man wants to get laid, sooner or later. But mostly sooner."

"You're a total sleaze, Stingray."

"Guilty as charged. Anyway, if he's calling every night, Susan must have asked about him."

"I've told her he's a friend of Teague's who's learning poker." Pausing for a couple of breaths, I added, "Which is true, mostly."

"Lindsay, she's sixteen-years old," Stingray said, finally beginning to gasp. "A man's been calling your house every evening for the past four weeks, and it's just about learning to play poker? Come on, get real."

"Well, I don't think Susan would mind if I had a bit of a social life. She's come to terms with her father's death pretty well." I switched my treadmill to cool-down mode and began to towel off. "Actually, she's meeting Sullivan this weekend."

"How so?"

"He's coming up to see his daughter and invited Susan and me to dinner at Eddie V's. Said it was payback for all the pointers I've given him over the phone."

"Cool. What are you wearing?"

"Come on, it isn't a date."

Stingray rolled her eyes and frowned. "What are you wearing?"

"I don't know."

"Lindsay, as soon as we get off these treadmills, I'm hauling your butt to Neiman's. Nothing prissy, just something reasonably stylish and flattering."

"You're saying my wardrobe isn't flattering?"

"Sweetie, when's the last time you bought a new outfit?"

"I dunno, a while, I guess. Maybe before Curtis died."

Stingray raised her eyebrows.

"OK, maybe I could use an update on a couple of things."

———————

A mid-afternoon drizzle accelerated into a downpour by early evening. When the doorbell rang, my heart did one of those "thump-thump," night-of-your-very-first-kiss things, reflecting the nervousness I'd felt since breakfast. Sullivan stood outside my front door holding a dripping umbrella in one hand and a bottle of *Riesling* in the other. Between his elbow and side, he shielded a box of chocolates from the rain.

I reacted with the diplomacy of a third-grade girl and blurted, "You look wet."

"Well, hello to you, too, Lindsay." Wearing a coal-black sweater, which flattered his silver hair, Sullivan looked as handsome as I remembered. "May I come in, or should I stand here and drown?"

"Oh, come in. I'm so sorry."

We retreated to the kitchen, where I opened the bottle of wine and offered him a seat at the breakfast bar. Susan was busy in her bathroom putting the final touches to her hair. She'd been a little confused about the purpose of the evening's dinner, but her confusion evaporated upon learning we were dining at Eddie V's. None of her friends had been there, and it would lend certain "coolness" to her reputation.

Sullivan nodded toward the glass of wine I'd poured. "I know you prefer dirty martinis, but I've never acquired the taste, frankly." He seemed fidgety. Maybe he had his own thump-thump thing going on inside his chest.

"Truthfully, I'm not that big on martinis. They're just a part of our good-luck ritual." I shrugged. "You know us gamblers. Stingray drank a couple of them one afternoon, and that evening, she drew hot and won big."

"Obviously, a direct correlation," Sullivan noted.

"Obviously. Since then, the night before our private party, everybody drinks dirty martinis for good luck."

"That's funny." He seemed to relax. "You know, I have a pair of lucky socks. Wear them whenever I play poker."

"Wouldn't washing them get rid of the luck?"

"Who said I washed them?" He raised his glass and clinked it with mine. "Here's to dirty martinis and dirty socks."

My thump-thump thing mellowed into a gentle, comfortable purr. "You know, I never asked how your daughter's waltz and two-step date went."

"All right, I think. She's always had good instincts about people. Worked for me in customer service during college, and learned a lot about people."

I glanced outside at his BMW, now being pummeled by the rain. "She drive a fancy car like yours?"

"Nope, a Dodge Ram pick-up, which, if I didn't own the dealership, is what I'd drive. Sullivan smiled. "Kind of like being called 'Queen,' it's part of the image."

Susan wandered into the kitchen, and Sullivan stood. Later, I explained to her it was a sign of good manners, an alien concept among the young males who normally visited our house. After introducing himself, he presented Susan the chocolates and thanked her for allowing her mother to spend time teaching him the finer points of poker. The sixteen-year-old hesitated, broadcasting a slightly dismissive, "whatever" look. That prompted a deadly "you-have-better-manners-than-that" glare from me. Understanding my message, she accepted the box, saying, "Thanks. I love chocolate."

"Nope, a Dodge Ram pick-up, which, if I didn't own the dealership, is what I'd drive. Sullivan smiled. "Kind of like being called 'Queen,' it's part of the image."

After Sullivan and I finished our glasses of wine, I toured him through our 1920's bungalow, which Curtis and one of our poker buddies restored between gigs. Susan tagged along, and in the living room, she pointed out a mahogany coffee table her father crafted in his shop behind the garage. "When I was little, I used to pretend it was a diving board and jump feet-first off of it," she said. "Mom told me not to, but sometimes when she was gone, Dad let me, if I promised not to tell her."

Resting on its glass top was a framed photo of Susan and her father taken just after they'd ridden the Texas Giant roller coaster at Six Flags, a few months before Curtis became ill.

"He was a handsome man," Sullivan said, turning to face Susan. "I can see him in your eyes."

"Yeah, everybody says that." She held up her hands, playfully. "But I also inherited these snow-cone-shaped fingers from Dad. At least that's what Mom always calls them."

Sullivan laughed, shrugging his shoulders. "Well, they look normal to me. Guess I'm just not a good judge of finger beauty, huh?"

I said, "Hey, while you guys are standing there debating snow-cone fingers, I'm starving to death. How 'bout some dinner?"

Sullivan looked toward the window. "Looks like the rain's letting up."

On the way to dinner, Sullivan and I talked about Fort Worth being the kind of place where a person could mosey over to the Stockyards and grab a steaming plate of enchiladas and a cold beer, or dress to the nines for an atmospheric dinner at a sophisticated place like Eddie V's. "I know I sound like a Fodor's commentator, but Cowtown's the best city in Texas, hands down," I said.

Sullivan clownishly scrunched his face. "No way it's better than Houston."

"No offense, but Houston's traffic reminds me of congealing Jell-O. Plus, you have 150% humidity every summer."

"Can't argue with that," he said.

"I like Austin the best," Susan interjected from the back seat. "Dad took me there, and we watched the bats fly out from under the bridge."

Sullivan nodded. "I have to admit, I'm intrigued by bats, but also a little scared of them. Maybe I've watched too many vampire movies. Guess that's why I'm more of a book person." He looked in the rear-view mirror at Susan. "So, do the vampire movies these days still have bats?"

"No," she said, "but they have wolves."

"I like wolves." Sullivan pulled near the curb at Eddie V's. "Maybe I need to go to the movies a little more often," he said, letting us out so he could park the car.

While we waited on Sullivan, Susan and I admired the handsomely marbled foyer. My daughter, having borrowed a lime-green party dress from one of her friends, looked sixteen going on twenty-one. As for my outfit, Stingray made good on her promise to spend some serious jack at the Fort Worth Neiman's. Thanks to her sense of style and the eight pounds I'd worked so hard to lose, my violet-colored ensemble made me feel attractive for the first time in years.

Just before Sullivan returned from parking the car, Stingray phoned. "How's your date going?"

"Come on, I told you it wasn't - "

"Right," said Stingray, her voice flat. "Well, I hope you have better luck with him than I'm having with Joaquin."

"Did he finally ask you out?"

"I told him I'd sign up for another six-months of personal training, if he'd take me to dinner."

"And?"

"We had dinner." She paused before begrudgingly adding, "But no dessert."

"Stingray, you need to find another prospect."

"Lindsay, this guy's a Greek god, I'm telling you."

"Gotta go, Stingray. Remember, Venus-What's-Her-Name lost her arms chasing after some Greek dude."

At Eddie V's, the conversation was light, with topics ranging from Susan's interest in becoming a cancer researcher to our upcoming poker party in New Orleans the following weekend.

"Teague asked me to sign up," Sullivan said. "In fact, I've already mailed him the advance fee."

Although we had discussed this possibility on the phone, his confirmation was news to me. "So, you're going to New Orleans? That's great," I said.

Susan twirled her hair with her fingers, antsy body language I'd seen dozens of times when she mentally processed seemingly random bits of information. Her eyes darted between my new ensemble, then to Sullivan, and back to my outfit.

Finally, Susan asked Sullivan how long he'd been playing poker.

"Off and on, maybe fifteen years. Nothing serious until the past year or so."

"Are you going to New Orleans just because of my mother?"

Like someone knocking over a party's punch bowl, her comment resulted in twenty seconds of tension, with Susan and Sullivan silently eyeing each other.

Finally, Sullivan answered, in a soft, but steady, voice. "Susan, I play because I enjoy the game. And, quite frankly, I also enjoy being around your mother."

Susan's countenance morphed from luke warm to stone cold, but her voice burned white-hot. "I hope you don't think she'd go out with you, because she won't," she growled, as if Sullivan had threatened to desecrate her father's corpse. "Dad is the only man Mom would ever be with. Do you understand that?"

Sullivan looked at me, seeking rescue from the ambush. My chest tightened, just as it had in Curtis' hospital room four years earlier, my throat and voice locking down. As much as I wanted to intervene on Sullivan's behalf, the words simply would not come, my silence unintentionally validating Susan's cruel words.

After enduring another ten seconds of palpable hostility, Sullivan, looking completely devastated and humiliated, broke the logjam. "OK, Susan, I understand how you feel." Taking a sip of water, he continued, as if nothing had happened. "By the way, what colleges are you considering? I hear A&M and UT have the best science departments in this part of the world."

We hurried through the remainder of the unexpectedly surreal dinner, a gun-shy Sullivan steering the remaining conversation to safe, fluffy topics.

As he drove us home, I decided not to confront Susan about her outburst until the following morning. In my bedroom, after spending a couple of hours second-guessing myself, I flipped on the television and watched reruns of old game shows.

At breakfast, I maintained a non-confrontational voice, as if we were discussing a school assignment or feeding the cat. "Susan, there's something we need to talk about."

She launched a preemptive salvo. "Mom, there isn't anything to discuss. You don't need to be dating." She poured Cheerios into her bowl and added milk. "You're 42, and it's gross to think about you running around with a man, particularly some old guy like Sullivan. Do you want my friends thinking my mother's a tramp?"

Her words were a searing iron pressed to my heart. "Susan, I'm not certain I even want to date Sullivan, or anyone else, for that matter," I answered, my voice doing its best to remain steady. Pouring myself a cup of coffee, I took a seat beside her at the breakfast table. "But, it is a possibility, and I should have talked to you in private. I'm sorry if I put you in an uncomfortable position."

Susan shoved her cereal to the other side of the table, sloshing milk over the edge of the bowl. Folding her arms, she stared straight ahead, her eyes misting over and refusing to engage mine. She hissed, "Dad would be so angry at you, right now."

Even though waves of guilt, sadness, and hurt splashed over me in a matter of seconds, my poker-table mask managed to hide those emotions. I mopped up the splotches of milk with my napkin. "Susan, you love your father as much as I do. But he's gone, and life has to move on."

No longer misty, her eyes cascaded tears. "But, I miss him, Mom. I can't ignore how I feel," she sobbed.

"No, you can't ignore your feelings, Susan, but you shouldn't put them in control, either." Moving my chair closer, I gently placed my hand on hers and explained the heart-rending talk her father and I had in his hospital room just before he died; how emotionally paralyzed I'd been after his death; how much I missed him, even now. "I'd never do anything to dishonor your father's memory, Susan," I said, caressing her cheek. "You know that. And someday, when you're 42-years-old, I hope you'll be lucky enough to have someone special to ask how your day went or what you're having for dinner."

"Mom, you don't -"

"I've been lonely, and now I have a friend. That's all."

Sobbing uncontrollably and unable to listen any longer, Susan bit her lip and angrily shook her head. Quickly rising from the table, she bolted to her room. The door slammed, echoing dissonantly throughout the house.

I feared my statement, "I have a friend" would become "I had a friend," after Sullivan tripped over Susan's emotional land mine and no medic rushed to his aid. When he didn't phone that evening or the next, I struggled with calling and apologizing, or waiting to speak with him in New Orleans, finally deciding a face-to-face meeting was the sure-fire way to communicate my regret.

It seemed to be the longest week of my life, alternately beating myself for not standing up to Susan at Eddie V's and wallowing in self-pity. Stingray was in San Antonio visiting her sister, and ironically, the only other person I'd have felt comfortable talking to about the problem was Sullivan.

I missed the intimate, nightly conversations with my friend and realized he'd become an important part of my world. In one of our calls a week before Eddie V's, we talked about Curtis. "I'd never try to compare myself to him or compete with his memory," Sullivan said, "but, I also wouldn't pretend he didn't exist, or you didn't have a great life together." In yet another irony, he seemed just the kind of man Curtis was thinking about when we talked in his hospital room that day - respectful, kind, and funny - yet, as Las Vegas demonstrated, a real person, with faults and weaknesses. Even though it was unclear where a relationship with my new friend would lead, knowing how much I missed our nightly calls convinced me I wanted to find out. Somehow, Susan would have to understand that even though I was her mother, I was also a woman.

My daughter and I settled on an uneasy truce during the week, avoiding the uncomfortable topic itching to be a part of every conversation. Susan wasn't ready to talk; nor was I. By the time she packed for her grandmother's house on Friday, our mother-daughter sabbatical could not have come a moment sooner.

With Susan safely at Mom's, I drove to Dallas and flew Southwest to New Orleans, mentally rehearsing my apology to Sullivan no fewer than ten times. Fortunately, the people sitting on either side of me were Jehovah's Witnesses, too busy studying their Bibles to pay attention to my muted lip movements and facial contortions.

Our team headquartered at Windsor Court Hotel, directly across from Harrah's Casino near the French Quarter. Sophisticated and moneyed, a perfect ambiance for high-stakes poker. The evening before, the three partners met for dirty martinis in the Polo Club Lounge, the epitome of refinement.

Arriving late, Teague reported that five players, including Sullivan and Knife, were committed for tomorrow's game. "By the way, Stingray, I saw the way Knife was eyeing you in Vegas. Maybe the good doctor will offer you a free 'check-up' while he's here in town."

She frowned. "Cue Ball, I don't think so. If you share a bed with a doctor, you may as well be there by yourself. Trust me, I know doctors."

Teague said, "Stingray, is there any profession you don't know well?" He paused a second, waiting to time his punch line. "Oh wait, I guess you don't know much about personal trainers, right?"

She frowned. "Cue Ball, I don't think so. If you share a bed with a doctor, you may as well be there by yourself. Trust me, I know doctors."

She rolled her eyes. "Just give me time."

It was vintage Stingray, yet despite the one dollop of raunchiness, our conversation lacked its usual pizzazz, mostly because I wasn't fully participating. During our second martini, Stingray asked if something was bothering me. Never one to keep secrets from my partners, I described the disaster at Eddie V's. Both partners knew about my years of grief and depression. They'd watched me gradually heal to the point where I was now considering a social life. Without saying a word, Stingray rose from her chair and embraced me, as if we were sisters who'd lost a sibling. Teague, seemingly unsure if he should join in the estrogen-fueled hug, looked away and robotically stirred his martini.

The next afternoon, the first poker guest, Barrett, showed up at our suite about 1:30. A paunchy, ex-professional quarterback, he'd partied with us three or four times previously, winning the big pot once. Knife breezed in soon after, followed by "Chivo," a roly-poly, greasy-ponytailed Mexican from Guadalajara, who unconvincingly claimed to export pottery. The last to arrive was Ginger, a 50-something-year-old woman from Scarsdale, New York, with a diamond ring the size and shape of one of Stingray's carefully manicured nails.

By two o'clock, Sullivan still hadn't shown. Remembering what Teague said about a humiliated man sometimes going on the run, I second-guessed myself for not calling him earlier in the week. Breaking one of our rules about beginning on time, Teague decided to give our friend another half hour. At 2:35, he glanced at Stingray and me, and asked, "What do you think?"

Stingray deferred. "It's up to you, Lindsay."

Now, it was the pit of my stomach doing a sickening thump-thump. I said, "Let's play some poker. It's what we're here for."

At the professional level, Texas Hold'em demands complete attention and concentration, and I had neither that afternoon, my mind drifting between Fort Worth, New Orleans, and Houston. Elvis, were he with us, would have delighted in my playing like a complete donk.

The Mexican bankrupted first, followed by the diamond lady. I was next, relegated to making nachos in the kitchen with Teague. Knife, pissy as usual, busted after me.

That left Stingray, who seemed to have resurrected her A game, and Barrett, who had a much better day than he ever did in the NFL. After battling for three hours, they called a truce about midnight, the ex-jock leaving with a Detroit Lions travel bag stuffed with cash. Stingray, with just over $55,000 in earnings, saved our bacon; Teague and I felt like hoisting her on our shoulders and parading her around the suite for a victory lap.

The next morning, the three of us slept in, then hiked to a late breakfast at *Café Du Monde* in the French Quarter. Selecting a table under the outside awning, we savored our *cafe au laits* and *beignets*. Teague fidgeted, repeatedly tracing his finger over the logo of his coffee mug and pretending to read the Sunday *Times-Picayune*. Stingray, oblivious to our male partner's nervous behavior, concentrated on forking her pastries without dropping any powdered sugar on her linen blouse.

"So, what's on your mind, Cue Ball?" I asked, somewhat flippantly.

"Nothing, Queen."

"Baloney artist," I said, shaking my head. "I'm not eating another one of these zero-calorie buggers until you spill your guts. Besides, aren't you gay guys all about communication and openness?"

Teague put his newspaper down. "There you go again, stereotyping us," he answered, knowing I was teasing. He waited a few seconds, still outlining the logo, before finally fessing up. "OK, I might as well get this out of the way. The truth is, I went out on a limb."

"How so?" I asked.

He raised his eyebrows, looking apologetic. "I spent $5,000 of our money early this morning without consulting you guys."

Stingray dropped her fork on the table. "Wait a minute, Cue Ball," she said. "How come you're using the word 'our' instead of 'my?'"

Teague cracked his knuckles. "I called Sullivan and told him that, given the circumstances, we were refunding his $5,000."

"You're gonna make your knuckles big," Stingray said, gently slapping his hand, as if she were his mother. "It's not a problem giving Sullivan his money back, as far as I'm concerned." She glanced sideways at me. "You OK with it?"

"Of course. Just hate that I'm the cause."

"Glad you both agree, but there's a little more," Teague continued, looking at me. "I told him you were delivering the cash."

"What?" I nearly choked on my coffee. "A little more?"

"And, delivering it today, actually."

"Cue Ball, are you crazy?"

"I changed your ticket from Dallas Love to Houston Hobby." He tried cracking his knuckles again, but without success. "You arrive at two."

"Guys, even if I wanted to do that, I have to pick up Susan from Mother's."

Stingray patted my hand. "I can handle that. She can crash at my place overnight, and tomorrow I'll take her to school."

"I don't know if it's such a smart move."

"What?" Stingray asked. "You afraid I'll corrupt her? If you like, I'll take Susan to my convent's choir practice."

"That's not what I meant, Stingray, and you know it. I'm not sure going to Houston is such a good -"

"Idea," Teague interrupted. "Yes, it is." His voice rose in pitch and intensity. "In fact, it's a brilliant idea, if I say so myself."

"He's right." Stingray wiped a sugar mustache from her upper lip. "You told us you wanted to talk to Sullivan face-to-face. So, put on your big-girl panties and go do it."

"Thank-you, Miss Eloquence."

Teague said, "Yeah, put your big-girl panties on and get to Houston."

"I think I left them in Fort Worth."

"No problem, I'll lend you a pair," Stingray reached for another *beignet*. "Or, maybe Cue Ball will lend you a pair of his."

Whenever the temperature drops below 60 degrees in Houston, the fur-coat-and-Rolex-wearing residents in the River Oaks section of town declare war on winter and crank up their fireplaces to full blast. Mixed with organic, heavy Gulf Coast air, the oak and mesquite smoke generated an inviting, friendly fragrance, reminding me of trips Curtis, Susan, and I had made to the Christmas tree farm.

Parking my rented Camry in the circular driveway of an imposing, English-Tudor two-story, I savored the mildly acrid air. Dad once told me beekeepers used smoke to calm a nervous, buzzing hive; so, I figured what was good for bees must be good for someone thinking, *what on earth am I doing here?*

The polished-brass doorbell produced a deep-throated Westminster

chime, and a few seconds later, Sullivan, dressed in a jogging suit with a towel draped around his neck, unlatched the heavy wooden door. "I can't believe Teague asked you to come here," were his first words, mopping his flushed, sweaty face with the towel.

"Well, hello to you, too, Sullivan," I said, trying to sound upbeat.

"I'm sorry, how rude of me. Come in, Lindsay. I just finished running."

Without making any attempt at small talk, Sullivan guided me through the entryway to his living room, gesturing for me to have a seat on one of two damask-covered settees, placed parallel with each other. Separated by an ornate, glass-topped coffee table, we sat like mannequins, posing on crimson and gold-fringed settees, as stiff as the atmosphere in the room. "When Teague called and wanted to refund my money," Sullivan began, breaking the uncomfortable silence, "I suggested he mail me a check. But, he wouldn't have it any other way."

"Maybe he just didn't trust the U.S. mail," I said, smiling, trying to lighten the mood and mask my nervousness, "so he sent someone even less reliable." I leaned across the coffee table and handed him an oversized envelope stuffed with $5,000 in cash.

Responding with an almost-forced smile, he took the envelope. "You didn't have to do this," he said, placing the money beside him on the settee. "But, it's thoughtful, nonetheless."

"Sullivan, I was hoping you'd be in New Orleans so I could apologize in person for what happened at Eddie V's last weekend."

"No reason to apologize." His eyes focused on the coffee table. "It was a heartfelt response from a young girl who's protecting her father's memory and looking out for her mother, that's all." Still not looking at me, he swiped his face and neck with the towel and leaned to the back of the settee, body posture telegraphing his embarrassment and pain.

"No, that's not -"

"It was foolish to presume things would work out," he said, cutting me off. "I should have known better."

"Sullivan, let me -"

"You know, it was totally humiliating, that's all." he said, his voice cracking with emotion. Then, as if dismissing a telemarketer who had called during dinner, he added, "I'm sure you have a plane to catch."

Of all possible scenarios I'd played out in my mind, this was the one I'd most feared. Sullivan's emotions seemed to be taxiing down the runway, poised to fly away from any possibility of a relationship. Not knowing what to say, I mumbled, "Don't get up, I can see myself to the door."

Sullivan didn't react or respond, blankly staring at me, as if his feelings had already reached cruising altitude, on their way to a vacation destination where dead husbands and emotional teen-agers weren't welcome.

Rising from the settee, I moved quickly through the house, not daring to glance back at Sullivan, lest he see my watery eyes. Desperate to awaken from this living nightmare, I didn't bother saying good-bye and, once safely out the front door, practically sprinted to my rental car.

I backed out of the driveway, but stopped at the street intersection, the engine still running. My stomach felt as if I'd been emotionally disemboweled. Aside from what I'd been through with Curtis, I hadn't felt devastation like this since high school, when my best friend became pregnant by my steady boyfriend. Ten minutes and a packet of tissues later, I looked across the perfectly manicured lawn outside Sullivan's house, and the reality of never seeing him again struck me. Once more, I felt a hard, thump-thump in my heart; but this time, it wasn't the euphoria of schoolgirl flutters. It was more the dull scraping of why-did-life-have-to-be-this-hard.

Dad often said that if you're a gambler, it's best to have a short memory. "Forget your immediate loss," he would say, "and make it up in the next game. That's why you never bet the farm. There's always another game, another tomorrow, *if* you haven't lost all your chips."

Looping his words over and over in my mind, I kept thinking *but this isn't poker, Dad, this is my heart. Who could guarantee there would be another game tomorrow? What if my heart never again did that thump-thump thing?* Sitting there behind the steering wheel, my running mascara making me look like some sort of circus clown, I decided to break Dad's rule and bet the farm.

I composed myself enough to park the car and hike back to the front door. Taking a deep breath, I rang the doorbell, unsure of exactly what to say.

Sullivan cracked open the door and peeked outside, surprised I wasn't already gone. "Something wrong with your car?"

"I want a glass of wine. A really big glass of wine."

He seemed at a loss for words. "What?"

"I'm coming in the house, Sullivan, whether you invite me or not."

He opened the door, looking befuddled. "Are you OK? Is there something wrong?"

Stepping into the entryway, I cocked my head and pointed to my smudgy mascara. "Sorry, I look like Tammy Faye Baker on a crying jag."

"You look just fine," he lied, shrugging his shoulders.

"Where's your kitchen?"

Sullivan didn't answer.

"Damn it, where's your kitchen?"

"It's in the back of the house. Why?"

"You have wine back there, or do I need to drive somewhere and buy us a bottle?"

"It's only four o'clock, Lindsay."

"So?"

Sullivan's face began to soften. "I think there's probably a bottle or two in the refrigerator."

"In that case, open one."

"Yes, ma'am," he said, relaxing a bit and cracking a half smile. "Right away."

He led me down the hallway to the kitchen, a warm, sunny room with a large picture window framing a beautiful magnolia tree. While he opened a bottle of *Chardonnay*, I took a seat on one of the stools at his granite-slabbed bar.

"Look, Sullivan, I'm going to say something, and I don't want you interrupting me."

He raised his eyebrows. "Do I get to say *anything*?" It was a warmer tone of voice, which reminded me of the Sullivan I'd known from our earlier telephone conversations.

"No, you don't, so listen up. I came here to apologize. Even if we never speak again, I need to tell you I'm sorry about not sticking up for you the other night. Susan's response caught me off guard, and I completely froze."

Sullivan, quietly retrieving a stemmed glass from his cabinet, poured wine for me, but none for himself.

"I'm not sure how I'll deal with Susan's hurt and anger - counseling, with a psychologist, I don't know, right now - but she will not be in control of my life. Susan and I have a strong, loving relationship, and we'll handle it, somehow." I paused, threw back my head, and downed most of the glass in two gulps, like a movie cowboy swigging his whiskey at a saloon. "Sullivan, do you remember back in Vegas when Stingray and I saw you with that woman in the Petrossian?"

Sullivan winced. "Not one of my finer moments." He reached for a second empty glass in the cabinet.

"You said it was 'uncharacteristic.' And, you know what? Now that I know you better, it *was* uncharacteristic."

Pouring himself some *Chardonnay*, he seemed to process my logic.

"Sullivan, I've frozen up a time or two in the past, but what happened at Eddie V's was uncharacteristic of me." I took another swallow, further steeling my courage. "Do you understand what I'm saying?"

"Lindsay, I'm not interested in causing problems between you and Susan." He refilled my wine glass and seated himself on the barstool next to mine. "Or, creating more of a mess than I've already made."

"Well, you didn't make the mess; but even so, life can't be tidy and clean all the time. You know that. Susan will learn to control her anger, eventually. Until then, if she continues to play the guilt card, I'll deal with it." Growing more relaxed, I took a smaller, lady-like sip. "After all, I'm the parent, not her friend. And, I'm not willing to sacrifice my long-term happiness." I paused and chose my next words carefully. "Curtis wouldn't have wanted me to, and to do otherwise, would dishonor his wishes."

"I hope you wouldn't choose to have a social life merely to satisfy someone who's no longer around."

"No, I want to have a social life, Sullivan. If not with you, then with someone else." Taking a deep breath, I threw all my cards on the table. "But, I'd prefer to explore the possibilities of a relationship with you."

Sullivan read the sincerity on my face and silently contemplated my words for a few seconds, although it seemed longer to me. Then, as if his emotions had returned from their short vacation flight, he gently placed his hand on mine. "I'd like that, also," he said.

With the whir of a kitchen refrigerator providing the only sound in the room, I looked into his now-moist eyes and felt like a schoolgirl who'd received her first Valentine.

Trying to lighten the moment, I continued, "Of course, if you're not interested in me any longer, I suppose I could drive over to the Mississippi River and see Elvis."

Taking a moment to filter my little joke, he laughed, softly. "You wouldn't want to do that. I imagine Elvis' idea of a romantic evening would be driving his Chevy to the levee and drinking whiskey and rye." He leaned closer, within inches of my cheek.

Hoping he couldn't hear my pounding heart, I said, quietly, "So, Mr. Casanova, what's your idea of a romantic evening?"

Edging even closer, our lips nearly touching, Sullivan whispered, "Oh, I suppose the Chevy at the levee is fine, but I'm just not much of a whiskey-and-rye man." He smiled, and for the first time in four years, I savored the clean scent of a man's after-shave. "Maybe I should learn to like martinis," he said, his lips grazing mine.

Even though I wasn't sure if it was a kiss, it felt perfect. ✪

Starlight

"To the left of me, beyond a dozen empty tables, a shiny
Wurlitzer jukebox churned out a string of twangy country
and honky-tonk tunes, none of which I'd ever heard.
Each time a new song played, sparkly glass tubes and
columns inside the machine burst into a neon rainbow.
The small, two-person cocktail tables were cleared away in
front of the Wurlitzer, probably to create a makeshift
dance floor. On the other side of the jukebox, against the
far wall, 'Captain Zodiac' and 'Lucky Lady' pinball machines
stood back-to-back, as if they were oversized bookends."

FIVE

Starlight

Uncle Curtiss called Mama the day after my seventeenth birthday. Aunt Lucille had taken a turn for the worse, and if Mama wanted to see her older sister one last time, she'd better come to St. Louis right away.

Mama decided to ride the bus because she was "afraid of flying."

But now, thirty years later, I know it wasn't the real reason. Every Sunday for over two years, my mother had worn the same cream-colored dress to church, even patching a tear in one of the sleeves. Once, when I asked why she didn't buy something different, Mama looked away and said she didn't care for the new fashions. The truth - that five-and-dime store clerks barely made minimum wage - would have been much too painful.

Mama took Snapper, my younger brother, to St. Louis and wanted me to come along, too. It was July, and since I was mowing yards for nine or ten widow ladies, I had a good excuse not to go.

On Wednesday after Mama left, my best friend, Carl, stopped by the house all jazzed-up about the beer he'd bought at the Starlight Lounge the weekend before. No one asked to see his driver's license, and since I looked a lot older, he was sure I'd have no problem. Carl shot pool with a couple of offshore workers home from the Gulf and said it was more fun than anything he'd ever done. I asked if he'd take me there while Mama was gone, but he had dates with Darlene Cole the next couple of evenings. Things were heating up, and he didn't want to lose his momentum.

Mama warned me to stay away from the Starlight. It was a dive, she said, where all the "hard people" hung out - alcoholics, pool sharks, and prostitutes. "A boy could meet the Devil in that hell-hole and not even know it," she said, making me promise never to set foot inside.

Since I'd never broken a promise or lied to my mother, it was hard to concentrate on mowing the next afternoon. Mama taught me values and good manners - always "Yes, ma'am" and "No, thank you, ma'am" - which is why the widow ladies tipped me so well. I kept twenty-dollar bills rolled up in the front pocket of my Levi's, saving up for a glacier-blue '77 Trans Am I'd spotted at the Frontier Car Corral. That wad of money made me feel powerful, like some rich oilman from Dallas.

After losing Daddy, Mama was so afraid something would happen to Snapper or me, she kept us reined in, locked up like antique teacups in her china cabinet. While I understood how she felt, a teacup is of little value if it's never used. By the time I'd finished mowing that afternoon, I'd decided to open the china cabinet, even though it meant breaking a promise.

At sundown, I stood outside a ramshackle clapboard building, its white paint peeling in dollar-bill-sized chunks. Fidgeting under the neon sign that flashed red "Starlight" and then yellow "Lounge," I would see for myself if the place was as good as Carl said, or as evil as Mama thought.

Mama said she didn't know the exactly how Daddy died, only that he was shot during a patrol on the Mekong River. She probably knew more, but chose to shield her boys from the painful details. I was five when it happened; Snapper was three, too young to attend the funeral. We kept the flag from his casket in an oak and glass box on the table between our beds. Even now as adults, so precious is the keepsake, Snapper and I swap the flag every Christmas. Neither wants to deprive the other of the honor for more than a few months.

A week after my twelfth birthday, after watching news coverage of the fall of Saigon and the history of the war, I experienced what would become a recurring nightmare. From that day forward, a couple of times a month, the dream always unraveled the same way - the swirling river, the scrawny gooks ambushing his patrol boat, Daddy getting shot in the gut. He'd fall overboard, screaming and thrashing around in the water like a panicked bird caught in a snare.

That's when the dream grew even more intense. I'd be standing on the shore just a few feet away, but when I'd reach to pull him from the river, my arms wouldn't move. It was as if they were somehow disconnected from my brain. Daddy would struggle for what seemed to be an eternity, then silently stare at me one last time before turning glassy-eyed. His body would go limp and slowly sink into the blood-red water.

I told Mama about my dream the next morning during breakfast. She completely went to pieces, more so than at Daddy's funeral. I couldn't stand seeing her that way, so from that point on, I kept the dream to myself. But it didn't stop.

The Starlight's screen door shut behind me with a metallic slap, much louder than I intended. Neon beer signs glowed through a fog of cigar and cigarette smoke, the smell reminding me to wash my clothes before Mama came home, or else she'd ask where I'd been. Three ancient ceiling fans, evidently serving no purpose other than to stir around the smoke, revolved at slightly-different speeds, the middle one creaking and wobbling unsteadily on every turn.

I edged over to the counter - absent a bartender - and cautiously took a seat on one of the swiveling stools. The lacquered-wood bar, yellowed and pockmarked every few inches with cigarette burns, reminded me of the images of Vietnam I'd seen on television, with its tiny bomb craters and dark-brown foxholes. At the far end, a forty-something-year-old businessman cozied-up with a much-younger woman in a low-cut, black dress. With his tie loosened, he whispered to the sharp-looking blonde, who laughed every time he said something. The way the man rubbed his hand on her thigh made me jealous of Carl, who probably was doing the same thing with Darlene.

Still feeling nervous, I looked to the right of the bar, two black men - Mama still called them Negroes, but I knew better - smoked cigars and shot pool. The older one, probably in his fifties, wore a bright-yellow shirt with shiny-glass cufflinks and a Panama hat with a dyed-red chicken feather arching from the back. He strutted around, banty-rooster-like, holding his silver-handled pool cue in one hand and waving a plastic-tipped cigar with the other. The younger man wore a khaki work shirt with a "Cowtown Freight" logo stitched over the front pocket. Untucked and sleeveless, the sweat-stained shirt emphasized the man's sculpted biceps. I remembered him from one of the civil-rights rallies the black folks held in front of our church. The way he crouched and paced around the pool table reminded me of Sonny Liston, the heavyweight boxer, stalking his opponent.

Even though Carl had described the Starlight, I was surprised at how small and closed-in it felt. He said the Army used the building during World War II as a machine shop. Later auctioned as government surplus, its oak-plank floors, gouged with holes and dents where lathes and grinders rested twenty-years earlier, still smelled faintly of machine oil and grease.

After a few minutes, the bartender made his appearance from the back room. "Sorry, didn't hear you come in." His thickset glasses hung right at the end of his beaky, pinched nose. Bald, except for a shock of white hair in the middle of his shiny head, he reminded me of an elderly Woody Woodpecker. He asked, "Can I help you?"

Maybe because it hadn't been that many years since I'd watched Saturday morning cartoons with Snapper, the image of a geriatric Woody Woodpecker made me feel guilty, as if I had no business being there and should be home reading my Bible.

The bartender repeated his question, louder this time.

I tried to sound confident, as if I'd done this hundreds of times before. "I'd like a beer, please," and held my breath, waiting to be thrown out of the bar.

He squinted through the Coke-bottle lenses. "You're 21, aren't you?" It was more of a statement than a question.

"Yes, sir."

"Well, what'll you have?"

My heart pounded like a marching band's bass drum. "Schlitz." It was the only brand I could think of other than Coors, which wasn't yet available in Texas.

Standing in front of a platoon of jewel-colored bottles of liquor, he reached down to a whirring icebox, grabbed a dripping-wet can and thumped it on the counter. "You wanna run a tab?"

Unsure of what "run a tab" meant, I said I did. For some reason, I worried about Mrs. Waskom, the minister's wife, seeing me in the bar. That was about as likely as Vicki Oates, our school's head cheerleader, asking me to run off to Mexico for the weekend.

A mixture of guilt and anticipation swirled in my mind as I took my first-ever sip of alcohol. It tasted sharply bitter, much different than I'd expected, and for a moment, I wondered why people made such a fuss about drinking beer.

The bartender leaned under the counter and grabbed a plastic bottle of dishwashing soap. "Don't know that I've seen you here before."

I mumbled something about living in another neighborhood and gestured toward the pool tables, anxious to change the subject. "What's it cost to play?"

"Dollar a game. Each player." He squirted several shots of Ivory into a

stainless-steel sink. Turning on the faucets, the bartender stuck two fingers in the stream of water and adjusted the temperature with his other hand. "No leanin' on the tables, no jumpin' the ball, no drinks on the felt." He raised his eyebrows to encourage a response. "You want a table?"

"No, sir." Besides him, the only other people in the Starlight were the businessman and his fancy woman at the other end of the counter, and the two black men. "Looks like I'd have to play by myself," I said, not wanting to admit I'd never shot pool.

This wasn't the crowded, glamorous nightclub I'd imagined from the movies. To the left of me, beyond a dozen empty tables, a shiny Wurlitzer jukebox churned out a string of twangy country and honky-tonk tunes, none of which I'd ever heard. Each time a new song played, sparkly glass tubes and columns inside the machine burst into a neon rainbow. The small, two-person cocktail tables were cleared away in front of the Wurlitzer, probably to create a makeshift dance floor. On the other side of the jukebox, against the far wall, "Captain Zodiac" and "Lucky Lady" pinball machines stood back-to-back, as if they were oversized bookends. The Starlight didn't seem like a place the Devil would call home.

The bartender extended his hand. "The name's Preacher."

"Preacher?" I shook his hand, careful to give him a strong, manly grip.

"Yep. Well, truth be told, Douglas is my given name."

"But they call you Preacher?"

"Yeah, 'bout a hundred years ago, I got sent to the principal's office at school. I was so scared, I prayed out loud all the way down the hall, thinkin' how hard that man paddled." He smiled and shook his head. "After that, my friends started calling me Preacher. Guess the name just stuck."

"Makes sense to me." His story reminded me of my own trip to the principal's office a couple of years earlier. Mr. Levin scolded me hard and said I needed to be careful, so I didn't wind up like my Daddy. It scared me, even though I didn't exactly understand what he meant. When I told Mama what the principal said, she went to his office the next day and gave him a piece of her mind. I asked her what she told Mr. Levin, but she wouldn't say.

Preacher dipped several glasses into the soapy water. "So, you got a name?"

Taking another drink of the bitter liquid, I hesitated and considered answering with a fake name, but decided to tell the truth. "Wes. Wes Springer." I crossed my fingers, hoping he didn't know me from somewhere else.

"Your father Ellis Springer?"

His question hit me like a slap to the face. "Yes, sir, he was." I leaned back, closed my eyes, and swallowed the last of the beer, not wanting to look Preacher in the eye. If he had known my father, he probably also knew Daddy had two young sons when he was killed. If he bothered with the arithmetic, he'd realize I was underage.

"Thought so." Preacher paused his dishwashing and tilted his head, studying my features. "I can see Ellis in your eyes." He looked back down at the soapy water and said quietly, "Good man."

The prayer-like tone of Preacher's last statement made me wonder how well he'd known my father, but it wasn't the right time to ask. "Yes, sir," I said, afraid to make eye contact. "My father was a very good man."

Preacher took my empty can and pitched it in the trashcan, ten feet away. Then, leaning down to the cooler, he asked, "You 'bout ready for another cold Schlitz?"

After Daddy was killed, Mama told Snapper and me only the good things about our father, never anything bad. She made sure we knew he worked hard and that family and church were his first priorities. He had no faults, as far as my brother and I knew, other than being "overly generous," which, of course, wasn't truly a fault. Daddy seemed more like a life-sized cardboard celebrity, displayed in a theater lobby to promote the next Hollywood blockbuster. I wanted to know what the real man was like - not the perfect, church-going war hero, who wouldn't have stood on the shore, his arms paralyzed with fear, while his father drowned in a river.

Once, I asked my scoutmaster, Mr. Robertson, what Daddy was like; they'd grown up together and played on the same baseball team. He said my father was a "decent man, who'd just gotten a bum deal." Mr. Robertson looked uncomfortable, as if the "bum deal" wasn't just about Daddy getting killed. I wanted to ask him what he really meant, but instead, I pretended to be satisfied with his answer.

It was like the time Mama gave me a pair of socks for my fourteenth birthday and asked if I was pleased with my gift. We were short on money, and I tried my best not to look disappointed. "They're exactly what I wanted," I said, smiling. She chose to believe me, I think, because accepting the truth would have been much too painful.

A year or so after Daddy was killed, Mama's friends set her up on a couple of dates, but once the men realized two young boys came with the package, they didn't ask her out again. Aunt Lucille tried to convince Mama to move back to St. Louis, closer to Grandma and the rest of the family, and for a while, she considered it. Finally, Mama told her sister she'd decided to keep her boys right where they were; they had nice friends, a good church, and a stable school. Once Snapper and I were out of the house, Mama promised to move to St. Louis.

I felt so guilty about my visit to the Starlight, I stayed home on Friday night and watched television. Lucky for me, because Mama called about nine o'clock and told me Aunt Lucille had passed away earlier that afternoon. She'd seen her sister just before she drifted into a coma, which was "a blessing." Mama called lots of things "blessings" I never quite understood, and in this case, I didn't know if seeing Aunt Lucille was the blessing, or if her going into a coma was the blessing. Either way, I was afraid Mama would think I was being a smart-mouth if I asked. After the funeral, she planned to help Uncle Curtiss sort through Aunt Lucille's things; then, Mama and Snapper would ride the bus back home.

By Saturday morning, I was feeling much better about my trip to the Starlight. It was just a lounge and pool hall, not the Devil's hall, and I hadn't met any of the "hard people" Mama warned me about. It reminded me of the time when Snapper and I were younger and asked Mama if we could go down by the railroad tracks and watch the Texas Eagle pass through town. She said, "No, because if you get too close, you'll get sucked in as it comes by." Late one afternoon, when she'd gone to a ladies' prayer meeting, we snuck down to see it. Sure enough, we weren't sucked in.

At noon, Carl stopped by Mrs. Moore's, where I was mowing, and asked if he could bring Darlene over to my house because he was "getting real close." I knew what that meant, so I told him I'd be gone by five and would leave the back door unlocked. I figured I'd be doing Carl and me both a favor by going back to the Starlight.

By four thirty, I'd showered and changed into a fresh pair of Levi's, a big lump of cash jammed in my front pocket. My guilt completely gone, this time it didn't bother me when the Starlight's screen door loudly banged my arrival.

Preacher, a white dishtowel draped over his arm, greeted me as I mounted one of the swivel stools. "Schlitz?"

Impressed that he'd remembered, I felt like one of his regulars. "Yes, please." Then, feeling slightly cocky, I added, "And start a tab, OK?"

"Sure thing."

The Schlitz was less bitter than before, but still not smooth as I'd imagined. It would take a full decade for me to acquire an appreciation for beer.

Even though it wasn't yet dark outside, the bar was crowded and looked more like what I'd seen in the movies. Players swarmed around four of the five pool tables. At one, the sharp-looking woman, whom I'd seen two days earlier with the businessman, flirted with a shaggy-haired, grizzly bear of a man. He wore a black-leather vest with the words "Road Warriors" embroidered in thick gothic letters across the back in orange and yellow stitching.

At the pinball machine, a cowboy, maybe six-foot-five, waged war, one hand furiously working its flappers, the other hand occasionally slapping the metal case. Every few minutes, Captain Zodiac temporarily surrendered and offered the shrill ding-ding-ding of a bonus round, prompting the cowboy to shout out an enthusiastic "Yeah, boy!"

Against the background noise of cue sticks striking balls and people talking and laughing, it seemed everyone was having fun, with the Devil nowhere in sight.

After about twenty minutes, the man with the red feather in his hat eased onto the stool beside me. Smelling as if he'd just come from the barbershop, he ordered a Pabst.

Preacher reached down to the cooler and fished out the beer. He nodded in my direction and said, "Roosevelt, this here's Wes Springer."

Setting his silver-handled pool cue against the bar, Roosevelt clutched the bottle of Pabst and lightly clanked it against my can of Schlitz, as if he were offering a toast. "Nice meetin' you," he said, then leaned back and guzzled half of the beer.

"He's Ellis' boy."

That seemed to grab Roosevelt's attention. He stared at me, sizing me up before finishing his beer with a noisy gulp. His bloodshot eyes were sticky, like they belonged to an old man in a rest home. "Ellis was a damn-good pool player."

I told Roosevelt I'd never known my father played pool.

He lifted one of his plastic-tipped cigars from his shirt pocket and removed its cellophane wrapper. "Ever' Saturday night, regular as clockwork. Sometimes on Friday." He laughed gently, almost wistfully, and shook his head. "Ellis and I made a lot of money hustlin' kids like you." He silently motioned for another Pabst.

I wasn't sure if he was serious. "You guys hustled?"

Roosevelt struck a match against the counter, lit his cigar, and blew out the flame. "Damn straight. Ellis and me played some mighty-fierce games against each other - twenty, sometimes fifty bucks a pop." He threw the blackened match on the floor. "Until we figured out we could make lots more money workin' together."

Preacher set another Pabst on the counter.

Roosevelt closed his eyes and took the first puff from the cigar, seeming to enjoy the mellow pleasure it brought him. "So, your old man didn't teach you to play?"

"No, I've never played. Always thought it would be fun, though."

"I can show you a few shots." He smiled, revealing two silver-capped front teeth. "Even some your old man taught me."

I was wary. "I don't think I ought to."

"Just showin' you how to play." Roosevelt took a long drag from his cigar. He leaned his head back and exhaled slowly, sending a thin trail of smoke toward the wobbly ceiling fan. "Nothin' else." He stubbed his cigar in the ashtray, stood,

and motioned for me to follow.

In spite of what he said, I feared this would lead to something involving money. Popping open another Schlitz, I reluctantly joined him at the unused pool table.

Roosevelt chalked-up his fancy cue stick, its luster now dulled after thousands of games. I asked him where he'd gotten it.

"It's my baby," he said, caressing it as if it were a child. "Won it back when we had big-time eight-ball tournaments in here." He pointed at the silver handle. "See, it's got 'Starlight' engraved right here."

Roosevelt used his unusual cue stick to show me how to break, when to use angles and combination shots, and what it meant to "scratch." He talked easily and steadily, and three beers later, I'd learned the rules for eight-ball, nine-ball, and one-pocket. I was years away from ever beating him in a game, but at least I hadn't totally embarrassed myself.

"You know, boy," Roosevelt said, as I followed his instruction on sinking a bank shot, "you got some good instincts. Real good instincts."

Growing more relaxed and somewhat dizzy from all the beer, I asked Roosevelt to tell me more about how he and Daddy ran their games.

"Aw, we just worked soldiers home on leave and college boys too big for their britches. Never anybody with young kids to feed." He chuckled. "People always thought I was the one lookin' to get at their money, 'cause I'm black. Your old man didn't look like no hustler, him being clean-cut and all, which is why ever'body wanted to match him. Figured they could take him real easy." Roosevelt's two silver teeth appeared to flash as he grinned. "Big mistake. The soldier boys would play me, and I'd win a few games, throw one or two. Then, Ellis would show up, actin' like he'd had one too many beers and flashin' a roll of money. I'd take him for several games, whup his ass real good."

"What happened then?"

"Ellis'd say he wanted bigger stakes to make up his losses. Maybe a hundred dollars a game. I'd say I had to get home, and that's when one of the soldier boys would take my place, thinkin' they's gonna whup his ass, too. But, o' course, they didn't."

Our conversation was interrupted by the Cowtown Freight man, who sauntered up to our table. Holding a beer in one hand and a cue stick in the other, he asked, "Mind if I join the party?"

"No problem," Roosevelt said.

The muscled-up man seemed to know there was a roll of money in my Levi's. "You wanna go a dollar a ball?"

Swallowing hard, I said, "I'm not sure, man."

Roosevelt scowled at the Cowtown guy and said, "Lay off, Shag. Don't mess with the boy."

"He's yours, right?"

"No, that ain't what I'm saying." Roosevelt shook his head. "He don't deserve no hustle."

The Cowtown guy mumbled something and shuffled back toward the bar.

"Thanks," I said.

Roosevelt seemed amused. "No problem."

I chalked my stick for another round of eight-ball. "So, what happened with you and my Daddy?"

The look of amusement on Roosevelt's face dissolved. He said things were going well until they worked over a cocky college student, home for the Christmas holidays. Turned out, the college kid's father was the county judge, who wasn't too pleased about his son getting hustled for six-hundred dollars, but even more upset that a white boy had used a "colored boy" to help with the set-up. "So, one night the sheriff paid Ellis and me a little visit. Said the judge would slap us for illegal gambling, maybe throw in some other shit, if we didn't give the kid his money back. He'd also bust the Starlight."

"Did you return the money?"

"Hell, we'd already spent most of it."
Roosevelt paused, racking up a new game
after skunking me on the last one.

"Hell, we'd already spent most of it." Roosevelt paused, racking up a new game after skunking me on the last one. "We offered the kid half, but that wasn't good enough for the judge." He looked at me with his head slightly cocked to one side, as if deciding whether to tell me more, and then continued. "See, back then, the judge was head of the county draft board, and everybody and their dog was gettin' deferments. They's havin' a hard time fillin' their quotas, so the judge gave your old man the choice - join the Army, or get his ass thrown in jail so long, his hair'd turn white waitin' to get out." Roosevelt shook his head, lining up the cue ball and taking aim at the rack. "I always felt bad 'bout that, 'cause Ellis had two little kids at home." He struck the cue ball sharply, scattering the stripes and solids across the table. "Then, he went and got himself . . ." His voice trailed off.

"Killed." I filled in the blank, the word knifing at my heart. I pretended to concentrate on my first shot and hoped Roosevelt wouldn't notice my glistening eyes.

When I was able to look at Roosevelt, his filmy eyes seemed apologetic, as if he regretted the harshness of his words. Neither of us said anything more until the awkwardness was broken by the dinging pinball machine and the cowboy shouting, "Yeah, boy!"

We played a few more games of eight-ball, mostly in silence, but about eleven o'clock, I'd had my fill of the Starlight. I figured Carl and Darlene would be out of our house by then, and if they weren't, I'd tell them to leave.

I took the long way home that night. Opening the china cabinet had come with a steep emotional price - Mama's shined-up image of Daddy was now tarnished like a cheap "Made in Japan" children's toy.

In the weeks ahead, I would call Uncle Curtiss and question him about Daddy's hustling days. He confirmed Roosevelt's story and told me that Mama always blamed the Starlight for my father's death, not the Southeast Asians who ambushed his boat. My old scoutmaster and I had a long conversation about Daddy's "bum deal." Given a second chance, I didn't hold back on the questions about my father's past.

In those conversations, I finally learned the truth about Daddy. He changed from a cardboard celebrity, a war hero whose son could never measure up, into a man. A *flesh-and-blood* man. My father encountered the Devil, all right; but he wandered the halls of the county courthouse, not the pool hall.

After making it home from the Starlight that evening, I crawled into bed and stared at the wooden box holding my father's flag. Against the stillness of the room, the yellow, dappled starlight danced lightly against the glass, almost rippling, as if it were gentle, peaceful water.

I slept soundly that night and never dreamed about Daddy drowning again.

That was the last time I visited the Starlight. Early one Sunday morning about six months later, while no one was around, someone set it on fire. The old wooden floors were so soaked with machine oil, the whole building burned in less time than it takes to play a game of eight-ball.

I never told Mama about meeting Preacher and Roosevelt, and I'm not certain what became of them. A couple of years later, I read a newspaper story about a Roosevelt Higgins who'd been stabbed in a bar fight on the other side of town, but I wasn't sure if it was the same Roosevelt.

At the end of that summer, I decided against buying that blue Trans Am; instead, I used my money to buy Mama a new Sunday dress, Snapper a bicycle, and put the rest in savings for college. Mama was so proud of me. I'd become a fine man, she said, carefully emphasizing the word *man*.

Several years later, when I thought the time was right, my brother and I sat down over a pizza, and I told him what I'd learned about Daddy. Snapper was surprised, of course; but time and age had given us a different perspective on what it all meant. Even now, at Christmas when we transfer the flag, we laugh about our old man, the pool hustler. But it is a respectful laugh, not one of embarrassment or shame.

After Snapper left for college, Mama decided to move to St. Louis to take care of Grandma. I came over and helped pack her things. At the very back of her bedroom closet, hidden behind some cardboard boxes, an old tattered quilt rested

lengthwise on the floor. Unwrapping the quilt, I discovered a beautiful pool cue, its unused wood still glossy. Engraved on its silver handle was the word "Starlight."

Later that evening after we'd loaded the truck, I told Mama about finding the pool cue in her closet. She looked away for a moment, no doubt thinking of all it represented.

Mama said she wasn't sure where it had come from - maybe a garage sale. It was mine if I wanted it, she added, her eyes moist. It didn't mean anything at all to her.

I chose to take Mama at her word, just as she'd believed me years earlier when I thanked her for the birthday socks. Accepting the truth would have been much too painful. ✪

Serene Oaks Home Owners Association

Monthly Meeting

¡It's a Mexican Fiesta!

¡Ariba!

Enjoy ~~com~~ ... itas and tasty nachos

> The Presdt stated there is no
> association bylaw prohibitg members
> from Mowing or Maintang their yards
> early in the morng, or for that
> matter, late in the Evng; However
> a new bylaw could be implemented
> by a vote of 2/3 of the
> members in good standng.
>   Mr. Goldstein reminded
> attendees that Mrs. Blume's husband,
> Peter - a well-Known personal
> ijury attorney who once sued the
> First Baptist church over their
> inhumane treatment of asses in a
>   OVER

backyard

6:00 P.M. Sharp

SIX

*July Minutes of the Serene Oaks
Home Owners' Association*

The July 21 meeting of the Serene Oaks Home Owners' Association was held in Earlene Tennison's backyard, festively decorated with a Mexican fiesta theme. A total of 42 members and guests gathered on her new pool deck, enjoying the complimentary margaritas and tasty nachos.

➤➤

The meeting was called to order by President Geoffrey Thomas, who thanked Earlene for the miniature-sombrero party favors. The June minutes were read by the recording secretary, yours truly. For the eighteenth consecutive month, no corrections or additions were required, which, it is modestly noted, undoubtedly sets an association, if not a national record of some sort.

The president asked members to stand, join hands, and bow their heads in a moment of silent meditation for Vice-President Roberta Fay Gilroy as she continues to recover from her recent (and, hopefully, successful) Brazilian butt-lift surgery.

"Troublesome Pets" was first on the agenda. Janice Schaefer reported a wandering schnauzer has twice defecated in her flowerbed, completely devastating her prize-winning petunias. While expressing great empathy, the president questioned Janice as to how she knew a schnauzer caused the problem or whether it could have been a non-neighborhood dog or perhaps a wild animal. Although Janice wasn't 100% certain, last week she saw a suspicious-looking schnauzer express a lingering interest in the petunias, and judging by the size and composition of the "evidence," the crime wasn't committed by a coyote or raccoon. Members were asked if anyone owned a schnauzer. Ronald Hastings admitted he owned a miniature schnauzer, but it was well-behaved and only made miniature "deposits." The president reminded everyone of the association bylaw prohibiting a member's dog or cat from urinating or defecating on other members' yards or gardens without prior approval.

Next on the agenda was "Yard Signs Regarding Political Candidates or Social Policy." The president reviewed the association rules for the size and display of such signs. He received a letter from Ashraf Fayad, who recently purchased the English Tudor fixer-upper on Live Oak Drive, complaining about the hand-lettered placard across the street with the statement "My God Can Beat Up Your God." Ashraf's objection was that the slogan, displayed in Ira Goldstein's front yard, supported neither a candidate nor a social policy, but was merely a thinly veiled attempt to chase him out of the neighborhood. Asked to comment about the matter, Ira explained the sign had nothing to do with Ashraf, but was merely an expression of his support for Israel. The president, displaying the type of skilled diplomacy the members have come to appreciate, suggested Ira and Ashraf get together over a beer and kosher hot dogs, with the goal of working out a compromise on the sign.

After another serving of margaritas, the president moved to the next business item, "Rules and Dress Code for Parties." He reminded attendees that (a) parties should end by midnight, with the exception of New Year's Eve; and (b) events involving costumes, with the exception of Halloween, should be approved in advance by the association's executive committee. Of particular concern was the recent Roman toga party hosted by Ruth and Clark Osgood, which, unfortunately, was not pre-approved. Several neighbors complained about a large, inebriated centurion and his lusty Cleopatra, wandering aimlessly through the neighborhood, knocking on several doors before finding the Osgood residence. Clark gave his side of the story, saying the rule was "ridiculous and stupid" and that a strict interpretation of the rule would prohibit even Santa Claus from attending the Christmas party, because, technically, he'd be wearing a costume. Clark further argued, "The only reason this is an issue at all is that most of you are party-poopers and were not invited." Ruth offered a motion, which was seconded by Clark, to suspend the costume prohibition from the association bylaws. After a brief but intensely emotional discussion, the motion failed by a vote of 39 to two, with one abstention coming from the president.

The president asked if any member had heard whether a new dry-cleaning establishment was opening next week in the old pilates and yoga salon, as had been rumored at the last meeting. Ronald Hastings said he had talked to a nice couple from Bangladesh or somewhere in Asia, he couldn't remember where, who planned to open their store by the first of the month. They both had red dots on their foreheads, he reported, and seemed to be well groomed and very polite. Clark Osgood asked if he were to invite the new dry-cleaning couple to a party, would the red dots constitute some sort of a costume and need to be approved in advance? The president said that since the couple's red dots were most likely a part of their daily attire, it would not be considered a costume and thus exempt from the rule.

The next item of business was "Commendation of Jo and Pete Fagin" for taking quick action to repair their front-yard concrete fountain, after vandals, no doubt part of a fringe terrorist organization, chiseled away a certain anatomical feature of a cherub statue they evidently found offensive. A note left at the crime scene said, "Serene Oaks is full of smut! Clean up your neighborhoods pornography!" The president pointed out the absence of an apostrophe after the word "neighborhood," which, he said, probably meant the perpetrators had public-school educations. Members were warned the vigilantes could strike again and were urged to report any suspicious activity to the neighborhood security patrol. Margo Hastings said she had seen two Mormon boys bicycling through the neighborhood, but didn't believe they were the militant type.

The final item was "Ideas on Dealing with Mrs. Blaine." The president explained he was somewhat reluctant to make this an agenda matter, but after several homeowners mentioned the problem, he felt compelled to bring it before the entire body. Apparently, Mrs. Blaine chooses to mow her yard early in the morning, prior to sunrise, while wearing her "shorty pajamas" and slippers. Although it could not be confirmed by anyone present, she reportedly chooses not to wear undergarments, as well. Two neighbors - both female, it should be noted - have politely asked her to mow later in the day and to wear something more appropriate, perhaps a tasteful warm-up suit. Mrs. Blaine responded by saying she and her husband worked long hours and pre-dawn was the only time she could mow. In fact, her exact words were, "I'll mow whenever I damn well please, wearing whatever I damn well please."

Mrs. Blaine was invited to appear before the home owners meeting to present her side of the controversy, but she declined, in a less than gracious manner.

The president stated there is no association bylaw prohibiting members from mowing or maintaining their yards early in the morning, or, for that matter, late in the evening; however, a new bylaw could be implemented by a vote of two-thirds of the members in good standing. Mr. Goldstein reminded attendees that Mrs. Blaine's husband, Peter, a well-known personal-injury attorney who once sued the First Baptist Church over their inhumane treatment of asses in a live nativity scene, would love nothing more than "to sue the pants off the association." Recognizing the awkwardness of his pun, Mr. Goldstein moved to table the agenda item until the next meeting, and after a proper second, the motion passed unanimously.

After a final round of margaritas, the president asked for a volunteer to host next month's meeting. He announced the theme of the gathering would be a Hawaiian luau, which brought a polite round of applause from the attendees. Ashraf Fayad graciously agreed to open his home to the association, although he wasn't exactly sure what a luau was and would need to read up on it. Clark Osgood asked if wearing Hawaiian leis would technically fit the definition of a costume and would need committee approval in advance. The president, showing remarkable restraint, ruled Clark out of order.

There being no further business, the meeting was adjourned.

Respectfully submitted,

Jan Silverman-Rodriquez
Recording Secretary

Enchilada

"I READ ABOUT THIS INTERNET POLL ASKING PEOPLE TO RANK LIFE'S MOST EMBARRASSING SITUATIONS. THE RESULTS WERE CATEGORIZED BY COUNTRY, AND FOR PEOPLE LIVING IN GREAT BRITAIN, NUMBER ONE ON THE LIST WAS GIVING A SPEECH WHEN YOU ARE ILL PREPARED. "

SEVEN

Enchilada

I read on the internet that the worst job in America is being the Chuck E. Cheese mascot in one of their pizza joints. You wear this uncomfortable, scratchy rodent costume that hasn't been dry cleaned in months. Junior League moms, already feeling guilty about outsourcing their children's birthday parties, bitch about the pizza prices

➤➤

while their five-year-olds sugar-up on ice cream and cake. And if that weren't enough, you change into your rat suit in a mildewed restroom that smells as if a birthday boy just barfed up his mozzarella and pepperoni.

Still, I had to think there were days when dressing up in a giant rodent costume would have been preferable to being the assistant band director at Jesse Jackson Middle School. I tried to teach mouthy adolescents, their hormones turbocharged and operating in overdrive, how to make something besides squeaks come out of their saxophones and oboes. Most days I'd have been just as successful showing them how to levitate.

Sharonda, one of my pimply-faced clarinetists, had a crush on Jerome, a pimply-faced trombonist, and regularly passed notes to him during class. Rather than write back, Jerome's idea of romance was squashing his hand under his armpit to make farting noises. Sharonda just giggled and kept sending him more notes.

Where the trumpeters sat, and I use the word "trumpeters" loosely, it smelled worse than a cat's week-old litter box. All, except one, were boys and hadn't yet learned the rewards of daily baths and deodorant. The lone girl sat at the end of the row, her eyes typically focused on a *Seventeen Magazine* she'd sneaked into class and hidden behind her music stand. Even though I'd repeatedly told the little shits to stop, the boys regularly emptied their horns' spit-valves directly in front of their chairs, which made pancake-sized spots of slime that just added to the stench.

It wasn't exactly what I had in mind coming out of college. I wanted to be performing with a progressive-jazz band, staying in Hyatt Regencys, enjoying all-you-can-eat breakfast buffets, and working sold-out clubs in L.A. or Manhattan. I pictured afternoons when we'd tweak our second set, then lounge under an umbrella by the hotel pool, telling road-tour stories over a couple of European beers. After our evening performances, a slightly stoned groupie with pierced eyebrows would ask if I'd autograph her halter-top, maybe even follow me to my room.

Instead, I munched on a stale Twinkie, trying to figure out which one of my seventh-grade saxophone players had drawn a large pair of breasts on the back of his music stand.

Two years before, the music gods were smiling down on me. After three unsuccessful auditions, I was finally invited into the One O'Clock Lab Band at North Texas University, the top college jazz group in the country. For a performance musician, having the Lab Band on your resume practically punches your ticket into the big leagues. Then, apparently, I did something to piss-off the music gods because just after fall rehearsals began, I caught mono from a bushy-haired chick I met at a Zeta party. I dropped out of the band for three months, and by the time I recovered, my "temporary replacement" had become permanent. Just before graduation, when the One O'Clock musicians were lining up cross-country tours or auditioning for symphonies, I was interviewing to be a middle-school band director. Dallas ISD hired me in July, but only because their first choice backed out when she took a whiff of the band hall and threw up.

Even though my job paid state minimum, which wasn't bad for a single guy, I eventually planned to make a down payment on a house. Plus, my girlfriend, Janice, was pushing to get married, in spite of her mother's opinion that she'd made a humongous mistake dating me. Evidently, Mrs. Liggins thought all musicians took a sacred vow of poverty and her only daughter would be forever wearing

mismatched clothes she bought on sale at Dollar General. So, as insurance against her mother saying "I told you so," Janice made it clear she wouldn't be happy with a typical starter-diamond; specifically, nothing smaller than a carat *and a half* would do. When she left town for three weeks' training for a new cat-scan machine, I figured it was a good time to find a second job, one where I could use my musical talent to work evenings and weekends.

I stopped by a 7-11 and picked up a copy of *American Classified*, the tabloid rag that lists page after page of want ads. Between "High-Risk Body Guard Needed for International Assignments" and "Earn Tens of Thousands at Home While Your Computer Does All the Work," was a listing for "Weinstein Music Agency - Guaranteed Work for Professionals." During my lunch break, I called and set up an appointment after school.

Just off Harry Hines Boulevard in one of those strip malls where the storefronts have iron bars, the agency was sandwiched between the Hot Tropics Nail Salon and EZ Money Pawn. Two-foot-tall plastic letters spelled out each business' name on the metal awning, and even though the "N," "a," and "i" were missing in "Nail," their sun-bleached outlines remained on the overhang like disintegrated corpses.

Animated musical symbols decorated the full-length plate-glass door into Weinstein's. Masculine half notes, outfitted with cowboy hats and Wranglers, danced with cutesy quarter notes, to music provided by tuxedoed trombones and leering saxophones.

Inside, a man weighing maybe 300 pounds, sat with his feet propped on top of a no-nonsense wooden desk, reading a paperback book in one hand and holding a lighted cigar in the other. Dozens of fading black-and-white glossies lined the smoke-yellowed walls, a few framed but most mounted haphazardly with thumbtacks and pushpins. Many of the photos had "To Lou" written with a black felt-tip pen, along with a personal message, but none of the musicians were famous, or for that matter, even remotely familiar. Smelling like a giant humidor, the room looked as if it hadn't been cleaned since Count Basie played Birdland, long before I was born. Without bothering to look up, the large man greeted me with a low, almost-snarling voice. "You the trumpet man?"

"Yes, sir."

"Lou Weinstein."

"I'm Robert Phillips."

"They call you Bob?" Lou turned a page of his paperback.

"No, just Robert. I never much cared for 'Bob.'"

Lou swung his feet off the desk, making eye contact for the first time. With his head seemingly glued directly onto his shoulders without the benefit of a connecting neck, he reminded me of one of the bodyguards on "The Jerry Springer Show," the guys who break up the cat fights between the pregnant girlfriend and the pregnant wife. Lou asked, "You any good?"

"I made the One O'Clock Lab Band at North Texas. That's as good as it gets."

Lou grunted. "Well, Bob, if you're so good, how come you're not on tour?" He tilted his head back, blowing an enormous smoke ring into the air, and simultaneously balanced his cigar on a half-coconut ashtray, the kind I'd seen in 1940's detective movies. If this was some sort of territory-marking arrow, it hit the bulls-eye.

"Things didn't work out," I answered.
"If you want, I can get my horn out of the car
and play something for you."

"Things didn't work out," I answered. "If you want, I can get my horn out of the car and play something for you."

"Not necessary," he said, dismissively waving his hand. "If you're lousy, I'll find out soon enough."

"Yes, sir."

"So, you're looking for something part-time?"

"Yes, sir."

"I got a group that plays restaurants, weddings, that sort of thing. They need a trumpet player for a couple of weeks. Regular man's on vacation."

"No problem. I can handle that."

Rapidly exhaling small-scale puffs of smoke like a Lionel toy locomotive, Lou scribbled a phone number onto a scrap of paper and shoved it across the desk. "Here, the man's name is Carlos." He narrowed his eyes. "And don't screw up, OK?"

"Yes, sir. I'll call him tonight."

"You get hired, my fee is $250. Cash, no checks. Understand?"

"Is that standard?"

"No, Bob," Lou growled, sarcastically. "Nothing's standard around here. Usually I charge $500 to a first-timer, but you look like you couldn't find shit from shinola in the dictionary. So I'm giving you a freakin' break." He launched another billow of smoke towards the ceiling, propped his feet back on the desk, and started reading his book. "Now, beat it."

"Yes, sir."

———————————

I tried Carlos' number, but a woman said he wasn't there and I should try again after midnight. Since Janice was out of town, I passed the time by catching up on some two-week-old laundry and surfing through the late-night talk shows. Around 12:30, I decided to grab a Diet Coke and shake off the cobwebs a little.

When I switched on the kitchen light, two cockroaches I had named Brad and Angelina skittered across the linoleum floor and hid under the refrigerator. The first night I moved in, I got up for a glass of water in the middle of the night and accidentally crunched two of their cousins. After that, I made sure to turn on the lights. Such was life when you lived in a rented, 25-year-old trailer in tornado alley. The place was so crappy my girlfriend wouldn't even visit after dark.

I chugged the Diet Coke, grabbed my cell phone, and dialed. A man answered.

"Hello, is Carlos there?"

"Speaking."

"Carlos, I'm Robert Phillips. Lou Weinstein gave me your number. Said you might need a trumpet man."

"How tall are you?"

"Beg your pardon?"

"How tall are you?"

"About five-foot-ten, I guess."

Carlos wanted to know how much I weighed, and I said about 200, give or take a few pounds.

"Good," he said. "Actually, that's very good."

"Sir, with all due respect, I don't understand what my height and weight have to do with playing the trumpet."

"Costumes."

"I'm sorry?"

"We wear costumes," Carlos said. "You speak Spanish?"

"Not much," I said, pausing for a few seconds, trying to think of some Spanish words. "*Enchilada, adios, muy bien,* but that's about it."

"That's what I figured," he said, sounding slightly disappointed. "Well, we're rehearsing Wednesday evening at my place. Six o'clock. Can you come?"

"Yes, sir."

"You play *conjunto* or *mariachi* music?"

I paused again, considering whether I really wanted a gig that required me to wear a costume and play Mexican music. While I had a feeling Janice wouldn't approve of my playing with a *mariachi* band, I was certain her parents, both Who's Who in Highland Park and always uptight about their social standing, would be absolutely mortified if they found out. Then, as if the music gods were signaling me with the equivalent of a burning bush, Brad and Angelina peeked out from under the refrigerator and made a dash to the stove. "I can play anything, sir, if I hear it once."

In his mid-50s, Carlos Santiago, tall and regal-looking with silver-hair and ruler-straight posture, stood in his front yard talking with another man when I pulled into the driveway. His modest, bungalow-style home featured a columned, wooden porch, just like my grandparents'. The wrap-around porch looked pleasant and inviting, unlike the expressions of the men in the yard, who, I imagined, weren't very pleased Lou sent a *gringo* for their band.

Nonetheless, the men strolled over to my car, and Carlos extended his hand. *"Bienvenido a mi hogar."*

"I'm Javier Sanchez." He smiled, revealing a collection of uneven, gold teeth. "Don't worry, we won't test you," he said in heavily accented English.

It sounded like a welcome to his home, so I shook his hand and said, "You know, fellas, I sure hope you like my trumpet playing, because my Spanish isn't too *bueno*."

That broke the ice a little. The other man, a short, jellybean of a fellow who looked about ten years younger than Carlos, offered his hand. "I'm Javier Sanchez." He smiled, revealing a collection of uneven, gold teeth. "Don't worry, we won't test you," he said in heavily-accented English. "But, I heard you know how to say *enchilada*." Javier started laughing, and when he did, the wire-rim glasses on the end of his nose bounced rhythmically as if they were on a tiny trampoline.

"Yeah, you can just call me Enchilada."

Carlos, still serious and unsmiling, invited me inside. His wife, a small, soft-featured woman with whom I'd spoken on the phone, asked if I'd care for

something to drink. When I declined, she disappeared into another room.

We rearranged the den furniture, giving us an area to rehearse. An old-fashioned room with knotty-pine paneling - real wood, not the fake Wal-Mart crap - its central feature was a large, wall-mounted crucifix centered over a table decorated with candles, several family photographs, and an open, large-print Bible.

Javier began tuning his *guitarron*, an enormous bass guitar that looked nine-months pregnant. While I warmed up my trumpet, he looked at me and smiled, as if he wanted me to succeed, although I imagined he also thought *what in the hell are you doing here*?

Carlos, the lead guitarist, said their band's name was *Los Fabricantes de Musica*, The Music Makers. He explained that one of the other members, Jessie, who played violin and sang lead vocals, was working late and couldn't make the rehearsal. "Let's start with 'Spanish Eyes,' and see if you can keep up," Carlos said.

Fortunately, I knew the song from my high-school-band days and easily nailed it. When Carlos nodded at me to take a solo riff, I made a point to show off a little.

Javier, who plucked his *guitarron* while balancing it upon his considerable tummy, looked impressed. *"Para un chico blanco, usted puede jugar realmente la trompeta."*

For the first time, Carlos displayed a hint of a smile. "He says you're pretty good for a white boy."

We went through seven or eight more tunes, all of which were vaguely familiar or easy to pick up. Carlos always followed the same pattern: he announced in what key we would play and led with an instrumental version of the song's verse and chorus; Javier, filling in for Jessie, followed on vocals for two verses and a chorus. During that segment, I played background and Carlos harmonized. Then it was my turn: I improvised either a twelve or sixteen-bar riff on my trumpet, taking great care to give it a Latin flavor. We wrapped up the song as Javier, again filling in for Jessie, sang the third verse and the chorus while I ad-libbed a counter-melody. Once I heard Carlos play the tune the first time through, the rest was a piece of cake.

After we finished a run-through of "*Perfidia*," one of their most-requested love songs, Javier looked at Carlos and said, "*Encontramos a nuestro hombre.*"

I had no idea what Javier said, but he grinned and began laughing, his glasses once again bouncing on the trampoline.

For the first time all evening, Carlos laughed and nodded. "Yeah, we found our man, all right. Hey, *Señor Enchilada*, let's see if you can fit into some costumes."

———————

My *charro* suit consisted of a huge *sombrero*; a pair of hip-hugging black trousers, at least a size too small, with a gold stripe down the side; a blousy, white shirt with an hugely oversized, floppy bow-tie; and a cropped, blood-red jacket with rows of coin-like buttons and shiny, silver doodads. I felt like a matador with training wheels.

I looked just as ridiculous in the other costume. Javier jokingly called it the "I'm-gonna-cut-you-with-a-knife" look: a snow-white cowboy hat, about a half-size too small; a pair of canary-yellow, pointy-toed boots that, thankfully, actually fit; and a green, pearl-snap western-shirt embroidered with ornate, sequined wagon-wheels. Even though the vacationing trumpet player and I were approximately the same height, I was at least thirty-pounds heavier and could barely snap the shirt buttons. Standing in front of the mirror, I looked like the Mexican version of the Pillsbury Dough Boy.

The next evening, *Los Fabricantes de Musica* was booked for a conference reception in the Anatole Hotel atrium. Wearing my *charro* costume, with the trousers safety-pinned together, I pulled in to the parking lot outside the hotel. Carlos and Javier were waiting beside a late-model pick-up truck; standing with them was an attractive young woman, with long, onyx-colored hair. Also dressed in costume, she stood ruler-straight and cradled a violin in her arms.

"Hey, Enchilada, welcome to *Los Fabricantes*," Javier said, smiling.

"*Buenas noches*,' I said, offering the greeting I'd googled and memorized thirty minutes earlier.

The slender woman extended her hand. "Hi, I'm Jessie Santiago. Sorry I couldn't make it to rehearsal last night."

Caught completely off-guard, I said, "Nice to meet you, Jessie, but I assumed you were a guy."

She smiled. "Disappointed?"

"Oh, no, I didn't mean it that way."

"It's Robert, isn't it?"

I paused. "Well, all my good friends call me Enchilada."

She laughed, an easy kind of laugh, and said, "Well, Enchilada, I hear you're pretty good."

"Just keep your fingers crossed I don't ruin the group's reputation tonight."

Carlos said it was time to go inside, so we gathered our instruments. Javier walked with me toward the hotel's entrance, and I quietly asked him if Jessie was Carlos' daughter. "No," he said, "she's a *sobrina* - his niece." Then, teasingly, he told me to calm down - my eyes were popping out of my head - "*Los ojos salen de repente de la cabeza.*"

The acoustics in the Anatole's cavernous atrium were "live," and our music carried well, even though we had to battle the clinking of cocktail glasses and the scattered, feel-good laughter of pharmaceutical sales reps unwinding after a long day. The mostly-male, out-of-state audience, dressed in dark suits and

conservative ties, loved the band. More specifically, they loved Jessie's sensual voice and live-wire personality. Strolling among the party guests, we played a couple of songs at each cluster before moving to the next group. Fortunately, I kept pace with all the songs. After a solo riff on "*Cuando Caliente El Sol*," Carlos gave me a thumbs-up and appeared genuinely proud to have a gringo in the band.

At the end of our first set, we sat down at a table away from the guests, and I asked how long the band had been together. Carlos and his brother, Miguel, were Cuban and started *Los Fabricantes* nineteen years earlier. Six months ago, Miguel, who is Jessie's father, decided he was too old for the late-night gigs and retired from the band. Carlos said, "That's when we traded him for Jessie." He winked at his niece. "I think we did pretty well."

Javier, a cousin of Miguel and Carlos, started playing the guitar while he was living in an apartment complex in Garland. Some of his upstairs neighbors played in a band, and he began attending their rehearsals. Javier patted his stomach and smiled. "They told me I was built for the *guiturron* and it was built for me." Later, when *Los Fabricantes'* original *guiturron* player quit, Carlos invited his cousin into the family's band.

Jessie, a high-school Spanish teacher, began learning the violin at age four and sang with the band from time to time, starting at age twelve. She was in the middle of telling a funny story about her father, who was also her violin teacher, when one of the pharmaceutical sales reps, a porky, middle-aged guy, wandered over to our table. He looked as if he'd had one-too-many gin and tonics, and interrupted her in mid-sentence. Smiling and holding a drink in his left hand, the man leaned down and put his free hand on Jessie's shoulder. Even though he was wearing a wedding ring, he asked if she'd like to come up to his room for a drink later in the evening.

Almost in one motion, Carlos jumped up from the table and placed his arm around the porky man's shoulders, like a high-school football coach correcting one of his players. He whispered something to the slightly inebriated man, and although none of us could hear Carlos' little speech, the guy's face turned chalky-white, as if he were seeing his life flash before his eyes. The man quickly excused himself and left the cocktail party, like a dog with his tail between his legs.

Seemingly a little embarrassed by her uncle's protective intervention, Jessie didn't say anything at first. Later, when Carlos left to find the men's room, she rolled her eyes and said, good-naturedly, "Uncle Carlos thinks I'm still a little girl and not capable of telling a man to go to hell. That drunk was polite compared to the gang members I see every day at my high school."

Over the next two and a half weeks, *Los Fabricantes* played just about every night: birthday and engagement parties, Mexican restaurants, open-air street dances, a grocery store grand-opening, a customer-appreciation event at a car wash, and a fund-raiser at a Catholic bingo hall. Since it was Carlos' church, that one was a freebie.

Every night, in between breaks, Jessie patiently taught me Spanish words and grammar. Javier said if I wasn't careful, she was going to turn me into a full-fledged Mexican.

The audiences seemed to enjoy seeing a gringo in the band, and Carlos began introducing me as his "long-lost cousin from Spain," which always got a big laugh. Every night, in between breaks, Jessie patiently taught me Spanish words and grammar. Javier said if I wasn't careful, she was going to turn me into a full-fledged Mexican.

Driving back to the trailer late one evening, I made my nightly call to Janice. I'd told her about my new part-time job, but didn't mention the type of music we played, our costumes, or the attractive woman in the band. When Janice asked where we'd been playing, I mentioned the Anatole, thinking it sounded a little classier than a grocery store or a church bingo hall.

"I just love the Anatole," she said. "Wonderful atmosphere."

"Yeah, and you can't imagine how good the acoustics are in there."

"So, what's the name of this band you're playing with?"

"They're called 'The Music Makers.'"

I could hear Janice taking a drag from her cigarette. "Sounds kind of gay," she said.

"*Everything* sounds gay to you, Janice."

"I can't help it. It does sound gay, like some band my grandparents would have listened to 60 years ago. You know, Lawrence Welk or Glenn Miller. One of those old dudes."

"Well, they're very good, and not at all like you'd imagine." Clearly the understatement of the year, I figured once Janice got back to Dallas we could have a face-to-face conversation about *Los Fabricantes*. I asked if she still planned to fly back next Sunday.

"Yeah, we get back late that afternoon. Maybe we can meet for some Chinese or Thai?"

"That'd be great," I said, knowing that Carlos attended mass and didn't book gigs on Sunday evenings.

"You guys have something for tomorrow and Saturday?"

"Yeah, we do," I said. "We have a wedding reception Friday night. Saturday, we're playing a hotel party for some new ambassador."

Janice didn't follow up with any more questions, but instead babbled on about how she and a couple of other girls in her training class had gone out for drinks earlier in the evening.

It was hard staying focused on the conversation because I was thinking about the lie I'd just told Janice. We weren't really playing a wedding reception on Friday; in truth, we were playing a *quinceanera*, a "coming out" party for a fifteen-year-old Mexican girl. Kind of like a *bar mitzvah* for Jewish boys, Javier said Hispanic families often spent as much or more on one of these parties as they did on a wedding reception.

It was the second time in our relationship I'd lied to Janice. The first time was when I said I admired her father. The fact was, I couldn't stand the jackass. I always thought when I met my girlfriend's father for the first time, he'd take me back to his walnut-paneled study and offer me a glass of brandy. We'd settle into comfortable leather chairs, break the tension with some small talk about football, and eventually discuss my personal and professional goals. After an hour or so, my girlfriend would wander back to his office and ask good-naturedly, "What in the world are you men talking about?" We'd laugh, get up from our chairs, and walk towards the den. He'd put his arm around my shoulder, smile approvingly, and say to his daughter, "He's a damn-fine man, and you better take good care of him!"

Instead, when Mr. Liggins and I met the first time, he skipped the small talk and immediately went for the jugular, asking what I did for a living. When I answered I was an assistant band director at a middle school, he shook his head gravely and offered me a job at his concrete company, "where I might have some sort of a real future." Even though my job may be on par with being the Chuck E. Cheese mascot, at least I don't have to work for that jerk.

The *quinceanera* was like being teleported to Mexico City for two hours, even though we were actually performing on Dallas' east side in a VFW hall, badly in need of a power-washing and steam-cleaning. Although the organizers were not high on the economic totem pole, the affair was beautifully decorated and carefully choreographed. Fourteen formally dressed attendants, along with their handsome escorts, stood in the receiving line alongside the smiling honoree as she greeted her guests. Basking in the attention, the slightly chubby girl wore a glimmering rhinestone tiara and a lustrous white gown, in contrast to the dingy walls and water-stained ceilings of the VFW. Only one other gringo was there, a confused-looking man who was married to one of the girl's *padrinas*, or godparents. He spent the entire evening standing by the rusting swamp coolers, making sure the standby

beer kegs stayed cold. Between our songs, Jessie gave me a running commentary of the customs honoring the young lady who was "transforming" herself from a little girl into a woman: the presentation of the "last doll" of her childhood; the changing of her shoes from flats to high heels; and the champagne toast, called the *brindis*, signifying the *quinceanera's* official entry into adulthood.

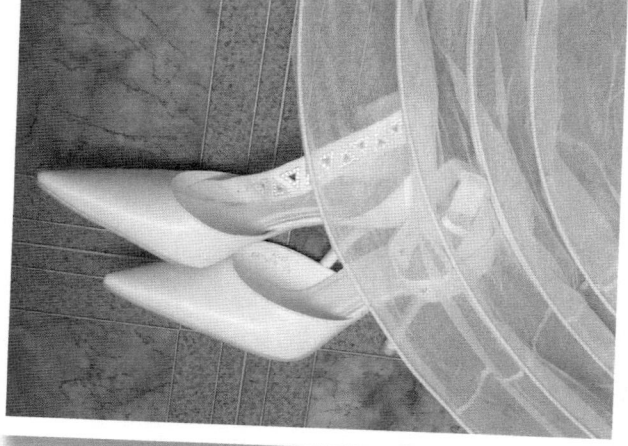

Sensing her pride in describing the traditions, I asked Jessie is she'd had her own *quinceanera*.

"Of course," she answered, smiling. "What kind of a girl do you think I am?" Her eyes looked mischievous, almost daring me to answer the question.

I was careful not to take the bait. "I don't know, what kind of girl are you?"

She smiled. "Not the kind to fall for someone who's already taken, that's for sure."

I had no idea how she knew about Janice; I hadn't mentioned my personal life to any of the band members. Maybe she was just playing a hunch, using her female intuition. If she was, my guilty look confirmed it.

Even though the Crescent Court Hotel was only ten miles from the VFW hall, it might as well have been on another planet, maybe another galaxy. Instead of the cracked concrete floors and chicken-coop-looking walls of the VFW, the Crescent had an ocean of polished marble, surrounded by elegant woodwork that a family of European peasants may have spent their entire lives carving. Rather than every-man-to-himself kegs of discount beer and Cheese-Whiz nachos, tuxedoed waiters served *Dom Perignon* to guests who nibbled on thin wafers topped with cucumber slices and caviar.

About 300 people, mostly wealthy campaign donors and corporate fat cats, gathered in the grand ballroom for the reception honoring the U.S. Ambassador to Mexico, himself a recent political appointee of the new administration. The lady in charge of the party, a razor-thin blonde who wore pink lipstick the exact shade of her silk suit, told Carlos our group should play "airy, traditional, Mexican folk music, but nothing radical like that *Chicano* stuff." Not exactly sure what constituted "radical" Mexican music, Carlos presented her with our play list, hoping it was sufficiently "airy." The pink-suited lady didn't know shit from shinola about music, as Lou would have observed, but said our songs "all looked acceptable."

Rather than stroll around from group to group as we had done with the pharmaceutical people, we were instructed to stand next to one of the three temporary bars, decorated to look like Mexican beach cabanas. Each guest received a sombrero and a miniature bullwhip as party favors. None of us could figure out the significance of the bullwhips, other than it had something to do with one of the sponsors of the event. Speaking in Spanish, Javier joked that maybe the bullwhips were illegal contraband confiscated by the border patrol. For the first time, I understood his wisecrack without having anyone translate. I said, also in Spanish, that maybe the miniature bullwhips had been the property of miniature *matadors*. Carlos started laughing and said if I kept learning Spanish, I could be another out-of-work Mexican comic.

The male guests, in their thousand-dollar Armani's and yellow power ties, looked a little peculiar wearing sombreros, but not nearly as ridiculous as the women with their black cocktail dresses, pearl necklaces, and diamond-stud earrings, all clutching their bullwhips as if they were the latest fashion must-have.

About fifteen minutes into our party, Carlos had the idea of playing "America the Beautiful," as a tribute to the new ambassador. Even though it hadn't been on our play list, we were pretty sure the pink-suited lady wouldn't mind. As soon as Jessie, in her strong, pure voice, began singing the words "O beautiful for spacious skies," the crowd grew quiet. Everyone focused their attention upon the beautiful woman of Hispanic descent, dressed in a folk costume, passionately singing about her home country.

When she sang the line "God shed his grace on thee," I spotted a couple of late-arriving guests making their way to join the crowd. It took a couple of seconds to recognize their faces, but once I did, my heart started racing. It was Janice's parents.

97

I read about this internet poll asking people to rank life's most embarrassing situations. The results were categorized by country, and for people living in Great Britain, number one on the list was giving a speech when you are ill prepared. In the United States, the top ranking was having a member of the opposite sex walk in while you're using the restroom, although the Brit's rated it as number five. That seemed a little odd to me, but maybe the British are accustomed to seeing members of the opposite sex do their business and don't regard it as any big deal.

They never spoke to me that evening;
not even a "Hello, nice to see you," or
"My goodness, what in the world are you doing here?"
I never felt so little in my life.

I'd much rather have had Janice's parents walk in on me buck-naked than see me in my *charro* costume. It took Mr. Liggins a few minutes to recognize me and make the connection, but when he did, he nudged Janice's mother and pointed me out. The way she looked at me, you'd have thought I'd just put a skunk in the ambassador's punchbowl.

They never spoke to me that evening; not even a "Hello, nice to see you," or "My goodness, what in the world are you doing here?" I never felt so little in my life.

When Janice called me from the airport on Sunday, I could tell her parents had already spoken to her. She suggested we meet at a Thai restaurant in Irving, and when I walked in, she was already sitting at a corner table, smoking a cigarette.

As soon as I kissed her hello, she said, "The Music Makers, huh?"

"I wanted to explain it to you in person."

She stared out the window, refusing to look me in the eye. "Why in the hell didn't you tell me the truth?"

"I was afraid you wouldn't approve."

"You were right about that."

"Janice, I was just trying to earn some extra money, that's all."

"Are there any other little secrets you haven't told me about?"

I considered saying I couldn't stand her father, but thought better of it. "No, there's nothing else. Look, I'm really sorry."

She took a final drag and smashed her cigarette in the ashtray. "Well, you should have considered how it would make me feel."

It was that final comment, one her mother could just as easily have made, that pushed me over the edge. Here I was busting my ass to earn some extra money to pay for a carat *and a half* diamond, just so I could be a part of a family who would degrade me for the rest of my life.

I looked at her and forced a smile. "You know, Janice, I wish you the best of luck in whatever life may bring you, but as for me, I just don't believe we belong together." And with that, I quietly rose from the table and walked out the door.

During seventh-grade band class, the word in the clarinet section was that Sharonda had dumped Jerome in favor of Lennis, a hormone-overloaded saxophone player and one of the prime suspects in the breast-drawing incident. Maybe Sharonda thought Lennis was more sophisticated since he knew what breasts were, even though she hadn't grown any herself.

While my boss, Mrs. Washington, directed the rest of the band in a tortured version of "My Bonnie Lies over the Ocean," I rehearsed the trombone section separately in a practice room adjacent to the band hall. We worked on their difficulty distinguishing between the fifth and sixth slide positions, something I've gone over with them probably 150,000 times. Jerome paid close attention and didn't appear to be distraught over getting dumped; in fact, I doubt he was even aware of Sharonda's new affections. Most likely, she would write Lennis notes for a few weeks, then move on to a tuba player or a drummer, or maybe even come back to Jerome. Such is the attention span of a thirteen-year-old clarinetist.

During the trombone sectional, I noticed two missed calls and messages on my cell phone. One was from Janice, but the other was a number I didn't recognize. When class dismissed, I went to the teacher's lounge and listened to the messages.

"*Robert, I'm not really sure why you got so upset last night, but if there's something you'd like to talk about, give me a call and let's work it out. Love you.*"

I pressed seven and deleted the message.

"*Hey, Robert, Charles Merrifield calling. I heard your band the other night at the Crescent Court, although at first I didn't recognize you. I'd forgotten how good you are. Give me a call first chance you get, ok?*"

Dr. Merrifield ran the One O'Clock Lab Band at North Texas and was one of my favorite professors in the entire music department. I figured he knew of an opening for a band director's position somewhere and was passing along the tip.

When I walked inside the trailer that evening, Brad and Angelina were in the middle of the kitchen floor, having a feast on a chunk of toast that had fallen off my plate. "You guys better eat while you can," I said. "I'm outta here in a few weeks." I decided to start looking for a house now that I no longer was buying a ring.

"I'll bet. Listen, I had an agent in my office last week who's looking for a jazz trumpeter to go on tour this summer with Harry Connick, Junior's band."

I rummaged through the refrigerator for a Diet Coke, sat down at the kitchen table, and hit the redial number on my cell phone. "Dr. Merrifield?"

"Yes, speaking."

"Robert Phillips. Sorry I missed your call today, but I had some trombones that couldn't get their fifth and sixth positions straight."

"Well, Robert, I appreciate your calling me back. Sounds like you had your hands full."

"Yes, sir, it's really life in the fast lane around here."

Dr. Merrifield laughed. "Hey, I enjoyed hearing you at the ambassador's reception Saturday night."

"Well, thanks. It's been kind of a strange gig."

"I'll bet. Listen, I had an agent in my office last week who's looking for a jazz trumpeter to go on tour this summer with Harry Connick, Junior's band."

"Really?"

"I think you'd be perfect. With your permission, I'd like to give him your name."

I took a deep breath, knowing I had somehow regained the favor of the music gods. "Dr. Merrifield, I'd be honored."

———————

I met with the agent for Connick's band late the next afternoon. Based upon my performance tape and Dr. Merrifield's strong recommendation, he offered me a job starting June 1, and I accepted on the spot. Maybe I could have held out for more money, but the pay really didn't matter. If it weren't for my bills, I'd have worked for free, maybe even paid them for the chance.

After school on Wednesday, I drove to Carlos' house for rehearsal. Everyone was waiting on the front porch when I pulled in the driveway. As always, Javier had a big smile on his face, and it struck me it wasn't going to be easy telling them about my new job.

"Hey, Enchilada, hope you've been practicing," Javier said.

"Of course, I've been practicing. What do you think I do all day long, work?"

"We got a fancy gig on Saturday, Enchilada. Big Mexican wedding. You gonna have to finally learn some *real* Spanish, not that fancy stuff Jessie teaches you." He started giggling. "Hey, maybe we can find you a nice bridesmaid to hook you up with. You know, one with big—"

"Javier," Jessie interrupted, "cut it out. He's already got a girlfriend."

"Oh?" Javier was surprised. "He never mentioned one to me."

"Actually, that's not true anymore," I said, looking directly at Jessie. "We're no longer together."

There was a long pause and my eyes started to glisten. I was tempted to look away, to hide my emotion from the others, but didn't. Finally, Jessie said, "I'm so sorry." And then, as if to reinforce her sincerity, "I really am."

"It wasn't a good fit, that's all."

"Better for you to know now, than figuring out you made a mistake twenty years down the road," she said.

"That's for sure." The mood had definitely downshifted to a more serious tone, and I figured I might as well give them the rest of my news. "Guys, this is hard for me, but I have something else to tell you." I took a deep breath and made eye contact with each of them. "You won't believe this, but I'm going on tour with Harry Connick, Junior's band starting in June."

"*Ah, felitanciones,*" Javier said, raising and clenching his fist in an old-fashioned black-power salute. Carlos and Jessie echoed his congratulations, but in English.

"Thanks, guys, but I wouldn't have gotten the gig if you hadn't taken a chance on me," I said, focusing my eyes on Carlos. "I can play with you another weekend or two, but then, I need to get ready for the tour. Plus, your "A-team" trumpet player should be back by then."

"Wow," Carlos said, "that's an opportunity of a lifetime." He started to say something else, but choked-up instead. Placing his guitar on the porch swing, he practically tackled me with a bear hug. "I'm so proud of you," he said, after we'd embraced in silence for a full minute.

Finally, Javier patted each of us on the back and said, "Come on, *hombres*, you guys are acting like Mexican women at a funeral. We've got some rehearsing to do."

We moved inside and practiced a dozen wedding songs, with the mood being businesslike and somber, not as jovial and easygoing as usual. At the end of rehearsal, Carlos and Javier went to the kitchen to review the band's bookings for the following week. Jessie and I packed our instruments, neither of us saying anything. Finally, Jessie snapped her violin case shut and said, "I don't know what happened between you and your woman, but you'll be fine." She smiled, gently. "You're a good man."

As much as I had felt an attraction to Jessie, initially, I knew it was better to leave our relationship where it was, good friends rather than anything more. "Thanks," I said. "Coming from you, it means a lot."

"So, does Harry Connick, Junior ever play in Dallas?"

"Yeah, I imagine he will at some point."

"Well, I just hope you'll remember your old friends at *Los Fabricantes*."

"Sure. Maybe I can get you guys some back-stage passes."

"That wasn't what I meant." Jessie had one of those men-just-don't-get-it looks on her face. "Remember your *family*, Enchilada."

It took a second for her words, and the full depth of her emotion, to take effect. It took a few more seconds for me to respond, to remember a specific word Jessie had taught me. Then, very slowly, so the pronunciation was correct, I said, "*Siempre*." Always. ✪

SAVED

"Moses strolled down the aisle, as if he were a drill sergeant inspecting his recruits. Standing within a few inches of people's faces, he asked 'Is it you, Brother? Will you answer the call, Sister?'"

EIGHT

Saved

Early Sunday afternoon on my ninth birthday, two elders from the Holy Gospel Church followed Daddy, Uncle Solomon, and me down a rutted, shadowy trail as crooked as the cottonmouth moccasins prowling Big Cypress Bayou.

Mother lagged the rest of us about thirty steps and joked that the men were walking so fast, she suspected they'd decided to go fishing rather than to a baptizing. I remember her

➡➡

shuffling along the trail as if she were playing a slow-motion game of hopscotch, carefully avoiding the claw-like briars and low-hanging pine boughs that could snag her new Sunday dress. She'd sewn it during the week - especially for my baptism - out of blue floral chintz purchased in Marshall, deciding to add a white-lace collar late Saturday night. Before leaving the house, Mother dabbed a drop or two of Jungle Gardenia on her neck. Given to her by Grandma Boykin on the day she married Daddy, it was the only perfume Mother would ever own.

A layer of pine needles carpeted the sometimes-slippery path that smelled of moist earth and decaying logs, a trail carved through the dense woods a hundred years earlier when the congregation used mules to haul drinking water to the church. Built in a clearing about two-hundred yards from the Bayou, the white-clapboard chapel received infrequent attention during the first century of its existence, and only then when Tadbaugh's Hardware donated cans of paint with expired dates. The original plans called for an imposing steeple with three bells; in its place stood a thriftier alternative, a makeshift cross, roughly hewn out of second-growth pine purchased from the sawmill on the state highway. Just as generation after generation in the East Texas congregation had set aside ambitions of more prosperous lives in Dallas or Shreveport, the high-minded plans for the grand steeple were eventually sacrificed for something less lofty and much more practical.

The trail to the Bayou spread wide enough for two people walking side-by-side, but not three, so I maneuvered to a position behind Uncle Sol and Daddy, and in front of the elders. Oak leaves, still sticky with moisture from the prior afternoon's rain, clung to the bottoms of my shoes, as if eager to hitchhike out of the woods to a drier, sunnier place.

The two elders were also Daddy's first cousins. The taller one, Malachi, a thin man with cadaverous cheeks and a gray beard as coarse as a wire brush, reminded me of a Civil War general posing in a tintype. Looking back 30 years later, what I remember most about him were his unforgiving eyes, the color of a shotgun barrel. I made it a practice to stare at the bridge of his nose whenever he quizzed me during Bible class. He paired off with the younger cousin, Thomas Ed, a raw-faced, red-cheeked man, who kept ledgers for the sawmill and wore the same polka-dotted tie every week to church. Thomas Ed toted a brown grocery bag with two freshly killed chickens inside, gathering the package under his arm as if he were carrying a football. The two cousins talked about President Eisenhower's heart attack and wondered if he would stand for reelection. Malachi allowed he could never bring himself to vote for a Republican, but Thomas Ed would give Nixon some consideration, assuming Eisenhower didn't seek another term.

Unlike the elders, who didn't seem to mind my listening to their conversation, Daddy and Uncle Sol spoke in the low voices they used when we hunted squirrels. Judging by the looks on their faces, whatever they discussed must have been important. Uncle Sol glanced over his shoulder from time to time, as if he wanted to make sure I lagged far enough that their conversation couldn't be overheard. I looked down, pretending to study a raccoon's skull I'd picked up on the trail, so they wouldn't think I was eavesdropping. At one point, I heard Daddy

use the words "special baptism," and at the mention of this phrase, Uncle Sol, the more hot-blooded of the two, bristled and said something that caused my father to stop dead in the trail and confront his brother. As they faced each other, Daddy, a massive man with the frame of a lumberjack, rested his hand on his brother's shoulder and answered him in a way that apparently settled the argument. Four-years younger than my father and not as tall or muscular, Uncle Sol nodded and placed his hand atop my father's hand, now grasping his shoulder as tightly as a pipefitter's vise. Until that day, I'd never seen two preachers argue, much less Daddy and his only brother.

Earlier that morning, Daddy had announced to the congregation that the afternoon's baptism would be a private celebration, limited to our family, with his first cousins acting as witnesses. After church, Uncle Sol's only son, Samuel, stayed at the chapel with his mother and the elders' wives. When the rest of us gathered to hike down the trail, I asked Daddy why Samuel and Aunt Rosalie weren't coming along. He said a six-year-old wasn't old enough to attend a baptism, which didn't make sense, as I'd been to several baptisms with children present much younger than Samuel. I kept quiet, because my father's number-one rule was never to question his authority on such matters; but still, I wondered.

When we neared the Bayou, I spotted three clumps of dead crickets floating on the water's surface, about a foot from the bank, matted together like decaying pieces of driftwood. The stench seemed to climb from the putrefying mass and blanket my face with the odor of death, chasing the scent of pines and Mother's perfume deep into the woods.

I felt sorry for the crickets, because from the earliest time I could remember, the insects held a special fascination for me. I called them "negro grasshoppers," not knowing the term was offensive until Army basic training a decade later. During the year I attended school, I learned that crickets comprised a special class of insects, more like katydids than grasshoppers. When Mother took over my education, she taught me how a person could determine the weather's temperature by counting the chirps a cricket makes in fifteen seconds. By adding

37 to the number of clicks, the sum total is the temperature in degrees Fahrenheit.

Mother, Uncle Sol, and the elders watched while Daddy and I stripped off our shirts, rolled up our pant legs, and left our shoes and socks on the exposed knees of a five-foot-diameter cypress tree. The elder with the grocery sack grabbed the dead chickens and hurled one into the mossy water about twenty yards downstream from where we stood, the other about twenty yards upstream, amid a cluster of floating logs and sticks. Daddy seemed to stare upstream at the chicken bobbing on the water, but it was hard to tell for certain. His left eye had a peculiar sideways cast, as if it were gazing in another direction. When he looked at you, the left eye made it seem as if he were always considering something else - as if half his brain were committed to the conversation with you, while the other half was thinking about something else. Samuel was also afflicted with a wandering eye, as well as my father's sister who died in childhood, but Uncle Sol and I had good eyes. Daddy said God created this imperfection to keep our family humble and to remind us of humanity's inherent flaws. While I understood his point, it seemed God could just as easily have given our family crooked toes or some other imperfection far less noticeable.

We waited about five minutes for alligators that might be roaming the area to roil the speckled-green surface and devour the chickens. When none appeared, my father and I waded into the murky water, to a level where my feet no longer touched bottom, but his did.

He latched his arm around my waist, holding me like a floating bait bucket, then leaned over and whispered, "Are you ready to meet Jesus?" It was an odd question, I thought, and after acknowledging I was ready, he kissed me on the cheek. When I looked up, it seemed both his good eye and bad eye somehow had managed to focus on me. His eyes were teary, and the expression on his face was not one of joy, as I expected, but one of sorrow.

Turning to the people standing on the shore, Daddy's eyes widened and he spoke in the Old Testament, Moses-like voice he could flip on and off as if it were a light switch. Almost shouting, he announced they would soon witness "the special baptism," which meant dying to the sins of man and to flesh, and being reborn into a new life in Christ. The new life could not begin unless there was first an end to the old life, he said, and being immersed in the water represented that mortal death. The immersion also represented reentering the womb to be born again into a new spiritual life. He asked everyone to bow and pray silently, and for a moment, the only sounds on the Bayou were the whizzing of a few mosquitoes and the distant, raspy scream of a red-tailed hawk. Daddy broke the calm by shouting "Amen," and immediately, the elders and Uncle Sol echoed with an even louder chorus of "Amen."

I took a breath and my father plunged me deep under the turbid water, one hand pushing my shoulders, the other holding my head. Even though the sound was muffled, I could faintly hear Daddy reciting the Lord's Prayer.

"Our Father Who art in heaven . . ."

But instead of a short dip under the surface, as I'd seen him do with others he baptized, he held me under much longer, continuing the Lord's Prayer.

"On earth as it is in heaven . . ."

When I tried to push up for air, he forced me deeper, the full strength of his body leaning against mine. My lungs burned red hot, ready to explode. Desperate to breathe, I panicked, flailing my arms wildly as my father continued what seemed to be the never-ending prayer.

"The power, and the glory, forever and ever."

When he said "Amen," Daddy pushed me down even harder, until my feet stabbed the slimy mud at the bottom of the Bayou. Struggling one final time to escape, I wondered what horrible thing I'd done to deserve being drowned. My thoughts flashed to the stinking crickets, and I saw my body floating alongside them in the filth, another piece of rotting driftwood. After that, I struggled no more.

The next thing I knew, Daddy, still alongside me in the Bayou, was shaking me and slapping my back with his hand, making me puke up the pea-colored water I'd swallowed. At first, I couldn't remember where we were, but then I heard the two elders on the shore applauding and shouting "Amen" and "Hallelujah." Uncle Sol, his head bowed and his back turned away from Daddy and me, did not applaud or shout, but knelt on his knees as if he were praying. A few feet from us, Mother, having jumped into the water, frantically extended her arms toward me, her blue dress now stained green with Bayou scum. Like me, the look in her eyes was one of utter terror.

———————

After the baptism, Mother sat with me in the back seat of our '52 Bel Air. As if shielding me from a hailstorm, she leaned over and wrapped her arms around me so tight, I thought my ribs might crack. Her tears moistened the back of my neck, and her skin, once fragrant with the scent of gardenias, now smelled of the Bayou, sour and fish-like.

Neither of my parents spoke all the way back to our wood-framed house, one of two on our road that wasn't brick. As soon as the tires crunched the gravel driveway, Mother, speaking barely above a whisper but in a voice as intense as any I'd ever heard, said I should find something to occupy myself. She and Daddy would be talking privately.

Inside the house, she closed the door to the back bedroom - more of a slam than a thud. I listened from the parlor, pretending to study my Bible in case Daddy later asked what I was doing. For more than an hour, Mother cried and wailed pitifully, like a stray cat caught in a varmint trap. When my father finally emerged from the bedroom, he quickly shut the door behind him, his face looking as if the blood had been drained from his skin. Mother wasn't feeling well, he said. She needed her rest.

At supper, Daddy scrambled a skillet of eggs - he wasn't good at frying them - and reheated the biscuits left over from breakfast. As we sat down to eat, he explained that during the first century of the Christian church, several devout sects baptized their new converts by holding them under the water so long, they experienced the sensation of drowning. The converts believed they were dying, which, after they were raised out of the water, made their baptism that much more significant. In their minds, they'd truly been given a second chance at life.

Daddy said his family continued to perform the ancient ritual for the males who had been specially chosen by God to become ministers of the Gospel. He clamped his hand on my shoulder, just as he had done to his brother on the trail. Grandpa Harlow, Uncle Solomon, and himself were baptized in this way, he said, and God had already chosen me for the ministry, which is why I'd received the special baptism. This sacred practice was not something ever to be shared outside of our family, not even with Grandma Boykin, because regular believers would never comprehend its extraordinary power. In time, he said, Mother's faith would grow strong enough to understand and accept what had happened.

I hadn't known I'd been chosen to be God's minister, so I asked Daddy how that could be. God had appeared to him in a dream, saying I would be anointed as a special servant to do "wondrous things" for the Lord. Even to a nine-year-old, it seemed strange that the Lord wouldn't have spoken directly to me in a dream, since I would be the one doing the great things. But as before, I dared not question Daddy on such matters.

When we finished the biscuits and scrambled eggs, I asked my father if I should check on Mother, still in their bedroom. He shook his head. We

should let her be, he said, but pray she'd grow stronger in the Lord.

The next morning, Mother cooked our regular breakfast of bacon and fried eggs, like always. But she and Daddy didn't speak or look at each other the whole time we ate.

———

Every night for the next three months - until the time she went away - I would try to block out the sound of Mother crying, sometimes wailing, in her bedroom. As Daddy instructed, I prayed that her faith, as well as mine, would continue to grow in strength. When I finished my prayers, I read the New Testament and concentrated on the wondrous things I must do for the Lord, now that I had been given a second chance at life.

———

About a week after my eleventh birthday, Daddy and I waited in the front seat of our Bel Air, its windows rolled down, while Miss Ellen changed clothes in our motel room. Careful not to touch the blistering-hot dashboard, I leaned toward him while he adjusted the knot on my blue-striped bow tie. The prior Christmas, I'd asked for a long tie, the kind the men wore, but Daddy thought it would make me look too old.

His right eye focused on my tie, but his wandering eye seemed to be gazing in the direction of the motel, and I imagined it was considering why Miss Ellen always took so long getting dressed.

He lightly thumped the knot of my tie with his middle finger. Even though four lost sinners had been saved during our weeklong crusade, Daddy said it hadn't met God's expectations. Tonight's service, our last before moving on to Biloxi, was my chance for redemption. "Son, you remember what *John 15:2* says?"

———

My father's eyes widened and he spoke
in his Moses voice. "And another branch
will sprout, one bearing much more fruit."
He thumped my bow tie again, harder this time.

———

"Yes, sir."

He fished a fresh pack of Dentyne from his shirt pocket and unraveled its waxy string. "Recite it."

In an instant, my throat tightened. "If a tree's branch doesn't bear fruit, the Lord will cut it off."

My father's eyes widened and he spoke in his Moses voice. "And another branch will sprout, one bearing much more fruit." He thumped my bow tie again, harder this time.

I wanted to answer, "I've done good things for the Lord," but my mouth was too dry to speak. A stick of Dentyne would have helped, but Daddy thought young people chewing gum was a sign of juvenile delinquency.

He glanced at his watch and lightly tooted the car horn for Miss Ellen. "The gospel needs to be preached strong tonight. *Real strong.*" The gum gave his breath a spicy scent, like cinnamon Red Hots. "The Lord expects five people - men, women, or children, it doesn't matter - to surrender their lives to the Lord Jesus Christ."

"Five?"

His good eye glistened. "You're not doubting the Lord, are you, son?"

"No, sir."

Daddy studied his watch, but continued his lecture. "Otherwise, you might antagonize the Lord. He'll cut off your branch and find someone else to produce the fruit."

As concerned as I was about antagonizing God, at least I could avoid meeting Him face-to-face until judgment day. There was no hiding from my father, especially if he believed I wasn't doing the Lord's work. Stone-faced, he'd sternly pronounce judgment, "He who spares the rod hates his son, but he who loves his son disciplines him promptly." Then, with misdirected eyes that seemed incapable of showing mercy, my father would slowly unbuckle his leather belt.

Daddy unwrapped a second piece of gum and popped it into his mouth. "I believe Miss Ellen takes longer to dress than the second coming of Christ." He honked the Bel Air's horn once more, this time for several seconds.

———————

Promptly at eight o'clock that evening, Daddy welcomed between 70 and 80 believers and curiosity seekers, most of whom fanned themselves with folded-up revival flyers. Muscular farmers and mill hands, dressed in blue overalls and company work shirts, sat next to sad-looking housewives and hardscrabble waitresses. Earlier in the week, Daddy and I, along with a high-school boy he hired for the afternoon, spent four hours setting up our two-pole, army-surplus tent next to the Piggly Wiggly parking lot. Miss Ellen, who began traveling with us soon after Mama went away, stayed in the motel room where it was cool. We stretched a long banner across the canvas wall nearest the Beaumont highway that read, *Hear The World Famous Boy Evangelist Tonight!*

Daddy worked the audience slowly at first, reminding me of a smooth radio announcer reading a Pepsodent commercial. "If anyone here tonight is oppressed or otherwise downcast, do not despair, brethren. In a few minutes, you'll hear Miss Ellen sing with a voice you'll know was heaven-sent. After that, you'll be blessed with a special word from God's own eleven-year-old messenger. Can I hear an 'Amen' to that?"

The audience responded weakly, as they always did the first time.

Daddy acted as if he were shocked by the crowd's response, announcing that last week in Galveston the folks practically shook the tent poles with their voices. He asked two more times before the audience finally shouted "Amen!" loud enough to make him smile.

It had been Miss Ellen's idea to feature me as the evangelist at our crusades. She called it a "hook," which would set us apart from other traveling evangelists. Daddy dismissed the notion at first, saying that even though I was destined for the ministry, I wasn't yet ready "to occupy the pulpit." But Miss Ellen possessed some sort of power over my father, and convinced him to try the idea at our crusade in Lafayette. That week, we drew bigger crowds and received larger offerings than we had all season long. After that, I became The World Famous Boy Evangelist.

Standing in front of the tent and already glistening with giant beads of sweat you could see from anywhere in the audience, my father reached into his suit pocket, unfurled a white handkerchief, and made a big show of mopping his brow. "This tabernacle, humbly made of man's cloth," he pointed at the olive-green canvas walls, "will soon gloriously transform in God's eyes to the marble and gold of a jeweled sanctuary." He paused and tilted his massive head upwards as if imagining the gilded ceiling above him. Closing his eyes, he lowered his voice to a breathy whisper. "Will you listen for His call? Will you receive manna from heaven, free for the asking?" Almost in mid-question, Daddy flashed open his misaligned

eyes and switched on his Moses voice. Shouting as loud as thunder, he recited the Lord's Prayer, which startled the congregation and made an old Mexican man nearly jump out of his metal folding chair. Hearing the Lord's Prayer always made my stomach knot, as I thought of my baptism in the Big Cypress Bayou.

At the exact moment Daddy hammered the final "Amen," Miss Ellen began a tender version of "Amazing Grace," right on cue. With a clear voice like hers, the musical accompaniment of a piano wasn't necessary, to say nothing of being too bulky and heavy for the trailer we towed behind the Bel Air.

Daddy thought Miss Ellen's singing helped to keep the people from "reaching the mountain" too early in the evening. "A good service always peaks at the end, not the middle," he would say.

After Miss Ellen led the crowd in singing two more hymns, Daddy prayed again, this time in his normal voice. The crowd bowed their heads and closed their eyes, except for the Mexican man, who seemed to be keeping watch in case Moses decided to shout again.

After Daddy finished praying in his normal voice, he announced we'd receive the evening's "love offering," the first of two offerings taken at every service. While Miss Ellen sang "Peace in the Valley," he paced the aisle holding a small, wooden apple crate, our makeshift collection basket. He offered the crate to each person, saying "God bless you" to those who gave folding money and nodding to everyone else. Sitting motionless on the front row and bowing my head, I prayed as hard as possible that five souls would be saved and the Lord wouldn't be antagonized.

Daddy returned to the front of the tent and lifted the apple crate over his head, toward one of the yellow light bulbs dangling from the center poles. Treating it as if it were filled with gold and silver, he presented the treasure chest to heaven, asking God "to bless and multiply these honest, humble gifts."

That was my signal to begin. I sprang from my seat and hurried to the four-foot square podium. My father said it was important to appear enthusiastic, as if I couldn't wait to proclaim God's word.

I preached about Daniel in the fiery furnace and stuck word-for-word to my sermon, not daring to incur Moses' wrath for "taking liberties with God's word." By the time I reached the part about Shadrack, Meshach, and Abednego, my black wool suit practically dripped with sweat, partly because of my nervousness about antagonizing the Lord, and partly because of the evening heat radiating off the nearby asphalt. After a week of gulf-coast humidity, my coat smelled like a soured dishrag.

Sitting on the front row, Daddy occasionally arched his eyebrows if I needed to raise my voice, or pursed his lips if I should speak softer. Even though I'd preached about Daniel dozens of times, there was always room for improvement, he said.

At the end of the sermon, I said, "If you're here tonight and do not have a personal relationship with Jesus Christ, it's time to come forward, here and now, and be saved. As the Lord rescued Daniel from Nebuchadnezzar's fiery furnace, He can save you from the fires of hell." Just as Daddy suggested after our services in Galveston, I added, "Will you choose eternal life . . . or damnation and eternal death?" I questioned whether "damnation" was a curse word and thus a sin. He recited several verses and said if the word was in the Bible, it was all right with the Lord.

When I finished the sermon, Miss Ellen invited the congregation to stand and join her in singing "I Surrender All." After two stanzas, no one stepped to the aisle.

Before the third stanza, the booming Moses voice interrupted the singing. "The Lord is speaking to someone, right this very moment. He's speaking to a lost, desperate soul right here in this tent." Daddy asked Miss Ellen to sing the rest of the hymn by herself, while everyone "quietly listened for Jesus' call."

Daddy paced the aisle, as if he were a drill sergeant inspecting his new recruits. Thrusting his chin within a few inches of people's faces, he probed, "Is it you, brother? Will you answer the call, sister?"

Most in the audience stared straight ahead, fanning themselves and avoiding the uncomfortable gaze of his misaligned eyes. But a couple of the men, brave enough to look the drill sergeant in his good eye, smiled confidently as he passed by.

During the next verse, an old woman, bent-over from arthritis, slowly shuffled from her metal folding chair toward the aisle. Wearing a flower-print dress with a yellowed lace collar - the same one I'd seen her wear every night that week - she clutched my father's hand. She was already saved, she said, but promised to rededicate her life to the Lord.

Daddy held the woman's hand and nodded at me. It was time to make one final plea. Above Miss Ellen's cream-textured voice, I urged the crowd to follow the woman's testimony and "be saved from the hell that surely awaits a sinner." It was so hot in the tent, the flames of hell seemed to be lapping just outside the canvas walls.

When no one else came forward to the altar, I repeated my warning about eternal damnation - with so much intensity this time, I felt dizzy. Despite my appeal, no one moved. Frightened about the punishment that surely awaited me because five people hadn't been saved, I began to weep, then cry, begging the congregation to answer Jesus' call. My tears were real, not onioned-up like Miss Ellen had suggested.

The wetness of my cheeks reminded me of how my Mother's tears moistened the back of my neck after my baptism, her embrace both shielding and comforting me. I remembered the times when I hadn't met Daddy's expectations and Mother saved me from his belt, shielding me in the same way. Feeling the heartache of missing her and now overcome by the heat, I collapsed to the canvas floor and wailed as Mother had done that Sunday afternoon, like a cat caught in a varmint trap.

It must have been a powerful witness, because almost immediately, three people responded and asked to be saved - an old farmer, a sickly-looking woman, and a pregnant girl with long, stringy hair. I rose to my knees and asked them to kneel at our makeshift altar, 2" x 10" pine boards propped up on concrete blocks. My father knelt beside them, whispering a prayer and placing his hand on each person's head, anointing them with the Spirit. When Miss Ellen

finished the last verse, Daddy announced that three souls had been saved, and as a "special recognition of this triumphant moment," we would receive an additional offering, the "celebration offering."

After the service ended, Daddy said we'd dismantle the tent the next morning and get an early start for Biloxi, where our next crusade began on Tuesday. Back at our motel room, Miss Ellen made bologna and cheese sandwiches, and we took turns using the shower. The Lord must have been satisfied with only three souls being saved, rather than five, because nothing more was said about branches bearing fruit. Nor was there any mention of sparing the rod and spoiling the child.

Later, Daddy said he and Miss Ellen were staying up late up to talk, which always meant I had to lug my sleeping bag to the back seat of the Bel Air. I didn't mind, because in that quiet place, I didn't have to worry about pleasing my father or the Lord. It would be years later -after I joined the Army - before I acknowledged and came to terms with the real reason I was always dispatched to the Bel Air.

That night, outside the motel room and lying in the back seat of the car, I watched crickets swarm on the rear window, shading a portion of the moonlight. One of the insects had somehow entered the car and struggled as he clawed on the inside of the window, desperate to join the others. Gently capturing the cricket, I opened the car door and placed him with his swarm. It made me feel good, as if I had a say in the creature's future.

I said my prayers, asking God to watch over Mother, wherever she was, and to bless our next crusade. Once we set up in Biloxi, I could save the other two souls, maybe even more. ✪

"Nobody caused any trouble, except a few Baylor Seminary students. Thought they deserved a *ministerial* discount."

NINE

Chicken Ranch Charm School

Bronco drove like a man in need of an exorcism, blasting along at 70 miles-per-hour down an Interstate 20 covered with ice as thick as a hockey rink.

"You just gotta treat the truck like it's a pro-jec-tile," he said, one hand on the steering wheel and the other clutching an empty can of Red Bull. "Don't hit the brakes, and you'll be fine." We whizzed past

➤➤

an overturned UPS truck in the bar ditch, packages littered across eight inches of snow. "See, that's what happens when you hit the brakes."

I clasped my seatbelt as if it were a strand of rosary beads. "Bronco, you just used the word 'projectile,' didn't you?"

"Yeah, pro-jec-tile." He rat-a-tatted each syllable, like a boxer training on a leather punching bag. "Learned that from my second wife."

"Connie?"

"Never got around to marrying Connie." My friend shook his smooth-shaven head. "No, Melissa was *numero dos*. Skinny, good-lookin' blonde from Wisconsin, with a great pair of headlights. Norwegian or Swede, I forget which. Up there, they drive on ice like this all the time. No biggie."

Bronco and I were brothers-in-law for fourteen months - my sister, Amanda, being the first entry in his matrimonial logbook. He's also the father of my niece, whom he treats as if she were heir to the British throne. Despite his divorce from Amanda and perhaps my better judgment, Bronco and I remained friends and fishing buddies. Had he gone to college, he would have been the social director at a party-hearty fraternity, always one toga away from being excommunicated from campus. Me, I was the late-night geek at the library, buried behind the stacks, trying to pull an A plus rather than an A in British Lit. Amanda said my relationship with Bronco reminded her of someone dumping a bag of salted corn-nuts into a crystal bowl of Russian caviar - too weird to imagine.

Our Chevy Silverado weaved around a car-hauling eighteen-wheeler with icicles the size of stalactites, then passed a redhead in a Hummer and a TxDot sanding truck, neither doing more than 30. The Hummer lady flipped us the bird, and the TxDot guy scowled with a go-straight-to-Hell-and-do-not-pass-Go stare. I grabbed the leather strap above the passenger door and instinctively pancaked my boot to the floorboard.

"There ain't no brake on that side of the truck, Earl," Bronco said, smiling as if he were an eight-year-old boy dropping a bullfrog down a girl's blouse.

I relaxed my foot, but hung on to the strap.

With the eastern sun glaring like a giant searchlight, Bronco adjusted the visor and appeared to squint, although it was impossible to tell for certain. Bronco's face looks as if a schoolyard bully grabbed a handful of his fleshy forehead and permanently mushed it down, right over the eyebrows.

"We should grab some breakfast," I said, as our truck skated across the Brazos River bridge. "There's a Waffle House up the road in Weatherford."

My friend glanced at his Safe-Driver-of-the-Year Timex, an award Greyhound's muckety-mucks would have unceremoniously snatched from his wrist, had they been present. "I guess so," he snorted. "We have two hours. Plus, she checked her luggage."

"You excited?"

With his oven-mitt-sized hand, Bronco reached into the ice chest wedged on the floorboard between our seats. "I dunno, man," he said, a bit hesitantly.

"Feelin' a little weird, I guess." He pulled a fresh can of Red Bull from the ice, steadied it between his thighs, and flipped the tab, all without taking his eyes off the road. "You know, me and marriage ain't worked so well."

"Maybe four's your lucky number."

He shook his head and grinned slyly. "I dunno, always heard seven was the luckiest."

A week ago, Bronco announced he was marrying Sheryl, an Iowa woman he'd met on an internet-dating site. For the past five months, they'd Ping-Ponged between Texas and Iowa every other weekend. Now in route to Dallas, Sheryl would rendezvous with Bronco and board a charter flight to Miami for a Caribbean cruise. The three-hour layover would allow just enough time for a quick sashay to secure a marriage license at the courthouse - with the wedding performed at sea by the ship's captain. After the honeymoon, the new bride would relocate to Texas, nail down a nursing job, and live happily ever after.

The prospective groom asked me to mule his truck back to Abilene, thereby avoiding the parking fees, which border on gangland extortion. With school on winter break and no teacher workshops to attend, I agreed to be Bronco's beast of burden. Of course, that was before the mother-of-all-blizzards blew in and I found myself white-knuckled with a demonic driver who considered his truck a pro-jec-tile.

"So, does this Sheryl lady know your divorce attorney gives you a volume discount?"

"Not funny, Earl. I've had hard luck with women, that's all." He hiccupped loudly, almost echoing in the tight confines of the mansmelling cab. "This is the first time I've ever been soul mates with a woman."

"Bronco, give me a break. Soul mates?"

"Well, you know, we learned what makes each other tick. She understands my spare time revolves around girls' softball and my extra bedroom's decorated in Hello Kitty stuff. I've learned Sheryl reads this guy Hemingway and loves lobster like they'll quit makin' 'em tomorrow."

"Wait a minute, Bronco. Do you even know what Hemingway wrote?"

"The point is," he said, ignoring my question, "I decided to really get to know Sheryl, instead of concentrating on all the physical stuff." He hiccupped again and guzzled the remainder of his Red Bull. "In the past, that's the way things worked with me and women." He paused, apparently realizing his last statement would include my sister. "Of course, it was different with Amanda."

I considered confirming that he always concentrated on the physical aspects of a relationship, but held my tongue. Bronco's failures with women, it appeared to me, centered on his obsession with the thrill of the "chase" rather than the everyday relationship after the "catch." It was why he always released the fish he caught, even the nine-pound-monster bass he snagged last spring.

Just then, the yellow and black Waffle House sign materialized on the horizon, the "W" dark and in need of a light bulb replacement. Not a moment too soon, since my stomach was growling like a tiger protecting a double order of bacon and sausage for her cubs.

I tell my sophomore English students that when it comes to breakfast, Waffle House is the roadhouse equivalent of Mecca, Rome, and Salt Lake City all wrapped into one. Usually, when I make a statement like that, they roll their eyes, never daring to admit their teacher might accidentally say something clever. I never take it personally because after teaching for eight years, I've learned the little darlings' eyes roll more than a slot machine at a stateline truck stop.

It's a pity some of my fellow teachers start their retirement-year countdown on their very first day on the job. My theory is these malcontents settled on teaching when their parents tired of funding never-ending college careers, or when more promising alternatives failed to develop. Me, I actually enjoy teaching - stamping out ignorance, as I call it. There's plenty of job security stamping out ignorance, since a fresh outbreak crops up every Monday morning and metastasizes after the Christmas holidays.

There's plenty of job security stamping out ignorance, since a fresh outbreak crops up every Monday morning and metastasizes after the Christmas holidays.

But thinking about my little academic angels was the least of my worries as Bronco whipped his truck into the Waffle House parking lot. By the length of three buttered waffles, we avoided a gray BMW slowly fishtailing on the glassy asphalt.

The sidewalks to the front entrance appeared to be salted, but apparently, one stealthy patch of black ice hid in ambush. Sure enough, I lost my balance, grabbed onto Bronco, and we tumbled to the sidewalk. Spread eagle, with me on top, we looked like ice dancers at the Gay Olympics who just failed compulsories.

"Get off," barked Bronco.

"Trust me, I'm trying." I unpretzeled myself and quickly scanned the parking lot for eyewitnesses. Unfortunately, I spotted a waitress inside the restaurant, pointing to us and laughing.

Bronco scrunched his face. "Earl, why did ya have to be so dad-gum clumsy?"

"Hey, it was black ice," I said. "This is exactly why you shouldn't be driving like a bullet."

"Not a bullet, a pro-jec-tile," he corrected. "See, instead of walking *through* the ice, you slammed on your brakes, didn't you?" His breath formed a mini-cumulus that quickly evaporated in the frigid air. "You have to listen to Bronco, son, and learn."

Inside Waffle House, the inviting aromas of bacon, coffee, and warm syrup formed a perfect atmospheric soufflé. A cheerful female voice, emanating from someone kneeling behind the counter, welcomed us as we saddled up on the swivel stools. Bronco's belly pushed against the buttons of his shirt, exposing hairy anatomy I'd just as soon not have viewed. Despite a physique that hinted at Michelin-Man DNA, Bronco attracted more females than a Barry Manilow concert. It was hard to figure. Maybe women loved the way Bronco made them feel about themselves - like they're the most beautiful, sexy creatures on the planet - or perhaps it was all the attention he paid them. Maybe women possess an odd little chromosome that makes them want to cuddle giant teddy bears.

It turned out, the friendly voice from under the counter belonged to the waitress who witnessed our tumble. Plunking two cups of coffee on the counter, she tried, but failed to suppress a smirk. "If I'd videoed you fellas, I'd have won $10,000 on America's Funniest Dorks," she said, her smirk mushrooming into a full-blown smile.

Bronco's cheeks turned the color of a packet of Sweet 'n Low. "Aw, there ain't no such show."

"Well, if there *were*, you could get superstar money," she teased. The 30-something-year-old sported the standard issue Waffle House uniform - crisp blue shirt under a black, slightly greasy apron, and a WH visor tagged with large political-style buttons celebrating Route 66, Santa Claus, and the American flag.

Flashing a rascal-like smile, Bronco nodded to our server and said, "How 'bout you just tend to your waitressin', and I'll just tend to my eatin'. That a deal?"

"Sure thing, Twinkle-Toes," she answered, scooping up the empty plate of the truck driver seated next to me. Bronco's always been a sucker for sassy women, and this one oozed enough to qualify as the Saudi Arabia of sass. I pictured the rusty sprockets slowly turning inside my buddy's primordial brain, as well as body parts farther south, greased up by the pheromonal WD-40 the waitress just squirted on the creaking gears.

We ordered breakfast and watched the thick-necked cook, who sported a Confederate flag tattoo just above the neckline of his wife-beater T-shirt. Performing on a grill no more than eight feet from the counter, he was a bubbified version of a Japanese hibachi chef, buttering toast, pouring waffle batter, and managing three different skillets of eggs. Even though the waitresses weren't communicating to him in Japanese, they used an equally foreign-sounding language to bark their instructions - "Mark triple, over well" and "Drop one hash brown, scattered."

Against the mild commotion of jabbering customers, clanking coffee cups, and sizzling sausage, my friend leaned over and whispered, "Check out the sunny-side-ups on that waitress, will ya?"

I grimaced. "Come on, Bronco, your new bride's arriving in a couple of hours. You can't be hound-dogging on your honeymoon."

"Hey, I'm just lookin'. No harm in that."

The waitress delivered our plates, nestling them on top of the laminated menus illustrated with tiny pictures of hamburgers and omelets, which also doubled as our placemats. Bronco leaned toward her and asked, "Is this weather cold enough for you?" Like most adult Texas males, his conversational icebreaker *du jour* usually involved weather or ball scores.

She deadpanned, "Mostly, but occasionally, I step into the walk-in freezer for a few seconds, just to get *really* cold."

Bronco grinned. "You single?"

The wedding-ring-less waitress threw up her hands as if she were under arrest. "Whoa, cowboy. You haven't even asked my name, and you're asking if I'm single?"

"Hey, if you weren't so stinkin' gorgeous, I wouldn't be askin'." Coming from most men, a cheesy comment like that would have sounded completely phony, but Bronco had a way of making it seem authentic and sincere.

She parried, "Normally, guys who hit on me this time of morning are either still drunk from last night or toothless. Open your mouth, will you?"

He opened his mouth for an instant, and quickly chomped it shut. Realizing she'd successfully pulled his chain, he smiled and said, "OK, you got me.

I'm Bronco. This is my friend Earl."

"Bronco? So did your parents give all the good names to their birddogs?"

Like listening to someone microwaving a bag of Orville Redenbacher, the conversation between Bronco and the waitress seemed to pop every few seconds. "No," he replied, "but if your full name was Claudius Ptolemy Jocasta, you'd tell the kids at school your name was Bronco. Otherwise, you'd get your ass whipped every day."

She smiled. "That's funny, Claudius."

Bronco asked, "You have a name?"

"Danielle, but my friends call me Daisy. You leave a nice tip, and you can be my friend, too," she said, hustling off to refill another customer's coffee cup.

We ate our breakfast, but Bronco's eyes never shifted from Daisy. She carried herself with a sense of purpose and appeared to enjoy her job - unlike some Waffle House waitresses with we'd-rather-work-somewhere-else demeanors. I know several sourpusses at school who could benefit from a heavy dose of Daisy's attitude.

After topping off our coffee cups for the third time, she asked if we'd care for anything else.

"No, better get going," I answered. "Guess we need our check."

Bronco chimed in, "Wish I could stay a while longer. Figure out how you got to be so dad-gum charming."

Daisy said, "That's simple. I graduated from the Chicken Ranch Charm School."

I choked on a mouthful of coffee. There was an uncomfortable five-second delay in the popcorn-quick conversation.

"You what?" I asked. "The Chicken Ranch as in -"

"Yep," she interrupted, *Best Little Whorehouse in Texas.*"

Wide-eyed, Bronco looked as if he'd swallowed his tongue, his teeth, and maybe his nose. "You were, um, employed there?"

"No, silly. They closed down, like, 30 years ago." She lifted a ballpoint from her blouse pocket and totaled our ticket. "But my mama worked there for a while. When I was small, she took me along sometimes, when she couldn't find a babysitter. The other working girls treated me like their kid sister."

"You're jokin'," said Bronco, still not believing what he'd heard.

"Nope."

I raised a condescending eyebrow, but kept mum, not wanting to be a total prude. This wasn't a topic normally discussed over morning coffee in the teachers' lounge at Abilene High. Granted, there could have been a reformed soiled dove or two teaching social studies or math, but they'd never admit to it, and certainly wouldn't be proud of it.

"Hey, boys, don't be so quick to judge," Daisy said, jutting her chin. "Those ladies taught me manners and how to appreciate the good qualities in every man, despite the fact he's visiting a place he shouldn't be visiting. Maybe the man's best quality is his heart, or he's a special friend to someone, or maybe he's funny, like ol' Bronco here, who slipped on the ice like a spastic penguin." She winked at my buddy.

He ignored her zinger. "My uncle told me about going to the Chicken Ranch. Said the place was real nice and proper, very clean. Nobody caused any trouble, except a few Baylor seminary students. Thought they deserved a *ministerial* discount."

"One of the ladies - I called her Aunt Rose - said the Baylor men deserved a *volume* discount," she chuckled, gently resting the check between our plates. "Every time I saw Aunt Rose, she brushed my hair with this soft brush, the kind you use on babies. Exactly 21 times, no more, no less. She told me brushing your hair with 21 strokes always brought a girl good luck."

"Yeah?" Bronco reached for his wallet. "So did brushing her hair bring Aunt Rose plenty of good luck?"

"Depends how you define 'good luck,' I suppose. She married this lawyer from South Texas who later became a state senator. Nobody ever knew where she'd worked or how she met her husband."

"I can't say that marrying a politician would be my idea of good luck," I interjected, feeling a little left out of the conversation.

"Anyway, Aunt Rose always told me there's a big difference between appreciating and flattering someone. Flattery's like sugar - it tastes good for a second or two, and then it's gone. But appreciation - *true appreciation* - nourishes a person and builds them up."

"Your Aunt Rose was a pretty smart lady," Bronco said. He counted out enough cash for the check, as well as an extra ten-dollar bill, which he slid under the coffee cup.

She glanced at the tip and smiled. "Well, thank you very much, Mr. Bronco or Claudius Whatever-Your-Name-Is. Just wish this wasn't my last day here, or I'd invite you back to see me again real soon."

His face wrinkled like the bacon frying on the cook's grill. "Oh? Where you going?"

"Don't know for sure. Maybe Houston or Galveston. Or back home to San Antonio. Who knows?" She reached across the counter and gathered our dirty plates. "But my rent's up," she said, glancing out the window toward the parking lot, "and it's time to make some tracks. Tomorrow morning, I'll eat breakfast, brush my hair 21 times, and decide where to go. Just need to let the highway ice melt a little."

Bronco's lips twisted to the side, as if he were thinking of a way to keep the ice frozen solid for a few more days. I'd seen him do it the day we went fishing and he reeled in that monster bass.

125

———

DFW Airport's older terminals look as if they were designed by the same architect who drew the plans for Lenin's Tomb in Moscow. Concrete, boring, and just plain ugly.

The airport security gorillas wouldn't allow us to wait in the loading zone, so Bronco and I orbited Terminal E, navigating the maze of icy airport roads and narrowly avoiding several slow-motion, fender-benders. Texans have about the same level of experience and competence driving on ice as Eskimos driving in dust storms.

Staring straight ahead, my buddy hadn't uttered a syllable since we left Waffle House an hour earlier. I felt fidgety, like Dr. Frankenstein waiting in the laboratory for his hulking creature to come alive and say something.

After the third orbit, Bronco finally broke his silence. "You know, Earl, I just don't know whether to scratch my watch or wind my butt about this marriage deal."

"Yeah?"

"I mean, I appreciate the fact Sheryl's a wonderful person," he said, as if he were reciting the guiding principle of the Chicken Ranch Charm School. "And, to tell the truth, I know more about her than my last two wives put together. But after thinking about it, maybe I'm making a mistake."

"Oh? So what happened to finally finding your soul mate?"

He scowled at me and refocused his attention to our pro-jec-tile.

"Bronco, all grooms get cold feet at some point. Brides, too, for that matter."

"Yeah, well, my feet are as cold as the ice on Interstate 20." He shifted uncomfortably in his seat. "The thing is, I need another wife like I need an extra hole in my head."

I considered asking why he hadn't performed self-psychoanalysis before asking Sheryl to marry him, but after my assy soul-mate comment, I kept quiet. Besides, who was I to offer advice? I hadn't maintained a meaningful relationship with a woman, it felt like, since Charles Dickens was in junior high.

Besides, who was I to offer advice?
I hadn't maintained a meaningful relationship
with a woman, it felt like, since Charles Dickens
was in junior high.

"I dunno," Bronco continued, shaking his head. "I just figured we'd cruise around the Caribbean, get married by the ship's captain, and, well . . . *enjoy* the honeymoon." He raised both eyebrows slyly, the universal male sign for you-know-exactly-what-I'm-talking-about.

"Did you guys ever talk about your life together after the honeymoon?"

"Sure, we talked. I mean, she talked and I listened. You know how women are." He looked at me and seemed to reconsider. "Well, maybe you don't know how women are."

"Just because I don't have a two-page list of ex-wives doesn't mean I don't know women," I said confidently, yet wondering if Bronco might be correct. My thoughts wandered to Marilyn, a personal trainer at the YMCA, who turned spazzy on me after we'd dated for a year - *casually* dated, so I thought. Evidently, she expected a ring for Christmas; instead, I gave her a new pair of Nike running shoes. She glared at me, then tossed the box on the carpet and growled, "So, is this your way of saying, 'Thanks for playing *Let's Make a Deal?*'"

My buddy and I completed another circumnavigation of Terminal E without sliding into anything. He said, "Trouble is, I already paid, like, four-thousand bucks for this cruise."

"Geez Louise, Bronco. Can you get your money back?"

He shook his head. "Non-refundable."

"Bummer."

"Yeah, big time. Plus, Sheryl's all excited and spun up about cruisin' on a boat with all those fancy people."

Before I could respond, Bronco's phone vibrated and played Elvis' "Hunka-Hunka Burnin' Love." "Hey, babe," he answered. "OK, stay put. We'll be there in, like, two minutes."

I said, "Guess we better pick up the future Mrs. Hunka-Hunka."

"Wait," he countered. "I've been thinking."

"What about?"

"I got an idea. I'm gonna tell Sheryl that Greyhound called, and with all the snow and ice, they need extra drivers to report in."

"Are you joking?"

With an expression that said he wasn't, Bronco rhythmically drummed the steering wheel with his sausage-sized fingers, as if he were thinking up the next chapter of his breakout novel. "So, when Greyhound called, I raised hell and told 'em I couldn't come in 'cause I was gettin' married." His lips twisted to the side again, just like at Waffle House. "But, they gave me no choice. Drive or lose my job." He raised his eyebrows expectantly.

With three ex-wives under his belt, Bronco had plenty of experience convincing a woman why the smudges on his shirt looked more like brake fluid than lipstick. But even for him, this Greyhound story was a stretch. I answered, "That's like using a kayak to fish for shark. Doesn't work."

"Oh, and here's the sweetener," he said. "You take my place on the cruise. The cabin's a suite, so both of you have separate places to sleep. While you're cruising around the Caribbean with Sheryl, I'll go back and talk Daisy into sticking around for a few days. Give us time to get to know each other a little better. Maybe a *lot* better."

"So *that's* what's on your mind?" I shook my head, displaying the most extreme look in my disgusted-look repertoire. "Come on, Bronco, you don't even know if this Daisy chick has a boyfriend. For all you know, she could prefer women to men."

He ignored my logic. "Sheryl gets to hang out on a big ship with all the rich people, and has someone there to protect her if anything goes wrong." He lowered his voice and added a gravelly edge. "But no monkey business, understand?"

"Bronco, you're completely nuts." I tapped my watch. "Let's get going. Your bride is waiting."

Standing outside Terminal E in the passenger loading area, I hoisted Sheryl's zebra-print suitcase into the backseat of the truck, avoiding eye contact with the two hunks of burning love. They kissed and mugged like two wrestlers locked in a clench, before finally breaking their clasps and climbing into the front seat, me in back.

Her hair tied in a topknot, Sheryl reminded me of a 35-year-old Pebbles Flintstone, minus the saber-tooth-tiger sarong. My buddy's always had a knack for snagging attractive women, and with Sheryl, he'd definitely maintained his streak.

After cranking the engine, Bronco didn't immediately pull out into traffic. Instead, while the truck idled, he spent five minutes or so gushing about Sheryl - how wonderful she looked, how just seeing her made him remember why he'd fallen so head-over-heels in love with her. He used the word "appreciate" no fewer than five times, fully embracing Daisy's Chicken Ranch philosophy, but perhaps forgetting her admonition that appreciating and flattering had two different meanings.

After his sugary preamble, he eased into his once-upon-a-time tale about Greyhound calling him back to work. As he jabbered, the bizarre scene reminded me of one of those 1930's screwball comedies the *Movie Channel* runs late at night, starring Cary Grant or Fred Astaire. Except it's hard to imagine Cary or Fred having the *cajones* to offer what Bronco dished out.

At first, Sheryl patiently listened to my friend's story, nodding her head and appearing to buy what Bronco was selling. But as the fairy tale grew more incredible, her eyes gradually narrowed, as if she smelled a skunk hiding in a brush pile. And then, like a farmer smoking out the varmint, she lit a match and asked, "Why don't we just skip the cruise and have a Justice of the Peace marry us?" Sheryl paused, letting the words sink into her fiancé's fleshy noggin. "I'll ride on the bus to keep you company. That's honeymoon enough for me."

Bronco stalled for a few seconds, long enough to conjure some lame excuse about Greyhound's rules, about as believable as Hey Diddle Diddle's explanation of the solar system. Edging the truck onto the road, he referred to the company as "heartless" and trolled the idea of Sheryl proceeding with the cruise, "since it's already paid for," but with me tagging along. I'd be there to keep her company and protect her, he told her, and because it's a suite, I'd sleep in the other room.

Sheryl stared at Bronco, her face frozen and expressionless, like a figure in a wax museum.

Bronco continued, "When you and Earl get back, I'll pick you up at the airport. Then, maybe in a couple of weeks, you can fly back down here."

The wax figure came alive, suddenly lifting her eyebrows to maximum height. "And just exactly what makes you think I'd spend several days in the same suite with a complete stranger?" Sounding like a skeptical prosecutor sniffing out a criminal's alibi, she tacked on, "To say nothing of it being a complete *male* stranger."

"Hey, Earl's a nice guy. We've been fishing buddies a long time," said Bronco, conveniently forgetting we were also brothers-in-law once.

Sitting quietly in the backseat during this uncomfortable exchange, I tried to sink into the upholstery and become invisible. Evidently sensing my discomfort, the newbie prosecutor slowly turned to me, the potential co-conspirator, and asked, "So, Earl, did you have anything to do with this?"

"Umm, no, not really," I stammered, looking and feeling guilty for having a friend who would pull such a stunt.

Evidently, my squishy answer negatively tipped the judicial scales against Bronco. Sheryl glared at my buddy, her demeanor morphing from blushing-bride-to-be into bridezilla. "OK, I get it, Claudius Ptolemy," she said, nail-gunning her words. "I *completely* understand what you're doing. And if that's what you want, so be it. Just take me to the charter terminal." She opened her purse, poked around until she found a wrinkled-up tissue, and then brusquely clicked the purse shut. "Earl, come along if you like. At least I'll have someone to keep me company."

An awkward twenty seconds of silence followed, as everybody in the truck waited for someone else to say something. A wrecker truck towed a crumpled Lexus past our truck, throwing slushy ice on our windshield.

Finally, I placed my hand on my buddy's shoulder. "Can we at least stop at Target? I'd like to buy a toothbrush, some underwear, and a swimsuit."

Sharing an armrest with a jilted bride on the two-hour charter flight to Miami made the trip seem more like two-weeks of bamboo-under-the-fingernails torture. We guzzled complimentary cocktails, courtesy of the cruise line, while Sheryl repeated sniffling mantras of "I can't believe I'm so stupid" and "I'm just happy I didn't marry that idiot." For the first seven or eight repetitions, I attempted to console her with "I'm so sorry," or "Yeah, you must feel really awful," but after that, I concentrated on the Sudoku puzzles and Mensa quiz in the back of the in-flight magazine.

Miami's Utopian weather - high 70's, sunshine with a few scattered clouds - contrasted sharply with Texas' current dark-side-of-the-moon temperatures. I imagined Bronco barreling down an icy Interstate 20 in his pro-jec-tile, with a terrified Daisy at his side, biting her fingernails and second-guessing her decision to accept a seat on an amusement-ride-gone-berserk. If my fantasy were true, Daisy wouldn't be the only one second-guessing a decision. During the first 24 hours of the cruise, I concluded that accepting Bronco's offer ranked as one of the top-five worst decisions I'd ever made, right after having a skull and crossbones tattooed on my shoulder. Sheryl spent the day boohooing in our room, gradually shifting from anger to acceptance on the scorned-woman continuum. During her crying jag, I made myself scarce, treadmilling in the fitness center and foraging lunch at the all-you-can-eat seafood buffet.

After overdosing on shrimp scampi and oysters on the half shell, I made buddies with a highly talented bartender on the Promenade deck and drank my weight in *daiquiris* and exotic *coladas*. By early afternoon, rough seas developed, causing the ship to pitch and roll as if Bronco were steering; fortunately, I scavenged two Dramamines from a chubby real estate lady from Nashville sitting next to me at the bar.

Just before sunset, with the Dramamine and daiquiris working their pharmaceutical alchemy, I declared war on the ship's casino. I found a worthy opponent in a joke-telling blackjack dealer, originally from England, who hoped to become a stand-up comedian in Atlantic City. Unfortunately, the Limey smelled as if he hadn't showered since the Titanic set sail from Southampton. Six hours later, he and I declared a cease-fire, agreeing to resume hostilities the following day - hopefully, after he'd showered and mega-dosed with Right Guard.

Around midnight, the seas calmed and I crashed on one of the plastic lounges by the adult pool on the Lido deck - not exactly a Sealy Posturepedic, but a place to horizontalize myself, nonetheless. And after consuming so many boat drinks I needed a Price-Waterhouse accountant to tabulate the final results, horizontalize felt like the perfect word choice.

The next morning, I traded my standard bacon-and-eggs breakfast for double shots of Alka-Seltzer and fresh air, then found my way to the door of my "shared" suite. I took a deep breath and tapped on the door.

Sheryl, wearing a pink jogging suit and tennis visor, cracked open the door six inches, but left the security chain stretched across the opening. Recognizing her roommate-in-theory standing in the hall, she adjusted the visor downward, probably an attempt to hide her puffy eyes.

I cleared my throat. "Uh, Sheryl, are you OK?"

"I guess so, considering this was supposed to be my honeymoon," she said in monotone, forcing herself to half-smile. "You know, I've decided to make the most of the cruise, get my mind off things. I'm thinking of exploring the ship and maybe catching a little sun out by the pool. Care to join me?"

"Sure, but I'd like to clean up a bit," I answered, worried about smelling as rank as the blackjack dealer. "You mind if I shower?"

"Of course not." She unchained the door. "Come on in."

Bronco booked one of the nicest staterooms on the *Royal Commander*, no small matter considering the size of a bus driver's paycheck. But with a shower the scale of an upright casket and only one queen-sized bed in the room, calling it a "suite" was like calling a two-seat Piper Cub a Boeing 747. Roomy, it wasn't. Earlier, after checking in and scoping out the suite, I noticed how uncomfortable Sheryl seemed, and so I immediately offered to sleep outside on the ship's deck. She quickly accepted my offer; with true appreciation, it appeared.

After I showered and changed into swimming trunks, Sheryl and I moseyed around the ship, exploring all eight decks of the massive, gleaming-white behemoth. It's beyond the comprehension of a mere mortal, let alone some nautical Einstein, to understand how 125,000 tons of steel, fiberglass, and sunscreen can stay afloat, not tip over and sink.

"First cruise?" I asked, as we passed the ship's Oriental spa.

"No, my second. Went on a singles' cruise about a year ago."

"How'd it turn out?"

She shook her head. "It was as if a troop of 30-year-old Boy Scouts were all trying to earn enough merit badges in sex to make Eagle Scout."

"Yeah?"

"I felt like a first-year Brownie by comparison. My town has exactly one blinking light, not even a full red light, so you can imagine how freaked out I felt.

Then, after that disaster, little ol' brilliant me turned to internet dating sites."

"I never tried the internet. Seemed so, well, fake."

"You'd think I would have known better. Men will write anything - absolutely anything - trying to convince you they're these sensitive creatures who care about your feelings and want to get to know the real you. But bottom line, most of them just want to make Eagle Scout."

The direction of our conversation made me feel uncomfortable, as over the years I'd earned a few merit badges of my own, so I steered our talk in a different direction - to the architecture and décor of the ship. Eventually, our exploring took us to the Lido deck, where we selected a couple of reclining lounge chairs only a few yards from where I'd crashed the previous evening. Before we could position our towels, a white-jacketed pool attendant - tanned to the color of parchment and beach-volleyball buff - supplied us with complimentary fruit skewers, cups of lemonade, and spray misters. Not just regular spray misters, but *Evian* misters.

My traveling partner slipped off her jogging suit to reveal swimming attire that definitely would have raised eyebrows in a one-blinking-light town. Undoubtedly chosen for the effect it would have on a honeymoon cruise, the cream-colored bikini was far more flattering than my white T-shirt and eight-dollar swimming trunks from Target.

Settling into her lounge chair, Sheryl appeared deep in thought while smearing Coppertone on her neck and shoulders.

Whether it was because of facing the direct sun or being caught off-guard by Sheryl's physique, I broke a major sweat, the first time I'd heavily perspired since volunteering for the dunking booth at the school's Halloween carnival.

Now smearing the cream on her arms, Sheryl looked at me and scrunched her face sympathetically. "Earl, you were such a good sport yesterday. I hope your evening wasn't a complete waste of time."

"No, it wasn't," I fibbed, mentally confirming that my casino luck wasn't any better on the ocean than it was on dry land.

"Bronco said you were a nice guy. At least he didn't lie about that."

I figured it was best to avoid any topic involving my buddy, so instead, I blabbered about the cold weather settling in on the Midwest and Texas, further validating the manly tradition of beginning every conversation with the topic of weather or ball scores.

Sheryl politely responded to my weather babble, but didn't stay superficial for long. Her voice lowered to a mellower pitch, the kind a goateed psychiatrist might use. "So, Earl, when you were a young boy, how did you think your life would turn out?"

Something in my brain immediately screamed, "Danger, Danger - Emotional Discussion with a Woman Just Ahead - Proceed with Extreme Caution." My mind darted to the last similar conversation I had with a woman - Christina, a dentist I dated last year. She and I had attended a history lecture at the local college, where the subject was "The Best and Worst Presidents in U.S. History." Afterwards at her condo, snuggling on the sofa and sharing cherry cheesecake, she asked whom I thought were the best and worst Presidents. I said the best ever was Washington, hands down, but I couldn't decide between Herbert Hoover and Jimmy Carter as the worst. It turned out, Christina's father and mother dropped out of college to work for the Peanut President's reelection campaign. In fact, Christina bragged, she was conceived in the back of a campaign bus during a whistle-stop trip through Florida, and would have been named James had she been a boy. I made the mistake of saying that her mother wasn't the only American who was taken advantage of during the Carter years, and from there, our high-minded philosophical conversation quickly deteriorated. In the space of fifteen minutes, I moved from snuggling and sharing cheesecake to being hustled out of her condo without as much as a goodnight kiss.

But since Sheryl's open-ended question had nothing to do with politics, I decided to take the plunge and answer the psychiatrist-esque question. "Well, when I was a little boy, I figured I'd become an astronaut and the second baseman for the Texas Rangers. You know, play baseball in the summer, and fly spaceships in the off-season. Then, I signed up for Little League, and after three years, it became obvious I couldn't hit a curve ball. Nor a fastball, or change-up, for that matter. And then, to really burst my bubble, someone told me our space shuttles had a nasty habit of exploding from time to time."

She nodded and squirted a few sprays of Evian to cool her cotton towel, which she carefully repositioned around her neck. "What did you want to be after you learned space shuttles blew up?"

"Then I wanted to become a barber. My fourth-grade year, this starving Great Pyrenees showed up in our backyard. Shaggy haired, matted with burrs, stickers, and all sorts of disgusting things. No one claimed the dog, so we adopted her and named her Lilly. A couple of weeks later, I sneaked out my mom's expensive scissors and trimmed Lilly's hair. My mother wasn't too pleased when she found out, but Lilly greatly appreciated the haircut, judging by the way she nearly wagged her tail off."

"So, what changed your mind about becoming a barber?"

"My older brother said barbers stood on their feet all day long and didn't make enough money. Took the wind right-out of my sails. I always loved reading, so after that, I figured teaching would make a good career." I nibbled a slice of watermelon from my fruit skewer. "Now I stand on my feet all day, look at shaggy-haired kids who need a haircut, and realize I still don't make enough money."

For the first time since we left Dallas, Sheryl laughed. The smile on her face, relaxed and gentle, made me smile, also.

"How about you?" I asked, plucking the last piece of cantaloupe off the stick. "What'd you want to be when you grew up?"

"Oh, that's easy. I always wanted to be a cat doctor. We had lots and lots of kitties around the house, strays and purebreds alike. We may as well have been the neighborhood animal shelter. But the thing is, when one of the cats died or ran away, it was just too painful. I'd cry for days."

"I know exactly what you mean. I cried a hell of a lot more when my yellow lab died than I did when most of my relatives passed away . . . maybe that tells you all you need to know about my family. Amanda, my sister, says our idea of a successful family get-together is getting through the whole day without breaking out the dueling pistols."

She acknowledged my joke with another smile and signaled to the pool attendant for a refill of her drink. "I thought about being a physician, because even though your patients die from time to time, they aren't as innocent or defenseless as animals. Unfortunately, organic chemistry, as well as my tendency to party a wee-bit too much, got in the way of med school. So, I settled for becoming a nurse." The attendant cruised by, delivering fresh lemonade for Sheryl and an extra fruit skewer for me. She continued, "That's the story of my life . . . always settling. Never taking the big risk and going for broke. Maybe it's why I chose someone like Bronco."

Her statement about taking risk reminded me of my fear of applying for a teaching position at the junior college. I shifted uncomfortably in my seat, anxious to avoid the subject of risk taking. "So, what was the attraction to Bronco all about?" It was a question I'd been dying to ask, given what I'd come to observe about Sheryl.

"Funny you ask. Several of my Iowa friends who met him face-to-face asked me the same question, so I'll tell you what I told them. Some men are attractive because of their physical appearance, which obviously isn't the case with Bronco." She paused, then sipped her lemonade. "But with him, he always seemed so emotionally transparent. He's not ashamed that he plays American Girl Dolls with his daughter or that he always cries on Christmas Eve. Bronco's always complimentary to me and appreciative of me. He was considerate and kind - he loves cats almost as much as me. You just naturally want to be with him. So, in that way, he's *extremely* appealing and sexy."

"Bronco likes cats?" That information was as hard to accept as hearing Bill Clinton had vowed celibacy so he could enter the priesthood.

"He's completely unlike the men in my hometown - emotionally constipated corn farmers, who think women should be content raising hogs and staying pregnant."

"Come on, they can't all be that way."

"You'd be surprised. The funny thing is, I convinced myself that despite his previous stumbles with women, I could be the one Bronco would grow old with." She shook her head and laughed gently, a sarcastic kind of chuckle. "Is that naïve or what? Apparently, your friend was like those guys on the singles' cruise, only interested in earning another merit badge." She sighed. "You know, I really have better judgment than it appears."

It was hard to argue with the merit badge comment, knowing my friend's history with women and his current bloodhounding of Daisy. "You lived in Iowa all your life?"

"Yep, corn fed through and through. My parents divorced when I was thirteen, and Dad left for Wyoming to work in the oilfield. Mom was killed by a drunk driver three years later, which wasn't a good time for a girl to lose her mother." She took a deep breath, as if taking in the memory of her mother, then released it slowly. "I guess no time is good, but it was especially hard for me. Dad was busy with his new wife and baby, so my junior year, I moved in with my aunt and finished high school in another county. But there, I was always an outsider, the one who was never invited to sit at the lunchroom table with the cool kids.

After that, I think I was looking for Prince Charming to ride up on his white horse, sweep me off my feet, and take me to his castle."

"Did he ever show up?"

"Well, right after high school, I married a guy, Ronny, who I thought was Prince Charming. Good looking, state champion wrestler, and made decent money as a diesel mechanic." Sheryl's body tensed slightly, as if someone had secretly placed small pebbles under her towel. "But the fairy tale didn't mention he left his dirty underwear on the floor, as well as socks, pants, and every other item of clothing he owned. It also didn't mention Ronny's bad habit of forgetting to show up for work once or twice a week."

"Ouch. How long did it take you to figure out it wasn't going to work?"

"Six years," she said, repositioning herself in the lounge chair, still trying to avoid the pebbles. "My brain kept telling me that he was a good man, with good qualities, and I could help him become so much more than he was. Like the stray cats, I could somehow save him. Anyway, I went to college, became a nurse, but Ronny just never matured beyond the emotional level of a nineteen-year-old." She shook her head. "Guess you'd call me a slow learner."

"Or a hopeless romantic," I said, recognizing a bit of myself in Sheryl - except my weakness was believing I could magically transform chronically underachieving students into potential Rhodes scholars. "You and Ronny have any kids?"

I winked and said, "I know it's hard to believe that with my stunning good looks, I'm still single, but I am."

"No, although I thought I was pregnant once. Thank God, it turned out to be a false alarm. But that little episode convinced me I needed to move out before it happened for real." She glanced at her lemonade, signaled to the pony-tailed attendant, who promptly glided over to our chairs. Sheryl leaned toward the man, mentioned she wanted to switch to rum punch, and then turned back to me, almost in one motion. "What about you, Earl? Have you ever found Princess Charming?"

I winked and said, "I know it's hard to believe that with my stunning good looks, I'm still single, but I am."

"Oh, come on now, you're a nice-looking man." Sheryl now looked comfortable in her lounge chair, finally ridding herself of the imaginary annoyance under her towel.

"I don't know about that. Ever since I broke the head off my sister's new doll at her tenth birthday party and she called me 'an ugly monkey face,' I've been a little insecure about my appearance. But thanks for saying so."

She twisted her mouth slightly, not unlike Bronco when he reeled in the big fish. "Earl, you didn't answer my question about finding Princess Charming."

"OK, OK," I said, wincing into a half-smile. "Over the years, there were a couple of possibilities for a permanent relationship, I suppose, but I always found some reason to avoid marriage. Looking back, I was probably too picky. I have several women friends now, mostly teachers at school. But the truth is, I'm not looking to mess up a good friendship by falling in love with one of them."

"That's such a typical male comment," she said, rolling her eyes in a playful way. "So, that makes you Mr. Confirmed Bachelor, right?"

"No, not at all. I'd love to find someone. But being Bronco's best man once or twice makes me tread very lightly on the whole marriage thing."

"Yeah, I can see how it would." The attendant delivered the rum punch, and Sheryl nodded her thanks. Biting her lip slightly, she steeled her eyes. "I just don't understand why Bronco suddenly got cold feet. There has to be more to the story." She stirred her drink with the straw, staring at the punch as if it were an oracle. "Earl, was he seeing someone else? Not that it matters, frankly."

I mentally parsed how to answer Sheryl's interrogation. Not wanting to betray my buddy, even though he was a total weasel, I also didn't want to lie to Sheryl. Technically, Bronco wasn't seeing anyone else, unless a flirty, 45-minute visit to Waffle House qualified. On the other hand, he certainly *wanted* to see someone else. And, for all I knew, he'd already convinced the woman with the Chicken-Ranch charm to stick with her job at Waffle House rather than move to Houston or San Antonio. My prolonged silence, brought on by my lifelong habit of analyzing everything to death, apparently answered Sheryl's question.

"Earl, don't bother. You don't need to say anything." She sighed with an air of resignation - less from being disappointed with Bronco's decision to flake out, it seemed, and more in having to start her search process one more time.

Switching from rum punch to frozen margaritas, Sheryl somersaulted through her emotions - hurt, disappointment, and relief - like a Slinky toy tumbling down a flight of stairs. I remembered enough from *Men Are from Mars* to know I just needed to listen and not try to fix things for her. Remaining silent was as difficult as sitting on the couch with my sister, listening to her sob and tell me she was divorcing the man who had become my best friend, and who would become a father in four months.

As for my choice of beverage, I stuck with Diet Coke. My brain would have thanked me, as it couldn't have taken another pummeling from the gauntlet it ran the evening before.

Even with half a bottle of sunscreen, my Iowa friend's fair complexion couldn't handle more than an hour or so of tropical sun, so we moved to the shady side of the deck. Her paprika-like freckles reminded me of a sophomore student, one of the perpetual underachieving little darlings I tried to challenge to seek more in her life. Feeling more relaxed with each other, Sheryl and I comfortably nested in wooden Adirondack chairs and began a three-hour, rapid-fire conversation on topics ranging from how silly political correctness had become, the differences between spirituality and religion, our mutual aversion to taking risks, and the writing styles of Hemingway versus Faulkner. For some reason, Sheryl was the first woman I'd ever had the nerve to reveal that my idea of a perfect afternoon was relaxing at the library and reading poetry behind the stacks - not exactly the most macho trait a man my age could have, but something I enjoyed, nonetheless. Maybe it was because I figured I'd never see her again after the cruise, or maybe I felt so at ease, I could be myself.

Sheryl and I also discussed our mutual tendencies to *analyze* rather than *feel* a relationship. Like me, she'd always listened to her intellect rather than her heart - which is why her brain told her to leave the diesel mechanic before a *bambino* came along. With Bronco, Sheryl had convinced herself that even though his matrimonial resume was paragraphs long and filled with questionable gaps, she would rely on her feelings of attraction to tell her what to do. Now, sitting husband-less in the middle of the ocean with a consolation prize she'd met less than 48-hours earlier, she regretted not paying more attention to her brain. "I'm not sure I was listening to my heart as much as just being lonely," she said. "You know, needing to have someone in my life."

I tried to lighten the mood. "Well, being single isn't all bad. In a restaurant, you can always find a seat at the bar if all the tables are taken."

"I understand lonely. I've watched enough late-night reruns of *South Park* to understand the concept."

She sighed. "Bottom line, I guess I threw away my judgment when it came to Bronco."

I tried to lighten the mood. "Well, being single isn't all bad. In a restaurant, you can always find a seat at the bar if all the tables are taken."

Sheryl leaned her head back and used a towel to dab the perspiration from the front of her neck down to the top line of her bikini, in a non-sexual, but highly sensual way. "Yeah, and a woman never has to worry about someone leaving the toilet lid up at night."

"That's such a typical female comment," I said, rolling my eyes in a copycat way.

Sheryl laughed. "You're funny, you know?" She looked down at her frozen margarita and swirled figure eights with her straw. "I'm glad you're here. I needed a friend."

At first, I thought Sheryl found my presence to be a tourniquet to stop her emotional bleeding, a way to divert her attention from the pain of making a bad decision about Bronco. That was all right with me, because offering a bit of consolation to an attractive woman wearing a fabulous bikini wasn't much of a price to pay for a freebie vacation. But the unvarnished sincerity of Sheryl's questions and her answers to mine signaled an interest in me as a friend, not merely as an emotional tourniquet.

At sunset, couples lined the railing, holding hands, embracing, and absorbing the magic of the flame-colored horizon, creating a scene which could have been included in a reality series for the *Hormones-Are-Raging Channel*. It occurred to me that the lovey-dovey duos could remind Sheryl that she wasn't on her honeymoon, so I made a battlefield decision and suggested the two of us go inside, change out of our bathing suits, and order a nice dinner.

"It's funny, but I bought a special dress for our first evening on the cruise," she said, as if she now regretted spending the money. "May as well get some use out of it."

Sheryl and I took turns using the "suite" to shower, change clothes, and afterwards, find our way to the ship's paneled Library Room. Her special dress turned out to be silky, fire-engine red, and low cut - emphasizing, as Bronco would

have said crudely, but accurately, her ample sunny-side-ups. Thinking of my friend and me, I remembered my sister saying we were caviar and salted corn-nuts mixed together. Bronco and Sheryl together reminded me of a can of Red Bull topped off with *Dom Perignon* Champagne.

At our table, with candlelight racing off the mirrors and the fine crystal, we faced the difficult decision of choosing between the steamed lobster and the filet mignon. Even though Sheryl loved seafood, and I normally preferred beef, I teased her to "shake things up" and "risk trying something different." Judging from the look in her eyes, she took my off-handed dare as symbolic of something much more significant. Accepting the challenge, she selected the beef, and to further drive home the point, ordered it rare. I chose the lobster, accepting her counter-dare, and decided my brain had rested enough to handle a glass or two of *Pinot Grigio*.

After the tuxedoed wine steward poured our glasses, Sheryl suggested we make a couple of toasts. Raising her glass next to mine, she said, "To Bronco, wherever he is. I wish him well."

My face flushed, my thoughts flashing to Bronco and Daisy. Were they cozied up at her apartment, soaking up each other's charms like hot syrup on a waffle? Feeling guilty for enabling my friend's bad behavior, but not so guilty I wanted to hurt Sheryl's feelings, I said, "Bronco's probably driving a bus somewhere in Arkansas, regretting his decision not to marry a wonderful woman like you."

Responding in an I-know-you're-covering-for-your-friend tone of voice, Sheryl said, "I doubt it, Earl, but that's all right." She lowered her glass, a philosophical look gracing her face. "You know, the one thing you and Bronco have in common is that you both appreciate your friendship."

"Funny you should mention appreciation," I said, remembering the admiring look on Daisy's face as she talked about Aunt Rose. "Remind me someday to tell you about something called the Chicken Ranch Charm School."

"You know the cliché about Texans," I said.
"Everything's always bigger there. This really isn't lobster,
but a Texas-sized crawfish."

Sheryl looked puzzled. "Why not now?"

"Definitely a story for another time."

She smiled. "OK, but I won't let you forget." She raised her glass again. "The second and more important toast . . . is to the bus driver's best friend."

We clinked our glasses solidly, creating a rich, ringing sound, which, for an instant, made me wonder if we'd cracked the heavy lead crystal.

"Now it's my turn to raise a toast," I said, clearing my throat dramatically, as if I were accepting an award at a black-tie dinner. "To taking risks. And ordering Iowa-raised beef and Texas-sized crawfish."

Sheryl arched an eyebrow in mock surprise. "What are you talking about? Texas-sized crawfish?"

"You know the cliché about Texans," I said. "Everything's always bigger there. This really isn't lobster, but a Texas-sized crawfish."

Sheryl shook her head and smiled. "Oh my, I thought Iowa pig farmers had a monopoly on bad, corny jokes, but evidently not." She gently placed her hand on top of mine and patted it gently. "Thanks for making me feel better this afternoon."

"I enjoyed the day, too." With the candlelight, the wine, and a charming dinner guest, I wanted to squeeze her hand in return, suggesting the possibility of some sort of future for us, but dared not. "Certainly a day I'll never forget."

"Me, either," Sheryl said. "You know, I feel so bad for you having to spend another night in one of those awful deck lounges. Why don't you stay in our suite?" She moved her fingers from the top of my hand toward my shirt cuff. There, slowly and deliberately, she unfastened the button. ✪

Life&Leisure

A Sign from Above?

Ask Mr. Mighty Brain

Editor's Note: After a three-month sabbatical to an undisclosed Central American country, where he cons on an unsuccessful coup d'état, Mr. Mighty Brain ret humbled, to The San Antonio Reporter-Gazette with wildly popular advice column.

Dear Mr. Mighty Brain,
My older brother, Fordyce, is an absolute grandmaster of colorful expressions and clever sayings. Unfortunately, I have zero talent in that regard and must admit to a bit of jealousy.

For example, last Sunday when I telephoned Fordyce to find out what he'd been doing lately, he said, "Working like a syrup-mill mule. But still so broke, I can't even pay attention." I asked if he was still going out with the cute manicurist from Longview. "Nope, not anymore." he said. "She

and made an immediate about-face. He began dieting, working out at the gym, and reading GQ and Esquire every month. The only downside was that he wanted Earlene to dye her hair auburn. On the other hand, Mr. Mighty Brain feels compelled to note that the blue-collared comedian, Larry the Cable Guy, has made a bazillion dollars with his big-bellied, plaid-shirt look. Of course, Larry the Cable Guy is funny. OK, mildly funny. Mr. Mighty Brain understands all that money has made Larry the Cable guy into a very handsome and charming man, in spite of his dysfunctional wardrobe.

Dictionary / Thesaurus

Aa

movies. Leonard, who I really my kid, doesn't n Air Jordan sneakers or anyway. Someday, w an adult, he'll be prou thanks to this big-as

Dear Mr. Mighty Bra
I could qualify as th an older guy who's of life's unpaved r dance hall or a b I haven't helped or another. I've times, best I ca at by a jealous his aim wasn' The other m my job at th an old tom porch. He

TEN

Ask Mister Mighty Brain -
A Sign from Above?

Editor's Note: After a three-month sabbatical to an undisclosed Central American country, where he consulted on an unsuccessful *coup d'état*, Mr. Mighty Brain returns, humbled, to The San Antonio Reporter-Gazette with his wildly popular advice column.

➤➤

Dear Mr. Mighty Brain,

 I could qualify as the "poster child" for an older guy who's traveled down a few of life's unpaved roads. There isn't a dance hall or a beer joint in San Angelo I haven't helped close down at one time or another. I've been married five times, best I can remember, and even shot at by a jealous husband. Thankfully, the man aimed through the wrong lens of his bifocals and missed.

 The other morning, as I was leaving for my job at the car wash, I encountered an old tom cat, asleep on my back porch. He had patches of fur missing here and there, with the rest of his mottled-gray coat infested with fleas. There were cuts and scrapes on the poor cat's leg, some of which had yet to heal. Blind in one eye, he made for a pretty sorry-looking creature.

 On the plus side, the tom cat seemed perfectly contented and purred when I reached down to check if he had a collar. He didn't, of course, but with his good eye, the old cat seemed to size me up - as friend or foe. Evidently, he classified me as a friend and didn't run away. I fed him part of a left-over Whataburger sausage burrito, which he promptly gobbled down. But when I returned home that evening, the tom cat was gone, probably moved on to someone else's back porch.

 Mr. Mighty Brain, my question is this: did I see myself in this old tom cat, and if so, what does it mean? Or, am I reading way too much into this casual encounter?

Signed,
No Angelo Angel

Dear Unangelic Angelo-type,

 Mr. Mighty Brain suspects that if you'd given the tom cat a bowl of milk rather than a half-eaten burrito, he'd still be on your back porch.

 Perhaps the Great-Sign-Giver-in-the-Sky has chosen to reveal to you, in this seemingly casual encounter, something about your prior relationships with females. Perhaps they, too, gave you "burritos," but for some reason, you were unsatisfied with the very best they had to offer. No, no, ultra-picky you preferred a bowl of warm milk, probably 2% or skim, non-generic, and organic. Or maybe a cold beer.

 Anyway, the point is this: that tom cat could be the equivalent of a burning bush in the desert or a road to Damascus experience. This could mean that even though you've wasted virtually all of your nine lives, there's still time to change.

 Or, it could mean you have mice under your porch.

Dear Mr. Mighty Brain,

I read where the Texas legislature passed a bill on third reading. My little brother passed a quarter once, but never a bill. We just studied digestion in eighth-grade science class, but I don't remember the part about passing bills. Sounds disgusting to me. Did I miss out on something?

Signed,
Grossed-Out in Galveston

Dear Gross,

Comparing the state legislature to one's intestinal tract is a wonderfully apt analogy. Once you become an adult and start paying taxes, you'll understand why. In the mean time, good luck with gym class.

Dear Mr. Mighty Brain,

My older brother, Fordyce, is an absolute grandmaster of colorful expressions and clever sayings. Unfortunately, I have zero talent in that regard and must admit to a bit of jealousy.

For example, last Sunday when I telephoned Fordyce to find out what he'd been doing lately, he said, "Working like a syrup-mill mule. But still so broke, I can't even pay attention."

I asked if he was still going out with the cute manicurist from Longview. "Nope, not anymore," he said. "She had more curves than a World Series' pitcher, but I'll tell you, she was as dumb as a blue Crayola. Truth be told, that cowgirl couldn't pour pee out of a boot if the instructions were printed on the heel."

Fordyce went on to tell me about a disastrous blind date he had with a dental hygienist in Kilgore. "I'll swear, the woman's hair looked as if it had been rescued from an animal shelter. When we danced, I was just thankful my rabies vaccination was up to date."

All the single women in our area find Fordyce attractive, and I'm convinced it's because of his mastery of these down-home idioms. Even though we're brothers, my DNA code obviously didn't include a silver tongue like his.

Mr. Mighty Brain, is there some school I could attend, or an internet site I can visit, where I could learn some of these witty sayings? I think it would help me with my love life, which isn't so hot right now.

Signed,
Tongue-Tied in Tyler

Dear T...T...T...T...Tongue-Tied,

So, your love life is colder than an Eskimo witch's heart? Mr. Mighty Brain would be happy to help - happier than Al Gore and Rush Limbaugh at an all-you-can-eat dinner buffet.

He (Mr. Mighty Brain, not Messrs. Gore or Limbaugh) suggests the following:

(A) Jot down some of your brother's wittiest bubba-isms and categorize them by topic - beautiful women, ugly women, incompetent co-workers, government policies, incredibly stupid government policies. No, wait, the last two are redundant.

(B) Tape the list to your forearm, much like an NFL quarterback does when his coach gives him a list of special plays (not to be confused with the index of bimbos' phone numbers he tapes to his other forearm). You'll want to keep your list tucked underneath your shirtsleeve, obviously.

(C) Practice politely coughing into your sleeve, allowing enough time to steal a quick glance at an appropriate expression. Then, casually toss-off the phrase into the conversation as if you'd just thought of it. Wallah! You'll appear just as bubba-fied as your brother. Granted, people may be inclined to offer you a cough drop, but that's a minor price to pay for your newly discovered popularity.

(D) Be sure to change the list every two weeks or so, lest you be accused of reusing the same tired material over and over, like Jay Leno.

Even though following this advice may seem stranger than a duck in Death Valley, Mr. Mighty Brain guarantees you'll have more success than a traveling salesman at a farmer's daughter convention.

Dear Mr. Mighty Brain,

My husband is nearing 55 years and has started wearing his shirts unbuttoned, showing off a t-shirt and a blue-collar worker belly. Since we live in the Abilene area, where dozens of retired Air Force men walk around in those "onesie" suits, I fear my husband may be in the early stages of wardrobe dysfunction. Can you offer any advice about how to remedy this downward spiral in attire?

Signed,
Concerned in Clyde

Dear Concerned,

Mr. Mighty Brain's second cousin, Delmont Mighty Brain, was similarly wardrobe-challenged a few years ago. His wife, Earlene, devised a clever scheme to deal with the issue. She sent Delmont an anonymous letter signed by "A Hot-blooded, 34-Year-Old Auburn-Haired Secret Admirer." She wrote, "I've had my eyes on you for a long time and have even fantasized about becoming special friends with a mature man. But lately, I've noticed your clothing choices have begun to deteriorate, and quite honestly, you've become a slob. Consequently, I may rethink who I dream about at night."

Bingo. Delmont read the anonymous letter and made an immediate about-face. He began dieting, working out at the gym, and reading _GQ_ and _Esquire_ every month. The only downside was that he wanted Earlene to dye her hair auburn.

On the other hand, Mr. Mighty Brain feels compelled to note that the blue-collared comedian, Larry the Cable Guy, has made a bazillion dollars with his big-bellied, plaid-shirt look. Of course, Larry the Cable Guy is funny. OK, mildly funny. Mr. Mighty Brain understands all that money has made Larry the Cable guy into a very handsome and charming man, in spite of his dysfunctional wardrobe.

Dear Mr. Mighty Brain,

As part of my court-directed community service, I was required to mow grass at the Lakeview City Cemetery. You really learn who your "friends" are when you're mowing at the cemetery, and mine stayed away.

At Lakeview, there are graves with all shapes and sizes of markers, and a few of them have these real fancy tombstones. It occurred to me that the people buried underneath might have been good-for-nothing S.O.B's like me, but had families who'd successfully covered up their loved ones' wasted lives by buying expensive monuments.

Well, I don't have a nice family, so I figured if I took the $30 a month I'll be spending on my son Leonard's child support over the next eight or nine years, and applied *it to a tombstone, I could have a real nice memorial marker. Maybe even topped off with a couple of those scary winged-things you see in old Dracula movies. Leonard, who I don't think is really my kid, doesn't need any more Air Jordan sneakers or video games, anyway. Someday, when Leonard's an adult, he'll be proud of his Daddy, thanks to this big-assed monument.*

Personally, I think it's a brilliant idea. What do you think?

Signed,
Chiseled in Stone

Dear Stoned,

Mr. Mighty Brain thinks he can save you some money. He knows an artist in Dumas who makes concrete statuary, like those large concrete leprechauns and gorillas no one in his right mind would ever buy. For $235 cash, the statuary artist will mold you a full-sized, concrete horse's ass to use as your tombstone. And, if you're interested in going first class, he'll carve one out of granite for an additional $400. Let me know if you'd like his phone number. ✪

ELEVEN

Press Six for Love

It was like standing in front of a South American firing squad and being refused a blindfold by a ruthless *Comandante*.

Shalonda, my psycho supervisor at the Wally World photo lab, summoned me into her glass-walled office just before eleven o'clock, not bothering to offer me a seat. As usual,

➤

the cloying fragrance of Chanel No. 5 saturated the air, since Shalonda practically bathed in her favorite perfume every morning. Not bothering to make eye contact, she stared at the computer screen, her fingers tap dancing over the keys. "We're letting some people go," she said smugly, "and you didn't make the cut. Turn in your badge at accounting." Still multitasking on her laptop, Shalonda aimed for the kill shot. "I know gay men can be pretty emotional, so don't cry in front of the other employees, OK?"

Brutal. Especially after three years of busting my minimum-wage ass for a retailer that piously displayed "Made in America" banners in their stores, then schemed with third-world sweat shops to manufacture 90% of their products.

My told-you-so sister said getting laid-off was actually a good thing. "It's about time. You've been stuck in graduate-school adolescence for years," she lectured. "Partying five or six nights a week. Plus, you were only using, like, a third of your brain at Wally World."

"Hey, grad school was stressful. I deserved a little time to decompress."

"If you decompressed any more, you'd be comatose." She glared at me just like the time I tried to shave our pet rabbit. "How much do you have in savings?"

I stalled for a few seconds. "I dunno, not a lot."

"Does it total five digits?"

"No."

"Four?"

"Umm, not really."

"Don't you think it's time to grow up and get a real-world job, something with a little *potential?*"

My sister was right, of course, but after six weeks of searching for jobs with potential and nary an interview to show for it, my three-digit savings shrunk to two. If that weren't enough, a couple of collection-agency gorillas knocked on my apartment door late one night and threatened to repossess my truck. That was all the motivation it took to shelve *potential* and concentrate on *right now.*

Swallowing my Masters-in-Psychology pride, I searched the phone book and found an employment agency promising "a guaranteed paycheck" within a week, which was as close to right now as I could find.

At the agency, the gum-smacking lady who filled out my paperwork mumbled something about my willingness to work in telemarketing.

"I've always admired the industry," I lied. "In fact, I've often considered it for a career."

Unconvinced, she trumped my lie with a bigger lie. "We have a fabulous company that needs someone immediately." She scribbled an address on an index card and thrust it toward me. "Can you start tomorrow morning?"

Just above the address, were the words "Alamo Psychic Hotline." My stomach felt as if I'd just eaten enchiladas topped with ice cream.

The agency lady maneuvered her gum to the front of her mouth and blew a Ping-Pong-sized bubble. "Interested?"

My mind flashed to the goons about to shanghaii my truck. "Sure."

"It's not in the best part of San Antonio. Be sure and lock your car doors, OK?"

There wasn't much to Dominic Fumagalli's three-minute-long job interview. A pasty-complexioned man with saggy, gerbil jowls and the physique of a beanbag chair, the owner of Alamo Psychic Hotline asked if I had any telemarketing experience.

"No, not really. But I'm willing to learn."

Studying his Blackberry rather than looking at me, Dominic asked, "You ever fooled around with Ouija boards, Tarot cards, or stuff like that?"

"Once, in junior high. A girl brought a Ouija board to a party."

He frowned, but didn't look up from his phone. "Look, here's the deal. I need a clairvoyant. My other one quit. You cool with that?"

"If it comes with a paycheck, I am."

"I have two other mystics you gotta work with. Don't cause any trouble, OK?" He reached into his shirt pocket and pulled out a toothpick, which he used to peck the keys on his cell phone.

"Got it."

Dominic made the mission clear. "It's all about keeping the caller on the line. They're mostly emotional women, drama-queen types. You have a girlfriend?"

"No, sir. Actually, I'm gay. Would that be an issue?"

He ignored my question. "The first three minutes are free. After that, it's $2.99 a minute, and you get half," he said, continuing to text with the toothpick. "Ask questions, make 'em clarify their answers, whatever it takes. Every minute you keep 'em on the phone, it's a buck-fifty in your pocket."

Later, I discovered the "free" minutes consisted of 30 seconds of synthesized music that sounded like Mozart on meth, followed by two-and-a-half minutes' worth of a pre-recorded Planet-Zoltar-like voice offering legal disclaimers and hypnotic-sounding instructions. "For information about dream interpretations and afterlife communications, press four. For celestial timing questions, press five. Press six for love and relationships."

Dominic appointed me the love and relationship guru, even though my last relationship with a female was in high school. For advertising purposes, my name would be "Saleem the Clairvoyant." Evidently, I was replacing Barabbas the Diviner, who'd quit the hotline to become a short-order cook at IHOP.

"Would 'Saleem' be a Turkish or an African name?" I asked, wanting to know my character's background, like a method actor understanding his motivation.

"I dunno," Dominic answered, faintly annoyed. "'Saleem' just sounds exotic. You come up with the story. Say you're part of an exiled royal family or somethin'. Maybe you're Rasputin's kid."

"Rasputin's been dead, like, maybe a hundred years."

"OK, so you're his great-grandson. Look, Einstein, the folks who call a psychic hotline don't know Rasputin from raspberries. Just come up with a story."

Dominic assigned me one of three cubicles he'd purchased at a bankruptcy auction in Houston. The size of garbage dumpsters, the stained-fabric panels emitted a faintly putrid odor, as if someone had puked on them. Centered in a windowless, fluorescent-lighted room, the cubicles were surrounded by a half-dozen tanning beds. Dominic's previous tenant from the other half of the building, San Antonio Tropical Tans, flaked-out on the rent, so he changed the locks and confiscated their equipment. By storing the casket-like beds in the psychic call center, Mr. All-American-Entrepreneur freed the vacant space for his new internet lingerie business.

Working together in a cramped work space, the other two mystics and I became car-pool chummy. Miss Cecelia, an African-American woman with a spooky resemblance to John Travolta, acted as Alamo's official seer. She interpreted dreams, communicated with the afterlife, and analyzed past lives. Unlike the other two of us, Miss Cecelia truly believed she possessed the gift of divination. She attributed her conjuring powers to a special rack of tubular wind chimes she periodically stroked, which worked best when she also burned "Louisiana swamp herbs" in a nearby ashtray. At first, I assumed the mysterious swamp herb was some form of marijuana, but based on my extensive experience as a party animal, the smoldering leaves and sticks represented nothing illegal.

Madame Z, our designated oracle, handled inquiries related to celestial timing, helping callers select lottery numbers, choose auspicious dates for weddings and divorces, and decide when to get pregnant and by whom. Madame Z covered her hair with a colorful, butterfly-themed headscarf and affected a sing-songy Caribbean accent whenever she spoke with a client, even though she grew up just outside of Little Rock and was busty and skanky enough to pass for a Presidential bimbo.

I decided that Saleem would be a sensitive, misunderstood mystic who'd discovered his gift of prophesy and intuition during his teen-age years, when he correctly predicted the winner of three-straight Kentucky Derbies. Madame Z pointed out that since 99% of our callers were female, it made more sense if Saleem had correctly predicted the winners of three-straight Miss America Pageants.

"So, do you ever feel lonely, or wish you had more friends?"

"I guess so." The caller paused. "Like all the time."

She sounded young, maybe sixteen or seventeen, judging by how often she used the word "stuff" and the phrase "he goes" rather than "he said." I continued my checklist. "Do you often feel insecure or depressed?" Seven-and-a-half minutes and counting.

"Well, sometimes. But not all the time."

"How often is 'sometimes?'"

"Saleem, what does this have to do with whether my boyfriend is gonna break-up with me?"

"It's *very* important, assuming you want a proper celestial reading. I mean, if it's just feel-good pabulum you're after, you've called the wrong clairvoyant. Me, I provide a thorough, accurate reading, so you get your money's worth." Eight minutes, definitely an improvement from my first-week average of five minutes per call. "Now, specifically, how often do you feel depressed?"

"Well, I'd say once a week," she said, sounding irritated.

"You sure?"

"OK, maybe twice a week."

"Does the depression last an hour or so, or does it go on for a day or two, Terry?"

"My name's Tammy, not Terry."

"I meant Tammy."

She shouted, "You're a total fake!" and hung up ten seconds before we reached the nine-minute mark.

Three weeks as a psychic and I'd made barely enough money to keep the collection gorillas at bay. I dined on cans of beans and weenies six days a week, splurging on a Big Mac on my day off. The other mediums sensed my frustration and offered moral support and practical advice. Miss Cecelia suggested I immediately write down the name of each caller, and Madame Z advised using dark metaphors whenever possible, thereby ratcheting up the spookiness factor. With their encouragement, I decided to stick around for another couple of weeks.

Two days later, my fortunes changed. A woman, who wouldn't identify herself, phoned the hotline and asked for a general reading about the men in her life. Her voice sounded familiar, but I couldn't identify it until she said, "I've been in ever-livin', ever-lovin' hell lately." It was an expression that Shalonda, the Cruella de Vil of Wally World, frequently used around her subordinates - mostly to belittle them. Once, when I issued a full refund to a customer on some blurry photos, Shalonda claimed it wasn't our fault the lady took lousy photos and I needed to grow an "ever-livin', ever-lovin' backbone." Another time, when I'd made an error on the cash register, she taunted, "You have the brain of an ever-livin', ever lovin' amoeba."

Worried that Shalonda would recognize my voice,
I stuck a pencil in my mouth, making it
sound as if I had a slight speech impediment.

Worried that Shalonda would recognize my voice, I stuck a pencil in my mouth, making it sound as if I had a slight speech impediment. I asked a couple of touchy-feely questions to burn some time and to make sure she didn't recognize me.

At Wally World, Shalonda didn't share any details of her personal life, except with Katie, our resident Mother Superior, who received confessions across the aisle in the electronics department. The irony was that Katie hated Shalonda as much as everyone else and couldn't wait to spill her guts to the rest of us lowly peons about our boss' diet of the month and complicated love life. Consequently, in addition to hearing about our boss' pomegranate and seaweed regimen, we also knew about Shalonda's suspicion that Harold, her live-in boyfriend, had been sneaking a tall redhead into their apartment.

To complicate matters, Shalonda's ex-fiancé was pressuring her to dump Harold and reunite with him, according to Mother Superior. A regular *Days of Our Lives* plotline, except with no commercials for personal-injury attorneys or feminine-hygiene products.

Armed with that tabloid-worthy information, I said, "It's apparent you're having difficulties with men. But, you're also having issues in your workplace, aren't you? Some unfortunate layoffs in your department?"

"Well, yes, that's true. Two or three losers, that's all."

"All of them?"

"Unmotivated bozos, every one."

Punched in the gut, I fought back. "Does your first name start with S-h?"

"You're pretty good. My name is Shalonda."

"I sense there's another female at work, someone with a strong personality, with whom you're able to confide. Someone not in your department, but very close by. I'm seeing a name beginning with the letter J. No, wait a minute, it's not a J. It's the letter K. Definitely a K, but I'm not certain if that's a first or last name."

"Katie. It's her first name. But everybody calls her Mother Superior."

"That's her. This Katie person, you can trust her completely. Her lips are silent as a tomb."

"I've always known I could trust Katie."

Score a punch for me. "I'm seeing another image, Shalonda. It's a woman, tall with red hair, knocking on a door. She's nervous. Almost fidgety. She knows she isn't supposed to be there."

"Yeah?"

"She's a very attractive woman, Shalonda. I'm talking slender and gorgeous."

"She is?"

"Absolutely stunning. Would you be the red-haired woman at the door?"

"Not even close. I'm a brunette, five-foot-three, and anything but slender."

"I see." Ten minutes into the psychic boxing match, I was slightly ahead on style points. "Shalonda, do you live in an apartment, an upper level?"

"Third floor."

"I'm seeing railroad tracks."

"Right next door," she said.

"You share the apartment with a male, correct?"

Shalonda sighed. "For the time being."

"I thought so. I see the male welcoming the statuesque woman into your apartment. I'm struggling to capture the first letter of his name. It just isn't clear right now." Eleven minutes and counting. "He's pouring her some wine. Looks like an expensive *Merlot*. Napa, upper end of the valley."

"What are they doing?"

"They just sat down on your couch. Wait a minute, Shalonda. It's an H."

"What?"

"The male's name. The first letter of the male's name is an H."

"That figures. How do you know these things?"

"I'm a clairvoyant, Shalonda. I've had the gift since my teen-age days, when I correctly predicted the winners of three-straight Miss America Pageants."

"That's amazing. Who do you think'll win this year?"

"Let's not waste your money on that subject, Shalonda. Shall we concentrate on the reading?"

"OK."

"The red-haired beauty just moved into your bathroom and stopped in front of the mirror. Oh, this is very odd. Give me some time to process this, please." I mentally counted-off 60 seconds, earning enough cash to upgrade the evening's dinner from weenies and beans to a Big Mac and fries. Punctuating my silence with an occasional "Hmm" or "Ah," I finally said, "This is most unusual. She's sniffing a bottle of your perfume. Chanel No. 5."

"What?"

"Yes, and the man is standing directly behind the red-haired woman and has lightly placed his hand on her shoulder. He's, he's . . ." I paused, allowing for 30 more seconds of celestial reception, enough to supersize the fries. "Are you sure you want to hear this, Shalonda? This could be a bit unpleasant."

"Of course, I want to hear it."

Perfect chance for a right uppercut. "He's dabbing Chanel No. 5 behind her ear. The perfume's practically dripping down her neck."

"No ever-livin', ever-lovin' way. I paid a hundred bucks for that bottle."

"Hold on. The man's saying something else." I took a deep breath and made a long whooshing sound as I exhaled, revving up the spookiness factor by several hundred RPM's.

"Saleem, what's happening now?"

"Harold just whispered to the red-haired beauty that he wants to sense how it smells on a sweet-natured person, as compared to a mean-spirited, vicious woman. Shalonda, he's not talking about you, is he?"

"Me? I don't know. I suppose he *could* be referring . . ."

"Granted, you don't sound mean-spirited to me, but there's no doubt the man's talking about the person he lives with."

"Yeah, yeah, I get it. But tell me more about the intruder-woman and the man."

"It's hazy, Shalonda. I'm sorry, but that's all the celestial energy I'm channeling at this moment. Unfortunately, it may take a second session to develop a thorough profile of their relationship."

She groaned. "OK, then, but before we end the session, I have a question about another man I know. He's —"

"Just a moment, Shalonda. There's so much negative energy in the force field, I'll need some time to refocus." At sixteen minutes and counting, this qualified as the longest reading of my psychic career. "OK, I'm receiving a more positive vibration now. Completely different from the first. I'm sensing the other man has something to do with a tic-tac-toe board, which is odd. That doesn't make any sense." Pausing twenty seconds, after the obligatory "hmm's" and "ah's," I said, "Wait a minute, it isn't the game itself, Shalonda, but the letter X that's inside the tic-tac-toe boxes. Do you have an ex-husband, perhaps?"

"Ex-fiancé."

"That's him. Yes, I'm getting a strong reading. Highly intense, with both positive and negative energies."

"What's going on with him?"

"He's conflicted, Shalonda. Your ex wants to make a change in his life. He wants to be closer to you. Does that make any sense?"

"Yeah, Ernie wants me to break up with Harold."

I jotted down Ernie's name. "But here comes the negative energy. While there's a part of him that sincerely wants to be back in your life, he also believes you're cruel and treat people badly. Bottom line, Ernie doesn't think you're a nice person. And, he doesn't think you'll ever change." I waited a few seconds. "This issue of your treating people poorly seems to be a trend, don't you think?"

"I'm not really a bad person, Saleem. Maybe a little too blunt on occasion, and people confuse that with being cruel."

Shalonda was as blunt as a guillotine. I kept her on the phone for another sixty-dollars' worth of wishy-washy information about her ex, recycling gossip I'd heard from Mother Superior.

Explaining that even though she truly loved Ernie, Shalonda broke their engagement because he was "too plain and predictable." She couldn't imagine being married to someone "so boring." Eventually, our conversation looped back to the more-exciting Harold and the red-haired woman.

"Saleem, I want to have a little talk with Harold and call you back in a couple of weeks. Could you channel another reading then?"

Although not technically a knockout, I'd won by a unanimous decision. "Of course, Shalonda. I'm always here for you. You can count on me."

Over the next fourteen days, my menu upgraded from weenies and beans to braised beef tips, topped with an assertive *bourguignon* sauce. After bringing my truck payments current, the repossession gorillas retreated to their jungle, and my bank balance rebounded to three digits, bordering on four.

Apparently, Shalonda recommended my extraordinary powers to her coven of friends and relatives, making me an overnight rock star with the coo-coo crowd. Like the *Starship Enterprise*, word of my "powers" rippled through the Oddball Galaxy at warp speed. Up to sixteen hours a day, I performed non-stop psychic readings, so hectic that Madame Z lent me her laptop to track client issues, their peculiar quirks, and my predictions for the future. I transferred my overflow calls to the other mediums, payback for the volumes of advice they'd offered me.

Following Miss Cecelia's lead, I invested in a rack of tubular wind chimes, similar to the one she used at her cubicle. At the beginning of a séance, she lightly strummed the chimes, generating an unearthly sound that would have scared the pea-diddle out of me, were I a first-time caller. Figuring a similar rack would help set the mood with my clients, I found one on eBay for six bucks. It arrived missing a fourth of its tubes, but Miss Cecelia took it home the prior evening and "loaded it up with plenty of south-Louisiana magic," as thanks for steering my overflow calls her way. She insisted on giving me some of her swamp herbs, pointing out that the wind chimes were useless unless I "breathed voodoo smoke."

Without a Mother Superior spoon-feeding me inside information on every caller, I assumed my star status would flameout quickly, so it was important to cash in on my celebrity while I could. The funny thing was, more often than not, callers instinctively knew the solutions to their problems and were subconsciously seeking validation. If a caller's good-for-nothing man was spending all his money on booze, bongs, or babes, I offered a prediction based on what the woman already knew on some level: things likely wouldn't change, so she could either swallow her pride and look the other way, or find another guy. A graduate-school professor of mine considered Shakespeare, of all people, the world's first published psychologist. Old Will nailed the concept perfectly when he wrote: "Our remedies oft in ourselves do lie."

For the first time in my career, I enjoyed work, and even though it was just a stupid psychic hotline, I finally put my $45,000 psychology degree to practical, although a bit sleazy, use. Plus, I was using 100% of my brain every day, unlike using only a sliver of it at the photo lab.

When Shalonda called back, she seemed upbeat - friendly, almost. It was as if we were old prep-school chums, fondly remembering our Exeter days over after-dinner brandies and cigars. "Saleem, you won't believe what happened."

I pictured the smirk on her face. "You had a polite little discussion with Harold?"

"I'm not sure I'd call it polite. More of a Salem witch trial."

"What'd he say?"

"Well, he denied the whole perfume thing. Said it was the craziest thing he'd ever heard. But I knew better. You'd channeled the whole scene."

"So, did he confess?" I asked.

"Yep, finally. Turns out, besides the red-haired girl, Harold was boppin' the apartment manager - also a redhead." She sighed. "Guess he had a thing for Miss Clairol."

"That's a lot of women to keep happy."

"Well, as of last week, he has one fewer."

"What about your ex-fiancé?"

Shalonda said she'd talked with Ernie several times over the past two weeks and was having dinner with him the following evening. She wanted a reading on how their meeting would go.

"Will you give me a minute to calibrate the celestial energy, Shalonda?"

"Of course, I will. Take whatever time you need."

Anxious to try my wind chimes, I gently stroked them a couple of times with my index finger and lit an ashtray packed full of Miss Cecelia's swamp herbs. "OK, Shalonda, I'm receiving something. It's faint, but the vibrations are definitely there."

"I love the wind chimes," she said, sweetly.

"It helps to focus and channel the incoming energy." It was strange hearing Shalonda be so positive.

"You know," she said, "I've made a big change in my life."

"Oh? What kind of change?" The fragrance from the ashtray seemed so mellowing, so relaxing. Remembering Miss Cecelia's advice, I breathed in the voodoo smoke.

"I didn't much like the person I'd become, Saleem. The men in my life were right. I was ugly to people, really mean. But I just couldn't help it."

"Yeah? You were mean?"

"So, I decided to transform myself. And I have. I've truly changed into a nice person."

That seemed as believable as Hannibal Lector announcing his conversion to vegetarianism. "Congratulations on your transformation."

"It's kind of a twelve-step program for me," she said matter-of-factly. "You know, live one day at a time, that sort of thing. It's all about change."

All the talk about change reminded me of the promises politicians continually make, when the "change" merely goes from your wallet to the government's. I took another breath of smoldering herbs and flicked my finger across the wind chimes again. This time, the strangest thing happened. At the tinkling of the last tube, I began to visualize a woman who looked like Shalonda, appearing as if she were a six-inch-tall hologram on my cubicle's desk. She was sitting with a man at a miniature table covered with a red-checked tablecloth. Over a dinner of lasagna and a bottle of *Chianti*, the Lilliputian figures came to life, animated actors on a diminutive stage.

The only time I'd ever experienced anything similar was when I had a nightmare root canal a couple of years ago and hallucinated on Vicodin and Valium. That night, on the shelf over my bathroom lavatory, cans of shaving cream and deodorant argued whether Pavlov or Freud had a bigger effect on the field of psychology. But in this case, I wasn't taking medicine, nor had I been drinking; I'd merely strummed the wind chimes and breathed the herbal smoke. "Shalonda, do you enjoy Italian food?"

"Love it. In fact, we're having dinner at Luigi's tomorrow evening."

The small man in the desktop tableau poured a glass of wine for the equally tiny Shalonda, who wore black Capri pants and a light-blue sweater. This whole scene registered an eight on the Richter scale of weirdness, where seven is considered la-la land. "Shalonda, have you decided what you're wearing tomorrow night?"

"Yep. Bought a new outfit yesterday. Why'd you ask?"

"Oh, just curious, that's all. Did you buy Capri pants and a blue turtleneck?"

"Saleem, you're amazing."

"Black Capri's?"

"I was a little worried how my butt would look in the Capri's, but I've lost four pounds this week, just by sticking to mangoes and anchovies. So, my butt should be OK, don't you think?"

"Your butt will be fine," I fibbed, thinking she'd be better off losing 40 pounds or buying a butt bra, assuming such an article exists.

In the hologram, little Ernie, a bookish-looking fellow with reading glasses perched on the end of his ski-slope nose, reached across the table and gently caressed little Shalonda's hand. He asked if they could "start over and try to make things work." Without hesitating, she blurted, "Only if you weren't so boring." It was as if little Shalonda hadn't received the memo about full-sized Shalonda's transformation into a kinder person. Or, more likely, the attempted transformation, like a cactus grafted to a pine tree, was doomed to failure.

Little Ernie rose from the table, threw down his napkin, and stormed out of Luigi's, leaving little Shalonda alone in the tableau. I strummed the wind chimes once more, and then, just like a fade-out at the end of an old-school rock-and-roll song, the ethereal scene slowly evaporated.

The flesh-and-blood Shalonda asked, "Saleem . . . Saleem, are you still there?"

Jolted back into our conversation, I stammered, "Shalonda, I think, umm . . . I think we need to discuss this transformation of yours."

"I feel so good - like a butterfly emerging from a cocoon," she said cheerfully, almost as if she were still trying to convince herself, as well as me.

As much as I despised Shalonda, it struck me that she'd at least acknowledged her problem and attempted to do something about it. Me, I'd been satisfied to party my life away while working at crappy places like Wally World and a psychic hotline where the cubicles smelled like vomit.

"Shalonda, how committed are you to this change?"

"Fully. Oh, I know I have to take it one day at a time, but it's already happened. I feel as if I'm a different person now."

"Then you have to promise me something."

"Of course, Saleem. Whatever you say."

"You have to promise to think before you speak tomorrow evening. If Ernie asks a question - any question - promise me you'll count to ten before responding. No, make that twenty."

"Why?"

"Think about the person you're choosing to become, rather than the person you've been in the past."

There was silence, about a minute's worth. Finally, she said softly, "Yeah, I understand what you're talking about."

"Shalonda, just promise me, OK?"

"I promise."

It was tempting to strum the wind chimes for a look at my own future, but after a couple of days of thinking it over, I decided against it. It was as if someone offered me a chance to know the exact date of my death. Even though some people would want to know, I wouldn't. Most likely, it was the realization that unless I changed - truly changed - my future would be a repeat of my past - a perpetual underachiever who never even won the employee-of-the-month parking space at Wally World.

As much as I hated to admit it, my sister was right - being fired from Wally World had been a good thing.

A week later, Shalonda called back.

"How did things go with Ernie?" I asked.

"I took your advice, Saleem, even though it was so hard counting to twenty. Ernie thought I was acting totally weird."

"He asked for another chance to make things work, didn't he?"

"Saleem, you're the most amazing psychic I've ever known."

"What'd you tell him?"

"I said there were some things we needed to work out. First, he needed to loosen-up a bit, maybe develop some hobbies or do somethin' else to make himself more interesting. But I wasn't mean about it, I swear. And second, I told him I was working on being a little softer with people, not so hard-edged."

"Wow, Shalonda, I'm proud of you."

"It wasn't easy, trust me."

"What's next for you and Ernie?"

"I dunno, Saleem. Bottom line, he's still a pretty-boring guy. People say you can't change the spots on a leopard, and I wonder if Ernie can successfully paint over his spots."

"Well, after a hard rain or two, you'll see if the spots reappear."

She laughed. "Hey, you mind if I come down to your office and meet you face-to-face? You know, thank you in person for all you've done for me."

She laughed. "Hey, you mind if I come down to your office and meet you face-to-face? You know, thank you in person for all you've done for me."

"I'm afraid if we ever met in person, my ability to interpret your future would be severely compromised. You wouldn't want that, would you?"

"No, I wouldn't."

"Shalonda, there is one other thing I wanted to mention about our talk the other day."

"Yeah?"

"You remember those people you laid off in your photo department a few weeks ago?"

Shalonda snickered. "The bozos?"

"Yeah, those guys. Well, if you and Ernie can change, don't you think they could, too?"

"I dunno, I guess so." She sounded as if she wanted to believe they could change, but wasn't sure. "Do you really think they could?"

"Shalonda, Saleem the Clairvoyant knows all. If he says so, *it will happen.*"

tWEEZ8

"She walked past a dry cleaner in Queens and spied a sleeping cat curled up in the window. Not pretty, not cute, nothing. Just a stinking housecat. But she wanted the cat, 'cause the girl's mental. This Vietnamese couple owned the dry cleaner, so Marta asked them if she could buy the cat. No, they said, not for sale. Why the hell not? Because it's our cat, they said, and you can get one just like it at the animal shelter for free."

TWELVE

Tweeze

The morning they gated me out, all I could think about was tweezin' my eyebrows. Not having sex, like Jermaine wanted, or hangin' with my homegirls. Just standing in front of a freakin' mirror, in a real bathroom with real tweezers - not two plastic spoons. My face looked like caterpillars were crawlin' across my eyebrows.

➤➤

Jermaine whined worse than a puppy needin' to pee. Been a long time, he said, and I was being unfair. Like he wasn't gettin' it somewhere else.

I said, you want to know what's really unfair, Jermaine? I'll tell you, 'cause I been totally schooled by the pros.

This Brooklyn bitch, prob'ly trippin' on smoky huff or crank, did three years for killing a cracker, who drag-assed on the subway stairs and made her miss the express. The next M train, she shoved the old man in front of the first car. Cut him in half. Legs and guts on one side of the rail, bloody neck and head on the other. Air in between. I asked her, why'd you do it? Hoochie mama just laughed. I dunno, she said. Guess I be PMS'ing or somethin'.

Then there was crazy Marta. She's walkin' her fat ass past a dry cleaner in Queens and spied a sleeping cat curled up in the window. Not pretty, not cute, not nothin' but a stinkin' housecat. But she wanted the cat, 'cause the girl's mental. This Vietnamese couple owned the dry cleaner, so Marta asked them if she could buy the cat. No, they said, not for sale. Why the hell not? Because it's our cat, they said, and you can get a hundred just like it at the shelter for free. But Marta wanted *that* cat. So, she swooped down, hawked it under her arm, and flew like hell down the sidewalk, the Vietnamese man chasin' and cussin' her. Trouble was, she's on probation for forgettin' to pay for a few things, and there's a couple of doughnut boys sittin' in a panda car who saw her. So, the little kitty-cat cost her three years of hard time. But you know what? All Marta ever talked about - all day long, every single day - was going back and finding that cat.

Now, you tell me, Jermaine, what's unfair? A hood rat slices a man in half, and a homegirl, playin' cards with a deck of 50, steals a lousy housecat. Guess what, both get rolled up for three years.

Then I said, chill out, homeboy. Take me somewhere so I can tweeze this freakin' caterpillar 'fore it drives *me* crazy. ✪

Jumping Off The Sunshine Bridge

"It happened back in the Bible days or maybe when Shakespeare wrote all those screenplays, I forget which. At any rate, I announced my plan to hire a couple of mourners who would throw themselves over my coffin and weep convincingly. I figured it would add color and levity to an otherwise somber occasion."

THIRTEEN

Jumping Off the Sunshine Bridge

A fortnight ago, Evette, *The Breaker of Hearts*, called at three in the morning, waking me from a mellifluous sleep - she hates it when I say "mellifluous" - to say she was done with me because I was a certifiable nutcase.

I told Evette the word "nutcase" should only apply to people like the idiot who sits behind the basketball

➡

goal on TV, wearing a rainbow-colored wig and waving a sign that says "John 3:16," or the fruitcake who had a crush on Jodie Foster and decided to impress her by shooting President Reagan.

Granted, I may do a few things that could seem a little quirky, but nothing that would warrant *The Breaker of Hearts* commanding me to jump off the Sunshine Bridge into the Mississippi River. I had to Google its height to determine whether she preferred I'd drown immediately or be swept away by the current and eaten by scaly reptiles. It turns out the Sunshine Bridge stands 170 feet tall, which means, most likely, I'd splat instead of splash.

And why did she choose an obscure bridge in Louisiana instead of one that's famous like the Brooklyn Bridge, the Golden Gate, or even the Bridge over the River Kwai? The only reason I could think of is that she knew I'd visited Louisiana once, with my sister, Winnie. We'd become intensely interested in hurricanes and decided to study a category-five storm first-hand. We met these offshore-rig workers at a hurricane-watch party in the cocktail lounge of the Lake Charles Holiday Inn. When the sheriff's office closed the bar, the roughnecks invited us to their room to continue partying. If *The Breaker of Hearts* thought I was a certifiable nutcase, she should have met *those* guys.

As luck would have it, the storm abruptly turned and missed Louisiana; but at least my mind was distracted for two solid days, which helped me deal with being unceremoniously dumped earlier in the month by Stephanie, *The Seductress of Men*. She wore six-inch-tall platform shoes with see-through plastic heels that were hollow and had a tiny lid on top where she could pour in water. If we went clubbing, Stephanie added a couple of small goldfish so when she walked around, everyone could see the little creatures swimming around in the heels. It made her look like a twenty-dollar ***** [crude word for lady of the night], but I never said that to her face. I'm not sure what she did with the fish afterwards, but knowing *The Seductress of Men*, she flushed them down the toilet, as she did to me, metaphorically speaking.

Back to Evette and me. We first met at the downtown post office after I developed an intense interest in commemorative postage and stopped in to purchase some masculine-looking stamps; some that didn't have Disney cartoon characters, intertwined hearts, or Judy Garland on them.

The Breaker of Hearts was working special services that afternoon. She smiled as I approached the counter. "How may I help you?"

"Do you have any manly stamps?"

"Manly? Well, we have flags. Those are manly."

I said, "Nothing against flags, but I find them a bit clichéd. I mean, everyone sends letters with flag stamps."

"Is there anything in particular you have in mind?"

"Maybe something with instruments of war, like nuclear submarines, battleships, or intercontinental bombers."

"Sorry," she said, "but I'll pass along your suggestions to the regional supervisor."

"Well, how about a stamp with a picture of Theodore Roosevelt or Ernest Hemingway? Those were manly men."

"Nope, nor do we have one of Sean Connery."

"OK, how about North American mammals, like grizzly bears, moose, or elk, but nothing small like squirrels or cotton-tailed rabbits?"

"No, we don't have any of those," she answered, "but we do have stamps with pictures of vintage cars with *huge tail fins*."

Now, I'm no psychologist, but I thought the way the little minx emphasized the words *huge tail fins* was a slight jab at my masculinity - as if my request for manly-looking stamps resulted from complicated issues I had with my mother, may her holy soul rest in peace.

So, to prove I was completely secure in my manhood, I decided to ask Evette out to dinner. After quite a bit of persuasion on my part, she finally agreed to the date. At the conclusion of a wonderful evening, I questioned *The Breaker of Hearts* if her huge tail fins comment was a veiled reference to the size of my manhood. She raised her eyebrows and said, "No, silly. I was talking about vintage cars, for crying out loud."

Despite our cautious beginning, Evette seemed to be as attracted to me as I was to her. She thought I was handsome and didn't find my extreme attention to detail all that peculiar. "I like a man who's free-spirited and quirky," she said, "and isn't a slave to what others think."

Even though we were totally different - like vinegar and oil - we blended well as a couple. Evette bonded with my sister, and for a while, everything went swimmingly.

Our problems first surfaced about a month ago, when I developed an intense interest in archaic words and ancient customs. After checking out several books on the subject from the library, I began sprinkling old-fashioned words into my conversation -"henceforth," "flummoxed," "rapscallion," and "mellifluous." It wasn't a political statement of any sort - I just thought it shameful the English language had become so coarse and full of boring words.

Over a late dinner at Red Lobster, I described to Evette the ancient custom of an aristocrat's family hiring professional mourners for the deceased's funeral as a way to demonstrate to the town folk how important their loved one was. I said, "It happened back in the Bible days or maybe when Shakespeare wrote all those screenplays, I forget which." At any rate, I announced my plan to hire a couple of mourners who would throw themselves over my coffin and weep convincingly. I figured it would add color and levity to an otherwise somber occasion.

She said, "Winston, for a man as smart and charming as you, that has to be the dumbest idea I've ever heard. You're not terminally ill or even sick. Plus, you'd have to pay for the mourners in advance and wouldn't even know if they showed up for your funeral, because you'll be *dead*."

My answer was that I'd talked it over with Winnie, and we concluded that when you're dead, your spirit sees everything that's going on. It would be as if you're one of those security systems in Wal-Mart where there's maybe a dozen hidden cameras rotating coverage onto a VCR, so you always know what's going on, including whether the professional mourners showed up.

She asked, "Ok, what would you do if the mourners didn't show up? Dress up in a white sheet and yell, 'Boo!'?"

I said I'd just contract with a reputable company with an established track record, and besides, Winnie would ask for a refund if they didn't honor the agreement.

Then, the argument shifted from hiring professional mourners to her criticizing my vocabulary. "It's just so goofy," she whined. "Like just now when you said Shakespeare wrote a 'screenplay.' 'Screenplays' are scripts for Hollywood movies. How can you not know that? And 'coffin.' Nobody is buried in a 'coffin' anymore. Winston, the word is 'casket.'"

I countered, "Well, if Shakespeare didn't write screenplays, how come *Romeo and Juliet* and *Hamlet* were movies?"

Evette called me a complete **** [crude word for male genitalia] and said movies weren't invented until about 300 years after Shakespeare wrote his plays and sonnets. And yes, Evette actually used the word ****. The woman is an absolute scalawag.

I said, "Henceforth, I shall continue using the word *screenplay* until they put me in my *coffin*." And that's when *The Breaker of Hearts* arose from the table, threw down her napkin, and stormed out of Red Lobster, completely unprovoked. I followed Evette from the restaurant to her car, and as she drove toward the parking-lot exit, I plopped facedown, right in front of her car. As she jammed on her brakes, I yelled, "I'd rather be flattened road-kill than face life without you."

She leaned out her window and asked, "What kind of road-kill, Winston? Flattened possum? Flattened raccoon? Flattened kitty-cat?"

Upon reflection, *The Breaker of Hearts* was mocking my intense interest in obscure details, but I didn't realize it at the time. Innocently, I answered, "Whichever you prefer, as long as it brings you happiness."

She fired back, "What would bring me happiness is to find a guy who could order dinner at Red Lobster without asking the waitress if they served organic porridge or roasted tubers." She said I was full of **** [crude word for excrement], then slammed her car into reverse and blasted out of the other parking-lot exit.

Around midnight, I phoned *The Breaker of Hearts'* apartment, hoping she'd settled down enough to accept an olive branch. When she didn't answer, I left a message on her machine, saying I planned to take poison "just like in *Romeo and Juliet*, the screenplay Shakespeare wrote."

I actually saw *Romeo and Juliet* with Claire, *The Bewitching Temptress*, whom I was dating at the time. Toward the end of the movie, when Romeo swallowed the poison, which is my favorite part, *The Bewitching Temptress* reached over and squeezed my hand. I told her I didn't care to hold hands at the movies, that I preferred to concentrate on the plot. Claire got all honked-off and said I was cold and distant and about as romantic as an eggplant. I thought comparing someone to an unpopular vegetable was unkind, although highly characteristic of a temptress.

After thinking over my suicide message for a few minutes, I decided it was a shade too Shakespearean, so I phoned Evette again and left her another voicemail, saying I was rescinding the first threat.

And so, at three in the morning, *The Breaker of Hearts* phoned, waking me from a mellifluous sleep, and told me to go jump off a bridge.

It seemed so natural to ask which bridge she wanted me to jump from.

"It doesn't matter," she said. "It's just an expression, for heaven's sake, like 'get lost' or 'go jump in the lake.'"

"Do you mean a draw bridge, a suspension bridge, or a causeway?"

She said, "OK, Winston, you win. How about the Sunshine Bridge? I read about it in some travel magazine."

"What river or body of water does the Sunshine Bridge span?"

"I don't know, it's in the South somewhere."

When I asked *The Breaker of Hearts* if she knew the height of the bridge and how fast the current ran underneath, she called me a certifiable nutcase and hung up.

Wondering what to do with my life post-Evette, I phoned Winnie, who has suffered through her own share of relationship problems. Her last boyfriend believed the Lord commanded him to ride a donkey across the United States while holding a "Jesus Saves" sign. Three months later, he'd traveled as far as Arkansas, camping out in roadside parks along the way. As he slept one night, someone stole his donkey and the "Jesus Saves" sign. Fortunately, the stupid ******* [crude word for illegitimate child] saved enough money for a bus ticket back home.

I briefed Winnie on the situation with *The Breaker of Hearts*. She said I needed to pick myself up by my bootstraps and jump back into life's boxing ring. I told her she was mixing clichéd metaphors and could do better. She answered, "Well, then, just remember that every dark cloud has a silver lining."

Like me, my sister has intense interests, so she asked if I was still focused on commemorative postage or whether I'd moved on to something else. I said I'd been studying ancient customs and archaic expressions and wanted to upgrade the quality of my speech patterns, but Evette didn't like me saying "thee" and "come hither."

"Winston, if you ask me, that relationship is toast." Winnie mentioned the possibility of introducing me to Ophelia, who'd just moved into the apartment next door to hers. "Actually, her real name is Tiffany, but she's having it legally changed to Ophelia because it's more renaissance-sounding." She said Tiffany/Ophelia had an intense interest in medieval reenactments and traveled almost every weekend to participate in some sort of faire or festival. "She's tall, very attractive, and has all these authentic-looking, hand-made costumes. Plus, I think she knows how to say all that thee-and-thou stuff."

(111)

> *"As a matter of fact, our apartment complex*
> *is having a pool party tomorrow night.*
> *You could come as my guest and I'll introduce you."*

"Well, Tiffany/Ophelia certainly sounds interesting, but I still have feelings for Evette."

"Maybe she'd take your mind off Evette. Divert your attention, like Moses did with the Red Sea. You know, that whole raised-walking-stick thing."

I told my sister that Moses *parted*, not diverted, the Red Sea, and with the possible exception of "that relationship is toast," she was having a bad-metaphor day. "But, you're probably right about meeting someone new. Maybe you could introduce me to this Tiffany/Ophelia person sometime."

"As a matter of fact, our apartment complex is having a pool party tomorrow night. You could come as my guest and I'll introduce you."

"Does Tiffany/Ophelia have any strange tendencies or interests? I don't want to get hooked up again with someone weird like Evette."

"No, she seems perfectly normal to me."

"OK," I said, "count me in."

"Just wear something nice and consider talking about something other than category-five hurricanes and commemorative stamps."

"A lot of women find hurricanes and stamps to be fascinating conversation topics, Winnie. Remember our trip to Louisiana to study hurricanes? And besides that, *The Breaker of Hearts* found stamps pretty-darn interesting."

"That's because she worked at the post office, Winston. I'm just saying that Tiffany/Ophelia may not find either subject all that fascinating. Since you're into ancient customs these days, why don't you talk about something medieval?"

In preparation for meeting Tiffany/Ophelia, I read all about the Abbots Bromley Horn Dance, one of England's oldest traditions dating back 800 years or so. Twelve guys, six of them carrying reindeer antlers, dance around the village of Abbotts Bromley to music provided by a man playing an accordion and a boy playing a triangle. No one remembers the purpose of the dance or what it symbolizes; it's just that they've carried on the tradition for nearly a thousand years.

When I arrived at the apartment complex, Winnie and her next-door neighbor were poolside, among a group of about ten other people. Standing beside the punch bowl, my sister introduced me to Tiffany/Ophelia, as attractive as Winnie had advertised. After shaking hands, I immediately sought clarification on the proper name to call her.

"Why don't you call me Tiffany for now," she said. "Later, if we hit it off, you may call me Ophelia."

That sounded a little strange. Why would I need to call her one name in the introductory phase of a relationship, then something else "if we hit it off?" What if we didn't hit it off? Would I forever be relegated to calling her Tiffany, while her inner circle of friends called her Ophelia? And who, exactly, would make the determination of whether the relationship had hit it off? Would it be her unilateral decision, or would I have some input?

"So, Tiffany, my sister tells me you're very interested in medieval reenactments."

"Yes, my lord, I am," she said, smiling and dipping into a mini-curtsey. "Do you know anything about the medieval period?"

"In a way, I suppose. Lately, I've been studying archaic words and ancient customs, trying to ginger-up my otherwise boring language."

"Ginger-up?"

"Well, spice up my language, I meant. You know, Shakespeare constantly added new words and definitions when he wrote all those screenplays."

Tiffany/Ophelia smiled. "I like a man who's not afraid to take linguistic risks. Most men are so, well, *hoi polloi*."

Winnie interjected, "Winston is anything but *hoi polloi*. He puts his pants on one leg at a time."

I said, "You'll have to excuse Winnie. She's been stuck in cliché hell all this week."

Tiffany/Ophelia nodded in agreement. "So, what ancient customs interest you most?"

"Well, most recently, I've been investigating the Abbots Bromley Horn Dance in England. I find it quite fascinating."

"You're joking."

"No, why would I joke about something that serious?"

"Well, Abbots Bromley just happens to be one of my favorite ancient rituals. A friend and I toured the festival together, several years ago," said Tiffany/Ophelia. "It's in September, you know. Have you been?"

"Actually, September's the prime season for hurricanes, and I rarely venture too far away from the coast, in case a category five develops."

At my mention of hurricanes, Winnie rolled her eyes at me and shook her head as if to say, *I told you to talk about something besides stamps or hurricanes.*

"You're interested in hurricanes? I've always found them fascinating," said Tiffany/Ophelia. "Were you there for Katrina?"

"Of course. Also Hurricanes Ivan, Dennis, and Ike."

"That's impressive. We seem to have a lot in common."

"We certainly do, Tiffany. And, I've always thought attending a renaissance faire would be the perfect way to spend a weekend. Assuming, of course, I had someone to escort."

"Winston, henceforth, call me Ophelia."

Concentrating on making my voice as mellifluous as possible, I answered, "Of course, my lady," and bowed slightly to *The Beautiful Enchantress.* ✪

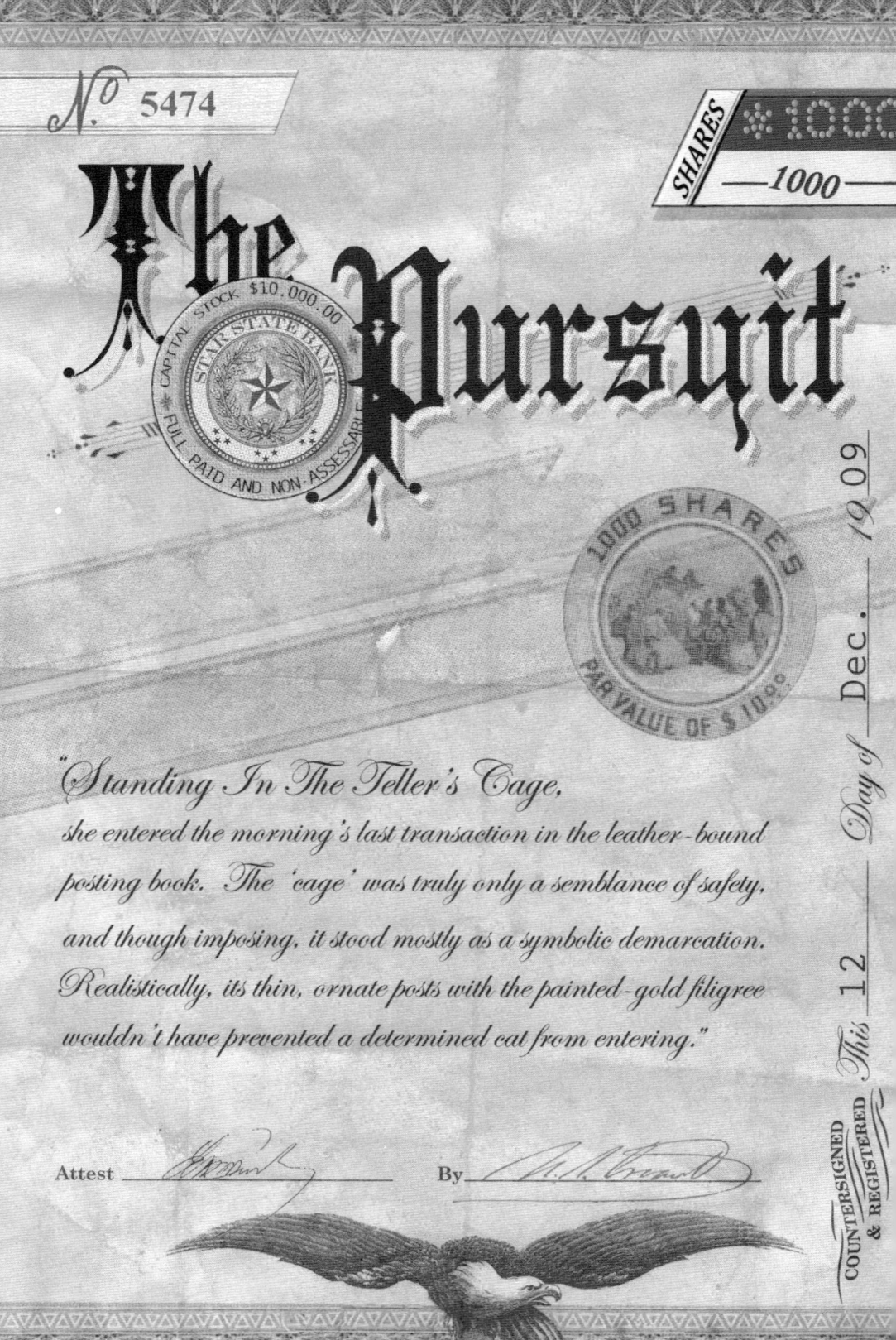

No. 5474

SHARES ✳1000
——1000——

The Pursuit

CAPITAL STOCK $10,000.00
STAR STATE BANK
FULL PAID AND NON-ASSESSABLE

1000 SHARES
PAR VALUE OF $10.00

"Standing In The Teller's Cage,
she entered the morning's last transaction in the leather-bound
posting book. The 'cage' was truly only a semblance of safety,
and though imposing, it stood mostly as a symbolic demarcation.
Realistically, its thin, ornate posts with the painted-gold filigree
wouldn't have prevented a determined cat from entering."

Attest _____   By _____

This 12 Day of Dec. 1909

COUNTERSIGNED & REGISTERED

FOURTEEN

The Pursuit

T.E. Hamilton hated this time of the morning. It wasn't so much walking through the weeds to the privy, or shivering when his bare skin settled against that damp wooden seat. No, it was excusing himself from Miss Barr and then leaving the bank.

She knew, of course, where he was going and how long he'd be gone.

➤➤

Mr. Hamilton considered it downright humiliating, like having to ask the teacher's permission in a one-room school, and blushed at the mere anticipation of this daily embarrassment. He wished the bank could hire an additional employee; that way, he could slip away without feeling compelled to announce his departure. But ever since Mr. Coolidge was elected President, profits hadn't been all that grand for the Star State Bank. Besides, Miss Barr was entirely capable of handling the cashier's duties by herself. So he endured.

"Would you excuse me for a minute, please?" As usual, Mr. Hamilton did not wait for her response.

Miss Barr smiled to herself as the bank president closed the back door, knowing how embarrassed this always made him feel. Clearly, he was in charge and could simply leave without any comment, but both of them knew he never would. *What odd creatures men were,* Miss Barr thought, reminding herself of the benefits of never marrying (and at age . . . well . . . "thirty-ish," never intending to!). She deeply admired Mr. Hamilton; in fact, he was the sort of gentleman she might have considered had she ever contemplated matrimony in earnest. And even though her employer was a portly fellow, Miss Barr found no fault in that; she considered herself rather "large boned."

Standing in the teller's cage, she entered the morning's last transaction in the leather-bound posting book. The "cage" was truly only a semblance of safety, and though imposing, it stood mostly as a symbolic demarcation. Realistically, its thin, ornate posts with the painted-gold filigree wouldn't have prevented a determined cat from entering.

183

Just as she completed the posting, Miss Barr heard what sounded like a small pebble strike the windowpane just behind her right shoulder. Instinctively, she whirled and looked out the window, assuming it was a young truant, absent from school.

But there was no one outside, and Miss Barr thought it might only have been the wind. When she turned back to her ledger, a man was standing in front of the teller's cage. He faced away from her, toward the bank's front door, as if he were expecting someone else to enter.

She hadn't heard the door open, which normally made a distinctive, unoiled creak, a helpful sound, which alerted the two bankers whenever one of the town's 200 residents entered the building.

The latest customer wore a bulky overcoat, as heroic soldiers wore in the Great War.

"And how may we be of service to you, sir?" The teller purred in her financial voice.

The man spun around. Miss Barr's first thought was not one of fear, just confusion. *Odd, he's wearing a red bandana over his face*, she thought, *like the one we used during Blind Man's Bluff at Lula Mae Webster's party last New Year's Eve.*

"This is a robbery, ma'am," the man rasped through the cloth. "Give me your cash. I don't mean you no harm."

Miss Barr was not amused. Even though she occasionally caught herself daydreaming about the drama of a potential bank robbery, Mr. Hamilton was always the lead actor. Now, for all she knew, a whole gang of desperadoes surrounded the bank, and Mr. Hamilton was still out back - indisposed. It was as if the main character had disappeared after the first act, and the understudy, who hadn't memorized the script, was assuming his role.

Emptying the cash drawer in the teller's cage, she noticed the robber's hands quiver slightly as he placed the money into the pockets of his overcoat. Unable to determine whether he had a gun, and certainly not wanting to press the issue, she did manage a glance out the front window. A black Model T Ford, a spare tire attached at the rear bumper, idled in front of the bank, pointed south in the direction of Moline, another no stop-sign town. Relatively rare in this remote stretch of Central Texas, a car so shiny and new, like this one, stood out like a prize-winning watermelon in a cantaloupe patch.

After Miss Barr reluctantly handed the last of about $300 of the institution's precious cash to the nervous-acting bandit, he motioned toward the bank's vault with his free hand, keeping the other one hidden in his pocket. "Get in there," he said, "and be quick about it."

Afraid of what might happen if the man carried a gun, Miss Barr silently prayed the robber wouldn't shoot as she shuffled into the steel vault. She had so much to live for - her card parties, church, a wonderful vegetable garden. And who would take care of her aging mother?

The cast-iron door closed with a solid thud, plunging her into darkness.

Miss Barr, grateful to be alive, listened but could not hear the creak of the front door opening and closing.

"MISTER HAMILTON! M-I-S-T-E-R H-A-M-I-L-T-O-N!" she yelled, definitely not in her financial voice. "P-L-E-A-S-E, MISTER HAMILTON," she pleaded, only to hear her voice resonate in the echo chamber of the vault. *What on earth could possibly be taking him so long?*

Like many women, Nettie Hamilton repeatedly chided her husband about his loss of hearing. But like most men, he had been simply too vain to admit his deficiency, particularly to his children and certainly not to his friends. And, even more certainly not to Miss Barr, of all people. He heard what he needed to hear, thank you.

If it hadn't been for the embarrassment issue, Mr. Hamilton had to admit he enjoyed this quiet break in his day. He finished the World Series article in *Collier's* and neatly stacked the magazine on top of the older issues of the *Saturday Evening Post.* Ambling toward the back door of the bank, he refocused his thinking from the Yankees' infield to whether the gin would work as much cotton as last year.

With his first step into the bank, Mr. Hamilton realized something was not exactly right. Miss Barr, normally there to offer a silent nod as he returned to his desk, was nowhere to be seen, and the vault was closed. He hurried behind the railing to the teller's cage, and immediately discovered the cash drawer open and, to his great disappointment, empty.

Mr. Hamilton crossed the room to the vault as quickly as a man of his size possibly could. He swirled the dial faster than he had ever done, all the while praying to find Miss Barr alive and unharmed. With heart-pounding anxiety, he swung the door open.

"Mister Hamilton, I'm so sorry."

"Are you all right?"

"I was so scared." Her normally steady voice quivered with emotion. "Mr. Hamilton, I think he had a gun!" Even though her black ordeal lasted only two or three minutes, it seemed like two or three hours. Any notion that she was safe took a well-deserved backseat to her emotional retelling of what *could* have happened. Miss Barr quickly described the robber and the automobile with the small spare tire. "I'm sure they're heading toward Moline," she said, regaining her composure. "I'm so sorry, but there was absolutely nothing I could do."

Mr. Hamilton immediately thought of Frank Soules. In addition to being Chairman of the Board of the Star State Bank, he was a trusted friend. Most importantly, he lived on a ranch not far from the Moline road and owned an automobile. If he acted quickly, perhaps Frank could intercept the thief or at least follow him to his hideout. But it wasn't yet noon, and Frank was hardly the sort of man to come in early from his chores.

The banker rang the switchboard operator, Lizzie Garret. Without explaining any details to the always inquisitive and all-knowing woman, he blurted, "Lizzie, there's an emergency. I need to speak with Frank Soules. Immediately."

———————

Frank Soules and his two grown sons, Henry and John, were branding and doctoring calves that day at the main pens near the headquarters' house. Working with livestock brought out the best and worst elements in men: cooperation, frustration, anger, and satisfaction. That day was no exception.

Frank, a widower, shared the house with John and his wife, Maurine. The old rancher thought as much of his daughter-in-law as he did his boys. She was busy preparing lunch for the men when the telephone rang.

From the wooden porch of the ranch house, Maurine shouted that there was a telephone call for Mr. Soules. Henry and John continued to work the calves while their father sprinted to the house. Telephones were still somewhat of a novelty; people dropped what they were doing to answer a call.

A minute or two later, the brothers looked up to see their father scrambling toward the pens, waving his arms and hollering for them to stop what they were doing. Gasping for breath, he told the boys about the bank robbery in town and the thief's escape toward Moline. With the look of a ten-year-old boy about to stalk his first rabbit, Frank Soules challenged his sons to help track down the robber.

Henry instantly agreed, but his brother was hesitant. "Right now, I'd rather be a live coward than a dead hero," John opined, no doubt thinking of his young wife.

Frank and Henry didn't have the time, nor inclination to change John's mind. Frank ran back to the house to grab the Winchester while Henry hurried to get the automobile started.

When the son drove around to the front of the house, the father jumped in the passenger seat, his rifle poking out the window.

"Let's cut through the Bennett Creek crossing. We might catch him before he gets to Moline," Henry suggested to his father.

"Well, then, get moving!"

The "posse" followed a rutted trail across the low-water crossing and through the native pecan trees on the other side of Bennett Creek. Henry concentrated on driving in the rough, gouged-out trenches while his father bounced up and down trying to hold on to his hat with one hand and the Winchester with the other.

Ten minutes later, Frank and Henry arrived at the Moline road and decided to park behind a large cedar tree, which would hide them from the view of an oncoming automobile. But before they could position their vehicle, a black Model T Ford swept by. It all fit. The shiny new car had a spare tire attached to the rear end, and it was definitely driving toward Moline.

"That's him!" Frank shouted, and the pursuit was on.

Henry floorboarded their automobile onto the road and flashed his lights at the Model T. Frank stuck his head out of the window and waved his arms for the robber to pull over. The black Ford paid no attention.

The chase continued for several miles around curves and over low-water crossings. It was obvious to the self-declared defenders of justice that the desperado had no intention of stopping. *Sometimes difficult situations require daring solutions*, Frank surmised. If the nefarious criminal wouldn't stop voluntarily, he'd good and well stop with a little "persuasion." Still an excellent marksman, the old rancher leaned half-way out the window of his careening automobile, took aim, and bull's-eyed the Model T's two rear tires.

Lurching to the right side of the road, the shiny Ford pulled over to a dead stop. Frank's heart warmed with a satisfaction he hadn't felt in years. Even though his son's palms now dripped with adrenaline-fueled sweat, he could tell Henry was pleased with his part in the apparent capture of the fugitive. Frank then realized he hadn't considered their response should the outlaw actually decide to resist.

The Soules men cautiously climbed out of their automobile. Frank prepared for another shot, if necessary, and this one wouldn't be at a tire. The gravity of their situation abruptly settled upon him and Henry, who had been calmly branding rather benign, and certainly unarmed, creatures a mere hour before.

As the pair slowly crept toward the black Model T, the robber threw open the door. Frank, taking a deep breath, steadied his aim at the emerging figure.

It took only a second before the Soules men recognized the man, Lucian Pitcock, who now stormed toward them. He had an angry look in his eyes.

Frank and Henry swallowed hard because they both knew Lucian Pitcock was a farmer, a neighbor, and a deacon in the Baptist church, just for good measure. And he was certainly no bank robber.

But there was one thing the Soules men did not know about Lucian. He had just purchased a brand-spanking-new Model T Ford. It now sat glumly beside the country road with two tires as flat as Frank Soules' once-soaring ego, as a shiny black Model T whizzed by, on its way to Moline. ✪

FIFTEEN

Searching for Who Knows What

Jonas' dorkiness turned radioactive the moment he spotted the Empire State Building. "Gollee, that's a tall building." He whistled softly, as if he were a 1940's private eye and would add "swanky" to his description. "Tallest in the world."

"Nope," I said, white-knuckling next to him in the taxi's back seat. "Not even in the top ten."

➡

"Well, it's the highest in the U.S."

"No, Jonas, it's not. That ugly thing in Chicago is taller."

Like a disappointed child hearing his older sibling's revelation about the tooth fairy, Jonas didn't have the ammunition to argue. Instead, he asked our Jamaican driver to stop on the Queensboro Bridge. "I wanna take some quick pictures of the skyline," he said, oblivious to the apocalyptic traffic about to destroy us.

The dreadlocked cabbie glared into his rear-view mirror. "You crazy, mon?"

"Hey, it wouldn't take but a sec," Jonas pleaded. "I'll open the door, snap a couple of shots, and bongo-baby, we'll be done."

"Bongo-baby? What the hell does that mean?" The Jamaican swerved to avoid a bread truck. "You are crazy, mon."

"How 'bout an extra dollar on your tip?"

"You double crazy!" The driver floor-boarded the yellow cab across the bridge, pinging from lane to lane as if we were inside a giant pinball machine.

"That's kind of spiteful, isn't it?" Jonas whispered to me.

Miraculously arriving at the Marriott with our heads still attached to our shoulders, I felt like pulling a Pope and kneeling to kiss the ground. Jonas wanted to stiff the uncooperative Jamaican on his tip, but I handed the cabbie a five spot. "You can't mess around with those Caribbean dudes, Jonas," I lectured softly, as we lifted our bags from the trunk. "They'll kill you for a case of beer. Maybe a six-pack, if it's Red Stripe or a brand they really like."

We checked into our rooms and met in the lobby after changing clothes. Jonas was easy to spot. At six-feet-seven, he Paul Bunyan-ed above the other hotel guests, especially with his ever-present cowboy hat, adding another five inches to his TCU-football physique.

From across the lobby, Jonas bellowed, "Hey, Mac, what took you so long?" Like Bunyan's giant ox, Blue Babe, he bounded toward me and slung his arm around my shoulders, as if we were long-lost friends and hadn't spent the afternoon sardined together on an airplane. "Let's have a cocktail or six!"

"Jonas, it's only four o'clock. Three, Texas time."

"So? The convention doesn't start until nine tomorrow. That means we've got between ten and twelve hours to have a few drinks, party, and who knows what." Jonas smiled and bared his teeth, chimpanzee style. "Emphasis on the *who knows what.*"

I agreed, reluctantly, figuring we'd likely skip the first session anyway. This year's kick-off speaker, the same bozo we heard two years ago in Denver, would likely offer regurgitated pabulum about the fertilizer industry needing to adjust to a "fast-paced, ever-changing paradigm." As if we didn't already know what it's like being pummeled by third-world countries using nine-year-olds to bag their phosphates.

Jonas and I coasted over to the lobby bar a few yards away. Seconds

191

later, we'd inhaled our watered-down drinks and moved on, deciding the ten-dollar cocktails wouldn't lead us to nirvana anytime soon. Our second and third stops weren't much better, except for scarfing enough beer nuts and stale pretzels to qualify as dinner. Searching for the dessert course, we stumbled onto one of the classic Irish taverns in Manhattan - McSomething or other - and quickly realized we'd found the Promised Land - one illuminated by neon Smithwick's and Guinness' beer signs.

"I see a wee bit o' the emerald isle in front o' me." Jonas' drawled-Irish accent sounded as believable as Arabs and Jews locking arms and admitting the other side's been right all these centuries.

"Land, ho," I practically yelled over the glass-clinking din. The bar's mahogany walls, sandwiched with layers of yellowed varnish and decade's worth of cigar smoke, cast an amber, have-one-for-the-road patina. "Jonas, can you imagine the crazy pick-up lines these walls hear, ten minutes before closing time every night?"

He cocked his head and pointed toward the suit-and-tie attorneys, Wall Street types, and thick-necked, working stiffs who looked as if they all drove delivery trucks. "You think any of these Irish wear kilts and play golf?"

"That's Scotland, dummy. The Scots play golf. The Irish just get drunk and beat the ever-living crap out of you."

"Scotland, Ireland, Greenland, whatever. They all have goofy accents."

We parted the sea of faux Irish and nabbed two seats at the U-shaped wooden bar. The bartender, twenty-something and uber-attractive, greeted us. Wearing red-red lipstick and a low-cut blouse, she asked if we'd like a beer.

"Guinness draft, please," Jonas said, pulling off his Stetson and displaying it on the counter as if it were some sort of championship trophy. "And one for my buddy. We're from out of town."

"Never would have guessed," she deadpanned. "Welcome to Manhattan, boys. Your horses need any hay?"

"Nope," I answered, trying not to stare too long at the sexy, barbed-wired tattoo across her chest. "Just a little nourishment for their riders."

When she turned to fill our mugs, Jonas whispered, "I like her. She's spunky." The 1940's gumshoe in him could have added, "And she'd real keen and snazzy, too."

After half-a-dozen beers each, we learned that the Dutch tourists sitting on the stools next to Jonas spoke four languages and were apparently allergic to deodorant. They sipped *Chardonnay*, an outright heresy in an Irish bar, and yaw-yawed about how refreshing it was to have someone other than a Texan in the White House. No matter their politics, Europeans automatically subtract 30 IQ points from any American with a Southern accent. Reciprocally, Southerners deduct 30 hygiene points from Eurosnobs who don't regularly brush their teeth or think the definition of "cool" is sucking on the nub of an unfiltered cigarette.

Turning to the annoyances sitting on the other side of me, two porky Yankees' fans stressed about their upcoming series with the Red Sox. A Derek Jeter wannabe whined in Brooklynese, "Our pitching's gone completely MIA. Wit' the kind of money dos players make, we should go undefeated."

His Italian buddy, showing complete solidarity, belched his agreement. "Spoken like a true genius." Ten seconds later, he belched again, this time almost two-syllable's worth. "Oh, 'scuse me. Nice beer." Then, solemnly, almost as if he were remembering a fallen comrade, the Italian added, "Hey, wait a minute. How 'bout us raising a glass for Mr. Steinbrenner, may he rest in peace."

The Yankees' farm team clinked their mugs and toasted the recently departed owner. "Wherever he is," said the wannabe, crossing himself Catholic style. "Great man. Shoulda been President."

It was tempting to tape their conversation so the next time someone complained about Texans being the most obnoxious two-leggers on the planet, I could whip out the recording and prove otherwise.

While Dumb and Dumber segued into a discussion of their previous weekend's sexual exploits, Jonas and I maintained radio silence. Based on his trance-like gaze toward the bartender, my buddy was fantasizing about future exploits of his own. Finally, Jonas beered-up his courage to ask if our bartender was single.

Surprised at his question, she reported being "happily partnered" to someone named Twizzle.

Jonas scrunched his nose. "His name is Tizzle?"

"No, Twizzle."

He stared blankly, as if she were speaking an obscure Mandarin dialect.

"*Her* name rhymes with swizzle," she said. "You know, like a swizzle stick."

"Oh," Jonas sighed, his confusion replaced with comprehension. Unhappy comprehension.

While the bartender resupplied the Jeter wannabe and Italian with fresh brews, Jonas rolled his eyes, a la a sixteen-year-old being lectured for wearing too much eye shadow. "I dunno," Jonas muttered softly. "Just seems such a waste. I mean, an attractive woman like her being gay."

"Why would you say that?" I asked. "How can it be a waste?"

"Well, it's a waste of good looks, that's what I'm sayin'."

"Jonas, it isn't a waste for a woman to be attractive and gay. Why shouldn't they be both? Besides, everyone in this bar probably assumes *you're* gay, what with the big cowboy hat and boots."

He shook his head like a dog shaking off a bath. "Hey, no one would ever think I'm gay."

"Jonas, this is New York City. Didn't you see the movie 'Urban Cowboy'?"

"No way. You and me got more testosterone in the tips of our pinkies than those Yankee guys have in their whole-dang-fat-assed bodies."

"Those fat-assed Yankees probably think you and I are on a date." I leaned over and smooched Jonas on the cheek, making sure the kiss was loud enough the farm team could hear.

He jerked away, as if he'd been tasered. "Good lord, Mac, what the hell you doin'? Four hours in New York City, and you've gone queer on me."

"Take it easy, buddy, you're not my type," I said, savoring the shock on Jonas' face. "Just saying that people aren't always who they appear to be. Maybe the bartender's gay, or maybe that's some sort of armor she wears, so idiots like you aren't hitting on her all night long."

"I'm not an idiot, Mac."

"After six or seven beers, *every* man's an idiot. Me included. I just kissed my best friend, for God's sake, and we both love skirts as much as Herman Cain."

"Hey, let's find a table at the back of the bar, OK?" Jonas stood. "I can't face Yankee Nation after you just embarrassed the hell out of me."

After a detour to the men's room, where Jonas selected a stall as far from me as possible, we sliced and diced our way to an empty table near the back, chosen specifically because of its proximity to another table where two attractive women sat unattended.

Jonas asked our server, an overly tan woman with a Rosetta Stone of tattoos, if she would send a couple of beers to the nearby table. "Just tell them it's an award from a couple of guys who've voted them the best-lookin' women in the bar."

"Are you serious?" The battle-scarred veteran of the Cupid wars twisted her mouth a half-turn, perhaps deciding if her dignity had sunk low enough to carry out the mission. "Actually, that's so totally uncool," she rasped, "it might work."

Jonas clinked my glass. "Keep your fingers crossed. Maybe this is the *who knows what* we've been looking for."

A few minutes later, our deputized server reported that the two women appreciated the drinks and wondered if they'd be welcome at our table.

"Of course, they'd be welcome." Jonas waved his hat, bull-rider style, in the direction of the ladies. They responded with a demur nod. "Bongo-baby," he said to me, flashing his toothy chimpanzee smile.

"Jonas, if you have even a sliver of hope for later tonight, don't do that smile-thing again. Trust me on that, will you?"

"Got it."

As the two women approached our table, the tall, mini-skirted brunette smiled. "What a coincidence. We just voted you the best-looking men in the bar."

The other woman, a flashy-looking, blue-eyed blonde who looked as if her jeans were a size Perfect, added, "And, to tell the truth, it was hard deciding between First Place and Mr. Congeniality. So, we decided to interview the contestants personally."

"OK, let the interviews begin. I'm Mac, and this is my friend Jonas. I suppose if you join us, we'll be the best-looking foursome in this little slice of Ireland, right?"

"I dunno. It's pretty dark in here. Hard to see the other competition." The brunette extended her hand. "I'm Kristen, and this is Mia. Let me guess. You're from Texas, right?"

Jonas looked startled. "How'd you know?"

"The accent. Dead giveaway. Besides, I'm originally from Tulsa, so -"

"She can spot a cowboy a mile away," Mia interrupted. "She also knows all about cows or goats, or whatever it is you grow down there."

"She can spot a cowboy a mile away," Mia interrupted. "She also knows all about cows or goats, or whatever it is you grow down there."

Before Jonas or I could respond with something equally snappy, Kristen's cell phone rang. The call lasted only a few seconds before she flipped the phone closed. "Guys, I'm so sorry. I forgot about an appointment this evening. Gotta go."

"Dang, just our luck," said Jonas. He leaned toward Mia. "Can you stay?"

Mia shook her head. "We're in my car." She looked at Kristen. "I'll take you home."

"Don't worry, I'll grab a taxi," Kristen said. "It's my fault, after all. Why don't you stay and have a beer with the Lone Ranger and Tonto?"

"Hmm, I don't know." Mia hesitated. She smiled and asked Jonas, "Texans don't bite, do they?"

"Just where it counts." He started to do the chimpanzee thing, but caught himself just in time.

Kristen said, "OK, they've apparently been vaccinated for rabies, so you're in good hands. I better get going." She stood, gathered her purse, and turned to leave.

"Wait, Kristen, you have my car keys."

She fished the key ring from her purse and handed it to Mia.

"I hate having this clunky thing in my jeans," Mia said. "Makes my silhouette look so bad." She pitched the key ring to Jonas. "You mind keeping it for me?"

"Sure," Jonas said. "Nothing worse than a bad-looking silhouette. Besides, now you can't leave without me."

She smiled. "Smooth opening move, Tex. We'll have to see about that."

The two women exchanged careful-not-to-muss-your-hair hugs. Kristen whispered something to Mia, then maneuvered to the front of the bar and disappeared. Jonas quickly scooted his chair closer to the blonde, like a Klondike miner staking his claim.

It turned out that in addition to being a world-class flirt, Mia was an aspiring actress. She explained her appearances probably weren't in any movies we'd ever seen - minor roles in some "art movies."

"Which ones?" Jonas asked.

"Well, have you seen 'Atomic Tequila' or 'Bikini Legends IV'?"

"Guess not. You seen 'em, Mac?"

"No, but then, I missed this year's Cannes Film Festival."

"You're so funny." Mia winked at me, perhaps thinking of staking a mining claim of her own.

"Yeah, a lot of gay men are pretty funny," Jonas said dryly, drumming his fingers on the table.

"You're gay?" She looked at me and squirmed. "You certainly don't act gay. Besides, I assumed all you Texas guys were macho, manly-man types."

"You're gay?" She looked at me and squirmed.
"You certainly don't act gay.
Besides, I assumed all you Texas guys were macho,
manly-man types."

I figured Jonas was due his little payback. "Well, looks are deceiving sometimes. You know, Big Tex, the giant cowboy at the Texas State Fair, just came out of the closet. Who would have guessed he was gay?"

Mia seemed confused. "Big Tex is gay?"

I bounced up from the table. "Hey, looks like our server's gone AWOL. Everyone up for a refill?"

"Make sure the mugs are cold," Jonas cautioned.

I zigzagged to the bar and ordered another round for the table. Still on their original perches, the Yankee boys discussed the difficulty of finding a beautiful, sexy woman who also understood and loved baseball.

"I mean, why's it I can't find a woman who actually *understands* the infield fly rule, instead of someone who *pretends* to understand it?" The Jeter wannabe slugged the rest of his glass. "Is that askin' too much, for cryin' out loud?"

The Italian complained, "The last chick I took to a game felt sorry for the pitcher. The manager pulled him for giving up two consecutive dingers, and she thought they shoulda talked about their problem more."

While the Yankees blathered, I kept an eye on Jonas and Mia, magnetically inching ever closer. By the time our icy mugs arrived, the two of them were snuggling like mountaineers surviving a blizzard. It appeared that *who knows* what was becoming a definite possibility for my friend. Some chimpanzees have all the luck.

Holding on to three beers, I weaved through the increasingly rowdy crowd, as if juggling in a hurricane. By the time I made it to our table, Jonas' lips were within inches of Mia's, ready to seal the deal.

I clanked the mugs on the table, interrupting their romantic séance. "Hey, Jonas, what kind of Texas malarkey are you using on our new friend?"

He pretended to be annoyed. "Well, if you must know, I was telling Mia that peanuts aren't like pecans, filberts, or almonds, which grow on trees. Peanuts grow underground and are more properly classified as edible legumes."

"That silver tongue never ceases to amaze me," I said. "Mia, if he starts using the Latin names for plants, watch out. It's his way of talking dirty."

"Wow, you sure know a lot of stuff about food, Jonas," Mia cooed. "Are you some sort of astrology professor?"

"I think you mean 'agronomy.' But no, I'm not. Just a fertilizer salesman."

After another twenty minutes, it was obvious I'd become the third seat on their bicycle built for two. I was in the midst of offering to take a cab back to our hotel, leaving them to *who knows what*, when Mia interrupted me.

"You know, I really should be getting home myself," she said.

"You should?" Jonas seemed surprised. "It's still early."

"Yeah, I have an audition tomorrow. Need to look my best."

He leaned in for the clincher. "Like some company on your way home?"

Mia's attitude changed from flirt to flight. "You men are a lot of fun, and all, but I'm not a one-night-stand kind of woman." Her eyes narrowed. "I hope I didn't give you that impression."

Jonas' demeanor deflated quicker than a Macy's balloon after Thanksgiving. "No, not at all," he fibbed.

"How about if I gave you my phone number? Maybe we could go out tomorrow evening for dinner. You have a pen?"

"Sounds good to me." Jonas unclipped a Hercules Fertilizer ballpoint from his pocket and presented it to Mia as if were a gold-capped *Mont Blanc*.

She scribbled her name and phone number onto a napkin. "Oh, you have my keys."

Like the Japanese signing the formal surrender to World War II, Jonas handed the clunky key ring to Mia. He folded the napkin into his shirt pocket. "Just keep the pen. Maybe it'll remind you of me."

"You Texans are so funny." She leaned over and gave Jonas a peck on the cheek. "I better get going. Call me tomorrow."

"Nice meeting you, Mia," I said.

"The feeling's mutual." She smiled. "And, by the way, if you ever decide to go straight, look me up, OK?"

"Thanks, I'll keep that in mind."

Mia quickly meandered through the noisy crowd and waved good-bye, Miss-Universe style.

Not knowing how to comfort Jonas, I concentrated on my beer. "Wow," I said, after a minute. "I thought for sure you were on to something big."

Jonas drank the rest of his Guinness and thumped the empty mug on the table. "Me, too."

"Hey, how about going back to the hotel and getting a good night's sleep? Maybe you can call Mia tomorrow and set something up."

"Hey, how about going back to the hotel and getting a good night's sleep? Maybe you can call Mia tomorrow and set something up."

"I'm pretty sure it isn't a working phone number."

"What?"

"Besides, tonight's not over."

"I don't understand. You want to go barhopping? Don't you think it's getting kind of late?"

"That's not what I meant." Jonas cracked a microscopic smile. "Mia will be back." Jonas sounded like Sam Spade toying with the police chief who'd arrested the wrong man.

"Jonas, she's gone home. She has an audition tomorrow."

"She stole my wallet."

"Aw, crap, Jonas." I slapped my hand on the table. "You can't be serious."

"Yep. While you were gettin' our drinks, Mia started gettin' friendly. *Real* friendly. You know what I mean. About the time I got distracted, she lifted my wallet."

"I don't get it, buddy. If she stole your wallet, why on earth would she come back?"

"Bongo-baby." Jonas flashed his chimpanzee smile. "'Cause I kept her ignition key." ✪

Life&Leisure

Say, Kids, What Time Is It?

Ask Mr. Mighty Brain

Editor's Note: The recent indictment of the Chief Financial Officer of Mighty Brain Worldwide Investment Fund "shocked and deeply saddened" the award-winning columnist. The San Antonio Reporter-Gazette wishes to clarify -- contrary to persistent internet rumors -- Mr. Mighty Brain himself has not been charged with racketeering, money laundering, extorting, or any other crime. Nor is he the subject of any past or current criminal investigation. Other than contesting two past-due parking tickets from Providence, Rhode Island, he professes to be as law abiding as a New York City Congressman.

Dear Mr. Mighty Brain,
Help! My husband, Stanley, wants to take our retirement money out of the stock market in order to invest in "collectibles." During our 46-year marriage, he invested in several get-rich schemes – a camel dairy, a combination barbershop and ice cream parlor, and a horse mausoleum come to mind. His latest brainstorm makes all the other ideas look brilliant by comparison.

Stanley is convinced the Baby Boom Generation will wax nostalgic for 1950's toys, particularly anything to do with the Howdy Doody television show. In particular, he plans to corner the market on Howdy Doody lunch pails, Buffalo Bob autographs, and Clarabell the Clown replica seltzer bottles. Stanley says that rather than placing our retirement funds with Merrill Lynch, we'd have been better off investing in Heidi Doody (Howdy's sister) cookie jars. Given our track record with Merrill, he has a point, I suppose.

headed for Times Square. At one of the stops, an arthritic old man shuffled on to our car and warbled a mournful Mexican dirge of some sort. He couldn't dance and probably should have carried an oxygen bottle instead of an accordion. Muy malo! Mostly out of pity for the poor dear, we handed him a dollar for his effort.

Since we flew home, Mother has become convinced our subway experience of hearing a trio, a duet, and a soloist, on successive days and in declining order of enjoyment, was some sort of cosmic metaphor, a special sign that her life will soon be ending. Even though her health is excellent, she's [...]
funk which is [...]

badassicle tattoo on his chest. The tat looked like a giant brain, with some initials inside. I didn't get close enough to be creepy, but I think the initials were "MB." Was that you? If it was, you have Superman quads, dude!
Signed,
Pumped

Dear Mr. Pumped,
Mr. Mighty Brain is flattered, he supposes, to be mistaken for a muscled-up Superman with a badassicle tattoo. However, he considers gymnasiums and fitness centers to be Kryptonite [...]

SIXTEEN

Ask Mister Mighty Brain -
Say, Kids, What Time Is It?

Editor's Note: The recent indictment of the Chief Financial Officer of Mighty Brain Worldwide Investment Fund "shocked and deeply saddened" the award-winning columnist. The San Antonio Reporter-Gazette wishes to clarify - contrary to persistent internet rumors - Mr. Mighty Brain himself has not been charged with racketeering, money-laundering, extorting, or any other crime. Nor is he the subject of any past or current criminal investigation. Other than contesting two past-due parking tickets from Providence, Rhode Island, he professes to be as law abiding as a New York City Congressman.

➤➤

Dear Mr. Mighty Brain,

My boyfriend of two years, Lewis, calls me all sorts of pet names, which he thinks are endearing and loving. But the thing is, instead of something traditional like "Darling" or "Angel," he prefers "Sugar Dumpling," "Love Cookie," and "Honey Muffin." They always involve some sort of dietary theme, which makes me wonder if he thinks my thighs are too fat.

My pet name for Lewis is "Handsome," and I've suggested that "Sweetheart" would be appropriate for me. To his credit, he tries for a while, but then slips back into his old habit. Just last week at a Swiss restaurant, he called me "Sweet Cakes" in front of our server. I just about choked on the fondue.

Lewis is such a nice man in all other aspects, but this habit is getting on my nerves. I need your advice, Mr. Mighty Brain!

Signed,
Darling Angel

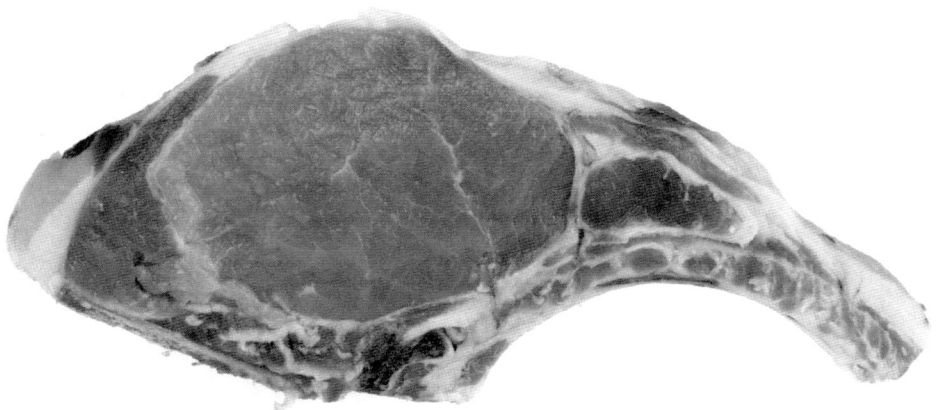

Dear DA,

While slightly off key, Lewis's charming use of pet names, or hypocorisms, sings of devotion and love. Mr. Mighty Brain reminds you it could be worse. The names "Thunder Thighs" and "Pork Chop" come to mind.

He suggests two alternatives. You could refer to your boyfriend as "Mr. Average" or "Nice-Try Lew" in the hope he would recognize how hurtful his monikers have become. Of course, you risk Lewis amping up your *nom de guerre* with something even more dietarily unflattering. Or, you could do nothing, on the assumption your relationship will eventually stagnate, and he'll refer to you not by some sugary nickname, but by "Hey, you" or "Good-Ol'-What's-Her-Face."

Hey, Mighty Brain,

'Sup, man? You work out at LA Fitness last Saturday afternoon? Pumping some serious iron? This muscled-up beast was there, with a badassicle tattoo on his chest. The tat looked like a giant brain, with some initials inside. I didn't get close enough to be creepy, but I think the initials were "MB." Was that you? If it was, you have Superman quads, dude!

Signed,
Pumped

Dear Mr. Pumped,

Mr. Mighty Brain is flattered, he supposes, to be mistaken for a muscled-up Superman with a badassicle tattoo. However, he considers gymnasiums and fitness centers to be Kryptonite storage facilities, populated by perspiring lieutenants of Superman's arch nemesis, Lex Luthor. Mr. Mighty Brain would more likely be confused with Clark Kent than Superman.

———————

Dear Mr. Mighty Brain,

Help! My husband, Stanley, wants to take our retirement money out of the stock market in order to invest in "collectibles." During our 46-year marriage, he invested in several get-rich schemes - a camel dairy, a combination barbershop and ice cream parlor, and a horse mausoleum come to mind. His latest brainstorm makes all the other ideas look brilliant by comparison.

Stanley is convinced the Baby Boom Generation will wax nostalgic for 1950's toys, particularly anything to do with the Howdy Doody television show. In particular, he plans to corner the market on Howdy Doody lunch pails, Buffalo Bob autographs, and Clarabell the Clown replica seltzer bottles.

Stanley says that rather than placing our retirement funds with Merrill Lynch, we'd have been better off investing in Heidi Doody (Howdy's sister) cookie jars. Given our track record with Merrill, he has a point, I suppose. Still, I'm not convinced our golden years will be all that golden if we're relying on Baby Boomers rekindling their love affair with a red-haired, freckle-faced marionette.

The only silver lining in all this is that Stanley is a regular reader of your column and has agreed to follow your advice on this matter. So, Mr. Mighty Brain, which will it be? Merrill Lynch or Howdy Doody?

Signed,
Stuck in Doodyville

Dear Stuck,

Cowabunga! As a youngster, Mr. Mighty Brain sat breathlessly each afternoon by the television set, waiting for *The Howdy Doody Show* and its opening signal, "Say, kids, what time is it?" He'd have traded his prized Ovaltine decoder ring for a seat in the Peanut Gallery quicker than Clarabell could honk his/her/its bicycle horn.

However, as influential as Howdy and his gang were on the Baby Boom Generation, Mr. Mighty Brain admits to having forgotten about them for the past three or four decades. Further, Mr. Mighty Brain, who considers himself a connoisseur of fine collectibles, has no desire to accumulate Doody memorabilia, even if deposited on the front porch of his cottage in a wicker basket with a note attached, reading "Take me, please." He is fairly certain most Baby Boomers share his viewpoint, as callous as it may be.

As a curious aside, Mr. Mighty Brain notes several similarities between Merrill Lynch, the investment company, and Howdy Doody, the wooden dummy. Both are anachronistic and slow-to-react, controlled and manipulated by someone else from high above (in Merrill's case, the federal government pulls the strings).

While Stanley's investment ideas may be more fundamentally sound than those of the Wall Street investment bankers, most of whom now wait tables in New Jersey, Mr. Mighty Brain must squirt seltzer water on this idea. He suggests placing your retirement funds with Mighty Brain Worldwide Investment Fund, assuming a new Chief Financial Officer can be recruited.

Dear Mr. Mighty Brain,

Some of your answers seem to be a bit mean-spirited. Are you eating plenty of fiber?

Signed,
A Concerned Reader

Dear Mother,

Fiber - along with organic coffee, hybrid cars, and Paris - is vastly overrated.

Dear Mr. Mighty Brain,

During a recent vacation to New York City, my elderly mother and I rode the subway each day to see the tourist attractions. On Monday, three Hispanic musicians boarded our train and serenaded us between stops with a guitar, bass, and accordion. As the train rumbled along, the colorfully attired trio sang catchy folk songs and even danced a Mexican hat dance. When they passed the sombrero among the riders, Mother and I contributed three dollars, one for each musician. We thought their mini-concert was muy bien!

On the ride to Central Park the next day, a different band, consisting of an accordionist and a guitarist, entertained us with Spanish ballads. These men didn't dance and were much less bueno *(musically speaking) than the trio. Nevertheless, we chipped in two dollars, following our formula from the prior day.*

On Wednesday, we headed for Times Square. At one of the stops, an arthritic old man shuffled on to our car and warbled a mournful Mexican dirge of some sort. He couldn't dance and probably should have carried an oxygen bottle instead of an accordion. Muy malo! Mostly out of pity for the poor dear, we handed him a dollar for his effort.

Since we flew home, Mother has become convinced our subway experience of hearing a trio, a duet, and a soloist, on successive days and in declining order of enjoyment, was some sort of cosmic metaphor, a special sign that her life will soon be ending. Even though her health is excellent, she's descended into a blue funk, which is quite unlike her. She's stopped attending domino parties and no longer calls or visits her friends.

Mr. Mighty Brain, had we given more than a dollar per musician, could this cosmic allegory have been avoided? What, if anything, should I say to Mother?

Signed,
Disturbed in Denver

Dear Disturbed,

Mr. Mighty Brain believes the cosmos responds in equally quirky ways, whether your donation is one or two dollars per subway musician. On the other hand, a three-dollar donation buys you a half-pint of intergalactic mojo, while four dollars practically guarantees you a star on the Hollywood Walk of Fame and a lifetime pass to Graceland.

Since you evidently possess the financial resources to visit the Big Apple without having to drain your bank account and declare bankruptcy, you undoubtedly have the wherewithal to hire a four-piece mariachi band to perform on your mother's front porch. Now, this next part is important: make sure (a) your mother's inside, moping about her life being essentially over; (b) the band members are festively costumed and all under the age of 50; (c) the hunky lead guitarist winks at your mother and suggestively mouths the words, *"Senorita es muy bonita."*

Tip them four dollars each, and your lifetime pass to Graceland is certain to follow.

Dear Mr. Mighty Brain,

I work in a 52-story office building. There's an unwritten code whereby people riding the elevators look straight ahead, keep to themselves, and don't engage in chitchat.

A few days ago, a young man (probably an intern, judging from his short-sleeved shirt and mismatched tie) boarded our elevator on the ground level. As people exited on each floor, he called out to these complete strangers, "Have a good one!" On each successive floor, he chirped the same irritating farewell, varying it only slightly by saying, "Have a good 'un!"

Unable to contain my annoyance any longer, I asked the intern, "What the hell do you mean, 'Have a good one?' Why can't someone have three or four of whatever it is you want them to have? How about a dozen?" He looked at me as if I'd dropped a cobra in the elevator. The other passengers stared straight ahead and said nothing.

When we reached my floor, I stepped out of the elevator, only to hear the intern loudly grumble to the remaining riders, "Gee, that guy was an old curmudgeon, wasn't he?" Before I could turn around and defend myself, the doors closed.

I haven't seen the intern again, so maybe he's back in college. Either that, or he's now using the stairs. Mr. Mighty Brain, am I really a curmudgeon? I thought I was just an ordinary citizen defending the rights of others to travel in peace, but now I'm having second thoughts.

Signed,
Grumpy in Houston (Maybe?)

Dear Houston Grump (Maybe),

Mr. Mighty Brain believes that throughout history, curmudgeons have been saddled with a bad reputation. These misunderstood patriots perform a service by commenting on the annoyances of life without kowtowing to political correctness or worrying about offending the self-proclaimed oppressed. In short, they call a spade, a spade. An idiot, an idiot.

Granted, the messengers of truth are sometimes a bit grumpy when they speak, but this grumpiness is often a superficial affectation, not an accurate reflection of their organic being. Mr. Mighty Brain is not entirely sure what the previous sentence means, but he loves the way it sounds, nonetheless.

And so, Mr. Mighty Brain has devised a simple test for curmudgeonry. If, after reading the following vignettes, you find yourself identifying with these examples of life's annoyances, consider yourself a bona fide curmudgeon.

1. You made a bargain with the devil and agreed to shop at Walmart. After avoiding the reptile from high school who now works in electronics, you drive your wobbly-wheeled basket toward the 87 checkout lines, discovering that - surprise, surprise - only two are staffed. You roll into place behind a grandpa with B.O. and a woman appeasing an ill-behaved preschooler who's throwing a stage-five tantrum because his mother isn't buying him M&M's. When you scowl at the kid, he glares at you and calls you a "Poopyhead." The mother smiles and says, "Isn't he just precious?"

2. Needing to book a flight out of town, you discover your computer is on the fritz, probably from all the red wine you spilled on the keyboard the prior evening. You phone the airline and learn that although Air Tarantula deeply values your business, the waiting time for speaking to an agent is approximately 57 minutes. Just as your patience wears Saran-Wrap thin, you're connected to a synthesized voice, which, for "security purposes," requires you to divulge your mother's maiden name, your hat size, and the name of the person you first French kissed.

Unfortunately, the computer has difficulty deciphering a Texas accent and transfers you to a trainee in Upper Mongolia. After ten minutes of explaining to the Mongolian that Washington is a state as well as a city, you hear a click as the line goes dead. When you call back, the waiting time is now 74 minutes.

3. After a co-worker suggests you join Facebook so you can "keep up with your old classmates," you're bombarded with 46 requests to become friends. Out of guilt, you spend the next four hours replying to mind-numbing emails from people you don't really like, reading narcissistic blogs from people you don't care about, and uploading photos you'll later regret. Early the next day, you handle 68 additional requests and responses. You feel like a lab rodent trapped in an evil-scientist's laboratory and want to strangle the co-worker who suggested you join Facebook, only to learn she now wants you to join Twitter.

4. Your original Air Tarantula flight was late taking off because the pilot was drunk and had to be replaced by someone more sober. Your plane lands 45 minutes late, and you dash through the airport, desperate to make your connecting flight. Completely out of breath, you arrive at the gate just as the agent closes the door to the jet bridge. Even though the aircraft won't leave for another twenty minutes, the frumpy agent says you'll have to rebook on a later flight. When you point out it will take her fifteen minutes to reroute you onto another flight but only fifteen seconds to open the door and let you board, she threatens to call security because you're "being abusive." Six hours later, you're jammed into the middle seat of the airplane, seated between a backpacking college student who hasn't showered in weeks and a ten-year-old girl with whooping cough. A surly Air Tarantula flight attendant, old enough to be your great-grandmother, offers to sell you a bottle of water for three dollars and a bag of stale peanuts for six. ✪

Rooming With Jose Cuervo
(Or How I Survived the)
(Oklahoma Writers' Conference)

9:00-9:45am	Welcome Address	Mrs.
10:00-10:45am	General Session	Writer
10:45-11:00am	Break With Exhibits	
11:00-11:45am	Breakout Session	Romar Does Y
11:00-11:45am	Breakout Session	The 00 Lessons from a r
12:00-1:00pm	Luncheon With Keynote	The Tw Dr. Gen
1:00-1:45pm	Breakout Session	
1:00-1:45pm	Breakout Session	Create A
10:45-11:00am		Social Me How to E
2:00-3:30pm	Break With Exhibits	
	Closing Session	
		Panel Dis Policy and

Unfortunately, the c
next to the Mother Ea
last year's banquet. Sh
screenplay about a vam
as a private eye.

ink Dracula meets Sam S
ned, and then proceed
ut of our table's convers
plaining the tedious a
rpiece. To top it off, th
ke a compost pile go

SEVENTEEN

*Rooming with Jose Cuervo
or How I Survived the
Oklahoma Writers' Conference*

The perky, twenty-something-year-old clerk hands me my room key and smiles, revealing a mouth full of gleaming-white, perfectly straightened teeth, which probably paid for some yuppie orthodontist's ski trip to Vail.

Her nametag reads "Ann-Marie," but could easily have been "Smokin' Hot." I reciprocate the smile, which is 100% recently divorced sincere.

➡

Straight from the Embassy Suites training manual, Ann-Marie says, "Don't forget our complimentary happy hour at five."

"Trust me, I know the drill on free booze," I say, a nanosecond later adding, "Will you be there by chance?"

Taking a moment to process my question, she answers, coyly, "Maybe. I normally go home about that time."

Fueling-up during happy hour, as well as tapping into my own tequila stash, is essentially my strategy of getting through the weekend, and it would be nice to include Ann-Marie as a further diversion. I've been dispatched to the Oklahoma Writers' Conference, where I'm a "shoo-in" to receive an award tonight for book of the year, according to Collin, my prissy but demanding publisher. Of course, that's the same thing he said last year, and I wound up with absolutely zilch. *Nada. Bupkis.* Not that I'm bitter or anything.

"It's the key to marketing your new book," Collin, the devil's second cousin, said last week. "Surely, you can park your assy attitude in Houston for a whole day, get off your arrogant high horse, and attend the awards ceremony."

"Assy and high horse? How clichéd," I said. "Collin, you can do much better than that."

"OK, then, quit acting like a narcissistic matador and get up to Oklahoma City."

Frankly, I'd just as soon have had an angry bull run over me as spend the weekend with writers, but unfortunately, I'm under contract to a guy who gets hand-me-down horns and red body suits from Satan. So, I surrendered my matador's cape and mirror, and booked a flight to Oklahoma City.

The lobby crawls with conference attendees, milling around the temporary display tables, manned, for the most part, by manuscript editors trolling for fresh meat. One of the hungriest, a nice-looking blonde dressed in a white lab coat, drapes a toy stethoscope around her neck and calls herself "The Book Surgeon." Apparently, she performs triage for aspiring writers whose manuscripts require appendectomies, lobotomies, or euthanasia. While the medical shtick is clever enough, her latex gloves seem a bit over the top, creating a fashion statement more reminiscent of a proctologist than a surgeon. Granted, I've known editors who've dealt with material so execrable, they *deserved* to be called a Book Proctologist, but hopefully, it wasn't because of anything I'd written.

The Book Surgeon recognizes me from across the lobby and gives me a thumb's up, silently mouthing, "Good luck." Even though she's parading around in a doctor's get-up and dispensing "editing prescriptions," she was actually one of the more normal people here last year.

At the table next to her is a pudgy fellow who bills himself as "The Word Astronaut." He poses awkwardly next to a poster-board sign, festooned with comets and swirling galaxies, which reads "Taking your manuscript to out-of-this-world levels!" Dressed in a stiff, NASA-looking space suit, he looks more like the Michelin Man than an astronaut.

After settling into my room and resisting the urge to guzzle my emergency bottle of Jose Cuervo Tequila, I wander down to the members' luncheon, and quietly slip into the back of the room, hoping to go unnoticed. Unfortunately, the only available chair is next to the Mother Earth chick I met at last year's banquet. She'd written a screenplay about a vampire who doubles as a private eye. "Think Dracula meets Sam Spade," she explained, and then proceeded to squeeze the life out of our table's conversation by tediously explaining the tedious details of her tedious masterpiece. To top it off, the woman's breath smelled like a compost pile gone horribly wrong. I'd have sliced off my little toe, maybe even my big one, for a mint to give her. Having learned my lesson, I always bring along Altoids, in addition to mosquito repellent, when visiting Oklahoma.

"No, please join us," she says,
scooting the chair out for me. "I'm Micki.
We sat together last year. Remember?"

"Is this seat saved?" I whisper, hoping Mother Earth won't remember me.

"No, please join us," she says, scooting the chair out for me. "I'm Micki. We sat together last year. Remember?"

I'm tempted to respond by offering an Altoid, but decide against it. "Sure, you had the vampire screenplay."

Excited I remember her, albeit for the wrong reasons, Micki drones on about her latest project, something called "What Time Is It Where You Live?" I don't pay any attention to the genre or plot description, because after ten seconds she sounds like the adults on the "Charlie Brown Christmas Special," the trombone-like voices you can't understand.

Mercifully, our server delivers our food, granting me a reprieve from Mama Motormouth. It's is a repeat of last year's meal: half a pickle, a piece of red cardboard cleverly disguised as a tomato, and a turkey sandwich so stale, survivalists may have hoarded it for the Y2K scare.

A dour-looking woman, about as pleasant as a wildebeest, calls the meeting to order. In a flat, colorless voice, she introduces the incoming slate of officers, a herd of similarly unpleasant, unsmiling creatures. Undoubtedly, at their nominating meeting earlier in the year, the other wildebeests whinnied and pawed in the dirt, complaining about the "lack of new blood" in the organization. Of course, this was the same dentured-up committee who refused to include anyone in the new officer team who wasn't addicted to Metamucil.

Madame Wildebeest monotones the locations of the break-out sessions, a series of mini-seminars the conference program teases with "Does your bodice-ripper lack zest?" and "Create authentic alien dialogue!" Both sound weird enough, but I decide on "The 007 Session," pimped as "Lessons in writing cloak and dagger thrillers from a real-life, retired spy!"

It turns out, 007 is a former CIA paper-shuffler, a low-level desk jockey who'd never been issued a gun or a suicide pill, and probably kept closer tabs on the office water cooler than rogue nations' nuclear capabilities. Wearing an ill-fitting toupee so obviously fake, one of the agency's spy satellites could have identified it from outer space, the man's sole qualification as session leader, evidently, is his recent *AARP Magazine* article, "How to Retire Gracefully on a CIA Pension." Oh sure, his black turtleneck, always the sign of an award-winning author, turbo-charges his macho look, but unfortunately, supersized dandruff flakes on the sweater's surface betray a secret-agent *faux pas*. Five minutes before James Bond finishes his lecture, I sneak upstairs and break the seal on the tequila.

Emboldened by a couple of shots of agave juice, I decide to check out the bodice-ripping seminar, "Romance Writing and You." A standing-room-only audience of plump, middle-aged women, along with one person of indeterminate gender, are mesmerized and pied-pipered by the big-haired and over-mascaraed speaker at the front of the room. A serial divorcee, the woman reminds me of a *grand dame* Dallas TV anchor. Seeming to absorb vaporous caffeine from the audience, she paces back and forth, over-gesturing and raving about modern romance-writers blurring the lines between sensuous romance and salacious porn.

"The only exception to the 'show, don't tell' rule in romance writing," the *grand dame* says, waving her index finger, "is when you're dealing with sex." Almost pleading, she continues, "So, please . . . *please* leave it to your readers to imagine!"

I survey the room full of frumpy writers, whose daily exercise regimen likely consists of clearing paper jams from computer printers. It's a safe bet the only sex most of them will be having any time soon will be, in fact, imaginary.

It's 4:46 and I've plopped myself on a stool directly in front of the bartender. I ask, as politely as possible, if he'll open happy hour a wee-bit early.

"Can't," he apologizes. "Manager won't let me. They're pretty uptight about that, you know."

I slip him a ten-dollar bill and a bottle of *Cabernet* magically appears from under the counter. We chat about the freaky people attending the conference, such as the essayist who truly believes aliens have interbred with humans and are running our government. Of course, this premise is gaining credibility since the last election.

After we talk for ten minutes, the bartender asks, "So, what's a guy like you doing here?"

"What's that supposed to mean?"

He backtracks a little. "Nothing, really. Just that you seem, well, a little edgy about things. That's all."

"Lucifer's cousin made me come here. Says I'm a shoo-in for an award."

"Which one?"

I smile. "Second cousin, I think."

"No, man, which *award*?"

"Best juvenile book of the year."

He looks at me as if I have a third eye. "You're kidding."

"Nope. 'Randy and the Renegade Reindeer.' A slam-dunk best-seller, my publisher says."

"Oh," the bartender frowns, probably disappointed I hadn't written a Harry Potter sequel.

There's a tap on my shoulder, and when I turn around, Ann-Marie, the desk clerk, smiles.

I invite her to have a glass of wine, and a few minutes later, I ask if she'd enjoy going to

the awards banquet. She winces slightly, and I tell her it isn't really a date, just an evening out. I have no idea why I say that, but after the wine and four or five conversations with Jose Cuervo, it makes perfect sense.

"OK, I'll go," she says, surprising me. "I've done a little writing myself. Always wanted to know what real writers were like."

"Well, in full disclosure, Ann-Marie, I'm not sure how many real writers will be there. But, it's Oklahoma, so we'll at least get a decent steak."

She glances at her watch. "Give me an hour to run home and change,

OK?"

"You got a deal." I hand the bartender another ten spot and head up to my room to shower and tuck Jose into bed.

The awards ceremony is worse than I imagined, extending well past midnight. Although it could have easily ended two hours ago, Madame Wildebeest has allowed every winner, 24 all together, time for an acceptance speech. I'm sure even God and Jesus are bored to tears, having heard virtually every winner thank Them for (a) "allowing me to follow my dream of becoming a writer;" (b) "giving me the strength" to (fill in the blank); or (c) "providing me with a supportive husband and kiddos." Interestingly, the two male winners don't thank their spouses, probably because, like me, their wives left them for men with more rational and profitable professions.

Fortunately, my Cuervoed brain responds quickly enough so I don't stand and make a high-horse ass of myself.

Ann-Marie has been a real trouper, but since she's working tomorrow, my plans for later tonight are *kaput*. Still, she's an enjoyable dinner companion, and I'm considering a return trip to Oklahoma City under less goofy circumstances.

Finally, Madame Wildebeest, in her best Sominex-like voice, says, "And now, the award for juvenile book of the year." She offers the obligatory comments about "having so many quality entries" and "the judges struggling to choose this year's winner."

She announces the runners-up, and I quietly edge my chair away from the table, so it won't scrape the floor when I stand.

"And first place goes to Micki Gavin for "What Time Is It Where You Live?"

Fortunately, my Cuervoed brain responds quickly enough so I don't stand and make a high-horse ass of myself.

Amid the robotic applause from the bleary-eyed writers' group, Mother Earth strides to the speakers' podium. Turning to the audience, she gushes, "I just want to thank God for giving me such supportive friends." Then, looking directly at me, she adds, "And, you all know who you are."

Acknowledging Mother Earth's gaze with a smile as real as a cubic zirconia, I vowed to awaken Jose from his midnight snooze and engage him in an all-night slumber party. ✪

Walgreens
The Pharmacy America Trusts

7096468-AF

NO MORE OR LESS A MAN

HUDDLING BESIDE
THEIR TIRED-LOOF
BUICK, THE WOM
FLOUNDERED
THROUGH HER PUF
SEARCHING FOR
THE KEYS.
THE MAN WREST
WITH HIS WALKE
TRYING TO FOLD

MAY
DIZZI

THIS MEDICINE IS A(N) FILM-COATED WHITE
SCORED ROUNDED-SHAPED TABLET IMPRINTED WITH

EIGHTEEN

No More or Less a Man

The salmon-colored scar erupted just below the woman's throat and spilled down her alabaster skin, disappearing into a tasteful silk blouse. The cashier, years past retirement age, carefully slid my purchases across the scanner, treating the toothpaste and shaving cream as if they were fine china and delicate crystal.

➤

"Anything else?" she asked, her manicured fingers gently placing the toiletries in a Walgreens plastic bag.

I grabbed two Tootsie Pops from a display rack. "Better throw these in as well."

She smiled. "You don't look like a Tootsie-Pop kind of man."

"They're for my kids."

"How old are they?" Under the harsh fluorescent lights, her lineless face reminded me of an heirloom doll - a porcelain figurine accidentally dropped and broken, the pieces sutured together at her chest.

"Six and three."

"Great ages." She tapped the cash register's total key. "Three dollars, eighty-four cents, sir."

I glanced behind me. With no other customers in sight, I emptied my pocket change, selecting dimes and pennies for the exact amount. "Didn't get to tuck them in this evening. Guess I'm feeling a little daddy-guilt."

She sighed knowingly. "Enjoy them while you can. They'll be grown before you blink."

Gathering my plastic bag, I acknowledged her grandmotherly advice with a nod. "Yep. Grown up before you blink," I repeated, stealing one final look at the woman's scar, which attracted my curiosity. What caused the wound? Why was a woman of such refinement working the midnight shift in a store that smelled of shampoo and liniment?

The cashier casually traced the raised ridge with her index finger. "Ugly, isn't it?"

"I didn't intend to stare."

"That's all right," she said softy. "Heart surgery."

"How are you doing now?"

She waited a few seconds before answering, the silence of the empty store magnifying the pause. "Well, the truth is I'm not doing all that well, and I'm . . ." Her voice trailed off, as if she had more to say, but felt unsure if she could trust me with such personal information.

"I'm sorry."

Diverting her eyes from mine, the cashier stared at the counter and absentmindedly rearranged the pennies in a take-one-give-one ashtray. "It's just so hard right now. My daughter's in Michigan. Clarence lives in town, but he's too absorbed with his own problems to pay attention to anyone else's."

"Clarence?"

"My . . . my former husband. We were married 39 years." The cashier looked up from the pennies and wrinkled her brow. "Funny, even now I can't say ex-husband, for some reason."

The woman's body language hinted at additional chapters to the story, chapters she seemed desperate to retell. Although it was late, I decided to invest a few moments and hear more of her story. "So, what happened with you and Clarence?"

The cashier slowly shook her head, like a wounded war veteran remembering combat. She told me her husband, a deacon in their church, led the congregational singing during worship services. "They couldn't open the doors to that building without him being there."

"Baptist?"

"Third Street Baptist." Her eyes refocused on the penny ashtray. "And then..." She hesitated and softened her voice to a whisper. "And then... "

"Go on. I'm listening."

"And then one evening, I noticed a lump in Clarence's groin. At first, he refused to see a doctor, but it kept growing. Eventually, he had no choice but to see a specialist."

"What was it?"

"Advanced testicular cancer," she said bitterly, as if she wanted to punish the very words themselves. "His doctors advised radical surgery, but he refused the procedure. Clarence said he wouldn't be a man any longer." Her eyes moistened as she reached under the counter for a tissue. "Can you believe that?"

"It's hard to imagine."

She forced a smile. "I told him it didn't matter. He'd be no more or less a man to me."

The cashier's emotional transparency made me feel uncomfortable, as if my mother had revealed a dark secret about my father. But the woman's unvarnished honesty - her trust in me, a stranger - overrode my discomfort. "Did the doctors change his mind?"

"Eventually. But you know the sad part? He never went back to church." She folded the tissue and dabbed her eyes. "He said religion didn't matter to him anymore."

"Sounds like your husband was angry with God."

"I told Clarence he'd been treating God like a rabbit's foot or a lucky charm, but he wouldn't listen. Next thing I knew, he asked for a divorce."

"A divorce?"

"I think he directed his anger at me on some level, maybe because I found the lump. I don't know, really. He couldn't divorce God, so he divorced me."

The automatic doors swooshed open and an elderly couple entered. Wearing a faded housecoat and a flower-print scarf, the woman cradled the arm of her palsied companion, who balanced himself with a walker. The cashier and I paused our conversation, allowing the pair to pass the counter. The thin-faced man, his eyes cloudy with cataracts, relied on his wife for guidance to the correct aisle.

With the couple no longer within hearing range, the cashier continued. "Clarence and I divorced two years ago, but our retirement and social security aren't enough to cover separate households." She gestured to the wall of cigarettes and tobacco behind the counter. "No one would hire me but Walgreens. Thankfully, it's across town from my church. At least I don't see my friends here."

"I'm very sorry." My mind raced for something more profound to say, a few words of encouragement, perhaps. Nothing seemed remotely adequate.

"Then, six months ago, I had open-heart surgery." Her voice quivered. "Clarence was too wrapped up in his own self-pity to visit me in the hospital. He called and said it would stress him out too much. I said, 'Stress *you* out? Like it's a walk in the park for me?'"

"You have amazing strength," I said, magnetized again by the river-like scar flowing down this China doll's chest.

The elderly couple shuffled toward the checkout area. I stepped aside, allowing the wife, her hands arthritic, to rest a quart of orange juice and a dozen eggs upon the counter. Shaking, her husband reached for his wallet, but fumbled it to the floor. Bending down, I retrieved the billfold and handed it to the fragile man.

He smiled, a "Thank you," evident in his milky eyes. The old gentleman struggled to pay for the juice and eggs for his wife, a subtle but intentional act of chivalry, a display of manhood having nothing to do with virility or the absence of particular body parts.

After the elderly couple drifted out the door, I turned to the cashier. "You know, I'd better get home before my wife begins to worry."

"Thanks for listening."

"Things will be okay," I said, specifically not using the word *you*.

"Sometimes, I wonder." She handed me two more Tootsie Pops. "Give these to your kids. Tell them they're from a friend of their father."

I thanked her for the candy and gazed directly into the woman's misted eyes, careful to avoid the magnetism of her scar. "And may God bless you," I added. Not normally a religious person, my words - deeply heartfelt words - came as a complete surprise to me.

The cashier nodded in appreciation. "He just did."

Gathering my bag of toiletries and candy, I hurried through the pharmacy doors into the sticky, summer-night air.

Once in my car, I started the ignition, glanced in my rear-view mirror, and noticed the couple from Walgreens. Huddling beside their tired-looking Buick, the woman floundered through her purse, searching for the keys. The man wrestled with his walker, trying to fold it up. Finally unlocking the vehicle, the wife stowed the metal contraption in the back seat and opened the passenger door for her wobbling husband, who latched on to her arm and steadied himself. Bending down to lower himself into the car, the old gentleman hesitated, straightened up, and turned to face the woman. He kissed her tenderly on the forehead.

I reached for the plastic Walgreens bag and touched the rounded shapes of the Tootsie Pops inside. I thought of Clarence. I thought of what it meant to be a man. ✪

WEEK OF JUNE 12.

A New and Exciting Story,

Sweet Springs

FOR YOUR READING PLEASURE.

SET IN THE BEAUTIFUL AND WELL-DESIGNED
Grasshopper Bowl
(CAPACITY: 19,352)

STARRING: (IN ORDER OF APPEARANCE)

Sonny Slocum	Himself
Brenna Hobgood	Herself
Carole Simmons	Herself
Judge Ortiz	Himself
Sweet Springs Centennial Committee	Themselves
Butord Sargent	Himself
Conrad Stemple	
Bank President	} Himself
Grace Ann Sargent	
	Herself

ALSO FEATURING THE EXTRAORDINARY TALENTS OF
62 PAGEANT ACTORS AND STAGEHANDS:

Pony-Tailed Postal Workers, High-Booted Cowboys, Bubba-Fied Truckers,
Blue-Haired Country Clubbers, and an Emergency Room Physician.

Continuted on next page.

NINETEEN

Sweet Springs

Sonny Slocum breezed into the Denny's parking lot at the wheel of his top-down Corvette, each curl of his blond hair artistically jelled into position like a statue of a Greek god. Sporting a five-star-resort tan, wraparound-mirrored sunglasses, and a Hawaiian shirt unbuttoned to expose a forest of chest hair, the words "God's Gift to Women" might

➣➤

as well have been hand lettered in filigree across the door of the red convertible.

Straddling two parking spaces with his Corvette, Sonny snapped an aye-aye-captain's salute to Brenna Hobgood and me, the committee members assigned to greet him. Brenna acknowledged God's gift to women with an enthusiastic nod. Like a homecoming queen on a parade float, I waved mechanically and thought, *You cocky bastard, who in the hell do you think you are?*

Exactly eight weeks later, I would pen a note to my fiancé, telling him I'd be traveling for a few days - but not mentioning I'd be riding with the cocky bastard in the red Corvette.

———————

Sitting in the far corner of the non-smoking section of Denny's, all twelve members of the Sweet Springs Centennial Committee focused on the slides projected on the screen. Like a TV game-show host on autopilot, Sonny sailed through the PowerPoint presentation, completely mesmerizing his audience, including Judge Jay Ortiz, who usually nodded off during our meetings or diverted his attention to a 90-foot concrete grasshopper in the park just across the street. Silver-haired and 65-years old, he concentrated like a sixth grader hearing about the birds and the bees for the first time.

Brenna, my best friend and the manager of our local Barnes & Noble, leaned over and whispered, "Carole, I'll vote for Sonny Slocum's company no matter what he charges." She cut her eyes toward the speaker's trim waistline. "Can you believe that man's body?"

"Keep your britches on," I whispered back to my twice-divorced friend, who had a weakness for anyone with an Adam's apple. "He'd probably spend all evening preening in the mirror."

Sonny clicked to the next screen, an illustration of an Egyptian pyramid under construction, with hundreds of cheerful workers dressed in an assortment of color-coordinated, pastel loincloths. "Slocum Event Management produces a seamless, turn-key historical pageant," he explained. "We develop a script, direct the actual production, and help sell your sponsorships." Another screen showed a smiling Pharaoh, his arms folded confidently, posing on the steps of the completed monument. "Slocum lifts the heavy stones, but the Centennial Committee gets all the credit. You'll look like Pharaohs when we're done." Sonny paused, then faux-chuckled as he delivered the perfectly timed punch line. "Except we won't bury you inside the pyramid!"

Like a TV studio laugh track, we responded exactly on cue.

Zipping through the rest of his presentation, Sonny concluded the show by distributing a two-page proposal to the committee. His facial expression morphed from a television celebrity tossing off corn-fed jokes into a mortician assuring a family their loved one looked at peace. "Of course, we'll make certain the pageant maintains Sweet Springs' sense of decorum and dignity," he promised solemnly.

Brenna passed a note to me. *Dignity? I didn't realize having the world's largest concrete grasshopper was so dignified.*

I stifled a giggle and scribbled back. *Not to mention smelling like someone crop-dusted "Essence of Oil Refinery" all over town.*

Dissolving his funeral-home countenance, Sonny returned to his upbeat patter. "We've produced highly successful events in Austin, El Paso, and Midland. Now, the spotlight shines on Sweet Springs, Texas. The $52,000 cost," Mr. Velvet Voice said, "is a once-in-a-hundred-years' investment." He presented the final slide, a cartoon of three smiling businessmen clicking their heels as they delivered wheelbarrows of cash to the front steps of the Chamber of Commerce. "And here's the kicker. We'll help you raise the money faster than you can say Sweet Springs is one great town!"

With the directors murmuring their approval, Sonny asked if there were questions, and answered them with the finesse of a Broadway dancer. "Great issues you're raising," he schmoozed. "I had a feeling this was an intelligent crowd." Glancing in the direction of Brenna and me, the only women present, he winked. "Exceeded only by its good looks and charm."

Later that evening, the committee unanimously voted to hire Sonny Slocum as our Centennial Czar. After the meeting, I told Brenna he was the type of man who could buy a worn-out cotton rug at a flea market, claim its provenance was Persian, and offer you a bargain-basement deal on the 300-year-old classic. In your heart, you knew it was hogwash; but the words were so appealing, it didn't seem to matter.

228

Two months earlier, my septuagenarian partner, Buford Sargent, proposed that one of us serve on the Centennial Committee because of the good PR it would bring our insurance company. "Of course, if it'll interfere with your big wedding plans," he said, expertly spreading a thick layer of guilt, "then I'll volunteer myself." He coughed gruffly, subtly reminding me of his recent hospital stay.

Already feeling badly about missing so much work time, I surrendered. "I'll handle it, Buford. And don't worry, the wedding plans are pretty well cast in stone. Or at least moldable clay."

Still pale and drawn-looking, he paused, as if grappling for the right words to say. "Maybe your luck with men has changed." He raised his bristly eyebrows in an I-certainly-hope-so way.

"Maybe it has. Finally."

My ex-husband and I moved to Sweet Springs a week after we married. Freshly minted graduates of Sul Ross State, Joey rough-necked, and I landed a job with Buford's insurance company. While he bounced around in the oilfield, I worked my way into management and eventually bought half of the business. As an idealistic newlywed, I hoped to emery-board the rough edges off a husband who stored his fishing lures in our bathroom medicine cabinet and considered *Porky's Revenge* the greatest movie ever made. One afternoon, after discovering a truck's dismantled transmission in our bathtub, I realized Joey's rough edges were more like razor wire on top of penitentiary walls. Sitting on the edge of the bathtub, I blubbered through an entire box of Kleenex.

Buford, as much a father to me as a business partner, gently suggested I cut my losses before any baby Neanderthals came along. "Carole, don't live your life trying to change people who aren't willing to change," he'd said at the time. "Sometimes you need courage to make the tough decision, not worry about anyone else, and do what's best for *you*."

I took Buford's advice and never once regretted my decision.

After a couple of pointless relationships, Conrad Stemple entered my life. The youth minister at First Baptist church, he scored 110% on the decency scale, singing in the community choir and coaching Pee Wee Dribblers in his spare time. Two months after our first date to his church's Labor Day picnic, Conrad said he loved me and proposed marriage. It came as quite a shock, as up until that time, his greatest displays of affection had been holding my hand at the high school band concert and pecking my cheek when he said goodnight.

In contrast to Joey the caveman, Conrad watched *Discovery Channel* instead of reruns of *The Ultimate Fighter*, and studied the Bible rather than *Penthouse*. At 37 and on the backstretch of the Motherhood Derby, I thought Conrad seemed the best horse to ride - especially after handicapping the rest of the stable in Sweet Springs. Recognizing the cultural taboo of a professional woman in West Texas bearing a child out of wedlock, I accepted Conrad's proposal and assumed the romance would flower once we became engaged.

Between Christmas and New Year's, I helped chaperone his youth group to a Santa Fe ski resort. One night after the kids' curfew, Conrad and I met in his hotel room, microwaved some popcorn, and watched a movie together on the sofa. Leaning close to him, I casually suggested the idea of moving our physical relationship forward - if not to the black diamond run, at least to the bunny slope.

"Carole, ministers are supposed to lead exemplary lives," Conrad scolded, as if he were worried the senior minister of his church was hiding behind the drapes, ready to leap out and yell "Aha!" at the first indiscretion we might commit. "I hope you'll respect my wishes and wait until we're married," he said curtly, making me feel like an Old Testament harlot.

Not that I required a blast-furnace
physical relationship;
a Bunsen burner would have been just fine.

I'm sure Conrad didn't intend to hurt my feelings, but it was a defining moment in our relationship. There wasn't a mean-spirited bone in my fiancé's body, but there wasn't a passionate one, either. Not that I required a blast-furnace physical relationship; a Bunsen burner would have been just fine.

When we returned to Sweet Springs, I considered calling off the engagement, but knew my decision would tidal wave a church where the youth minister stood on a pedestal only inches lower than Joseph's and Mary's. Conrad would forgive me, but I doubted the other Baptists, several of whom were major customers, ever would. Many in his congregation were one-day-a-week Christians - scripture-quoting hypocrites who hated gays, uppity African-Americans, and any Jezebel who would leave their youth minister stranded at the altar.

So, I planned a late-summer wedding in the Baptist church. Conrad made reservations for our honeymoon at the Hampton Inn in Lubbock. I crossed my fingers, hoping he reserved a king-sized bed and not doubles.

With the energy of a springtime dust devil, the Sweet Springs Centennial Committee whirled into action. Six weeks before the Friday and Saturday evening performances, task forces mobilized for lighting, costumes, sound, scenery, and publicity. Brenna, along with the high school principal and Sonny, recruited 62 pageant actors and stagehands - pony-tailed postal workers, high-booted cowboys, bubba-fide truckers, blue-haired country clubbers, and even an emergency room physician.

The responsibility of helping Sonny raise sponsorship money fell to the president of First National Bank and me. With oil at $90 a barrel and rising, our assignment proved to be easier than the scenery committee's mission of constructing a ten-foot-paper-mache grasshopper, a replica of the concrete 90-footer across from Denny's. The committee rebuilt the prop's head three times before it resembled an insect and not an armadillo.

Sonny's home office in Omaha consulted with the local history teachers and the editor of the newspaper in developing the pageant script. Judge Ortiz and our beloved real estate diva agreed to narrate the action, as actors pantomimed 100 years of history in 90 minutes. One of the pageant's central themes would be Sweet Springs' transformation from a dusty afterthought of a town into a thriving, vibrant community - resulting from the discovery of the Grasshopper Oilfield. Unfortunately, the oil strike had zero effect on the dust.

A local rancher, Drum Mayfield, named the oilfield during the drought of the 1950's, when grasshoppers devastated everything in his pastures except tumbleweeds. Facing foreclosure, he sold his cattle at a substantial loss and leased the land to an oil wildcatter. Two years and 78 monster wells later, Drum turned the tables and purchased the local bank that had threatened his foreclosure. He also built a mega-mansion on the outskirts of Sweet Springs as tasteless as anything in Midland. Bouncing around his pastures in a Cadillac Seville, the rancher affectionately referred to the steel pump jacks as his "mechanical cows" and even assigned pet names to them - Hilda, Belle, and Blossom.

Mayfield, a deeply religious man, believed his good fortune resulted from divine intervention, as the Mormons thought God dispatched seagulls to Utah to eat crop-ravaging crickets in the mid 1800's. Just before the rancher died, and as a tribute to God's benevolence, he donated funds to construct a massive, concrete grasshopper on the outskirts of Sweet Springs. Mayfield hoped it would eventually become a tourist attraction; instead, the gray behemoth became the object of parody and ridicule by news organizations from *Fox News* to *Texas Monthly*. Even though outsiders loved to make fun of our grasshopper, we took pride in the giant insect. It was as if your cousin lost 200 pounds on the *Greatest Loser* reality show. You're embarrassed she's such a fatso, but stick up for her nevertheless. After all, she's family.

Set for early June, the pageant would be performed outdoors in the Grasshopper Bowl, our high school football stadium. Constructed with tax revenues generated from an underground ocean of oil, it featured state-of-the-art training facilities rivaling those of a major college. The school trustees instructed the architects to design the Grasshopper Bowl with seating for 19,352, exactly 50 more than Ratliff Stadium, home of our chief rival, Odessa Permian. Three years ago, the administration built a new campus, complete with junior varsity and varsity swimming pools, even though to this day, Sweet Springs has no aquatics team.

Three weeks before the centennial pageant, Brenna stopped by the insurance agency to renew her homeowner's policy. After chatting with Buford across the hall, inquiring about his health, she poked her head inside my office. "Hey, girl, you jacking up my premium so you can buy a bunch of fancy flowers for your wedding?"

"Yep, rare orchids from a rain forest in the Himalayas. Wait, the Himalayas don't have rain forests. Make it a Brazilian rain forest. An endangered rain forest." I gathered Brenna's paperwork and motioned for her to have a seat across from my desk. "Actually, your premium's the same rate as last year. A couple of minor adjustments, which I'll be happy to review."

"Don't bother," she said. "Just show me where to sign."

I handed her one of our freebie advertising pens. "So, how's it been to work with God's gift to women?"

"Carole, to tell the truth, I 'bout wet my pants when he first asked me to work with him," my friend gushed. "I told him I'd be more than happy to help with recruiting." Looking up from the policy's signature page, she raised an eyebrow suggestively. "And, anything else he needed help with."

I laughed. "OK, I'll bite. Did he accept your offer?"

"No, dang it. Maybe I should have been more direct." She tapped the plastic ballpoint against the policy and frowned. "Out of ink. When are you and Buford gonna spring for some decent pens?"

"Here," I said, handing her my platinum Waterford, the one Buford presented me when we became partners.

Brenna grinned. "Oh, this is much nicer!"

"Don't get too attached. I'm lending, not giving."

Scrunching her mouth, she butchered her signature as if it were a doctor's prescription. "It's just that Sonny always looks great, smells nice, and acts so, well, so *in charge* of things."

"That's what he does for a living, for cryin' out loud." I shoved a duplicate copy of the policy across the table. "Sign this one, too."

"The men in Sweet Springs are like this stupid ballpoint pen. Dried up and boring. Sonny's like this Waterford. You know, *stylish*."

"Brenna, you're acting like a schoolgirl with a crush on the quarterback of the football team. Trust me, Sonny Slocum has more notches in his bedpost than I have in my comb. And I have a very long comb."

"Well, it's pretty much a moot point. I don't think I'm his type."

"Oh? So, tell me, just exactly what is Sonny Slocum's type?"

"Beats me. Maybe it's you," she said with a bit of an edge. "He wanted to know your marital status."

"I hope you mentioned Conrad."

Brenna shrugged her shoulders. "I told him you were engaged, but that didn't seem to bother him."

Gathering the policies, I folded her copy into a manila envelope. "Brenna, just don't make a fool of yourself, OK?"

Rising from her chair, she nodded, but not convincingly.

Two days later, Sonny phoned and asked if we could strategize over two more sponsorship opportunities.

Even though it was a busy day, I met him at Leo's Café for the lunch buffet. Our other fundraising cohort, busy entertaining bank examiners, couldn't attend our meeting. Sonny and I cruised through the array of salads and entrees. When we returned to our table, he outlined his thoughts on the best candidates for the sponsorships. I offered an additional prospect, one of our long-time insurance customers.

At the mention of my client, Sonny smiled. "Carole, I've heard nothing but positive comments about your agency. Everyone in town says you're the best, hands down."

"Well, Buford's a legend in this business. I've just been lucky enough to tag along."

"From what I hear, Buford may have built the car, but Carole Simmons supercharged it."

"Supercharged? Come on, Sonny, you know us girls don't know anything about cars."

He smiled, leaned forward, and cocked his head slightly. "May I ask you a personal question?"

I grimaced. *OK, here it comes. Get ready for a mirrored-ball-at-the-prom moment when he asks if I'd like to dance.*

Without waiting for my answer, he continued. "Of all the nice people I've met in Sweet Springs, you don't seem to fit. I mean, it's a great place and all, but have you ever thought about living somewhere else?"

His question surprised me. Despite the ladies-man, say-anything-it-takes reputation I'd assigned to him, he seemed totally sincere. "Sonny, since the day I came here, I've found Sweet Springs to be a good place. Sure, there are places more cosmopolitan. More exciting, maybe. But we have good people here. Good schools, good churches." Conscious of how many times I used the word *good*, I continued my mantra, nonetheless. "And I make a good living here. Of course, it is hard to get good sushi around here, living this far from the coast. It's more like fishing bait."

He chuckled. "I don't know about the sushi, but I agree Sweet Springs is a good place. Sonny's gray eyes seemed to laser into my mind. "But the question, are you really happy here?"

"Why wouldn't I be? Happiness is a relative thing, you know."

"It doesn't have to be." He took a long sip from his iced tea. "I decided long ago to choose to be happy every day. Rain or shine. Rich or poor. Life's too short to be miserable."

"Come on, Sonny, you can't be happy every day of your life. Doesn't work that way. You can't always be Bubbles the Clown. Sometimes, you take what life gives you."

"Sorry, but I don't agree with that at all." Sonny turned in his chair and gestured toward the buffet line. "See all that food over there? All kinds of wonderful choices. I think life is like that buffet. Trouble is, most people pass through the line and go home hungry. Me, I fill my plate every day I'm alive. Not only the *good* food, but the *great* food. Sometimes I go back for seconds."

Finally, he spoke. "A minute ago, you talked about all the good things in Sweet Springs. I guess your fiancé falls into that category?

I smiled. "Well, if you go back for seconds, don't you pack a few pounds on your butt? Maybe get indigestion occasionally?"

Sonny laughed, revealing the whitest teeth I'd ever seen a man have. "OK, occasionally you get a little indigestion. But it's worth it."

The waitress delivered our check, and I assumed we were finished with our meeting. Gathering my purse, I prepared to leave, but Sonny shifted uncomfortably in his seat, as if there were something else he wanted to discuss. It was the first time I'd seen a movement of his that wasn't completely confident and choreographed.

Finally, he spoke. "A minute ago, you talked about all the good things in Sweet Springs. I guess your fiancé falls into that category?"

"Conrad's a fine person."

Sonny seemed to study my eyes, processing my response. "Yeah, I've met him. Straight arrow." He paused again before asking, "You love him?"

"Come on, you're sounding like a *Cosmo* writer. Why would I marry someone I didn't love?"

"You don't have to defend your answer, Carole. I just asked if you loved him."

Instinctively, I swallowed, a reflex I hoped Sonny didn't notice. "Of course I love him."

He nodded in the direction of the buffet line. "Does he make you happy?"

My thoughts flashed to the Santa Fe ski resort, and I tried not to project the gnawing in my stomach. "If Conrad didn't make me happy, I wouldn't marry him."

Sonny didn't seem to be convinced. "If that's true, then he's a very lucky man." He glanced at the lunch check and reached into his wallet. He chose a couple of tens and tapped the cash against the table, almost as if he were asking a blackjack dealer for another card. "You know, with all the stress of a wedding, it'd be nice to take a couple of days and clear your mind. Relax a bit, maybe sort a few things out." The poker player in him paused for a moment, then tapped the cash against the table one more time. "I'm leaving for New Orleans the Sunday morning after we finish the pageant. You're welcome to come along for a couple of days. No strings attached. No one has to know."

Driving to work the next morning, I felt a mixture of guilt and anger. It was as if an interior decorator walked into your home and said your furniture was dowdy and you needed new drapes. You'd be angry and would want to say, *Damn it, the floral sofa belonged to my mother; the wing-backed chairs were the first pieces of real furniture I bought on my own; and the drapes are all I can afford right now.* But, you feel a little guilty because the interior decorator nailed it perfectly. And even worse, you find yourself attracted to the man, even though you're old and wise enough to know better.

I wasn't naïve enough to think Sonny's invitation to New Orleans came with no strings attached. In fact, considering the lack of passion in my life, the fringe benefits sounded pretty darn attractive. Still, Sonny's offer reminded me of the rattlesnake roundup our chamber sponsored every spring. Professional snake handlers protect themselves with heavy gloves and boots because they know the snakes will bite, if given half a chance.

Settling in at work, I listened to a phone message from Grace Ann Sargent, my partner's wife, saying she'd taken Buford to the hospital. I phoned her back and left a voice mail saying I'd stop by later in the afternoon to check on them.

I finished at the office shortly after lunch and drove out to our regional hospital. A state-of-the-art facility, it was a healthcare magnet for the small, dried-up communities in our area. I popped over to the maternity ward and admired the newborns, always a part of my hospital ritual, before taking the elevator to the patient wing.

Grace Ann stood outside the door to her husband's room. As soon as I saw her dulled, ashen-colored face, I knew Buford was gone.

I reached out to Grace Ann. "I'm so sorry."

She collapsed into my arms. We embraced in silence.

———————

Although my partner and I often discussed business continuity in the event of his passing, those conversations seemed like scenes from early silent movies - grainy and disjointed. Eventually, I would file a life insurance claim with Regency of Boston. Always a planner, Buford arranged for the company's insurance to purchase his share of the business, leaving me with 100% ownership. As a symbol of my love and appreciation for him, I signed the claim form with my Waterford pen.

The funeral at the Methodist Church, a week before the pageant, was one of the largest in Sweet Springs' history. The crowd filled every seat in the sanctuary and spilled over to the prayer garden, where two video monitors broadcast the service. Seeing the number of people who mourned the loss of one of their own, reminded me of my conversation with Sonny, when I repeatedly used the word *good* to describe Sweet Springs. Without a doubt, it had been the right word to use.

Grace Ann asked me to be one of Buford's pallbearers, a mark of respect previously reserved for males in our community. As far as I knew, I was the first woman in Sweet Springs to be so honored.

Near the end of the funeral, the minister asked everyone to join hands and recite the 23rd Psalm, a long-standing tradition at our community's funerals. Most in attendance didn't bother to consult the printed words.

At the graveside interment, the other pallbearers and I filed by the bier and removed our boutonnières, placing the white carnations on top of the mahogany casket. Waiting outside the funeral tent, Conrad, looking handsome in his pinstripe suit, reached out to hug me. Careful not to let his chest touch mine, his well-meaning, but stiff movements reminded me of a giant erector set my nine-year-old nephew would construct. In my mind, I fast-forwarded to a day - one of those *good* days - when Conrad would learn I was pregnant and embrace me in the same robotic manner.

Friday night's centennial pageant delivered a smash hit, seamlessly blending a frontier spirit with old-fashioned patriotism. Beginning with a vintage-aircraft flyover, a former Army Ranger, now our local Lutheran minister, parachuted from one of the planes. Trailing grasshopper-green smoke from his Evel-Knievel-like jumpsuit, he landed on the 50-yard line and delivered the ceremony's opening prayer. The festivities ended with the high school band forming a giant grasshopper on the football field. As the musicians played "God Bless America," a dozen trick riders, carrying twenty-foot-long cloth streamers, weaved their ponies through the insect's wings, creating the appearance of the grasshopper taking flight.

The appreciative audience responded with a three-minute standing ovation, then hurried to their cars just in time to avoid a blistering thunderstorm. Everyone performed flawlessly, but the showstopper turned out to be a troupe of four-and-five-year-olds, costumed as tiny grasshoppers, skipping and hopping across the football field. Encouraged by the crowd's cheering, the star-struck preschoolers refused to surrender the spotlight and had to be herded back to their mothers.

Even with a soggy field, Saturday's performance ran smoothly, except for one minor foul-up midway through the performance. The head on the paper-mache grasshopper, evidently waterlogged by the previous evening's rain, began a slow-motion droop, as if it had become hungry and decided to nibble the grass. Brenna, helping to corral the rambunctious preschoolers on the sideline, instinctively rushed on to the field and steadied the grasshopper's head for the last half of the show. Judge Ortiz paused his narration and ad-libbed with a perfect quip about Sweet Springs having a female version of the little Dutch boy sticking his finger in the dike and averting disaster. The crowd roared with delight, and Brenna's do-whatever-it-takes response seemed a fitting metaphor for Sweet Springs transforming a potential disaster into something good, just as Drum Mayfield had done 50 years earlier.

The pageant ended with a fireworks display and an invitation from Judge Ortiz to attend Sweet Springs' *bi-centennial* event. "Ya'll come back to the Grasshopper Bowl, Saturday at 8 pm, 100 years from tonight," he

231

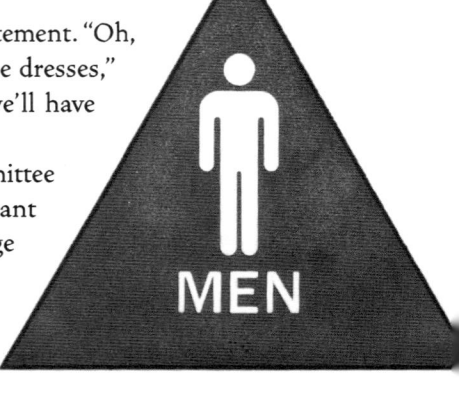

explained with typical West Texas understatement. "Oh, you ladies can go ahead and wear the same dresses," the judge deadpanned, "'cause by then, we'll have forgotten what you were wearing tonight."

Afterwards, the Centennial Committee hosted a party at Leo's Cafe for the pageant cast, crew, and volunteers. A hodgepodge of cowboys, nurses, truck drivers, and teachers jammed into the main dining room, clinking drinks and reliving the evening's fun. Conrad and I watched as Brenna, evidently still trying to become the next notch on Sonny's bedpost, fortified herself with a half-dozen *Chardonnays*. She'd managed to peel her target off from the rest of the crowd, cornering him in front of the hallway leading to the restrooms. Sonny steadily inched backwards, finally escaping Brenna's advances by disappearing into the men's room.

After twenty minutes of mingling with the other volunteers, Conrad announced he needed to "get a good night's sleep for church tomorrow." I followed him to his car, and as usual, he ended our evening by grazing a kiss to my cheek. He'd pick me up at my house tomorrow night at seven, he promised, and we'd have dinner at *La Paloma*. Conrad knew it was one of my favorite restaurants.

Back at the party, I spotted Brenna, now wobbly from too many glasses of wine. I offered her a ride home, but Judge and Terri Ortiz had beaten me to the punch. Acting like orderlies at a mental institution, they locked arms and escorted my best friend to their car.

With the party winding down, I decided to visit the ladies' room and head home. Just before I opened the door, Sonny made his break from the men's room, where he'd taken refuge.

"Is Brenna still here?" He glanced nervously about the reception area.

"You're safe," I answered, slightly embarrassed by my friend's behavior. "You looked like a wounded gazelle a few minutes ago. I though the lioness was just about ready to pounce."

Obviously relieved, he sighed. "Hey, I was on my way to thank you for helping with the fundraising," he said, "but Brenna cornered me. Carole, we couldn't have done it without you."

"Sure you could. You guys are pros."

"That's nice of you to say." His brow furrowed. "By the way, I'm so sorry to hear about your partner."

"They don't make men any better than Buford. I'll miss him."

Sonny paused and took a deep breath. "I'm still leaving for New Orleans early tomorrow morning," he said calmly. "My offer still stands. No obligation on your part - I promise."

"Unfortunately, my *Mardi Gras* costume hasn't come back from the drycleaners," I said, trying my best to laugh him off. When he didn't smile, I continued, "Sonny, even if I were inclined to clear my mind for a few days, it wouldn't be appropriate tagging along with you. You do remember I have a fiancé, don't you?"

He twisted his mouth slightly, as if he were nervous. "You're calling off the engagement, aren't you?"

Sonny's words stunned me. After several seconds of awkward silence, which only seemed to answer his question affirmatively, I blurted, "Why would you say something like that?"

"It's true, isn't it?"

"Sonny, it's none of your business."

"Look, even if you don't go to New Orleans with me, you're making a mistake with Conrad." Sonny shook his head. "I saw it in your eyes when we talked about him. He doesn't make you happy. And the worst part is, he never will."

His words made me feel as if my insides were falling out of my body. I wanted to argue, and, in some odd way, stand up for Conrad. But in my heart, I knew Sonny had discerned more about me in five minutes of conversation than Conrad Stemple had discovered in the six months of our engagement.

He moved to within a few inches of me, almost as if he wanted to touch. "I'll make you a deal," he said softly. "Tomorrow morning at eight o'clock, I'll stop by your house. Put your suitcase on the front porch and I'll know you're coming with me. Otherwise, I'll keep on driving."

At six the next morning, in one of the most irrational decisions of my life, I packed my suitcase. It was the Samsonite I'd purchased for the ski trip to Santa Fe.

Sonny would be a diversion, three or four days of blast-furnace hedonism, an escape from grieving over Buford's death and questioning my decision to marry Conrad. I'd phone Brenna and my office staff on Monday, telling them my aunt had taken ill, and I'd be visiting her until Thursday. Should any problems arise, they could reach me by cell phone or email. My office staff would be thrilled the boss was leaving town for a few days, but Brenna, inquisitive to the point of being nosey at times, would ask me about the details once I returned to Sweet Springs.

Over toast and black coffee, my stomach churned as if I were starting the first day of kindergarten. I checked my make-up twice and decided my shoes looked too sensible and boring. After trying on three pairs, I settled on strappy sandals I hadn't worn since my first marriage.

At seven thirty, I agonized over whether to call Conrad or write him a note. Running out of time and fearing an extended phone conversation, I scrambled to find my Waterford.

Conrad, I'm going out of town for a few days. I need to get away and sort some things out. Please don't contact me while I'm gone. We'll talk when I get back. Carole.

I folded the note and taped it to the front door, where Conrad would find it when he picked me up for dinner. Taking a deep breath, I rolled my suitcase onto the porch, in clear view of the street.

After checking the mirror one last time, I debated whether my sandals seemed too youthful for someone my age. *It's not an insurance convention, it's a fling in New Orleans. The sandals are fine.*

I gathered my wallet and keys, and remembered the Waterford I'd left on the kitchen table. Like my purse and lipstick, it traveled with me everywhere. When Buford presented the elegant pen to me, he said I was one of the most courageous people he'd met in his 50 years in the insurance business. Always someone who paid attention to small details, he had the word *Courage* engraved on the barrel. "Even when yours runs thin at times," he said with an impish grin, "you'll always have a little courage with you."

Turning the barrel of the pen over and over in my hand, I thought about what a good man my partner had been - never afraid of the future and always willing to make difficult and sometimes unpopular decisions. Buford also believed I had the courage to make difficult choices, and that I, too, was a *good* partner. Focusing on that pen, I realized I was running away from making a painful decision - the opposite of the characteristic Buford had seen in me years earlier.

Feeling a different energy, I sprinted to the front door and retrieved my suitcase and the note. Peeking through the curtains so no one could see me, I waited, gripping the Waterford pen with a force that turned my knuckles white. A minute later, a red convertible cruised the street and stopped at my curb. The driver, a man with perfectly mussed hair, adjusted his mirrored sunglasses and stared in the direction of my front porch. Tapping the Corvette's horn a couple of times, he glanced at his watch, and then drove slowly down the street and out of sight.

While Sonny Slocum didn't seem to be the kind of person who would patiently wait for something he truly wanted, I decided I could. ✪

LEARN TO SAY...

"NO WAY, JOSE"

BY DR. NOLAN WESTON

LACK CONTROL OVER YOUR LIFE?

Are the numbers on your credit card worn smooth from overuse? Tired of always being the one to cook Thanksgiving dinner?

Learn why saying "No" to others is really saying "Yes" to yourself.

You'll discover ten useful tips, illustrated with cheerful, easy-to-remember examples, guaranteed to clear your path to a fabulous job, top-rated credit scores, and fulfilling relationships.

OTHER BOOKS BY DR. WESTON:

- MY SELF
- TAKE IT EASY!
- WHO'S DRIVING THIS BUS?

THE WEST COAST'S **NUMBER-ONE** SELF-HELP BOOK.

TWENTY

Learn to Say "No Way, Jose"

Learn to Say "No Way, Jose"

Preface

Lack control over your life? Are the numbers on your credit card worn smooth from overuse? Tired of always being the one to cook Thanksgiving dinner? Because of people like you, dear reader, I've written **Learn to Say "No Way, Jose,"** *which remains the West Coast's number-one self-help book.*

In these easy-to-read pages, you'll learn why saying "No" to others is really saying "Yes" to yourself. You'll discover ten useful tips, illustrated with cheerful, easy-to-remember examples, guaranteed to clear your path to a fabulous job, top-rated credit scores, and fulfilling relationships.

Congratulations! You've taken the first step in gaining control of your life.

Dr. Nolan Weston
Carmel, California

Eighteen months ago, I bought a copy of **Learn to Say "No Way, Jose"** from a bulldog of a door-to-door salesman. Even though I didn't really want to buy anything from the guy, I figured it was the one book that might actually be useful. The fact is, I had a major problem saying "No" to people.

My $100-an-hour therapist called it "habitual people pleasing." After two years and $2,400 worth of counseling, Phyllis didn't cure my problem; but at least she gave it a name.

My need to please people was so intense I sent Oprah $25 to feed homeless cats after Hurricane Katrina, and I despise cats. A neighbor talked me into caring for her two scarlet macaws, even though my allergies go berserk around birds. If telemarketers had a Pushover Hall of Fame, I'd be enshrined with a life-sized statue. Once, over the span of 72 hours, I purchased two Veg-O-Matic slicers (to this day, still in their boxes), a personal sound amplifier (I'm not hard of hearing), and *The Complete Collection of Funky 60's Soul* (I'm as white as a Styrofoam cup and dance like one, too).

Even my own family took advantage of me. My older sister sold me enough Amway cleaning products to fill up half my storage closet - even a case of industrial-strength detergent for cleaning outdoor fireplaces, which I didn't need because I live in an apartment.

"Trust me," she said, "one of these days, you'll own a fabulous home with a couple of outdoor fireplaces, and then you'll thank me."

245

Self-Help Tip #1

When someone makes a request of you, it is perfectly acceptable to ask for time to consider matters before giving a response. That way, you can remind yourself the decision is entirely yours. Later, after thinking things over, you can politely, but firmly, say "No." Example: "Let me have a few days to think about investing in your Ethiopian ostrich and chinchilla farm, Carlos. I'll give you an answer next week."

I repair lottery ticket machines for the semi-sovereign state of Texas, although personally, I'd just as soon pitch silver dollars into the Brazos River as spend money on lottery tickets. My territory covers Fort Worth to Austin, which means I spend a week in steak-and-potatoes country, followed by a week in organic-quiche land. Smack-dab between the two cities is Waco, where I live - or, Wacky Waco, as some of us natives call it. Believe me, between all the Baptist Holier-Than-Thous and the Chicken-Fried Bubbas, it more than lives up to its nickname.

In Austin, I stayed at the Holiday Inn Express, the one on 290. That's where fifteen months ago I met Cynthia, the assistant manager. From ten at night to eight in the morning, she ran the front desk. Over the course of my every-other-week visits, we chatted every day. She was cute - great smile, nice personality, but slightly on the chubby side. Not as fat as Rosie O'Donnell, but a bit meaty in a few places. *Real* meaty in a couple of others.

Cynthia graduated with a home-economics degree from Texas State and kept the hotel's back-office TV tuned either to the *Home & Garden* or *Food Channel*. In her mid-30's, she'd never married, and I quickly learned her biological clock was ticking louder than Big Ben at midnight.

Three weeks after we met, I popped down to the lobby early one morning for a sweet roll and coffee. Cynthia was tidying up the breakfast area after a pack of junior-high girls, part of a gymnastics team staying at the hotel, had devoured most everything in sight. The leotarded nymphs left the buffet counter littered with milk-soggy Cheerios, wadded-up napkins, and pulverized bran muffins.

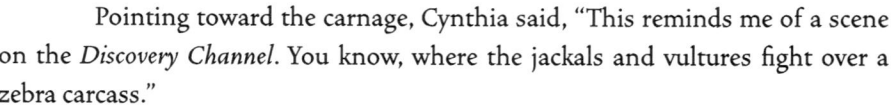

Pointing toward the carnage, Cynthia said, "This reminds me of a scene on the *Discovery Channel*. You know, where the jackals and vultures fight over a zebra carcass."

"Yeah," I said, "except the jackals probably have better manners."

Smiling, she grabbed the tongs, airlifted the one remaining cinnamon roll over to a black plastic plate, and offered it to me. "Aren't these just fabulous?"

"Best hotel breakfast anywhere, hands down. It's why I come here."

She raised an eyebrow. "Oh? I thought it was because you enjoyed seeing me."

"Well, of course, I like talking to you." I knew she was flirting, but I wasn't really interested in anything more than a hello-and-good-bye relationship.

"After work sometime, maybe we could go out for a drink."

"I'm not really much of a bar person, actually." It was a feeble rejection, about a "3" if I'd been scoring on Olympic rules. Maybe a "6" if I were a Russian, judging one of my countrymen.

"That's good, I'm not either." She seemed relieved. "I only mentioned it because I figured you liked going to bars. Most men are like that, you know. Me, I'm more of an IHOP or Starbucks girl."

"Yeah, I like IHOP, too." I wanted to reel in my words as soon as they left my mouth. Unfortunately, a rewind button isn't standard equipment on a male.

"That's cool. You want to meet for pancakes this afternoon?"

I stalled for time, remembering **No Way, Jose's** first self-help tip. "Umm, can I get back to you on that?"

"Sure," she chirped. "It's not like I'm trying to pressure you or anything. Just thought it'd be fun to hang out."

Five minutes later, as I dumped my plastic plate and coffee cup in the trash, Cynthia asked, "Well, now that you've had time to think, what about pancakes and decaf this afternoon? Maybe 5:30?"

I surrendered quicker than the French army. "Sure."

That afternoon we met at IHOP. After making small talk about our waitress' triple-pierced lips and barbelled tongue, Cynthia leaned across the table and playfully scrunched her nose. "You know, I've never heard you talk about a girlfriend."

"My work schedule pretty much puts the kibosh on any kind of social life."

She smiled, as if she were aiming an emotional Taser gun towards my chest. "Well, maybe you'll find someone while you're on the road." Cynthia gently rested her hand on mine, doing her best to close the sale.

Now fully Tasered, I placed my other hand on top of hers. "Yeah, maybe so." In the time it takes a time-share salesman to offer a "no obligation" vacation trip to Padre Island, I acquired a girlfriend.

Because of our schedules, Cynthia and I had to see each other between five and nine o'clock in the evenings. We'd have dinner, catch a movie, just normal stuff. Even though I wasn't attracted to her at first, her upbeat attitude worked like a super-charged magnet. When I wasn't in Austin, we talked on the phone every day. Even after I started dating Judy Lynn.

Self-Help Tip #2

Nonverbal assertiveness can reinforce your ability to say "No." Try looking into the other person's eyes and shaking your head as you say, assertively, "No, Claressa, I don't care to sneak your marijuana-infused Milk Duds into the movies."

The Texas lottery was marketed to a gullible electorate on the notion it would "benefit our school children" by providing extra funding for education. That's about as believable as bragging you talked Sasquatch into wearing a bikini and posing for your family's vacation photo.

Those of us who repair lottery machines have a special kinship. It isn't easy working in nasty truck stops where half the toilets haven't flushed correctly since Al Gore invented the internet. Basically, we install machines anywhere people spend cash. My boss said the Texas Lottery Commission would place machines in orphanages and nursing homes, if the payback was enough.

Six weeks after Cynthia and I began dating, I met Judy Lynn at one of our regional training workshops. The seminar speaker, who had a personality as plastic as VISA, assigned each person to a table, so we could "brainstorm ways to reduce overhead and operating expenses." Along with two other been-there-done-this-crap technicians, Judy Lynn and I drew the table at the back of the room.

Right after we were seated, she said, "Well, number one on my list would be to eliminate totally useless seminars like this."

Our group erupted in laughter, all of us veterans of mind-numbing meetings that were as helpful as lobotomies. Hearing the commotion, the clueless speaker eased over to our table. With a televangelist's sincerity, he asked, "Hey, guys, you getting a good dialogue going?"

Straight faced, Judy Lynn returned serve. "We were just discussing how beneficial this process could be."

Everyone at our table solemnly nodded in agreement.

"Su-per du-per," he said, his voice practically dripping with oil.

Judy Lynn lived and worked in Dallas, which has enough gambling-addicted losers to justify a full-time technician. Tall and rangy, her dishwater-blonde hair hung three inches below her shoulders - basically, a boots-and-blue-jeans-wearing woman who evidently classified make-up and lipstick as possible carcinogens.

Unlike me, Judy Lynn didn't seem to have a problem saying "No." She told our table about her boss recently asking her to fill in for a vacationing Lubbock technician. She couldn't find a babysitter for her four-year-old, so she declined the assignment. The boss wouldn't take "No" for an answer and said her job would be in jeopardy. So, Judy Lynn chinned up to the guy and told him to kiss her "freakin' pink bohunkus." He looked at her as if she were speaking Mandarin Chinese. She said, "In case you didn't study redneck in school, buddy, 'bohunkus' means 'ass.' I assume you're familiar with the color pink."

Our table broke out in laughter again. By this time, the seminar speaker realized we were a school of caffeined piranhas and left us alone.

That evening after the workshop ended, the four at our table headed to a local dive for supper. The sign outside the entrance read, *If You're Satisfied With Our Service, Tell A Friend. If You're Not, Keep Your Mouth Shut Or Joey Will Beat You To A Pulp.*

Once inside, one of the other guys asked Judy Lynn if she was married.

"Not anymore," she said. "If somebody thinks doing time in the penitentiary is hard, they ought to marry a 'hobosexual.'"

I asked, "You mean homosexual?"

"Nope, straight as a two-by-four. But he always looked like a bum." She shook her head. "I'm no Miss America, but he actually went out of his way to look scraggily. Everybody on TV was talking about these stylish 'metrosexual' men at the time, so I started calling him a 'hobosexual.'" Judy Lynn rolled up the sleeve of her blouse, revealing a red, heart-shaped tattoo with the word "Danny" inscribed in black gothic lettering across the center. Pointing to it, she said, "I was pregnant as Arkansas trailer trash, and three weeks before the baby came, the son-of-a-snake disappeared. Left me high and dry. No child support, no forwarding address, nothing but this ignorant-looking tattoo. He even took the spare tire from my truck."

A slight ripple of discomfort seemed to wash over the three of us men, no doubt caused by our thinking about the various women we'd done wrong at one time or another. Gradually, the conversation returned to lighter topics, such as the flavor-of-the-month rumor about the Lottery Commission installing machines in funeral homes. At the end of dinner, the two other technicians said adios, leaving Judy Lynn and me by ourselves. She suggested we go somewhere for a nightcap. Although I was attracted to her sense of humor and ability to say "No," I felt guilty about two-timing Cynthia. Shaking my head, I tried to be assertive, as the self-help book suggested. "You know, Judy Lynn, I really should be getting back to the hotel."

She scoffed. "For crying out loud, I'm not asking you to sleep with me, just have a drink. If you don't like liquor, we can grab something else. Maybe a cup of decaf."

It was as if a weeping Sally Struthers herself had requested a donation to feed starving Mongolian children. How could I resist?

Self-Help Tip #3

Instead of directly refusing the person's request, suggest an alternative. Example: "Elliott, instead of playing Russian roulette with that pistol, perhaps we could visit a shooting range and take a round of target practice. It would be more amusing and considerably less bloody."

Once I dealt with the guilt, dating two women in different cities was a piece of cake. But over time, it became more like eating cake plopped on top of beef stew. Individually, the foods are fine; together, they have a tendency to cause a serious case of indigestion.

Whenever I worked the Ft. Worth area, I drove over to Dallas to see Judy Lynn a couple of times a week, usually staying over for the weekend. Mindy, her little girl, was shy around me at first, but gradually warmed up after I renounced my dignity and played Barbies with her one evening.

Judy Lynn kept me laughing with her half-a-bubble-off-plumb view of the world - like the bumper sticker on her pick-up truck that read *"Yes, Six Miles Per Gallon. Got a Problem With That, Hoss?"*

Because of her ex-husband pulling a Houdini, Judy Lynn seemed anxious to find a replacement daddy for her little girl. I became the *numero uno* candidate one weekend when I gave Mindy several mini-bottles of Holiday Express shampoo and a couple of cheesy toys I'd bought at Wal-Mart. In return, she colored and presented me with pictures of "money-monies," the four-year-old's term for lottery machines. After that, Judy Lynn started wearing make-up and telling her friends about finding a "good man" she could "settle down with." If she'd known about Cynthia, I'd have moved from "good man" to "scum of the earth" quicker than Al Sharpton elbows his way to the front of a news camera.

The first time Judy Lynn came to Waco, her mother babysat Mindy. Her visit to my apartment seemed more like a background check, as if she were searching for chopped-up body parts stashed in my freezer. Of course, even if I'd dismembered a prior girlfriend, there wouldn't have been room in there because of all the Amway food supplements I'd purchased from my sister.

Cynthia was also a bit apprehensive about her first visit to my apartment, but seemed more uncomfortable with my bachelor décor than discovering a freeze-dried ex-lover. In fact, on her second trip, she brought a new mold-resistant shower curtain and a dried-floral centerpiece for the coffee table, replacing the priceless orange traffic cone from my college days.

Cynthia worked every other weekend at a daycare center, getting her "baby fix," as she not-so-subtly called it. On non-work weekends, she wanted to cocoon and cook - preparing exotic appetizers, fancy main courses, and complicated desserts - the whole nine yards. Basically, if Martha Stewart ever started a suicide cult, Cynthia would stand in the rose-garden gazebo, bullhorn in hand, directing the other sect members as they drank the mango-and-hibiscus-infused Kool-Aid.

One weekend, Cynthia whipped up two pans of lasagna *Florentine*, the recipe courtesy of the *Food Network*, as well as two chocolate-pecan pies, recipe courtesy of her grandmother in Houston. We ate one lasagna and pie, and saved the extras in the freezer.

Two weeks later, Judy Lynn traveled to Waco and suggested we picnic at a state park near Lake Whitney. While rummaging through my refrigerator, she discovered the frozen lasagna and thought it would be perfect for our little outing.

Feeling my face flush, I kept my cool. Right out of **No Way, Jose's** playbook, I suggested an alternative. "How about we pick up some pizza or fried chicken, instead? It'd be right on the way."

"But I'm in the mood for Italian."

"Pizza is Italian."

"No, it isn't," she said, with a men-are-so-stupid tone in her voice. "*Americans* invented pizza. We just gave it an ignorant name that sounds Italian."

I wanted to pause our conversation while I read ahead in the playbook, but there wasn't time.

Naturally, we took the lasagna to the picnic, and afterwards, Judy Lynn said she was impressed with my cooking. "You're the first man I've ever dated who could cook something besides hot dogs and boiled eggs."

"Well, to be honest, I didn't make the lasagna myself." A slight understatement, and another example of males needing to be equipped with a rewind button.

"Oh? Who did?"

There comes a point in every relationship where a tiny, courtesy lie is appropriate; in this case, a Godzilla-sized falsehood was required. "Actually, my mother made it."

"Well, she's a great cook." Judy Lynn seemed to believe the lie. "You suppose I could get her recipe?"

"Umm, I don't think she uses one. But I'll ask."

I hoped the issue would die, but a week later, Cynthia visited my apartment. She poked around in the freezer, searching for her made-from-scratch masterpiece, and asked what I'd done with the lasagna *Florentine*.

Fortunately, I'd prepared for her question with another Godzilla. "Well, I defrosted the freezer, Cynthia, but after I unloaded all the food, I forgot to put the lasagna back." I shook my head gravely and scrunched my nose. "It smelled pretty nasty after three days on the counter."

Cynthia looked at me as if she were encountering a three-headed alien. "I can't believe you actually defrosted your freezer."

"Yeah, it needed it."

She shook her head. "You had a traffic cone for a centerpiece on your coffee table and a science experiment growing on your shower curtain, but you know how to defrost your refrigerator? You're the first man I've ever dated who even knew it needed defrosting." Peering inside the freezer again, Cynthia pushed aside the boxes of World's Finest Chocolate I'd purchased from the local 4-H club. "So, how come the pecan pie's still here?"

I'd forgotten about the pie, and was fresh out of Godzillas. "How about if we go to this really nice Italian place I know? They've got the second-best lasagna in Waco, next to yours. Then, we can come back here and have pie for dessert."

She smiled. "OK, but why don't you just fess up and say you got hungry and ate the lasagna? That would have been OK with me."

Self-Help Tip #4

Practice saying "No" in front of a mirror, so the words flow easily and naturally. Rehearse such phrases as "Thanks for asking, Natasha, but I'm afraid an eyelid piercing wouldn't work for me," or "No, Dikumbu, I don't care to order a three-year subscription to American Unicycle Magazine."

After avoiding a midair collision over the lasagna incident, I needed to spill my guts to someone. I considered calling my sister, but knew she'd sell me more of her Amway stuff. Phyllis, my therapist, was the logical choice. Even though I'd skipped several counseling sessions, I called and asked for an appointment ASAP. She seemed a little irritated I'd "abruptly stopped our regular visits," but agreed to see me the following Saturday.

Located in the basement of her 1950's-era split-level, Phyllis' counseling office always smelled of lavender air freshener, which seemed to emanate from the adjacent bathroom. It made me wonder if the anticipation of my visit triggered some sort of gastrointestinal response from the therapist.

As usual, Phyllis asked me to sit on the couch, while she held court at her desk. "So, how are you *feeling* right now?" She lit a cigarette. "Oh, I think I asked you previously, when you kept consistent appointments, if you minded if I smoked."

"Sure, go right ahead," I said, even though I wished she wouldn't.

"OK, then, let's get started." A large woman, Phyllis constantly snacked on a bag of Cheetos between cigarettes. When we shook hands, I always felt like wiping mine, lest they acquire a slightly orange hue. Between the chain-smoking and looking like Moby Dick's little sister, she obviously had her own problems saying "No." Like a lot of therapists, she was great at pointing out others' issues; not so good in recognizing her own.

I took a deep breath. "Well, my life has become pretty complicated lately. I'm dating two women, one in Dallas and one in Austin. And, it's beginning to cause some issues."

"Like what?"

"Well, for starters, they're about as opposite as you could imagine. One drinks Lone Star Beer in a can, wears Levi's, and mounted a gun rack in her truck. The other one drinks organic green tea, loves Capri pants, and keeps a crocheting project in her Prius in case she gets stuck in traffic. It's as if I'm dating a roller-derby queen one week and a debutante the next. The thing is, I think I'm in love with both of them."

Phyllis casually waved her cigarette in my direction. "Wow, you do have some issues."

I explained the lasagna episode and how stressed I'd become keeping up with both women's likes and dislikes. "Basically, I need a spreadsheet."

"A spreadsheet?"

"Yeah, to track which topics I've already discussed. I have to focus and think through every answer to every question they ask me. The pressure's getting to me."

I spent most of the hour session responding to endless variations of the same question from Phyllis: How did I feel about the situation? How did I *feel* about commitment? How did I *feel* about Cynthia? Judy Lynn? Both women were wonderful, I said, but in very different ways, and I didn't really want to choose between them.

"Have you considered telling Cynthia and Judy Lynn about the existence of the other?" Phyllis took a drag from her cigarette and exhaled through her nose in a slow, calculated manner. "I mean, wouldn't that be the honest, straightforward thing to do?"

"Frankly, neither of them would respond very well to that information. I'd either be tied up with a lariat rope and drug behind a pick-up truck or suffocated with a spinach and artichoke soufflé."

"OK." She plopped a Cheeto in her mouth. "Then the question is how would you respond to losing them?"

It was vintage therapist psychobabble: never any concrete solutions, just open-ended questions. "Well, Phyllis, I suppose I'd respond by wearing out my PlayStation on the weekends, all alone, because both of them would trash me like an empty beer can."

She glanced at her watch and forcefully snubbed her cigarette into an ashtray. "I'm sorry, but it looks like we're out of time for today." Rising from her chair, always her signal it was time to pay up, Phyllis asked, "Do you want to call me when you're in the midst of a crisis, or would you like to schedule something for two weeks from now?"

Earlier in the day, I'd stood in front of a mirror, just like the book said, and practiced saying, "No, Phyllis, I'm not coming back anymore unless you give me some solid advice I can really sink my teeth into." Instead, I said, "Ok, how about ten o'clock, two weeks from today?"

Self-Help Tip #5

Remember to separate refusal from rejection. You're turning down a request, not a person. "I have nothing personal against you, Harriet, but I'm simply not interested in trudging outside in this blizzard and scooping the dog poop in your backyard, while you sit by the fire, sip hot cocoa, and address your Christmas cards."

The following Monday morning, I waited to check in to the Holiday Inn Express behind a guy wearing an airline pilot's uniform. In his early 30's, the lanky man had a receding hairline with a widow's peak that looked like the Florida peninsula. As he checked out, the pilot mentioned something about flying to New York City later in the morning.

Cynthia said, "Oh, this is the week for the New York Fancy Food Show. I'd give anything to see all the crazy new food ideas."

The pilot joked that he'd love to give her a free ride, but the flight was completely sold out. He picked up his receipt and stepped around the corner to the elevator.

As usual, I was chipper. "Hey, Cynthia, speaking of freebies, how about a free room tonight?"

"Darn. I'm fresh out." She smiled. "Come back in two weeks and see if I have any by then."

I raised one eyebrow and winked. "Should I try sweet-talking the night clerk?"

"That won't get you a free room, but it'll get you a nice dinner later this evening."

"That's a deal. Six o'clock?"

"Great. I saw a bread pudding recipe on Paula Deen's show I'm dying to try."

Cynthia seemed busy. I said I'd see her later that evening, picked up my bag, and walked around the corner to the elevator. Just as I pressed the "Up" button, the door opened and the pilot, carrying an overnight bag and a briefcase, stepped out. As we passed, he nodded and disappeared around the corner.

Before stepping into the elevator, I realized my laptop was still in the car, and since my expense reports were due, I decided to retrace my steps and retrieve the computer. Walking toward the lobby, one step from turning the corner, I heard the pilot's voice.

"Hey, Cynthia," he said. "Thanks again for a great meal."

I stopped in my tracks.

"Glad you enjoyed it," she said.

"We have another lay-over a week from Wednesday. I think it's my turn to buy dinner."

"That would be wonderful." Cynthia sounded enthusiastic. A little too enthusiastic.

"How about Chinese?"

She laughed. "Well, if you're buying, I'm eating."

Somewhat shell-shocked, I decided to abandon the laptop and returned to the elevator. Pressing the second-floor button, my face felt warm, almost sunburned, as if I'd stayed too long on a Florida beach. I never cared for the Sunshine State, nor widows' peaks, for that matter. In fact, in my nighttime prayers later that evening, I'd ask God to smite Florida with a category-five hurricane as soon as possible.

It turned out to be a long morning. I repaired a lottery machine in a convenience store where the collective IQ of the three employees wouldn't have totaled triple digits, and after that, I stopped by a Vietnamese supermarket and lunched on a delicious mystery-meat burrito. For all I knew, the burrito could have been prepared with Fido, Fluffy, or road-kill possum, but I didn't care. It tasted great.

At five, I hurried back to my hotel room and reread parts of **Learn to Say "No Way, Jose"**, focusing on the sections that encouraged assertiveness. After showering and changing clothes, I drove over to Cynthia's place, my mind still obsessed with Florida widows' peaks.

Her brick and stone duplex is a couple of blocks off William Cannon Drive, in an area known for massive live oak trees and recent UT graduates looking to snag their first billion. When Cynthia opened the door, I smelled garlic and basil, which turned out to be wonderful-looking pastry appetizers, almost too beautiful to eat. Almost, but not quite.

In the kitchen, Cynthia worked alone on our salads, after politely refusing my obligatory offer of help. She rinsed the Romaine and chattered about the prior weekend, spent weeding her herb garden and pickling several jars of beets and carrots.

As she meticulously tore the lettuce into silver-dollar-sized pieces, I steered the conversation to what I'd been fretting about all day. "So, Cynthia, seems like a lot of airline people stay at your hotel these days." It was the oblique approach to interrogation, kind of like the beady-eyed IRS agent asking you to explain your deductions for monthly trips to Vegas for "church work."

Cynthia said, "We have a nice contract with American and Continental." She opened the refrigerator and grabbed a plastic jug of homemade Caesar dressing. "We get maybe 40 rooms a month out of the deal."

"You ever get to know any of those people? I mean, on a personal level?"

She stared vacantly at me for a moment, then remembered to trickle the dressing over the lettuce.

"For instance, do you ever socialize with any of them, that sort of thing?" Inwardly, I smirked, proud of being so assertive.

She turned away from me, toward the refrigerator, evidently unwilling to look me in the eye. "Well, yes, I have and will."

"Have and will?" My tone of voice sounded like a tenured Ivy-League professor baiting an ill-prepared freshman into giving another shoot-from-the-hip answer. "That's an *odd* choice of words."

She opened the refrigerator and returned the dressing to the shelf. Still not facing me, her voice seemed as warm as ice-water. "That means I've socialized with one person in particular, and will continue to do so in the future." Cynthia's don't-you-dare-go-there button had definitely been pressed. Maybe even pressed and held down for a while.

"Male or female?" I asked innocently.

She turned toward me and took a deep breath. "Well, I guess now's as good a time as any to tell you. I've been seeing another man. A pilot for American."

I tried to act surprised. "Wow, Cynthia, I had no idea. You like him?"

"Yep. He's a nice guy. I don't like him as well as you, obviously, but at least he's . . . *marriage material*," she said, carefully enunciating each syllable of the last two words.

"He's *what?*"

"You heard me. Marriage material." She opened a cabinet drawer, pulled out a pair of wooden tongs. "I'm 34 years old. Every time I've brought up the idea of marriage and children, you act like I have some sort of horrible infectious disease." She tossed the salad, glaring at me as if *I* were the one with leprosy or the plague.

"Hey, that isn't true. You know I love you."

Cynthia opened a package of croutons and aggressively sprinkled them over the salad. "You say you love me, and I'm sure you do on some level, but the truth is, I'm interested in something permanent. And you aren't interested in marriage. Right?"

I tried to focus on **No Way, Jose's** tip on refusal and rejection, but Cynthia wasn't following any of the examples I'd memorized. "Well, sure, I'd like to get married."

"Then let's get married, OK?"

"I don't know about the timing, Cynthia, that's . . . "

"See what I mean?" She whirled away from me and tossed the salad tongs into the sink, making an uncomfortable clattering sound. Turning on the faucet, Cynthia aggressively squirted Palmolive under the stream, creating a small mountain range of bubbles. "You always avoid the subject."

"Hey, I'd like to talk about marriage . . . at some point."

The salad tongs probably wondered why they were getting such an angry scrubbing. Cynthia asked, "OK, how about now?"

"Well, I suppose -"

"Here's the deal," she interrupted, whirling toward me. "Since you evidently won't ask, I'm asking you to marry me." Cynthia quickly dried the tongs and her hands with a paper towel, disappeared into her pantry and retrieved a Julia Child calendar. Her eyes now misty, she flipped it to June and pointed at the Saturdays. "If you're serious, choose a date." Teary-eyed, she thumped the calendar with her index finger. "Choose a date, damn it!"

We stared at each other, neither of us speaking. It was as if a weeping Clint Eastwood had cornered me and was pointing his .45 at my head, daring me to blink.

"Well," I swallowed, "getting married on the 13th might be bad luck."

Through her tears, Cynthia's eyes blazed hot. White hot.

I folded like a summer lawn chair. "OK, let's go for the 20th." It was more surrender than agreement, like when the door-to-door Cutco salesman talked me into buying a "once-in-a-lifetime" set of deluxe carving knives.

The tension now broken, Cynthia put her arms around me and gave me a long, tear-flavored kiss.

"Ok, I accept," she said, now smiling. "You want anchovies on your Caesar?"

Self-Help Tip #6

Avoid placing yourself in situations where the word "No" even needs to be said. If you find yourself in front of a North Korean firing squad, being asked for your final words, you've obviously put yourself in an inadvisable situation. The problem could have been avoided by vacationing in Ohio rather than in the world's largest insane asylum.

By the time I left Austin late Friday afternoon, Cynthia had mobilized into full-battle alert, planning our wedding. Her dining room was transformed into the equivalent of the Pentagon's War Room: sample books of wedding invitations carefully positioned on one end of the dining table; sheet-music options for the vocalist and harpist in formation on the other end; brochures for caterers, photographers, florists, and limousines neatly organized, one category per chair; and white swatches of silk, satin, and taffeta aligned on the floor according to style and fabric weight. The only things missing were high-definition monitors tracking the current GPS positions of her bridesmaids.

On the two-hour trip back to Waco, I figured I could tell Judy Lynn about

my engagement to Cynthia, or invent a story about being gay and deciding to come out of the closet. Realistically, there wasn't a choice. I would drive to Dallas the next morning and explain the situation, face-to-face. Man to woman. Hopefully.

Judy Lynn lives in the Oak Cliff section of Dallas in an older, leafy neighborhood with modest, but well-maintained homes. Sometimes we spent Saturday afternoons working in her yard, while Mindy, attired in her "just-like-Barbie" bathing suit, ran back and forth through a pulsating garden sprinkler.

Just before noon on Saturday, I pulled my Jeep into Judy Lynn's driveway. She and Mindy were waiting for my arrival, sitting on the front-porch steps, laughing and blowing soap bubbles. It was as if they were starring in a commercial for Hallmark greeting cards.

I hollered, "Hey there, girls, I could see those huge bubbles two blocks away."

Mindy ran and threw her arms around my neck.

Judy Lynn strolled over to join us. "I'm glad you're finally here," she said. "Mindy's talked about you non-stop for the past three hours."

I presented the little girl with a package of puppy and kitty stickers I'd grabbed at a convenience store. Mindy grinned as if she were a sixteen-year-old, getting the keys to a brand-new Porsche.

Judy Lynn grabbed my hand and squeezed it. "I don't know what mojo you cook up, but she thinks you're pretty special."

Even though I also thought Mindy was very special, I had the presence of mind not to blurt it out. Maybe the evolutionary process for the first rewind button for males had begun.

Walking to the house hand in hand with Judy Lynn, Mindy one step behind, I felt guilty, knowing what was about to happen - like a Mafia turncoat preparing to testify before Congress, minus the witness relocation program.

In the kitchen, a Domino's Pizza box rested on the oak breakfast table. Judy Lynn poured Mindy a glass of milk and asked if I'd like a beer. I preferred iced tea, I answered, thinking alcohol and jilting a woman probably weren't a good combination.

As each of us ate a slice of the pizza, Judy Lynn recounted her week repairing machines on the north side of Dallas, mostly in the Plano area, the cultural polar-opposite of her neighborhood. "One of the high schools over there looks like a car dealer for Lexus and BMW." She sighed. "I can't begrudge the parents, I guess. I'd probably do the same for Mindy, if I could. Except it'd be a Silverado pick-up truck."

"I doubt you would," I countered. "Your head sits a little straighter on your shoulders than most of those power-hungry, i-parents'."

"You're probably right," she said. "Still, it'd be nice to have the temptation of spoiling your kid."

Mindy, her mouth half full of pepperoni, asked me, "What did you do this week?"

I'd thought about what I would say to Judy Lynn about Cynthia, but hadn't considered Mindy. "Well, I worked on 'money-monies,' like your mom does, and then spent some time with a friend." I figured now was as good a time as any to break the news about my "friend" Cynthia and get it over with.

"Does your friend have a daddy?" Mindy abruptly hijacked the topic, as only a four-year-old can do.

"Well, yes," I said, deciding not to include "she does."

Mindy finished her glass of milk and asked, "Do you have a daddy?"

"Yes, but I don't see him very often. He lives a long way from here."

"I want you to be my daddy," she said, matter-of-factly, as if deciding she preferred pepperoni over mushroom pizza. "Could I have more milk, please?"

Desperate to change the subject, I answered, "Sure, I'll get you some." Standing up to retrieve the milk carton from the refrigerator, I glanced at Judy Lynn, my eyes pleading for a get-out-of-jail-free card. Rather than bail me out, she raised her eyebrows and looked amused. I refilled Mindy's glass, returned the carton to the refrigerator, and sat back down, all without saying anything else.

With smudges of red pizza sauce outlining her lips, the little girl reached for another slice of pepperoni, replacing it with the uneaten crust of her last piece. In the same tone of voice she used to ask for another glass of milk, Mindy continued her line of questioning. "So, will you be my daddy?"

Judy Lynn looked at me. "She's asked me that question every day this week. I told her she needed to talk to you."

I put aside my slice of pizza and smiled at the little girl, hoping not to crush her spirit. "Well, I'd really like to be your daddy, but - "

"Yea!" Mindy squealed with delight. "Mommy, I knew he'd say yes!" Before I could finish the rest of my sentence, she jumped out of her chair and ran to me, planting tomato-colored kisses on my cheek.

I stuttered. "Well, what I meant - "

"I love you," Mindy said, with a four-year-old's innocence and sincerity.

It was game, set, and match. By now, the little girl had crawled on my lap, her head snuggled against my chest. It was as if a Night of the Living Dead zombie had gobbled my brain, leaving me incapable of independent thought. "I love you, too," I said, nuzzling Mindy's sweet-smelling hair and looking affectionately at Judy Lynn. "And I love your mom, also."

Judy Lynn beamed. "You know, I have some vacation days the last week of June. Maybe we could slip off to Vegas, do the whole wedding-chapel thing. My mother could keep Mindy. How about it?"

"Sure," I said, unable to resist. "I know the 27th is a Saturday."

Self-Help Tip #7

Ignore the feelings of guilt that may cause you to say "Yes" when you should say "No." Guilt is never a valid reason to agree to someone's request. Let the other person know his entreaty unreasonably plays on those feelings. Example: "Sylvester, you're dangling my pet goldfish above the fish bowl, and while I feel guilty about him suffocating, I simply won't donate more money to your Congressional reelection campaign."

Phyllis tilted her head backwards to a 45-degree angle, purely for dramatic effect, and lazily blew a smoke ring into the air. "So, do you plan to wear the same tux to both weddings?"

Sitting on her couch and feeling a world-class jerk, I felt as if I were about to be paddled and expelled from elementary school by the principal, Mrs. Beelzebub.

Phyllis was relentless. "You know, I rarely criticize a client, but in your case, I'll make an exception. It seems you haven't listened to a single word I've said over the past two years."

"It's not like I haven't tried," I pleaded, failing to mention that **Learn to Say "No Way, Jose"** hadn't helped me, either.

"Perhaps you should consider finding a therapist you respect, someone you'll listen to." Stabbing her cigarette stub into an ashtray, she reached in her desk drawer and pulled out a small bag of Cheetos.

"Phyllis, are you firing me as a client?"

Unable to open the Cheetos bag with her fingers, she placed it in her mouth and ripped the cellophane with her teeth. "Well, it isn't in my nature to fire a client, but honestly, I don't know of anything else to suggest." She picked out a Cheeto from the bag and pointed it toward me. "I recommended you tell both women about the existence of the other, but you didn't agree. Just look where that's gotten you."

She was right, of course, but changing therapists wouldn't solve my problem, nor would studying more self-help books. While shaving that morning, I realized I needed someone to coach me through the actual process of coming clean with both women. "Phyllis, I've been thinking. How about if I invited Cynthia and Judy Lynn to sit in on one of our sessions? I think I could tell them the truth if you were there, holding my feet to the fire."

"You're joking, obviously."

"No, I'm not."

Phyllis looked as if she'd swallowed the whole bag of Cheetos. "Well, that's highly . . . irregular," she stammered, "and I'm not sure if it meets professional standards, quite frankly."

I tried to look as desperate as possible, which wasn't difficult, given my predicament. "I've thought about it, and basically, you're my only hope."

"One woman at a time?"

"No, both at the same session. I'm afraid I'd lose my nerve otherwise."

"You'd be asking for *big-time* trouble." Phyllis continued to feast on the Cheetos. "Plus, how would you convince them to come?"

"I'd say it was pre-marriage counseling. You know, maybe some sort of a compatibility workshop."

"Compatibility workshop?" Phyllis shook her head. "You'll need something better than that."

"Ok, but once Cynthia and Judy Lynn were in the same room together, I'd tell them the complete story about my habitual people pleasing. You could intercede if I strayed off message or if things got out of hand. Call the sheriff, I guess, if things really got out of hand. But I think it has a good chance of working out."

Phyllis munched on the last Cheeto, deep in thought. "Well, perhaps it *could* fall under 'joint conflict resolution,' which is covered in my professional code of conduct." Still thinking, she wadded the bag and threw it in the trash. "I suppose as long as you don't involve me in any lies and jeopardize my professional credentials, they could join us for a session. Of course, you'd need to pay the hourly fee for both your guests." Phyllis opened her desk drawer, found a match, and lit a fresh cigarette. "How about next Saturday at ten?"

Self-Help Tip #8

If saying "No" is too difficult, try saying it in another way. Example: "Gee, Sven, I'm sure it would be enjoyable serving on the Organizing Committee to Bring the Olympics to Fargo, but I simply don't have any more room on my calendar."

263

Talking Cynthia into pre-marriage counseling was a snap. Her older sister had done it with her third husband, and they were still together. A minor miracle in itself, she said. Cynthia thought my idea revealed my "feminine, sensitive side . . . but in a positive way." She even suggested coming to Waco on Friday, but the thought of spending the prior evening with either of my fiancées made me feel guilty, so I said I had to work late. I gave her Phyllis' address and asked that we meet at her office.

In contrast, Judy Lynn was skeptical. "Seriously, you want us to go to pre-marriage counseling?" She snorted in disbelief. "Isn't that where I have to list the five things I like about you, and you list the ten things about me that are as annoying as hell? Then, we hold hands and sing 'Michael, Row the Boat Ashore?'"

"No, I just thought it would be a smart thing to do. With your hobosexual ex-husband, I figure maybe you have some issues that need to be explored. I probably have a few issues of my own we should discuss." Actually, it was just one other "issue."

Somewhat reluctantly, Judy Lynn finally agreed to the session. Her mother couldn't babysit Mindy until Saturday morning, which fit the plan perfectly, but she didn't want to meet at Phyllis' office. "Why can't I come to your place, and we could ride over to your little 'séance' together?"

I told her my apartment was being exterminated, and in a way, it was true. I was finally dealing with the rat who lived there.

Self-Help Tip #9

When asked to do something you'd rather not do, it may be best to acknowledge your problem to the other person and admit your difficulty in saying "No." Example: 'Andrea-Louise, babysitting your twin Rottweilers for a month may be a reasonable request for some people, but as someone who's afraid of dogs - even poodles - I want to say 'No.' Yet, because you're my friend, I'm having difficulty turning you down. I hope you understand and respect my problem."

Saturday morning, my stomach felt as if I'd eaten a bowl of lead bullets the night before. Arriving a quarter-hour early, I waited for my fiancées in Phyllis' basement office. Just before ten o'clock, Judy Lynn and Cynthia arrived within a minute of each other. Apparently, they were both standing on the porch outside the office, poised to ring the doorbell, when Phyllis opened the door and greeted them.

I heard Cynthia say she was there for pre-marriage counseling and asked if there had been a scheduling error.

Phyllis said it was a group session and they should come in and make themselves comfortable.

Judy Lynn, outfitted in cowboy boots, blue jeans, and a pearl-snap shirt, led the way down the stairs into Phyllis' office. Looking hesitant at first, she smiled broadly upon seeing me. "Hey, hoss, you ready for all this touchy-feely stuff?"

Cynthia, wearing a strand of pearls more suitable for a formal tea, followed two steps behind. She seemed taken aback by Judy Lynn's familiar-sounding greeting. "Excuse me, but do you two know each other?"

Hearing Cynthia's comment, Judy Lynn abruptly whirled around and asked, "What do you mean 'Do you two know each other?'"

Before Cynthia could answer, Phyllis, who was trailing the pair, interceded. "Ladies, why don't we all sit down and get started." She'd placed folding chairs in front of her desk and suggested we sit in a circle, facing each other. Phyllis continued, "I appreciate everyone coming this morning, and I'd like to begin by talking about the need to maintain an open mind. Let's not be harsh or judgmental, and remember to be respectful and listen to everyone's point of view."

"Wait a minute," Judy Lynn said, gesturing toward the chairs as she sat down. "There aren't enough grooms here."

"Yeah," Cynthia said, taking a seat. "What's going on?"

I'd assumed there would be more time for chit-chat before launching into my confession, an obvious miscalculation. "Uh, actually, Judy Lynn's right. There aren't enough grooms here."

"I don't get it," Cynthia said, shifting uncomfortably in her chair, and looking around at each of us. "What are you people talking about?"

Phyllis nodded toward me, as if to say, "You're on, buddy."

"Ok, here's the deal," I began. "I have a problem saying 'No' to folks. Actually, it's a serious problem, which is why I've been seeing Phyllis for two years."

"Actually, on and off for two years," Phyllis corrected.

Both Judy Lynn and Cynthia sat stiffly erect in their chairs, like suspicious, stone-carved creatures guarding an Egyptian tomb. With a dead guy inside.

Things weren't going as smoothly as I'd fantasized. Taking an extra-deep breath, I went for broke. "It's also why I've been dating both of you over the past several months. And, it's why I agreed to marry both of you."

It took Cynthia a second or two to comprehend the message. A look of recognition, immediately followed by hurt and betrayal clouded her face. "You're . . .

you're a total, disgusting ... slime ball." She fumbled in her purse for a tissue and began to cry.

Dry-eyed, Judy Lynn glared at me as if she'd just seen a reincarnation of her hobosexual husband. "Have you gone totally nuts?" Then, raising her voice 50 decibels, she shouted, "You worthless piece of garbage!"

Now leaning over in her chair, head in her hands, Cynthia sobbed hysterically.

Phyllis handed her a box of tissues and said, "Ladies, why don't you take a minute to compose yourselves, then perhaps we can discuss how - "

"I'm not staying," Judy Lynn interjected. "I'm driving home to tell a four-year-old girl that another good-for-nothing man has broken our hearts." She popped up from her chair, like a child's jack-in-the-box, and without acknowledging anyone, bounded straight for the door.

"Wait a minute, Judy Lynn," I pleaded. The door slammed before I could finish my sentence.

"I'm leaving, also," Cynthia gasped between sobs, raising her head and glowering at me. "You know, I had actually found someone with real marriage potential. An honest, decent man," she said, almost hiccupping the words. "And I gave him up for you?" She slowly rose from her seat and clutched her purse, her posture precise and resolved. "Nice meeting you, Phyllis." Then, narrowing her eyes, Cynthia hissed, "Don't you *dare* ever speak to me again."

The door slammed a second time, and Phyllis and I sat in unnatural silence for a full minute. Then, the plump therapist silently rose from her seat, ambled to the other side of her desk, and rustled around in one of the drawers until she found two bags of Cheetos. One for her and one for me.

Self-Help Tip #10

When all else fails, try using humor to say "No." Experiment with using an outrageous catchphrase to convey a negative response, such as "No Way, Jose," "Only when pigs fly," or "Not by the hair of my chinny chin chin."

After experiencing a debacle worthy of two segments on *The Jerry Springer Show*. I chose the Hampton Inn as my new Austin headquarters. Even though it lacked Holiday Inn Express' world-class cinnamon rolls, it also didn't have a possibly homicidal ex-fiancée lurking near the reception desk.

Seven weeks later, Cynthia's Facebook page announced that "after an ill-advised relationship with a wannabe bigamist," she'd regained her senses and found "the love of her life." She and the Florida widow's peak were planning a November wedding, with a "round-the-world honeymoon, thanks to American Airlines." That was painful to read, of course, since I still cared for Cynthia. But it also meant her biological clock would only need to be recalibrated by five months, making me feel considerably less guilty.

As for the Cheeto queen, Phyllis and I were through. After searching for an excuse to end the useless therapy sessions, she'd given me the perfect way out, by firing me as a client.

Judy Lynn was a different matter. Because of our line of work, I knew we'd eventually cross paths. A month after the fiancée fiasco, the Lottery Commission Pooh-Bahs offered an optional skills-development class in San Antonio, but I called in sick. Five months later, they scheduled a mandatory training workshop at the Dallas Hyatt Regency, and I had no choice but to attend.

During the morning session, Judy Lynn was her normal self, asking slightly irreverent questions of the instructors and offering homespun sayings that kept the entire group laughing. At the mid-morning break, everyone stepped outside the conference room and gathered around the coffee and juice table.

Standing behind her as she filled her coffee cup, I said, "Judy Lynn, you still have the touch. Thanks for keeping these know-it-all instructors in line."

She turned around, seemingly surprised to hear my voice, and gave me a quarter-smile. Maybe a half-smile. "You know, they really should record these guys and put out a CD to help people with insomnia. They'd have a slam-dunk Grammy."

I laughed. "So, how's Mindy doing these days?"

Judy Lynn's half-smile grew to a three-quarters-smile. "She turned five and started kindergarten. Already teaching the class, I think. Next week, she'll probably move up to the principal's job."

Her joke made me realize how much I missed being around the little girl. "Please tell her hello for me, OK?" I grabbed a cup and began filling it with coffee.

Judy Lynn's face clouded. "No," she said, "I'd rather not." She hesitated. "Maybe in a few years . . . when she understands life a little better."

Her words were crushing, and although I wanted to walk away, I didn't. "Look, you have no idea how sorry I am for what happened."

"I'm sure you are, in your own way."

"I'd love to have a chance to explain what happened, Judy Lynn. I know it wouldn't change things, but would you let me take you to dinner? Just dinner, nothing more."

Judy Lynn blew on the hot coffee and took a sip. She blew on it again, almost stalling for time and measuring her exact response. In a low-pitched voice, colored with gravel-textured emotion, she said, "No way, Jose." Then, Judy Lynn turned and hurried back to the meeting room.

Epilogue

By now, you've read and studied all the tips for mastering the art of saying "No." The rest is up to you! Will you continue allowing other people to dictate your choices? Will you let others run your life? Or, will you seize command and become the master of your future? The choice, dear reader, is yours!

Dr. Nolan Weston
Carmel, California

It would be nice if this saga had a happy ending, like the cavalry riding in to save the wagon train from certain doom. But the truth is, it doesn't.

The irony is that when Judy Lynn turned me down for dinner that day, her words had a more galvanizing effect on me than talking to Phyllis for two years or memorizing the ten tips from **Learn to Say "No Way, Jose."**

By always being the habitual people pleaser, I had, in the long run, pleased no one. Certainly not myself. Maybe the only way I would lick my problem was to grow a backbone and take charge of my life. One day at a time. One door-to-door salesman at a time, one neighbor's request at a time, one fiancée at a time.

It didn't happen overnight, but gradually, I took a few baby steps - saying "No" to the telemarketer who tried to sell me a Jazzy power wheelchair, for example, and turning down a "house party demonstration" for Excalibur fruit dehydrators.

In time, I even worked up the nerve to call my older sister and tell her I wasn't buying any more of her Amway cleaning products and food supplements. Funny, her reaction was, "You know, I wondered how long it would take before you finally wised up to this overpriced stuff." Then, after a long pause, she said, "That reminds me, I'd love to come over and show you a new line of wonderful aromatherapy products I'm now offering - fragrant bath salts and herbal body scrubs. Everything's natural and organic, of course, and reasonably priced."

"No, Sis, that doesn't work for me - unless you'll accept a case of fireplace detergent as payment." ✪